# MIMIC ARCANIST

## ASTRA ACADEMY BOOK II

## SHAMI STOVALL

# CONTENTS

Published by
**CS BOOKS, LLC**

This is a work of fiction. Names, characters, places, and incidents either are the product of author imagination or are used fictitiously, and any resemblance to actual persons, living or dead, business establishments, events, or locales, is entirely fictional.

Cover Design: Darko Paganus

Editors: Amy McNulty, Nia Quinn, Justin Barnett

**IF YOU WANT TO BE NOTIFIED WHEN SHAMI STOVALL'S NEXT BOOK RELEASES, PLEASE VISIT HER WEBSITE OR CONTACT HER DIRECTLY AT**

s.adelle.s@gmail.com

ISBN: 978-1-957613-13-0

*To John, my soulmate.*
*To Justin Barnett, who is way too good to me and helped so much.*
*To Gail and Big John, my surrogate parents.*
*To Drew, my agent.*
*To Henry Copeland, for the beautiful leather map and book covers.*
*To Mary, Emily, Scott, James, Ryan & Dana, for all the jokes and input.*
*To my patrons over on Patreon, for naming the Academy.*
*To my Facebook group, for all the memes.*
*And finally, to everyone unnamed, thank you for everything.*

# A Recap of Events

Last time in the Astra Academy series, Gray Lexly was plagued by monsters in his dreams.

Right before Gray would die from these monster attacks, Professor Helmith from the famed Astra Academy was there to protect him. Unfortunately, Helmith disappeared just as Gray was to about attend the Academy himself.

After entering the Menagerie, and bonding with Twain, a cat-shaped mimic, Gray promised himself he would find Helmith somewhere on the campus. Gray was joined by his twin brother, Sorin Lexly, as well as a quiet girl named Nini Wanderlin. Sorin bonded with a knightmare, and Nini bonded with a deadly reaper. Together, they were a trio that all the other students thought strange.

When Professor Helmith finally showed up to teach class, Gray realized she was an imposter. Determined to get to the bottom of this, he ignored most classes that discussed the abyssal hells to focus on his investigation.

Gray spoke with several professors at the Academy. The oft-hungover Piper, the stiff Leon, and the mysterious Professor Zahn, a man building a powerful teleporting gate in the basement of the Academy.

And while Gray thought the monsters in his dreams were no longer a problem, during his investigation, he was attacked by a monster in the woods. Through a long string of questions and after searching the Academy, he realized someone was targeting the eldest twin in sets of siblings, and Gray just so happened to be the eldest himself.

When Gray told this to Leon, the man informed Gray that Zahn was also a twin.

Gray thought he had allies to help him unravel the mystery, but when he put his faith in Zahn, he was betrayed. The professor was also a mimic arcanist, and he was using his eldrin to attack people in their dreams—specifically Gray and other older twins. Zahn needed the souls of older twins to activate his Gate of Crossing and enter the abyssal hells to find his brother, Death Lord Deimos.

Leon, Nini, Sorin, and Gray fought Zahn, Deimos, and Seven, a doppelgänger arcanist pretending to be Helmith, in the basement of the Academy. Gray and the others just *barely* defeated Zahn and the Death Lord, but only after Gray was sliced up by the Death Lord's trident and nearly killed.

And Deimos wasn't destroyed, he was simply sent back to the abyssal hells...Gray and company closed the gate, but Zahn managed to flee with his life. Seven was killed, and the true Professor Helmith returned to Astra Academy.

However, in the process of destroying the gate, it was shattered into thousands of pieces. The many shards scattered to the winds, presumed harmless.

Gray, confident he could return to the Academy as a normal student, didn't give the fragments much thought.

And now it's time to continue the story in *Mimic Arcanist*.

# CHAPTER 1

## WELCOME BACK TO ASTRA ACADEMY

I had only been a student at Astra Academy for three weeks.

It was the best place I'd ever lived in my life. Granted, I'd only lived in two places: the Academy, and on the Isle of Haylin. My home isle was small, and my father, a candlemaker, had made sure we did the same old thing, every day—forever. He made candles, dreamt of candles, talked about candles, and generally avoided anything that smelled of progress.

Astra Academy had been anything but predictable and boring. Cloudy peaks, star shards raining from the sky, telekinetic laundry rooms... Death Lords in the basement. Every room in the Academy was far more interesting than my old home.

Even the boys' washroom was a delight.

I stood in the large room, all alone except for Twain, just admiring my surroundings. The floor was covered in rough tiles to prevent slipping. The walls were bare, and the windows were set high. Glowstone chandeliers kept the room bright, despite the dark night sky. Steel pipes brought water into the Academy, creating baths and showers.

Plumbing. That was what they called it.

My home isle didn't have this wondrous *plumbing*. We had tiny little washrooms with stoves with which to heat our own water.

My eldrin, Twain, sat on the edge of a brass bathtub. He was a mimic, but he resembled a kitten. An adorable kitten. His orange fur practically matched the metal. He stared at me with two differently colored eyes: one gray-blue, one pink.

"What're you waiting for?" Twain asked as he tilted his head.

He had long ears with tufts of fur—like a lynx's. And no tail. It was just a little bob.

I thought his tiny nub-tail made Twain cute, but he didn't like whenever I mentioned it.

"I just want to make sure we're alone," I said, my voice echoing around the massive room.

The washroom was designed for forty people, bare minimum. There were several showerheads on the far wall, and numerous tubs, all separated by short privacy walls. A rack of towels and washcloths stood in the middle of the room, making it easy for everyone. And the place was clean —too clean, to be honest.

The housekeeper was an overachiever.

Once I was certain no one was looking, I slowly peeled off my shirt and trousers. I hated looking at myself. When I glanced down, it was only briefly. I set my focus on the showerhead and stood under the water as soon as it was warm.

My thoughts drifted and darkened. I glanced down.

Scars covered most of my body. Gnarly, twisted scars. The worst one was across my gut. I ran my fingers over it, my hand shaking. My scarred skin felt *thinner* than the rest of my body. It felt like, if I weren't careful, it would just tear open, and my insides would spill out across the floor.

It didn't help that I had memories of seeing my own insides.

Death Lord Deimos—who I had thought was nothing more than a myth a month ago—had sliced me open with his trident. Just thinking about it caused me to shudder.

"My arcanist?" Twain asked. "Are you okay?"

"Yeah," I said with a casual shrug. "Absolutely."

"Hm."

He didn't believe me. That was fine. I was, technically, totally fine. I wasn't bleeding. Nothing hurt. My life wasn't in danger. I just had an overactive imagination. The Death Lord wasn't coming back. I was fine.

4

Totally. Completely. Fine.

"Hey, Gray!"

The shout caused me to nearly jump out of my skin. I practically gasped as I stumbled forward into the wall, my heart pounding in my chest. I whirled around, one arm over my scar on my gut, and one arm raised. I wasn't really a fighter, but I wouldn't go down without a fight, that was for sure.

Fortunately, it was just my twin brother, Sorin.

I let out a long exhale as I slowly relaxed. "What's wrong with you?" I snapped. "I told you I wanted to be alone."

My brother walked across the washroom, the shadows flickering around his feet with each step. He wore a white shirt that contrasted nicely with his black hair. It wasn't big enough, though. The shirt was straining to keep itself together. It was a valiant effort, but I suspected the shirt would eventually lose the battle against Sorin's pectorals.

My brother was just *large*.

Mostly muscle, but he seemed to have a layer of softness around his body that gave him a barrel shape. Not really defined, yet still intimidating. He was taller than me, too. I hated that. I didn't tell anyone, though. We were *twins*, after all. Why had Sorin gotten all the height and muscle? Shouldn't we have been more identical?

Instead, I was a few inches shorter, and lithe.

We shared the same inky locks, tanned skin, and gray-blue eyes, though. Everyone always commented on that. Even my mother, right before she had died, had remarked on my strange eye color. Hence, my name: Gray. Not a very happy naming story, but I cherished it nonetheless.

Sorin stopped near the rack of towels. The darkness shifted across the tile floor, pooling around his feet.

"I just heard something exciting," Sorin said with a smile. "I couldn't wait to tell you."

I stood back in the stream of water, impressed with how it just kept coming. Did the Academy ever run out of water? I didn't want to test my theory, but I suspected not.

I lathered up my hair with soap. "What's so exciting that you would stand around and watch me wash just to tell me?"

"Ah, c'mon. This is important." Sorin held up a finger. "We're going on a trip. Our whole class. For approximately one month."

"Where did you hear that?"

"From Captain Leon." Sorin leaned onto the towel rack. It creaked under his weight. "Also, it's a special trip. *We will sleep outside in the dead of night, huddle close, blankets tight.*"

I groaned as I tossed the soap to the side. "Stop with the poetry, I'm begging you."

"*We shall sit by bonfires, admiring flames, tell stories and play games.*"

After rinsing myself, I turned off the water. The squeak of the metal as the valves closed intrigued me. How many pipes were in the wall, out of sight? I shook away the thought as I headed over to the towel rack.

With a sigh, I said, "You used twenty-five words, and I don't even know what you're attempting to tell me. Poetry isn't an effective method of communication."

Sorin handed me a towel. "Captain Leon said it was a *camping trip.*"

"See? Do you see how easy that was?" I rubbed my body down, and then my face. "Well... what's a camping trip, exactly?"

"Remember those twenty-five words?" Sorin grinned. His smile could light up a dark cave. "Apparently, we're going to learn how to *survive out in the wilderness.* And make campfires. And tell stories. Oh! And also, we're going to help build a schoolhouse and a tavern for a little village on the edge of the empire."

I threw down the towel. "We are?"

Sorin nodded. Then he stood straight. "Yeah. Apparently, we're going to learn all about cultivating the land, and what it means to be arcanists who graduated from Astra Academy. Captain Leon seemed excited. He said it's the headmaster's idea to help out places that don't have arcanists living there."

"Huh."

"And apparently, there are highwaymen in the area. Captain Leon said we might have to handle the problem."

*Highwaymen* was just another term for bandits. They were individuals —sometimes arcanists—who pretended to be local authority. They would demand tolls from people who wandered down roads all alone. If the people didn't pay, the highwaymen would just rob them.

They were nothing but thugs and would probably run at the sight of Astra Academy arcanists.

I grabbed my clothes and pulled them on.

Twain leapt off the tub and then scurried over to the towel rack. He jumped up and landed on a rung next to me. His gracefulness was on full display. "I don't like this. We have to sleep outside *and* deal with highwaymen? Ew."

The shadows around Sorin's feet fluttered at the edges. A gruff voice emanated from the darkness. "Learning the art of survival is important for any arcanist."

"Says the knightmare who doesn't have to sleep on the ground because you can't even sleep." Twain huffed.

A suit of shadowy armor lifted out of the darkness. It wasn't a complete suit—it was missing parts of the legs and arms—but otherwise, it was a full plate suit made from the shadows themselves. The empty helmet and feathery black cape made the armor seem evil or haunted, but I knew that wasn't the case.

Thurin was my brother's eldrin—a knightmare.

My brother had a mark on his forehead, as did all arcanists. A seven-pointed star with a cape and shield laced between the points. It was a shallow etching on his skin, just like mine.

Well, not exactly like mine. I had a shallow etching on my forehead of a seven-pointed star, but that was it. My star had no creature. A mimic arcanist's mark shifted to whatever their mimic was transformed into. And since Twain wasn't currently transformed, mine was currently plainer than most.

Thurin threw back his black-feather cape. "An arcanist must gather all the skills he can in order to be a force for good."

Sorin nodded along with his words. Then he pointed to his eldrin. "Did you hear him, Gray? You should be excited. This will be an amazing trip. You'll see."

"Our whole class is going?" I stepped around the rack and headed for the door. Twain leapt onto my shoulder before I got too far away.

Sorin followed me, his smile never waning. "That's right. Nini, Raaza, Knovak, Phila, Nasbit, and Ashlyn!"

Thurin kept pace as well, the clink of his shadowy armor echoing throughout the empty washroom.

"Exie isn't coming?" I asked.

Sorin let out a short sigh. "Oh. Right. *Her.* Yeah, she's coming, too."

"Hey, cheer up. Maybe she'll accidentally fall into the bonfire."

Sorin gave me a sideways glance. We exited the washroom, but he didn't acknowledge my joke. He didn't like it when I got "too mean," as he so lovingly put it. Exie wasn't really someone I worried about offending, though. She never seemed to care if *she* offended anyone else, after all. And she had made it clear several times that she didn't like Sorin or me.

But still—I had promised Sorin I would try to keep any sarcastic commentary to myself. He was a kinder, gentler person than I was, and that was a good thing. Without Sorin's noble disposition, I probably would've gotten into a *lot* more trouble as a kid. And even now, as an adult.

My brother happily embraced the role of *moral compass.*

"Oh," Sorin added. "And Professor Helmith will be joining us."

I caught my breath. "Really?"

Now *that* was good news. I had joined the Academy because of her. She was just so wise and magical and interesting—she knew so much about mystical creatures, and about the world. My whole first week, she hadn't really been here. And I hadn't spoken to her much afterward. Now we would be taking a trip with her?

"I knew you'd want to hear about your honeysuckle," Sorin said as he punched my arm.

I shoved him back. "I told you. Professor Helmith's not my *honeysuckle.* If you keep saying that, I'm gonna get angry. And she's married."

Twain purred as he nuzzled the side of my neck. "Who is your honeysuckle, then? Is it... Ashlyn?"

I covered Twain's little kitten face with my hand. He barked out a "*Hey!*" as I playfully squished him against my shoulder.

"I think this will be loads of fun," Sorin said, patting me on the back. "And you're still young. You don't have to be too worried about who your honeysuckle is quite yet. Who knows? Maybe you'll experience love at first sight or be caught up in a whirlwind of romance."

I ran a hand down my face. "I'm sure this camping trip will be an *event*, especially after that speech." While my time at the Academy had been mostly fantastic, there was always the possibility something could go wrong.

But I was optimistic.

Professor Helmith would be there. Probably Captain Leon as well.

What could go wrong?

# Chapter 2

## Camping Trip Prep

Sorin and I traveled the halls of Astra Academy until we arrived at the dorms for the first-year students. There were four rooms: two for the girls, and two for the boys. Each room had ten beds, and enough wardrobes and chests to fit ten people's belongings. Despite that fact, the boys' dorms weren't equally split.

Four of us shared one dorm room, while ten others shared the second.

It wasn't difficult to see why the numbers were imbalanced.

Sorin, Raaza, Knovak, and I were all the lowborn islanders. We had bonded with our eldrin here at the Academy because the headmaster had been gracious enough to pay for our voyage. He had also given us the opportunity to see multiple mystical creatures and participate in their Trials of Worth. If it hadn't been for him, the four of us likely would've never attended this prestigious Academy...

The other ten male students were all nobility, apparently. Or something. I wasn't entirely sure. I didn't much care for lineage or birthright. If they didn't want to associate with me, I didn't want to associate with them.

Sorin reached for the doorhandle to our dorm but stopped before opening it. Then he turned to me and placed a finger over his lips.

It was the dead of night. Only the evening lanterns kept us company.

"We don't want to wake them," Sorin whispered.

I nodded once. "I know. I've been doing this for a while now."

"Showering at night?"

"Yeah."

My brother furrowed his brow. "I knew it." Then he tightened his grip on the doorhandle. "But why?"

For a long moment, I said nothing.

Twain twitched his long ear. It tickled my neck. "Gray doesn't want anyone to see his scars."

Again, I squished his little kitten face with the palm of my hand. "Don't listen to him. I just like my privacy."

My brother glanced between us and frowned. "What's wrong with your scars? You should be proud. You saved everyone in the school from a Death Lord. Kind of."

I crossed my arms. "Look, it's just weird, okay? Arcanists aren't supposed to scar."

"Why not?"

"We heal faster than mortals. And Doc Tomas used his magic to stitch me back together. There shouldn't be a trace left over from the attack, and yet..." I glanced down at my shirt, my mind picturing the twisted scars on my body. "I just wish they weren't there."

Sorin nodded once. "Well, maybe we can find an arcanist who can help you." He slowly pushed open the door to our dorm. Light shone from within, and my brother's eyes widened. "Is someone awake?"

We both stepped inside, our eldrin in tow.

A single lantern was lit at the far end of the room. Despite the late hour, Knovak and Raaza were still awake. And for some reason, they were both... trying on clothing?

Knovak, who slept in the bed closest to the door, had donned a full pompous ensemble. He wore red pantaloons, a black vest, and a puffy white shirt. He had topped it all off with a pointed hat straight out of a book depicting old-world wizards. A small mirror sat on the dresser next to his bed, and Knovak admired his own reflection for a few seconds before turning to face us.

His dirty-blond hair had been combed back, and most of it was hidden under his hat. He had a plain face—a forgettable one, really—but his forehead carried an arcanist mark, his star laced with the image of a unicorn.

Knovak forced a smile. "Oh, the Lexly twins. You've finally returned." Then he turned his back to us and focused his full attention on the positioning of his vest.

I had said we were all lowborn islanders, but Knovak was in a bizarre situation. He came from a rich family of merchants. The Gentz family. He *loved* his fancy clothing and food and summer vacations, and boy did he love to regale us with tales about how large his house was.

It had really upset Knovak when all the other mainland nobles hadn't immediately made friends with him.

"What's with the outfit?" Sorin asked as he walked by.

"Haven't you heard?" Knovak straightened the sleeves of his puffy shirt. "We'll be traveling to a far-off town to represent Astra Academy. We should look our best."

"I thought it was a tiny village without a schoolhouse?"

"That's true..."

Knovak stopped sprucing up his shirt and stared at it. Then he hurried over to his wardrobe and hastily went through a few of his outfits. He settled on a black silk shirt and compared it to his body, measuring his arms against the sleeves.

"I shouldn't wear white," Knovak muttered to himself. "That'll get too dirty."

I walked by, not bothering to get involved in the conversation. Our school uniform was a velvet robe of blue and black with hints of silver. I suspected we wouldn't wear it while we were neck-deep in construction materials.

Raaza's bed was in the middle of the room. Like Knovak, he was trying on clothes, but unlike Knovak, Raaza's seemed more... practical. He wore a straw hat with a wide brim, and a pair of thick leather trousers. He also had on a tunic that seemed light and breathable.

Raaza was a kitsune arcanist. His star was marked with the foxlike creature woven between the seven points.

His kitsune, Miko, sat on his bed, watching as he dressed. Her red fox coat appeared glossy in the lantern light, and bits of flames flickered around her black paws. The fire wasn't real. It didn't burn the blankets or damage the bed in any way.

"I like this hat," Miko said with a tilt of her head. "When you stare at the ground, it shields your eyes. It's so mysterious!"

Raaza grabbed the brim of the hat and fidgeted with the edge. He didn't reply.

"Is *everyone* excited for this camping trip?" I asked as I kept walking. My bed was at the far end of the dorm, near the gigantic window.

"I'm not excited," Raaza snapped.

He glanced over at me, his dark eyes narrowed. The man never seemed to smile.

"You're not excited?" I asked. "*At all?*"

"This is a waste of our time." Raaza removed his hat and threw it on his bed next to his eldrin. "I came to this Academy hoping they would teach me in the art of combat and magical mastery. I don't care about some tiny village in the middle of nowhere."

I half-laughed. "Wow. What a hero. A true role model for everyone to aspire to emulate."

Raaza just glared at me.

He had scars on his face. Small ones. Like something with claws had gone for his eye and just barely missed. Raaza had gotten them long before he had become an arcanist, but they still reminded me of my own scarring.

Miko stood and then walked in a circle around the bed, her fox tail swishing as she moved. "My arcanist already knows how to survive in the wilderness, thank you very much. There's little for him to learn on this trip."

"And it's a month long," Raaza said with a groan. He patted his eldrin on the head. "I'd rather stay here and learn more about our magics."

Most nights, Sorin and I slept next to each other. I walked past my brother's bed and went to my own. When I sat on the edge of the mattress, Twain leapt off my shoulder and landed on my pillow. Then he used his claws to knead the casing. He practically ripped it all up while I just glowered at him.

"Why are you *so* obsessed with fighting?" Knovak asked from across the dorm. He had changed into his black silk shirt and was now admiring himself as he spoke. "We live in a time of peace and prosperity. The God-

Arcanists War is over, the arcane plague no longer haunts the land or troubles the mystical creatures. There's little need for combat proficiency."

Raaza scoffed. "Are you serious? The basement of the Academy was blown open like a ship hit by a cannonball because a Death Lord was about to rampage out of control down there. How am I the only one who understands the importance of combat training?" He threw his arms up and sat down hard on his mattress.

"Captain Leon did mention the possibility of highwaymen," Sorin interjected. "I mean, sometimes combat is necessary to stop scoundrels."

Raaza nodded once and gave my brother a brief smile. "Yes. Exactly. That's a real problem." Then he straightened his posture. "Wait, are we really going to deal with highwaymen? Ourselves?"

He sounded a little *too* eager for my taste, but what did I know? Maybe highwaymen gave him those scars and now it was payback.

The room went quiet for a moment.

Sorin didn't interject himself into the conversation. Sorin's knightmare sank into the shadows, out of sight from everyone else. As Sorin ambled over to his bed, he shrugged. "Captain Leon said the whole trip would be a learning experience. We need to cultivate and protect the land. He made it sound like we'd be dealing with *all* the problems."

"Good." Raaza turned away. "Good," he repeated, his voice softer, almost inaudible.

I just sighed. This was going to be an interesting trip, for sure.

Then Raaza shot me a glare. "You agree with me, don't you, Gray?"

"In theory," I said, shrugging.

I had never learned how to fight. I figured I would use whatever magic I could mimic if there was ever a problem again in the future. That probably wasn't the best plan. Raaza had a point. If I had been forced to fight Death Lord Deimos—rather than just exploding the gate he had been walking through—I would've died faster than a fish in the desert.

"You're all soft." Raaza grabbed his kitsune and brought her into his lap. "You'll see things my way once you experience the harshness the world has to offer."

Knovak dramatically rolled his eyes. "Yeah, yeah. No one has *ever* had it as hard as *you*. We're all simpletons for not wanting to become brooding warlords." Then he leaned in close to the mirror and picked at his eyebrows, making sure they were just right.

Raaza rubbed at his face, his frown deep. It seemed like he had choice words for Knovak, but he held them all back.

"I think you should focus on learning diplomacy on this trip," Knovak commented, either unaware of Raaza's anger, or he just didn't care. "You could use some."

Raaza gritted his teeth. "You can shove some feathers up your—"

"Hey, hey!" Sorin leapt in between them, smiling. "No need for any of that. We're all new arcanists, in the same class, sharing the same dorm. We should help each other as allies, not squabble like bickering children." My brother glanced over at me. Then he motioned for me to join the conversation.

Why did everyone want *my* input? It was a *camping trip*, not an *end of the world event*. Couldn't we just... go with the flow?

The door to our dorm slowly creaked open. Everyone stopped what they were doing to glance over. Who was entering at this hour? No one else lived in this dorm, and it was well beyond curfew.

A girl walked into our dorm.

It was Nini.

While I hadn't known her long, she had quickly become friends with both Sorin and me.

Nini held the door open so her eldrin could enter. She had bonded with a *reaper*—a bizarre mystical creature of death and ruin. His name was Waste, and he was nothing more than a floating cloak, seemingly worn by an invisible man. The edge of the cloak was tattered and threadbare, and a small chain hung from inside the dark red folds of cloth.

The reaper also had a scythe. The weapon floated around the creature, twirling and moving, seemingly on its own. Waste had a hood, but it was empty inside, just as the knightmare was an empty suit of armor.

Sorin turned to face her, his smile fading. "Nini? Is everything okay?"

Although it was impractical most of the time, Nini tended to dress in several layers of clothes. She wore a tunic, a shirt, a jacket, and her robes—and that was only on her torso. She also wore long pants, boots, and a pair of glasses, practically covering every inch of her small body.

Her bloodred hair fell to her shoulders, but even that was almost swallowed by the collar of her large coat.

Nini fixed her glasses as she muttered, "I heard about the camping trip and, uh, wanted to speak with you all about it."

"The girls are coming as well," Sorin stated. "You didn't want to speak with them?"

"They'... not really my friends. I don't think they want to speak with me about anything."

"You're not supposed to be in here," Knovak said with a sweeping gesture to the room. "This is an area for the boys. Only boys. You'll need to leave."

"Oh, yikes," I said, unable to hide my sarcasm. "That means Miko needs to go. Sorry about that, Raaza."

The little kitsune stood in Raaza's lap, her faux flames flaring around her feet. "I'm allowed to be with my arcanist! It's my right as his eldrin. Besides, his magic will be weaker if I'm too far away..."

"That's different." Knovak placed his hands on his hips. "Eldrin are different. Stop trying to confuse the issue."

"Relax, everyone," Sorin said as he leapt over an unoccupied bed and then jogged over to Nini. "We're not asleep yet, right? Let's just all talk about the trip together. It'll be fun." He placed a hand on Nini's shoulder and offered a bright smile.

Although Nini wasn't one who emoted much, she managed a small smile of her own when my brother drew near. Her reaper hovered close, his chain rattling. He reminded me of a snake, warning anyone who would attempt to do his arcanist harm.

Knovak huffed. Then he glanced around. "Everyone has their eldrin with them? You know they're supposed to sleep in the treehouse." He pointed to the back window. "It was specifically designed for them."

The treehouse was a massive structure that wrapped around most of Astra Academy. The branches of the colossal redwood had been carved into walkways that connected with most of the windows. Mystical creatures came in all sizes—some large, some tiny—and instead of changing the structure of the Academy to accommodate all of them, the treehouse had been built with their needs in mind.

It had waterfalls, shallow pools of water, lush gardens, and dark cave-like spaces so each creature could find its own special accommodations.

"Miko will go to sleep in the treehouse once we're done packing," Raaza stated. He gently stroked his eldrin's fur. "Besides—we were undertaking some magic training together, and I prefer to do it here."

Nini grabbed the edge of Waste's cloak. "I just... feel better with my eldrin around."

Sorin pointed to the flittering shadows around his feet. "My eldrin doesn't sleep. And also, he likes to hide in the darkness, so I think it's perfectly acceptable to keep him with me."

Everyone turned to face me.

Twain had curled up in the shreds of my pillow long ago. He stared at everyone else with wide eyes.

I grabbed my blankets and threw them over my eldrin. He barked out a "*Hey!*" as everything settled over him. "Nothing to see here," I quipped.

Knovak frowned, his eyes narrowed. "Fine. *I'll* be the only one who follows instructions. Clearly."

The others half-laughed and turned away, obviously not in the mood to argue about it. I preferred that. It was irrational, but I didn't want to send my eldrin away. Ever since the attack in the basement, I had been afraid of *something* coming out of nowhere to get me. Either from my dreams or from a nearby open window. I carried this lingering dread from the attack.

It felt like the terror from the abyssal hells hung around like a dark fog through the halls of the Academy.

I shook the thought away and patted Twain through the blanket. Despite being buried in the sheets, he purred.

A camping trip away from Astra Academy started to seem a little more appealing to me in that moment.

# CHAPTER 3

## TRAVELING THROUGH GATES

Morning.

A new dawn.

Light cascaded through the giant window, brightening the dorm. I slid off my bed and dressed before Twain even awoke. Then I scooped up my kitten eldrin, and my small bag of belongings, and headed for the door. Everyone else had already left the room, leaving me and Twain as the last to depart. It surprised me—had everyone else gotten up before sunrise?—but I didn't dwell on the situation long.

Anxiety hounded me. It crept up my spine and across my scalp, giving me goosebumps. I hurried into the common room between dorms, wanting to see someone, I didn't care who. The thought of being alone just didn't sit right.

Luck was on my side today. People stood around the common room in small groups.

I walked around large, blue couches set up in a pleasant half-circle near another large window. Pathways to the treehouse were built into most sills, allowing for eldrin to come into the Academy from the outside. The window was shut, keeping the cool air at bay, but the glass was clean and polished, and it was easy to forget it was even there.

There were twenty-seven first-year arcanists attending the Academy.

Nine of them were in my class—Class One. The common room connected all dorms, and while I didn't really know the other first-year students, I was happy to have them around. They chatted with one another, most wearing their velvety robes.

Were all the classes going camping?

It didn't look like it.

Sorin had told me to pack for the trip, which was why I had a bag slung over my shoulder, but none of the other classes had any of their belongings on them.

"Shouldn't we be heading to the lake?" Twain asked. Then he yawned, his little kitten body shaking as he did so. "That's where Sorin said we should meet him."

I smiled as I said, "There's someone I want to speak with."

"Really?"

I stepped around the other first-years until I reached the far couch. Ashlyn and Phila sat together, conversing in hushed voices. When I approached, they both fell silent and turned to me.

Ashlyn's blonde hair was tied back in a ponytail, secured with a decorative strap of leather woven into her locks. She wore a pair of tight white trousers under her robes, along with a black vest and similarly colored shirt. For some reason, she reminded me of an adventuring scholar.

It was probably her athletic build and keen gaze. She also had a pouch tied to her belt, and a backpack stuffed with supplies sitting on the cushion next to her.

Ashlyn stood and gave me the once-over, her blue eyes quickly darting over me. Then she frowned and placed a hand on her hip.

"You don't look prepared," she stated, her voice flat.

I wore my usual outfit: a simple pair of trousers, boots, and a tunic. My school robes were over my shoulders, but they hung loose. My clothing wasn't as neatly tailored as hers.

Compared to Ashlyn, I probably looked like a vagabond.

"Good morning to you, too," I sarcastically said with a slight bow.

A growl of irritation caught my attention.

Ashlyn's eldrin—a typhoon dragon—came into the common room through the window. I hadn't heard the window open or felt the cold winds of morning, but the dragon had walked along the branch of the gigantic treehouse and slid into the room.

The beast's scales came in every shade of blue, from the indigo of twilight to the deep aqua of the ocean. He was a dragon of the water, which meant he didn't have wings. Instead, Ashlyn's typhoon dragon had large fins across most of his body.

Ecrib. That was his name.

The dragon was as large as a couch, and when he came stomping over, his claws scraping across the stone floor, several students leapt out of the way.

"Is this *kitten arcanist* giving you trouble?" Ecrib asked as he sauntered around his arcanist. The tip of his tail twitched as he shot me a glare with his golden eyes.

"Ha, ha, very funny," I said as I rolled my eyes.

Twain puffed his fur until he was nothing but a large ball of fluff. "I'm a kitten who can kick your tail, I'll have you know."

The gills on Ecrib's long neck flared as he hissed. I stepped away, concerned we might get into an actual fight.

Ashlyn patted her eldrin's shoulder. "Calm down. It's too early for this." She eyed me again. "I just think Gray needs to rethink what he's wearing for the trip." She pushed her bangs to the side, revealing the arcanist mark on her forehead.

Her seven-pointed star had a typhoon dragon—fins and all—laced between the points.

When Phila stood from the couch, she startled me.

I had forgotten she was even there.

Unlike Ashlyn, who had the muscle and physique of an adventurer, Phila was delicate. Her long, strawberry-blonde hair went all the way to her waist, and it practically glistened in the morning light as she ran her long fingers through it.

Phila had an artist's expression. Wide-eyed and dreamy, like she saw the world differently than the rest of us. With a smile, she tilted her head and met my gaze.

"I think Gray is perfectly prepared for this trip," Phila said. She gestured to my ill-fitted clothing. "No matter the weather, he's sure to be comfortable." Then she pointed to my small bag. "And he isn't encumbered by unnecessary weight."

Ashlyn glanced between me and my bag. She maintained her dismissive frown. Her dragon joined in the frowning.

"You've participated in a camping event before, right, Gray?" Phila asked. "You must've experienced so many."

I narrowed my eyes. "What makes you think that?" And hadn't Sorin said it was a camping *trip* and not a camping *event*? Did she even know what she was talking about?

"You're an islander, aren't you?" Phila patted her lower lip with a single finger. "You must sleep outside and in small tents all the time. That's what my nursemaid said. She said the islands flood with water from storms. Well, the islands without arcanists protecting them, that is."

I bit my tongue to prevent myself from getting too sarcastic.

What did Phila know about island life?

Phila wore a similar outfit to Ashlyn's. Tight, white pants. A beautiful black vest. But she wore a pink shirt underneath, one fashioned from silk and decorated with tiny beads around the collar and sleeves. Her family had coin to spare—it was obvious—and from what I knew of Phila, she had grown up in a palace, far from the Academy.

She knew nothing about the Isle of Haylin.

Sure, we had storms. And yes, sometimes we had to go to the storm shed to weather the downpour, but that didn't mean we slept on the ground or in tents! Camping wasn't *an event* we participated in because— where would we have gone? The island wasn't large enough to justify sleeping in a location other than home. I could walk from one side of the island to the other in less than a day.

"We should emulate Gray," Phila said as she crossed her arms. She glanced me up and down, taking her time to examine my clothing. "We don't want to look like we're new to this. I want to blend in. I want to look like an islander."

Ashlyn half-smiled and shrugged. Her dragon wrapped his tail around her legs, holding her close, his mouth somehow also curled in a smile, like Ecrib knew exactly what she was thinking.

"Captain Leon said the student who earned the best marks on this trip would be given a special trinket made by the artificers here at Astra

Academy." Ashlyn patted her eldrin. "So, while Gray may be more comfortable, I'm not here to relax. I'm here to win."

She said every word with the intensity of a challenge.

Twain puffed his fur, obviously feeling the same.

A trinket was a minor magical item, but they were still useful and rather expensive. I had never owned one. Winning one from this camping trip would be a fantastic way to show the elitists of the school that I was a contender to watch, even if I had been raised on a backwater island.

"Well, I don't know if your fancy clothing will make up for your inexperience," I said. Even though I knew nothing about building schools, camping, or dealing with highwaymen, Phila and Ashlyn didn't know that. "This is second nature to Twain and me. We already have this in the bag."

My confidence seemed to shake some of Ashlyn's away. But her hesitation was quickly replaced by fire. She huffed and then smiled, as though eager to get this started.

"I underestimated you before," Ashlyn said, sweet but cold. "Your tricks won't catch me off guard this time. And I'm already number one in our class."

"It's a friendly competition, then. May the best student win."

We locked eyes for a couple of seconds. Phila glanced between us, a slight frown on her face. My shoulders started to hurt from the strain of keeping my posture as straight and tall as possible. Competing with Ashlyn would be difficult—but I wasn't going to let her know I was thinking that.

Phila brushed back some of her long hair. "Well, while the two of you are dueling over honor, I shall investigate the natural phenomena of our destination."

Ashlyn turned to Phila, her eyes narrowed. "What natural phenomena?"

"I asked the professors why a tiny village existed out in the middle of nowhere. They told me it was because of the waterfalls. They're magical, and the locals bathe in them."

"Why?" I asked.

She shrugged. "I don't know. That's why I need to investigate." Phila smiled afterward, her attention drifting with her imagination.

Interesting.

"My arcanist," a soft voice called out. "I have your things, my arcanist."

We all turned to spot Phila's eldrin—a beautiful coatl. He was a five-foot-long corn snake with white and orange scales and beautifully colorful wings, much like a parrot's. What was his name? *Tenoch.* Yeah. That was it.

Coatls were considered rare and powerful. Once Tenoch was fully grown, I assumed he would be gigantic, but right now, he was just a hatchling. His wings were the size of a raven's, and his body was thin.

Which was awkward because Tenoch was *attempting* to drag Phila's backpack across the ground. He had his little snake tail wrapped around the straps, and he struggled to haul the overly-stuffed bag even just a few feet.

"I'm almost there," Tenoch said with a hissy wheeze. He yanked the heavy backpack half a foot more across the stone floor. "Don't worry, my arcanist. I have this."

Ecrib huffed and then stomped over. Typhoon dragons were so large that, even as a hatchling himself, Ecrib was more than twenty times the size of Tenoch. Ecrib grabbed Phila's backpack with his claw and effortlessly lifted it from the floor. Phila's coatl—too stubborn to let go—dangled from the strap of the pack. The coatl spread his wings and flashed his fangs, hissing at the dragon.

"It's my *sacred duty* to help my arcanist," Tenoch shrieked.

"You're pathetic," Ecrib said as he carried the backpack—and the coatl—over to Phila. "This will be faster."

"I should catch up with my brother." I turned away from the comical scene, allowing my shoulders to relax. My irrational fears about the abyssal hells had disappeared, and now all I wanted to do was spend time with Sorin.

"Wait," Ashlyn said.

I stopped and glanced over my shoulder.

"Let's go together."

Phila, Ecrib, and Tenoch all turned to me. There was a tense moment where they exchanged strange looks. For some reason, I suspected they thought this was an odd arrangement.

"Sure," I said. "Let's go."

Ashlyn hefted her backpack onto her shoulder and then jogged over to my side.

"Hmm," Twain said as he snuggled into my arms. "They better keep up!"

That was an ironic statement coming from a kitten who refused to walk himself anywhere. I had to carry him, either on my shoulders or in my arms, lest he wildly complain.

Once the others had joined us, we all traveled together through the halls of Astra Academy.

The plan, apparently, was to take the Gates of Crossing to an area close to our intended destination. I spotted the rest of Class One out on the docks of the nearby lake. Astra Academy had been built along a mountain range. Parts of the campus were located on several peaks, including one that was permanently awash in thick, white clouds.

The mountain lake near the Academy had five Gates of Crossing fixed in the water. Each gate was an impressive circular ring made of metal, all of them large enough to allow for a three-masted ship to sail through. The Gates of Crossing were shaped like an ouroboros—a serpent eating its own tail—and engraved across each were images of rizzels. Those ferret-like creatures were masters of teleportation, and their magic was the key to the gates.

I found my brother on the edge of the dock, standing a few feet from the others as he examined the water. The rest of our class stood around on the wood planks of the pier, none of them saying a word to the others.

A single boat was prepared for travel. It wasn't anything impressive—just a single mast, and no real hold to speak of. It was a fishing boat, nothing more.

Was it going to take us through one of the gates?

Sorin turned to face me as I came walking down the dirt path.

"Gray," he said with a smile. Then he held out his arms and embraced me as soon as I was close enough. "You're finally awake!"

The morning sun hung low in the sky. How was I late? This was still considered *early*.

I returned Sorin's embrace, but that just meant Twain was squished between us. My eldrin made disgruntled noises until we broke apart.

Using poetic rhythm for his speech, Sorin said, "*With the sun as our ally, and the wind as our friend, we shall brave the unknown, where we shall transcend.*"

I grabbed Sorin by the collar of his robes and pulled him to the side. "You need to stop that," I said in a hushed voice. "And we're not using the wind to travel. You remember the Gates of Crossing, don't you? We're teleporting."

Sorin pulled his robes from my grip and then patted his clothing back into place. He wore the same outfit as I did—our father hadn't had much to give us before we had gone to the Academy—but Sorin's barely wrapped around his barrel-like body.

"I remember the gates," he said, his voice low. "The wind was more of a metaphor for travel."

The shadows shifted around my brother's feet as his eldrin moved around. I ignored the darkness and instead pointed to one of the nearby Gates of Crossing.

"You should come up with a tribute to one of those." I shrugged. "They're powerful artifacts. Impressive feats of magic."

"Yeah, but..."

My brother's eyebrows knitted together.

But he didn't finish his sentence.

"What's wrong?" I asked.

In a whisper, Sorin replied, "They remind me of the upside-down gate."

The *upside-down gate*.

According to legend, the abyssal hells had been sealed closed with an upside-down gate. That was why the gate in the basement had been upside down. Professor Zahn had done his research and had gone way out of his way to make the perfect portal. The Gates of Crossing in the lake were similar to the one Zahn had created, but each was slightly smaller and had been made with less magic, apparently. They wouldn't take us to the abyssal hells.

I hoped.

"You liked the gates when they brought us to Astra Academy," I said.

"But..." Sorin rubbed at the back of his neck. "I just don't think I'll be able to think of something epic and poetic when all I can imagine is the abyssal dragon and the Death Lord."

"C'mon. Nothing is as epic as a Death Lord."

Nothing was as terrifying, either. But I didn't say that. I wanted my brother to focus on concocting some other poem or phrase so he would be distracted for the travel. *He* liked spinning words into cute little poetic sayings, but I suspected no one else appreciated it. They all probably thought it was silly and childish. I was just trying to save my brother from the inevitable embarrassment.

"I guess you're right," Sorin eventually muttered. "Death Lord Deimos was impressive, even if he was dark and frightening. I'll try to use him as inspiration for something."

"I think it's for the best," his eldrin said, the knightmare's voice drifting up from the shadows, disembodied and haunting. "You should turn your fears into a battle cry to intimidate your foes."

"Also, poetry is like any other skill," I said. "You gotta practice in order to get good. You can't just rhyme things together and call it art. That's insulting. You need to really invest yourself into the words. People don't pick up a sword one time and call themselves a swordsman. That takes time and practice. Same with poetry."

Sorin nodded as he stared at the darkness around his feet. "Yeah... You're right. I need practice. And I need to learn more... I need to progress."

I liked this. Perhaps Sorin would cut down on the number of times he burst out into random poetry.

I patted Sorin's shoulder. "All right. Let's get this whole camping trip over with." I turned and glanced around, searching for Captain Leon and the professors.

Where was Helmith?

# CHAPTER 4

## SAFE TRAVELS

I didn't see Professor Helmith anywhere.

Guardian Captain Leon was obvious, though. His short, white hair fluttered in the wind like a dying flame. He stood on the gangplank of our fishing vessel, his armor shining in the morning sunlight. It wasn't a full suit of metal armor—just the chest piece and a shoulder pauldron. He wore sturdy trousers, leather gloves, and an impatient expression.

"Listen up," Captain Leon shouted. "Everyone should form a line and file onto the boat. Keep your belongings with you. We won't be on this ship long."

He had a neat beard on his chin, and he stroked it as everyone in our class slowly complied with his command. Captain Leon's skin had known the sun for years. It was tanned and leathery, and he seemed like the sort of person who thrived away from civilization. The mark on his forehead was a seven-pointed star with a three-headed dog woven throughout.

A cerberus.

When Captain Leon caught me staring, he narrowed his eyes. "You Lexly boys doin' okay?"

Occasionally, he seemed to speak with an accent. I wasn't sure where he was from. Not the islands, that was for sure.

"We're fine," Sorin said as he waved his hand. "Thank you!"

"Why are you thanking him?" I whispered as we took our position at the end of the line.

"For looking out for us."

I held Twain close to my chest and lifted an eyebrow. "Maybe he thought we were troublemakers."

Sorin shook his head. "Nah. Captain Leon has been asking about us all the time since..." My brother lowered his voice as he said, "*Since the basement.*" Then he resumed his normal volume. "I think he's just worried about us."

I hadn't thought of that. It made sense. Captain Leon had almost died fighting Zahn; the doppelgänger arcanist, Seven; and Death Lord Deimos. If Leon hadn't been there, I suspected Sorin and I wouldn't be here, either.

"Nini?" Captain Leon called out. He pointed at her. "You okay?"

Nini walked over and took her spot in the line right behind me. She kept her gaze down as she nodded. "I'm fine."

"Good," Captain Leon replied with a huff.

Nini had also been in the basement. Sorin's theory held more weight, it seemed. Captain Leon was concerned about all three of us. Which was unexpectedly kind of him, if I was being honest. He tended to rely on yelling as his primary form of communication.

"The Academy looks horrible," Nini whispered as she turned around and squinted.

Everyone in line turned to glance up at Astra Academy.

It sat on the top of the nearby mountain, its black, stone walls, giant windows, and pointed towers a glorious sight to see. Except for the massive hole in the lower section of the back wing. It was a destroyed wreck—a gaping wound left over from the battle with the Death Lord. Zahn's modified Gate of Crossing, the one that had led to the abyssal hells, had exploded so thoroughly that bits of it had gone everywhere, including through the stone walls.

Headmaster Venrover had summoned some of the professors' arcanists to help repair the damage, but they hadn't yet arrived, apparently.

At least the treehouse was still in one piece. None of the exploded gate had ripped through the colossal redwood that grew on the eastern side of the Academy. Even from our spot on the docks—at least a mile away from the tree—I spotted the many rooms and personal spaces for mystical creatures all throughout the trunk.

"You were here less than a month, and already you ruined the place," someone said.

The prissy tone and snooty commentary were instantly recognizable. I slowly turned to face Starling, the unicorn. The little foal clopped his hooves on the pier and swished his ivory mane back and forth. His horn, made of pristine bone, was still small, only a few inches in length. Once Starling was a fully grown unicorn, it would be an impressive sight, but right now, he was just a baby horse, practically all legs.

Knovak patted Starling. I didn't know when Knovak found the time, but he had altered his pointed hat to include a small stitching of a unicorn's head, complete with the horn. I suspected he had done that because half his arcanist mark was covered by the hat.

"I'm surprised the headmaster didn't have you help clean it all up," Knovak commented.

I just narrowed my eyes into a sardonic glare. "You know it wasn't *me* who made a gate to the abyssal hells, right? It's not *my* fault there was an explosion."

Starling lifted his little muzzle into the air. "Hm! I'm sure you had some hand in it. I've seen the way you Lexly twins operate. *Shady.* You use all sorts of questionable methods. If my arcanist and I had been there that night, we would've handled things in an organized way, thank you very much."

I opened my mouth to lash out with something sarcastic, but Sorin quickly placed a hand on my shoulder. He knew me too well. I bit back my commentary.

"I bet you two would've been great to have during the fight with the Death Lord," Sorin said, smiling through it all. "I heard unicorn arcanists used to be honorable knights, known throughout the lands."

"Now they're just washed-up nobles," I commented under my breath. Sorin jabbed me with his elbow. I held back the rest of my statements.

Knovak grabbed the brim of his cap and turned away from us.

Sorin and I couldn't ever seem to get along with that guy, it seemed.

"Hurry up now," Captain Leon said, jerking me out of my thoughts. "We should be sailing out soon."

One by one, our class funneled onto the fishing boat.

Ashlyn first, with her typhoon dragon, Ecrib.

Exie second. She liked to keep herself in Ashlyn's shadow whenever possible. She wore a long, white dress, which was probably the single worst outfit someone could wear on a trip to build a school, but I wasn't about to say anything. I'd just laugh to myself whenever she attempted to do anything.

Exie's eldrin, an erlking by the name of Rex, flew through the air behind her, leaving an illusion trail of afterimages. His wings were like a peacock's, and his little body was covered in fancy clothes. More illusions? That was what erlkings were known for, after all.

Phila was third on the ship, followed by her coatl—still dragging her overstuffed backpack and breathing like a bellow.

Raaza and his kitsune leapt up the gangplank afterward. Both of them seemed quick and nimble, and Raaza hadn't packed much outside of what he was wearing. His large hat shielded him from the sun.

Knovak and Starling both pranced onto the ship. They were made for each other.

Sorin and Nini managed to get on the gangplank next. My brother smiled at Nini the entire time. He whispered something to her, and she giggled. Her reaper, Waste, floated nearby, but he didn't need to walk on the pier or the plank of wood. Waste just floated along, untethered by gravity. His empty cloak body was still disturbing, though, even if it was intellectually interesting how he moved about.

That left me and...

Nasbit.

He was a golem arcanist, and his eldrin, a sandstone golem by the name of Brak, stood on the pier. Nasbit's eyebrows were knitted, and he continually wrung his hands together, even as I walked by him.

He was a portly fellow—large and pillowy, like a sack of grass. Nasbit wore the fine clothing of nobility, just like Ashlyn and Phila. Silky shirt. Tailored vest. Pants that fit a little too snug. His velvet robes were tied shut in the front, probably to hide some of his gut, but I wasn't judging. People came in all shapes and sizes, after all. And there were more important things in life to worry about than one's silhouette.

"Aren't you getting on the ship?" Twain asked as we walked by.

Nasbit exhaled. Then he gestured to his golem. "I'm not sure if Brak will make it up the gangplank."

Brak was a hefty mystical creature. It was made of large stones all held together through magic. Bright gold flecks of dirt were speckled throughout the boulders of its body, glittering in the sunlight. The golem had no eyes or mouth—or fingers or toes. It was just a massive beast, a little over four feet tall.

It was... heavier than all the other creatures, including Ashlyn's typhoon dragon.

"I'm sure it'll be fine," I said with a wave of my hand.

Nasbit poked his fingers together and then frowned.

"*What's wrong with you two?*" Captain Leon snapped. He stood on the deck of the ship, glaring at us like we were insane. "Just get aboard!"

Nasbit and his golem didn't move, however.

"You heard the captain," I whispered.

"I'm worried." Nasbit kept his voice to barely a breath of volume. "What if I break the gangplank? I'll make a fool of myself. I mean, the others already make fun of me for my weight..."

I hadn't heard of that. It didn't surprise me, though. Sometimes people were cruel and made fun of anything they could see.

With a sigh, I glanced down at Twain. My mimic stared at me for a long moment before realization dawned upon him. Once Twain understood what I wanted, I glanced back at Nasbit. "I'll go up first. I'll make sure the gangplank can support your eldrin's weight."

Nasbit frowned in confusion.

That was when I dropped Twain to my feet. I closed my eyes and concentrated on our surroundings. The magic in the nearby area felt like threads to me. *Strings*. They all led back to a source. I just needed to tug on a specific thread—to make the connection taut.

I picked the stone golem.

With all my focus, I tugged on Brak's thread.

Twain meowed. Then he bubbled and shifted, his whole kitten body practically exploding outward in a burst of rock and sandstone. He grew large, his fur disappeared, and then so did his facial features and claws. He warped into an exact replica of Brak.

The star on my forehead—normally empty—filled with the image of a stone golem.

Nasbit's eyes grew wide. "Oh! You're going to test the gangplank for me?"

I patted his shoulder. "Glad you're keepin' up."

Before he could reply, I briskly walked up the gangplank and stopped on the deck of the ship. Everyone from our class watched as Twain lumbered up after me. His stone stomps strained the plank of wood. It groaned in protest, but it never broke.

The handful of sailors on the ship watched, their mouths agape.

I hadn't realized how amusing this was.

Once Twain was on the ship, he shimmered and shifted back into his kitten form. The rocks disappeared, and his orange fur puffed back out across his body. A veil of magic faded from his body as he dashed over to my feet.

My arcanist mark changed again, reverting to an empty star. The shift never hurt, but I felt it every time—my skin rearranging itself.

"It's all good," I said, loud enough for Nasbit to hear me on the pier. "This whole ship is sturdy. I like it."

Nasbit and his stone golem shuffled onto the ship a moment later. None of the other arcanists paid attention—they were now focused on Captain Leon, who held a star shard in his hand.

The star shard wasn't large—it was just the size of his thumb—but it sparkled with the brilliance of a dozen stars. The inside of the shard was filled with magic and power, and it captured the attention of everyone in the vicinity.

"Now that everyone is finally aboard," Captain Leon said, obviously holding back a quip, "it's time to go over a few things. We'll be heading to the very edge of the empire, far from most roads and civilization. Then we'll camp near a tiny village known as Red Cape. We'll be learning the art of survival, as well as the beauty of cultivation and community service."

He made the last part sound as dull as mud.

The rest of my class must've felt the same way, because not a single person said a word, not even while Leon waited in silence. Was he expecting a round of applause? Why the pause?

When no one did anything, Leon cleared his throat and continued.

"Treat this camping trip like one long extended class session. We'll be practicing our evocation, and I'll also be teaching you all your manipulation abilities. As a cerberus arcanist, I evoke fire, and then I can *manipulate* fire. Some arcanists manipulate different things—unrelated to their evocation—and while some of you have already begun expanding your magical knowledge, I would recommend you wait for my instructions."

Raaza groaned loud enough to be heard from the Academy's tallest tower.

The heavy stomp and huff of a large creature drew everyone's attention away from Leon. I glanced over my shoulder and spotted a fully grown cerberus running down the pier. It was Sticks, Leon's eldrin. The three-headed dog was a massive creature. His black-and-rust fur—thin and shiny—barely covered the dog's rippling muscles.

Sticks galloped up the gangplank and then hurried over to his arcanist's side, two of his three heads panting. The third head—the one in the center—carried a small pouch in his mouth.

Sticks also wore a saddlebag, something typically meant for horses. Both bags were stuffed full of supplies.

Captain Leon patted his eldrin on the head. Sticks wagged his long tail, practically whipping Knovak in the face. Fortunately, Knovak stumbled out of the way just in time.

"Now that we're all here, I have an announcement," Captain Leon said with a smile. "We will have a competition, of sorts. I'll be awarding points for your performance during the trip. The individual with the highest score at the end wins a trinket."

The ship filled with whispers and excited murmurs. Ashlyn and I exchanged a knowing glance. When our gazes met, I smiled. She answered with a smirk.

"Oh, one last thing." Leon held up a hand. With a cold and serious tone, he added, "There are rumors of highwaymen near our target destination. If we should stumble upon these fiends, it will be our job to handle them. As your instructor, I will give you clear directions when—or if—the time comes."

Raaza perked up at this announcement, like it had been specifically crafted for him. His eldrin flashed fire from her feet as she danced around him.

Captain Leon gave us all a final once-over. "And that's it. Let's set sail!"

But there was someone who still wasn't here.

"Wait," I called out.

Everyone turned to face me, even Sticks, all three heads.

"Where's Professor Helmith?"

The others in my class quickly exchanged glances and snickers. Someone whispered, "*Of course he's anxious to see her.*" Someone else commented, "*Does he ever even think of anyone else?*"

Captain Leon ignored the hushed murmurs. "She'll be joining us there," he said. "No need to worry about it."

I wanted to make a joke about how Leon hadn't recognized the signs that Helmith had been in danger before, but again, I just kept it to myself. Sorin wouldn't appreciate a sarcastic quip, and the, *what would Sorin do?* test seemed to be working so far. I was trying to keep my sardonic comments to myself.

"I was just curious," I said.

Captain Leon walked to the bow of the ship and planted a foot up on the railing. He grimaced slightly, and I suspected he hadn't stretched that far in some time. "We, er, are ready to set sail," he said through gritted teeth. Leon didn't move from his position. I suspected he couldn't without rolling to the side.

The sailors knew what he wanted, though. They set our little fishing boat in motion. The single sail carried us toward the Gate of Crossing in the center of the lake, and while Leon remained at the bow the entire time, it wasn't long before we were nearing the silver ring of metal.

The star shard in Captain Leon's hand glowed a bright white. He tossed it onto the deck of the ship.

And that was when we sailed through the ring.

# CHAPTER 5

## FOX FIRE PRACTICE

The etching around the Gates of Crossing glowed with the same
light as the star shard

The brightness blinded me.

I held up an arm to shield my eyes. Where were we going? The
moment the ship teleported, I stumbled forward, shaken. The light
vanished, and I regained my ability to see. We had arrived at another body
of water. It wasn't a lake, but the ocean. *An* ocean. I wasn't sure which.

The waters were a vivid blue laced with green, the white foam at the
edges of the waves a welcome sight. I missed the fierce waters of the ocean.
They were beautiful and deadly at the same time. If sailors weren't careful,
the waves would claim their lives.

Twain leapt up to my shoulder. He dug his claws into my clothing.
"Where are we?"

I chuckled to myself. Then I pointed to a spot beyond the bow.
"There. See the shoreline? It's that dark spot. It's probably Red Cape."

"Look at those waves!" Twain's fur puffed out, making him into a
spherical orange mass. "And all that salt! *Yuck.* I hate everything about
this."

"I love it."

Twain's ears went flat against his skull. "Boo. I don't like it when we disagree."

I patted him along his back, scratching near his bobtail. "Then I'll just have to change your mind, won't I? How much do you like... fish?"

His ears immediately perked back up. "More than I like breathing."

"Then I've got good news."

The ocean winds picked up, breezing across the deck. Leon and his cerberus stood near the bow, both staring at our intended destination. Leon had his hands on his hips like this was the start of an epic adventure.

Exie walked across the deck and approached me. The gusts played with her white dress, practically tangling it around her legs. Exie stumbled once before correcting her posture and huffing in irritation. Her erlking flew next to her, occasionally spinning in the air after a strong blast of wind whipped by.

Her curly, chestnut hair was pinned down to keep it from flying about. Exie had a knack for maintaining her regal beauty, even in the worst of conditions.

She was definitely the prettiest one here.

It wasn't much of a competition, though. The others in our class didn't seem too concerned with appearances. Well, that wasn't true. Knovak was definitely invested—he just wasn't as good as Exie in the execution department.

"Good morning, Gray," Exie said as she walked up to my side. "How are you?"

Even her speech felt rehearsed and polished.

"Pretty good." I shrugged. "No nightmares, which is all that matters, right?"

Exie forced a laugh and then waved one of her hands. "So true." Then she cleared her throat. "But the real reason I came over was because you're an islander, right? I was hoping—because I'm not very well versed in all this—that you might help me once we reach land."

"Help you do *what*?"

"You know. Find my way around. Assist me in all the physical tasks. Help me with the assignments so I can gain points. Introduce me to the local arcanists. That kind of thing."

"I've never been to Red Cape." I offered her a shrug. "It's not an island. It's just a port city on the coast. I have no idea who the arcanists are."

"But you can find them?" Exie narrowed her eyes. "I just need your help, Gray. A simple *yes* would suffice."

"A simple *please* would go a long way, too."

I probably shouldn't have been sarcastic. Exie's mood soured in real time, her frown forming in a matter of seconds. She really didn't like me. I didn't much care for her, either. She had been rather rude to Nini, even making her cry, and I had never forgotten it.

Rex, her erlking fairy, fluttered close. "Your disrespectful attitude is unbecoming of a student from Astra Academy." He had a cute little voice that undercut his chiding. "My arcanist asked for your assistance. A chivalrous and noble arcanist would have accepted in an instant."

Twain cuddled his kitten body close to my neck. "Uh, I'm pretty sure anyone can walk around a port and ask for the local arcanists. She doesn't need *our* help."

Erlkings were strange little creatures. They were fairies—with humanoid bodies—but Rex's skin was an odd color, similar to ash. Despite that fact, his face grew red as he clenched his little fist. Then he waved his hand, and an explosion of bugs flew straight for Twain and me.

I leapt backward, flailing my arms, completely caught off guard.

Twain hissed and swiped his claws.

Bees, wasps, mosquitoes, and gnats swarmed around my head, landing on my cheeks and crawling toward my eyes. The sudden panic actually gave me a moment of clarity.

Erlkings evoked illusions.

None of this was real.

With my heart pounding, I forced myself to stop flailing around. Twain was a little slower to catch on. His claws dug into my shoulder as he took turns swiping with his left and right paws, his fur puffed out to its fullest extent again.

"I'm so sorry about that," Exie said as she grabbed her erlking out of the air. She hugged her eldrin close. "Rex is just a little touchy. You understand." With a smug smile—like she delighted in my panic but didn't want to admit it—Exie patted Rex on his head.

The bugs vanished just as quickly as they had appeared.

Twain gulped down a breath, his eyes wide, his pupils dilated.

"Well, I'll be on my way, then. Sorry to bother you." Exie wheeled around on her heel and strode off down the deck of the ship, her dress threatening to catch around her legs a second time.

She went straight for my brother.

I almost wanted to storm over and tell Exie to leave my brother alone, but that was ridiculous. My brother was a grown man. He could make his own decisions. I was certain he would be kinder than I had been. Sorin never turned someone down if they asked for help—even if their request was preposterous.

Twain huffed as he twitched his whiskers. "I don't like illusions."

"Do you know anything about them? What if you transformed into an erlking?" I laced my fingers together and then rested my hands on top of my head. "That's an evocation we should master in our free time."

"I don't know. It seems... difficult."

"It'll be fine. We can do anything we set our minds to."

Twain turned to face me, his eyes narrowed. "I can't tell if you're being serious or not."

I shrugged. "Hey—I'm just trying to be optimistic. Also, I made some pretty big claims in class about being the most magically powerful one here, and it would be embarrassing to mess up now."

Twain snorted out a little laugh. "I think you need a better reason to become a talented arcanist. *Not embarrassing yourself* seems too low a bar for us." He puffed out his chest. "We're amazing, and we need amazing goals to aspire to."

I turned my attention to Ashlyn. She stood at the starboard railing of the ship, her typhoon dragon by her side. She waved her hand over the side, and water splashed up to greet her palm. Was she practicing her manipulation? Could typhoon dragons control water? It made sense.

Even now, she was practicing.

It made me angry, but in an excitable way. It wasn't the same frustration I felt with Exie. This was different. When I glanced over at Ashlyn and saw her practicing, it made me think, *Why aren't I doing that?*

It made me feel like I was falling behind.

And I couldn't have that.

Determined to improve my own magic, I headed for the port side of the ship. On my way, someone *else* hurried to speak with me.

Raaza.

The scarred man practically tackled me onto the deck. He hurried over, his kitsune hot on his heels. They were by my side in an instant, Raaza's face set in a glower, his kitsune's eyes also narrowed, mimicking his mood.

"Gray," he said. "I thought we would teleport closer to port."

"Professor Helmith told me the Gates of Crossing are set up far at sea to safeguard against crashing. Ya know—so people aren't surprised by what they find on the other side of the port."

"That's fine. And logical. But now it'll be a good thirty minutes before we're docked." Raaza grabbed the brim of his wide hat and shielded his eyes from the sunlight. "I don't want to waste that much time. Train with me. Help me get better."

I almost made the same joke I had made with Exie—no one wanted to say *please* anymore—but Raaza wasn't even asking. He was demanding. Did it really matter? I had been about to train anyway.

"All right," I said.

"Good." Raaza half-smiled. "My fox fire is unique and special. Since I can create tangible illusions, the possibilities are endless."

"Why do you need my help?" I asked.

"Because my imagination will be the limitations of my fox fire, and you're an individual who likes to think outside of the box. Help me think of useful ways to use my ability."

Raaza held out both hands, palms facing skyward. A burst of red fire lit up our portion of the deck, but just for a moment. When the flames died, both his hands held a gold coin each.

"I've seen your coins before," I said. "Can you make anything else yet?"

"Not currently... Coins were the first thing I manifested, and since then, it's like I've had a mental block. It's the only thing I can create."

With a shrug, I said, "Well, you can use those to *buy* things." Then I half-laughed.

That didn't amuse Raaza, though. He just shot me a glare.

"Way to think outside the box," he snapped. "If you have the mind of a common thief, I'll go elsewhere."

I sighed. "It was a joke. Besides, I can't help you unless I know the circumstances you're in. Are you creating coins in the middle of combat? Or are you in town?"

Raaza's kitsune, Miko, trotted up to me, her fluffy tail swishing. "I have a scenario. We're hunting down a villain. No, wait! *Highwaymen.* We're hunting down the highwaymen."

She leapt into the air and landed with all four feet spread, as though on the prowl.

Then Miko continued. "Then the highwaymen stop at a river," she whispered, her voice harsh and overly dramatic. "And we want to sneak up on them. How would you use fox fire?"

Twain purred slightly as he said, "Oh, I like this." His eyes grew wide, and his pupils expanded to circles. "It's like we're detectives, trying to bring in the villains."

Although Raaza had come to me asking for solutions, he held up a finger to answer Miko. "I could throw the coin into the water to distract them. While they're investigating, I can sneak up from behind."

Miko smiled.

"The villains might just think it's a fish," I said. "Then they would ignore it, and you've wasted time."

Raaza slowly nodded. "True."

"Just because you're limited to creating coins doesn't mean you have to think about them like coins." I grabbed one out of Raaza's hand and then held it up between two fingers. I turned it around until one side caught the sunlight and glinted. "See that? You could hang the coin in a tree so it catches the light. Then the villains would see the twinkle in the forest and get intrigued. As they stomp over to your hanging coin, you're lying in wait with plenty of traps."

Raaza's eyes went wide. "Traps. *Yes.* Exactly."

A bell rang out across the ship.

"We'll be pulling into port soon," Leon shouted. "Everyone, gather your things and meet me on the quarterdeck. We'll be disembarking shortly."

Although I wanted to spend more time with Raaza and his kitsune, I handed him back his fox fire coin and shoved my hands in my pockets. The bug illusions the erlking had created didn't have any tactile sensations. Despite the fact that I had seen the creepy crawlers on my cheeks and hands, I hadn't really felt them. My mind had just filled in the blanks for the few moments I had been panicked.

But Raaza's fox fire was different.

The coin had been very tangible. Even the light had bounced off it, acting as though it were real.

There were so many possibilities with that—Raaza was right.

How could I use it to my advantage? I would have to think about it for a while.

# Chapter 6

## Shadows Under The Waves

Our ship neared the shores around Red Cape.

And *wow*—it was sad.

They had a grand total of ten buildings. And *building* was a generous description. One little shack had a tarp for a roof, and another "building" had mud walls and was half in the ground, like a cooler shed used to keep meats cold. Perhaps that was what it was. So, eight buildings and two ramshackle locations likely used for storage.

And a single road.

The village didn't even have a proper port or harbor. Our ship was literally too large to get near the coast, so dinghies were prepped and readied for our convenience. Everyone in class gathered near the edges of the ship, waiting their turn to get into one of the tiny boats.

Ashlyn, Exie, and Phila all shared a boat. Ashlyn's typhoon dragon just slipped into the ocean, though. He swam alongside the small vessel, manipulating the waters with his magic, helping it speed toward Red Cape.

Nasbit and his stone golem got their own dinghy. It made sense. The golem was heavy, and the boat strained when the hulking pile of rocks climbed inside. Nasbit whispered supportive words to his eldrin the entire time.

Raaza, Knovak, and Captain Leon stepped into the third dinghy. Leon's eldrin, Sticks, was so massive that he practically took up half the boat. The monstrous cerberus dog wagged his tail at a fearsome rate, his three heads glancing in all directions—but especially at the seagulls overhead.

The birds squawked incessantly.

Sticks didn't like that much. His exhales were laced with embers as he glared daggers at them.

That just left me, my brother, and Nini. That suited me. Sorin was a comfortable presence, and Nini was a fine conversationalist. The three of us piled into our boat, and I realized we had plenty of room.

Sorin's knightmare hid in the shadows.

Nini's reaper didn't weigh anything. It just hovered around the boat like a ghost.

And Twain was a kitten. He sat on my shoulder like a parrot sat on the shoulders of pirates.

Our dinghy could've held up to six people, which meant we had plenty of space to stretch out and relax. That also suited me. With a smile, I motioned to the water.

"Twain, transform into a typhoon dragon." I pointed to the waves. "If Ashlyn and the others are going to arrive early, we should try to catch up."

Twain frowned. "We haven't really learned how to use magical manipulation properly yet." Then he leaned in close to my ear and whispered, "Remember that one time we tried to manipulate things and we practically died?"

"It wasn't *that* bad," I whispered back. "C'mon. Let's try."

My little orange kitten fluffed himself up. Then he glanced at the water and glared.

He didn't like getting wet. *That* was why he didn't want to do it. Everything made sense now.

I patted his head as I kicked my feet up onto an empty seat. "Never mind, actually. We should just relax and enjoy the short trip to shore."

Sorin held both oars. He was large for his age, and while he was barrel-shaped and not defined, he was definitely muscular. "Everyone, hold on," he said with a huff as he rowed us closer to the shore. "I might not have water manipulation magic, but I think I can get us there quickly."

"Don't strain yourself," Nini said. She gently touched his shoulder and frowned. "It's just a short trek."

I glanced over at the shore. If Sorin rowed hard, we'd be there in about five minutes.

"It's okay." Sorin exhaled as he rowed again. "I have a sea shanty for this very occasion." He huffed as he propelled the boat forward. "I wrote it myself."

"How does it go?"

Sorin smiled wide. The winds played with his black hair, giving him the appearance of a swashbuckling arcanist. It was like he had been made for this life.

"*Oh, there once was a crew that loved a song,*" Sorin sang out. "*The nights were cold, and the days were long. They filled their time with rum and beer, and covered the seas in their lustful cheer.*"

Nini giggled, but she hid most of her face in the collar of her oversized coat. She did that from time to time—hiding herself in the mountain of clothing. I wanted to ask her why, but had never found the time nor the place.

"I like this," Twain said, clapping his little forepaws in time with the lyrics.

I wasn't as into the singing. I glanced over the edge of the dinghy, content to stare at the water and just allow the light to seep into my tanned skin.

"*But then one day they disappeared,*" Sorin said, his tone never shifting away from upbeat. "*Was a monster they said and many feared! The oceans swirl with the dead, souls want vengeance, or so it's said!*"

The waters around our little boat rippled for a moment.

I thought I saw something move in the depths below us—a shadow of a large creature. It wasn't human.

There were many mystical creatures that dwelled in water. According to Professor Helmith, the ocean was where *most* creatures could be found, they were just difficult to bond with. So, that meant the swirling in the depths below us was nothing more than a creature stirring through its home.

Nothing more.

But for some reason, the hairs on the back of my neck stood on end. I rubbed at my gut, my hand shaky as I felt the thin scarring.

The abyssal hells...

It was the place all the dead went to. I had thought it was more of a story, but apparently, it was true. And according to all the legends, the gate to the abyssal hells was located at the bottom of the ocean, deep in a trench away from human influences.

But that just meant it was under us right now.

"*They say ghosts are vicious and cruel as well,*" Sorin continued to sing. "*They want more blood, and that means farewell.*"

The boat rocked slightly.

Sorin kept rowing—and he was picking up speed—but the jostling of our dinghy wasn't him.

Then I saw it.

A creature beneath the water. Something with scales and tentacles—like an eel and an octopus had merged into a single hideous monster. What was that? I had never seen a mystical creature like that.

And it was longer than our dinghy, and swimming so close.

But then it disappeared. Not into the depths, or out into the ocean. It just *shimmered* and seemingly vanished from my sight. The water rippled and shifted, but then everything went calm. Was it still there?

What was it doing?

What *was* it?

My heart raced as I sat up straight.

"Sorin," I muttered.

My brother caught his breath and stopped rowing. For a short moment, he just stared at me. And then, like any good sibling, he understood something was wrong. He scooted forward in his seat and got closer to me.

"Yeah?" Sorin whispered.

Twain tilted his little head. "Are you seasick? You're so pale. That's not like you."

Even Nini furrowed her brow as she gazed upon me.

With a powerful exhale, I glanced over the side of the boat. The calm waters were practically mocking me. No more shadows. No more bizarre creatures. No more movements. Just gentle tides all the way up to Red Cape.

After a long moment of staring, nothing happened.

I glanced back at the others. "I thought I saw something, but maybe it was just my imagination."

"You're sure?" Nini whispered.

Again, I glanced at the water. Nothing. "Yeah, I'm sure."

Sorin let out a long breath. "Oh, *whew*. I thought you were going to say the nightmares were back." He smiled widely. "I'm glad it wasn't that." He grabbed the oars again and rowed a little easier than before. "I need to write a sea shanty that *doesn't* involve the abyssal hells next time."

"I think it's for the best, my arcanist," Thurin said from the darkness at Sorin's feet. "Besides, it limited your lyric selection."

"Yeah, you're probably right."

While they discussed song choices, I closed my eyes and forced myself to calm down. What was I worried about? We were far from Astra Academy, and nowhere near the abyssal hells, even if we were sailing across the ocean. The gates were closed—I had exploded the Gate of Crossing that led to a Death Lord—and there was no way anything like that was around here.

No way.

A nervous chuckle escaped me. I was getting paranoid. That wouldn't do.

Then the dinghy hit the shore. Sorin chivalrously leapt out, pulled the boat up onto the rocky sands, and then offered his hand to Nini. She hesitantly took it and then stepped out. Once she was safe on land, Sorin grabbed me and yanked me out, almost without warning.

"Careful," Twain hissed as he clung me. "I don't wanna get wet!"

After I got to my feet, and Sorin moored the dinghy, we hurried over to the sad storage shed to meet with the others of our class. They had gathered around the mud walls of the tiny shed, most of them giving it odd glances from time to time.

Sure enough, it smelled of fish and blood.

Definitely a place where the people stored meat.

Captain Leon straightened his half-plate armor as he paced around. He glanced at the dinghies, and then at the small village. Sticks did the same thing, all three of his heads completely out of sync.

"What're you looking for?" I asked.

"I thought..." Leon shook his head and then squared his shoulders. "Never mind. It doesn't matter. It seems we're the first ones here, which is fantastic because now we can spend the next couple of hours hiking to our destination. This weather is perfect."

Everyone glanced up to the clear blue skies overhead. Not a cloud in sight.

We had been "in town" for a grand total of three minutes, and already, everyone was sweating. Well, except for the stone golem, who couldn't sweat.

"The mercy of shade has abandoned us," Sorin said in a deadpan tone.

Captain Leon ran a hand through his white hair. "Trust me, it's better than making the hike at night." He clapped his hands together once. "We're heading north, away from Red Cape, in order to set up camp near our eventual destination. Then we're going to collect some lumber and build a much-needed schoolhouse, understand?"

"Why haven't the good people of Red Cape come to greet us?" Knovak asked. He fixed his giant hat in place and made sure it was shielding his eyes. "We're all arcanists, after all. I figured they would *want* to see us."

"The people of Red Cape are typically busy this time of day. I'm sure we'll see some of them as we head through the village."

Exie raised a hand.

Leon pointed to her.

"I don't know how to build a schoolhouse," she stated matter-of-factly.

"But you know how to follow instructions, don'cha?"

"Well... I suppose."

"Then you'll do fine. Any other questions?"

Although I didn't really know her well, Phila turned to face me, her hair fluttering out with her quick movement. "I have a question for Gray."

I pointed to myself. "Oh?"

"Why don't you have your mimic transform into a rizzel and just teleport us to our camping destination? Then we wouldn't have to walk." Phila fanned herself and then sighed.

"Uh, well, I can try."

The rest of my class waited with bated breath. Except for Ashlyn and

Nasbit. They had both seen me attempt teleportation. I had almost killed us all.

That didn't mean I didn't want to try again.

I closed my eyes.

It wasn't necessary for me to close my eyes, but when I did, it gave me an extra bit of concentration. It was as though removing my sight allowed my brain to focus in on the magic all around me. I felt around for the threads—the strings of magic that fluttered off every mystical creature and arcanist.

My mimic abilities were different from everyone else's abilities. Whereas everyone else could evoke magic or manipulate things, I couldn't unless Twain was transformed.

If I mentally tugged on one of these threads, Twain would rearrange himself into the exact shape and size of the mystical creature whose powers I wanted.

But...

I scrunched my eyebrows together.

There were no rizzels close by. The only magic threads I felt were the nine people around me. Nothing else. No arcanists lived in Red Cape? It seemed that way.

With a powerful exhale, I stopped trying.

"Sorry, Phila," I muttered. "But we're too far away from any rizzels for me to use their magic."

She frowned. "You have a limitation? It isn't just *everywhere*?"

"Sorry. I mean, maybe I can extend the range once I've practiced enough." I wasn't sure about that, but it was something to look into. I wanted to be the best mimic arcanist anyone had ever seen. Especially the others in class.

"That was anticlimactic." Knovak huffed and then headed for the road.

His unicorn pranced along after him.

"Everyone, grab your things," Captain Leon shouted. "The faster we go, the quicker we'll be there!"

# CHAPTER 7

## ARCANE VEINS

T he hike wasn't as awful as I had imagined.

The pathway was well-worn, and trees grew on either side aplenty. With the shade as our ally, we made our way over gently rolling hills, away from the sad village of Red Cape.

And while the entire trek was uneventful, I knew the instant we had reached our destination. Not because Captain Leon had said something, but because everything changed. The vegetation, the trees—even the air was different.

For two hours, the grass had been green, and the oak trees had been vibrant and lively. Now the grass was teal, and the trees were thick and twisted. Were they even oaks anymore? Their long leaves seemed closer to willows, and their trunks were so thick, they could be hollowed out to make a small home.

And it had all happened in an instant, like we had stepped over some threshold and entered a new land entirely.

While everyone else in my class gawked and marveled at our bizarre new surroundings, Captain Leon continued forward as though nothing had happened. Perhaps the man was color-blind, or maybe he had other thoughts on his mind, but he barely even gave the nearby area a second glance.

The flowers were purple, the dirt a shade of dark red, and the clouds overhead were tinted orange.

"Do you know what this is?" I asked Twain.

My little kitten eldrin shook his head. "I've never seen anything like this!"

"It's like the world decided to color itself differently today."

"Maybe the woods are sick."

Captain Leon glanced around and then abruptly stopped. He wheeled around on his heel and rubbed his hands together. "Here we are, class." He motioned to the blue grass all around us, then pointed to the thick trees. "You might notice something strange about this area."

His cerberus circled him once before taking a seat, his tail wagging enough to kick up red dust.

"This place has been changed by the *arcane veins*," Captain Leon said matter-of-factly. "Think of it like a magical ore. Like iron. Only it shows up randomly and sometimes without warning."

Nasbit's hand shot into the air. His arm practically trembled with excitement, and he huffed out his breaths, barely restraining himself from speaking.

Leon pointed to him, his brow furrowed.

"Arcane veins are like star shards!" Nasbit blurted out. "They're rare phenomena that produce magical plants and materials. Whereas star shards fall to the ground from the sky, arcane veins sprout up from the ground. The veins are clusters of ore that look like rubies but are actually just crystalized magic."

A lighthearted giggle filled the air around us. Everyone glanced around, searching for the source. Although I didn't immediately see her, I knew the laugh like it was my own.

Professor Helmith.

I spun around just in time to catch her walking up the path.

She wore a dress as light and feathery as dew on a dove's wing. It trailed behind her, fluttering on the gentle breeze. Her inky hair swirled around her heart-shaped face, framing her cheeks and accentuating her lavender eyes.

Professor Helmith had the poise of a dancer and the regal bearing of royalty. When she approached our class, everyone parted to allow her through. She smiled at each person, acknowledging everyone.

Then our eyes met, and she giggled once more.

I hoped my face didn't redden, because I'd never hear the end of it from my classmates. I turned away as soon as possible and rubbed my face, hoping to hide even my expression.

I was glad Professor Helmith was here. Even though her magical abilities only dealt with dreams and sleep, I felt safer with her around.

When Helmith strode by, I took note of her shoulders. She wore a sleeveless dress that exposed her arms all the way to the edge of her collarbones. Blue and pink swirling tattoos flowed across her skin down to her wrists. The mystical tattoos were in the shape of storm clouds, stylized and glittering with power.

"Nasbit, you're correct," Professor Helmith said as she took her place next to Captain Leon. "You must've been studying."

Nasbit nodded once.

"Star shards are the magical component needed to make trinkets and artifacts—permanent magical items." Helmith held up a finger. "But the *ore* here has special properties that can *enchant* living creatures, such as arcanists and their eldrin, making them permanently more magical." She pointed to the glittering tattoos across her shoulders. "These markings here are enchantments that empower my magic."

A group-wide *oooh* swept through our class.

"But how does it work?" Raaza asked. "If we touch the ore, do we get enchantments?"

"No, unfortunately. The ore must be ground into a fine powder and made into an ink." Helmith smiled widely. "But there is one other way. Some mythical creatures carry enchantments on them. Like a sickness, it can transfer to those that interact with them. But that is very rare."

Captain Leon nodded. "It has gotten rarer and rarer since the God-Arcanist's War. I wouldn't bank on finding a creature in the wild with enchantments. Best get them with the ore and make your own, I think."

I had seen a few professors with the glittering tattoos before, but I had never asked what they were or why they had them. Now I knew. They were enchantments. Rare—very valuable—no doubt expensive.

Odd that Professor Helmith likened enchantments to a sickness, though. But maybe I was thinking too hard about that.

"All right." Leon clapped his hands together. "Drop your things here. This is your first assignment." He knelt and dug a hand through the blue grass. Then he stood, shook away some of the dirt, and showed off the thumb-sized rubies he had plucked from the ground. "See these? Bits of occult ore. I want you all to find more."

Everyone glanced down to their feet, myself included.

Twain squinted at the grass.

I didn't see any hints of rubies. Were we supposed to dig through the dirt? Were they everywhere here?

"These ores are more prevalent underground," Leon said.

Everyone continued staring at the dirt.

"But some filter up to the surface, causing all the strange coloration changes you see around us. Now, I'm going to give you all thirty minutes to gather as many of these little bits as you can find. Whoever finds the most gets a trinket, and whoever finds the second will get some points for the overall trip."

The talk of points got Ashlyn's attention. She stood straight, and Ecrib flashed his massive dragon fangs.

"I want you to use your evocation as much as you possibly can." Leon tucked the ore into his pocket. "Don't worry, you can't harm the occult ore with your abilities. It's very sturdy. You'll need to sift through the grass, dirt, and river to find these little bits, though. They should sparkle when you get close, makin' it easy to spot them when they're nearby."

I wanted to use more of my abilities, and it seemed everyone else felt the same way. Everyone stood close to their eldrin, poised to run off in every direction.

"Professor Helmith, Sticks, and I will be setting up camp while you're searching," Leon stated. Then he waved his hands around. "This will be the site we're staying at. You need to come back after thirty minutes."

Murmurs of acceptance ran through the group.

"Okay, then, what're you waitin' for? Your thirty minutes start now!"

I dropped my bags and waited to see where everyone went. Phila and Exie ran off together, Knovak continued down the road, Raaza went for the northern tree cluster, and my brother took Nini toward the sounds of water—likely for the nearby river.

Nasbit and his stone golem didn't hurry away like everyone else. They slowly headed toward the eastern cluster of trees, taking their time to search every inch of soil along the way.

That left me and Ashlyn. When I glanced over, I noticed she was glaring in my direction.

"Is something wrong?" I asked.

Ashlyn motioned to our surroundings. "Which way are you heading?"

"Whichever direction has the least amount of people."

"That was *my* tactic."

"Great minds think alike."

My quip-compliment didn't make her laugh, like I had been hoping. Instead, she narrowed her eyes further, evidently not amused by my antics. I wasn't about to lose to her, though. I just wanted to search around without fighting everyone else.

We didn't have many options at this point. We could go west—no one had gone that way—but south just went straight to a grouping of rocks. And they weren't strangely colored rocks, they were just normal, plain, brown boulders. A small hill that was pretending to be a mountain, really.

"The two of you should just go together," Captain Leon said, breaking me out of my thoughts. "That'll keep you both out of trouble."

That wasn't the most ideal solution, but I didn't mind it. If we gathered the same number of occult ore, would they split the reward between us?

Ashlyn sighed as she grabbed the neck of her typhoon dragon and then climbed onto his back. Ecrib was about the size of a small horse, and he could easily carry her weight. He happily stomped westward, his fin-covered tail swishing through the dirt as he went.

I glanced at Twain on my shoulder. "When can I ride on you?"

"Never." Twain licked his paw and then smiled. "You're *my* mount."

"We'll see about that in the future."

"Hmpf!"

Then I hurried after Ashlyn. Before I passed Professor Helmith, I slowed and gave her a knowing nod. She acknowledged me with a small wave, and then I quickened my step. Once I had reached Ecrib's side, I slowed my pace to match the lumbering dragon's.

The surrounding area was still bizarre to me.

Thick trees made the place seem like a maze. We traveled around a cluster of them, bringing us to a new field of blue grass. The trees seemed bloated, almost. Sap leaked from the bark in a surprising amount. Were they okay? It made me think they would explode if left untended for too long.

We walked together as a group for a few minutes, no one saying a word to each other. Should I be the first to break our silence? I decided not to. Ashlyn still seemed irritated we were doing this together, and I didn't want to add to her frustration with idle chitchat.

But...

She was the type of woman who would appreciate talks of strategy.

"So, here's my plan," I said, holding up both hands. "We carefully search a small area, rather than rushing around the place."

Ecrib stopped near a flat portion of the field.

Ashlyn hopped off her dragon. "Okay, Ecrib. Search this area." She stepped away and crossed her arms, never really acknowledging me.

I stood by her side and patted Twain on the head. What was her typhoon dragon going to do? He was a creature of the ocean, after all.

The monstrous dragon huffed. Then Ecrib slammed his claws into the strange grass and raked them through the dirt, gouging a huge chunk of earth straight from the ground. He was so large, and so strong, that the process was effortless.

Then he did it again, only in the spot directly adjacent to his last strike.

It was like Ecrib was plowing the field and prepping it for harvest—all by his lonesome.

He dug deep furrows into the ground, yanking up the dirt at impressive speeds and then chucking the clods around with little regard for where they landed.

"See, my thought was to just tear up as much ground as possible," Ashlyn said to me. There was a slight hint of amusement to her voice as she added, "You're more than welcome to go try your strategy elsewhere. The professors can't see us here—they won't know if we split up."

Then she casually walked over to a clump of dirt and sifted through it. At first, I thought she wouldn't find anything, but Ashlyn eventually pulled a small ruby-like piece of ore from the dirt.

One for Ashlyn, zero for me.

"Curse the abyssal hells," Twain whispered. "At this rate, she's definitely going to beat us."

Ashlyn turned around, her blonde hair shining in the afternoon light. She genuinely smiled—not smugly or arrogantly—catching me off guard with her beauty. A lump formed in my throat, and I didn't know what to say.

"Remember when we were tasked with finding star shards together?" she asked as she walked over to me. She held the ore up to the light, the scarlet inside glittering. "Sometimes I think these magical lessons are just chores in disguise, ya know? They could've just paid someone to come out here and collect ore, but instead, we're out here."

I chuckled, my voice awkward and strained. With a powerful couple of whacks to my chest, I cleared my throat. "Yeah. I remember searching for star shards."

"Someone tried to kill you out in the woods."

"Professor Zahn, the Death Lord's brother," I said. "*That* was who was trying to kill me."

Ashlyn's smile disappeared and she glowered at me. "You know, in the future, you can just ask for help. I'll help you. Ecrib will help you."

Her eldrin stopped digging up the field. He glanced up, his scaled snout covered in mud. He shook his head and flung it everywhere. "What was that, my arcanist?"

"You'll help Lexly if he needs help," Ashlyn said. "Right?"

"Of course."

"See? So, next time you're in danger, don't hesitate to ask for our help."

I lifted an eyebrow. "Did you just call me *Lexly?*"

"That's right." Ashlyn smacked me on the shoulder. "Everyone else calls you *Gray*. I want to use something unique."

She wanted something unique, huh? That was a good sign.

"Maybe I should start calling you *Kross,* then. Since that's *your* last name."

"No," Ashlyn said. "My family name isn't fun to say. Unlike yours. I like yours."

I wasn't that fond of mine, either, but if she liked it, she could say it all day long. I wouldn't mind that.

Now that her dragon had stopped, I stepped forward. "Twain." I held out my arm. "Are you ready? Let's show Ashlyn and Ecrib how to *really* find occult ore."

My eldrin stared at me with half-lidded eyes. In a quiet voice, he said, "You have no idea what you're doing."

"Play along," I whispered. "This will go great."

"I have a bad feeling about this..."

I set Twain on the ground. "Digging through the ground is fine, but it's slow. Allow me to demonstrate a superior form of searching." I pushed up the sleeves of my coat and shirt.

Ashlyn and her typhoon dragon watched with neutral expressions. I wondered if she would be impressed with my plan. I hoped it would work.

I closed my eyes and searched for the magical threads of the arcanists and mystical creatures all around me. One of them would have magics that could help. Illusions? Fox fire? Shadows? Fear? Surely, someone would have something...

Then I had a brilliant idea.

I tugged on a thread, and the arcanist mark on my forehead burned as Twain shifted shapes.

## CHAPTER 8

# FIRE AND BRIMSTONE

Twain's orange fur melted into black and rust. His head shifted until he had three, and his body expanded to the size of a small horse. Before our eyes, Twain became a muscular cerberus, expertly mimicking Leon's eldrin.

He was Sticks, just with Twain's mind.

My arcanist star shifted until a three-headed dog appeared in the etching. I rubbed at my forehead and then shot Ashlyn a smile. "Are you ready?"

She crossed her arms and lifted an eyebrow. Her dragon sat back on his hind legs and did the same, only adding a huff at the end.

"Go on," Ashlyn said.

I turned to Twain. His three dog heads just stared back at me. I stepped around him and then held out my hand. Evoking magic involved pushing energy from the body out into the world. I had seen Sticks in action before, just like I had seen Leon. Cerberus arcanists evoked powerful fire. And since Helmith had said the occult ore filters to the surface, the fastest way to fit it would be to clear away everything.

After a deep breath, I closed my eyes and pictured my magic leaving my body through my palm. Once the visual was in place, I pressed outward.

Fire erupted from my hand so quickly, and so intensely, I startled myself. With a flinch and a few steps stumbling backward, I set the field ablaze. Then I ended the evocation, my heart hammering.

"Oh, I see," Twain said, his voice identical to Sticks's gruff tone. "Like this?"

He opened all three of his dog heads and lit more of the field on fire. The flames washed over the strange grass and then swept up the trunks of the nearby trees. Smoke filtered into the air like disgusting pillars. Would Leon and Professor Helmith see that? Probably. Would they come over and stop us? Would they get angry?

I hoped not.

Twain stopped evoking flame and then glanced over at me. I covertly offered him a shrug.

"Uh," Ashlyn muttered. She stared at the fire and smoke for a long while before frowning. "Are you going to do anything about this?"

"In a moment," I said as I shook out my hand.

"You're going to burn down Red Cape before we even manage to build a school," Ecrib quipped. The typhoon dragon glared at me. "Is that your idea of getting out of work?"

I waved away his comment. "Are you two even paying attention? Look there!" I pointed to the center of the field, between a cluster of embers. Red bits of ore glinted among the flames, plain as day. "There they are. Three bits of ore."

Ashlyn rolled her eyes. "Okay, Lexly. Let's see it. Go get them."

I rubbed at my shirt. Twain glanced over again, his cerberus heads all frowning. I had seen Leon use his magic before. When he *manipulated* fire, he could effortlessly snuff it out. That was all I needed to do—snuff it out.

But I hadn't learned much about manipulation. It was about controlling magic outside of the body. The flames burning the field *should* be easy to manipulate, but I wasn't even sure where to begin. In an effort to buy time, I cracked my knuckles and smiled.

"Step back," I said.

Ashlyn and Ecrib took a step back.

Twain did the same. I shot him a glare. "Not *you*."

"I have a bad feeling about this," one of his cerberus heads muttered as he stepped up closer to me.

What was the best way to go about doing this? I shook out my hand a second time.

The problem with my mimic abilities was twofold. First, I needed to know how to use *everyone's* magic. While all the other arcanists at the school could focus on mastering one set of abilities, I didn't have that luxury. Evoking fire was *a lot* different than evoking terrors or even lightning. Second, if Twain mimicked an older creature, its magic was substantially more potent than a young creature's. And since I was a new arcanist, potent magic stung me.

The fire I had evoked from my palm left behind a subtle agony.

Until Twain was older, I made a mental note to avoid mimicking older creatures. I should've had him transform into Ashlyn's typhoon dragon. Ecrib was practically still a hatchling. I could handle his magic.

"Any day now," Ashlyn called out.

She pointed to the flames that were creeping their way across the field. The smoke had become a curtain that rose into the sky, blotting out some of the glorious sun. I sighed the moment I realized the professors would *definitely* see this.

I exhaled, and then held up my hand a second time. Picturing what I wanted the fire to do, I waved my arm around. At first, nothing happened, which was disappointing, but at least a tree hadn't exploded or something.

Then I tried again, this time *really* envisioning the flames snuffing out. I waved my hand.

Some of the fire answered the summons of my borrowed magic. A few embers ceased to be, practically winking out of existence. But large portions of the flames just moved around, dancing to the motions of my hands. The fire spread to the trees faster, and even grew in size.

How was that happening?

I stopped waving my hand, wondering if perhaps I should use *both* arms. Would that allow me to control more of the fire? Or just cause an inferno twice as fast?

"This isn't as bad as I envisioned, but this isn't *good*, either," Twain muttered.

Enough smoke wafted through the air that my eyes watered and I had to cough before speaking. "You're not helping."

Ecrib flared his gills. He wheezed and hacked and stumbled backward, away from the flames. "*End this*, kitten arcanist. Or I'll do it for you."

"You can snuff out the fire?" I asked. "Because if you can, now is a great time to do it."

Ashlyn snapped her attention to me, obviously shocked. "You can't do it?"

"Well... let's say I'm having a bit of trouble."

"Curse the abyssal hells!"

She dashed away from the clearing and ran full tilt into the forest. Ecrib turned and followed her, stomping through the undergrowth as fast as his fin-covered legs could carry him.

"Do you think they're running away?" Twain asked.

I shook my head. "Probably not?"

"Okay, well, focus! You can manipulate the flame. I know you can."

"You can, too," I said, motioning to the growing blaze. "I'd love your help."

"O-Okay. Together? On the count of three." One head said, "One." The second head said, "Two." And the last head yelled, "*Three!*"

Both Twain and I attempted to manipulate the fire. I pictured it dying this time—ceasing to exist altogether, as though it had never been here in the first place.

And that seemed to work.

The fire on the trees withered and died.

Some of the flames on the field vanished. Twain's ears perked up and his tail started wagging a mile a minute. "Look, Gray!"

"I know," I said with a chuckle. "We're doing it! We're manipulating the flames!"

Ecrib and Ashlyn came rushing out of the nearby trees. Balls of water floated in the air near them, twirling around as though gravity had abandoned a small fountain's worth of fluid. Ashlyn waved her arms and a head-sized ball of water hurtled through the air. It splashed across a small portion of the field, killing a segment of the flames.

Ecrib waved a clawed hand. Two more balls of water hit the fire on the grass. The blaze sizzled as it died, more smoke wafting into the sky.

There were only a few patches of fire now.

Twain and I used our newfound ability to manipulate magic to snuff them out.

"You can manipulate water?" I asked Ashlyn as she slowly walked over.

With a frown, she nodded. "You knew that."

"Well, I mean, you can carry it through the air? I didn't know *that*. A useful ability."

"If there's water nearby." She waved to our surroundings. "*Some* arcanists evoke the things they can manipulate. Like cerberus arcanists who evoke *and* manipulate fire. But typhoon dragons don't have that luxury. There has to be water *nearby*, or else I can't do anything with that."

"There's always water nearby." I gestured to the grass on the side of the field that was still green. "Plants have water in their leaves. Trees have water in their trunks."

Ashlyn narrowed her eyes in a sarcastic glare. "Yeah. Great. The tiny fragments of water inside the *grass* will really help quell a raging inferno. What insight you have. Your parents must be proud."

I snapped my fingers as I walked out into the charred part of the field. "I don't appreciate your sass." With a smile, I knelt and scooped up three bits of ruby-like ore. Then I quickly juggled them before tucking each into the pocket of my trousers. "Who has more occult ore? Me? Or you? Because with the power of *simple addition*, I've determined that I'm winning."

Ashlyn pursed her lips. With a chuckle, I ambled back in her direction. Something about gloating only felt good with Ashlyn. She wasn't like the others. They would have all gotten angry. Not her. Ashlyn would get *even*. I saw it in the way she slid her gaze to the surrounding area.

Twain bubbled and shifted.

His giant cerberus body melted away, the black and rust colors swirling back into orange. He became a small kitten once again, his giant ears pointed upward.

"I'm tired." He groaned. "Sorry, Gray. I *tried* to maintain the form longer. I really did."

I shrugged. "It's fine. Just help me find a few more pieces of ore."

A sharp moan echoed from the distant trees—the ones that had burned. I wheeled around on my heel and stared at the blackened trunks. Smoke continued to spill into the sky, creating a haze. When I stepped forward, I had to rub at my eyes and cover my mouth with the collar of my shirt.

"Did you hear that?" I asked no one in particular.

Another moan sounded from beyond the trees. The tone was agonized, almost frightened. Was someone injured? Had my flames actually caught someone? The horror of the situation sank into my thoughts. What if a villager from Red Cape had been strolling through the woods, and my evocation had accidentally burned them?

"Hello?" I called out.

A gurgled groan was the only answer.

I hurried forward, my heart beating so hard, my ears were filled with the thumping. Did we have any arcanists nearby capable of healing?

"Gray?" Ashlyn asked.

I pushed my way past the black trunks. "Hello?" I called out again, this time louder.

Sounds of splashing, followed by another moan.

"Gray?" Twain also yelled.

I coughed back some of the lingering smoke and glanced around. Was someone here? Perhaps it was one of the highwaymen everyone kept mentioning.

Then I saw it. The source of the noise. The creature groaning and splashing about.

It was a human corpse. A half-rotten body covered in flotsam and dripping mucus so thick, it might as well have been jelly. Its bone hands were sharpened into claws, and its skull had glowing eyes deep in the sockets. Fangs jutted out between normal teeth, and water occasionally sloshed out of the seaweed wrapped around in its guts.

What was this? It definitely wasn't a bandit.

I took a single step backward, my legs unsteady.

It was... something straight out of the abyssal hells.

Then the monster moaned again, and it lunged for me.

# CHAPTER 9

## THE MIDNIGHT DEPTHS

The half-rotted corpse slashed me across the left shoulder and part of my chest. Its claws sliced through my flesh as easily as it slashed through the fabric of my robes and shirt. I caught my breath and stumbled backward, the injury pulsing with sharp pain that lanced through my body.

I had felt this before...

Shaken, I fell backward and hit the ground in a sitting position, my right hand over the injury. This was exactly the kind of pain I had felt when Death Lord Deimos had hit me with his trident. The memories of that terrible event flashed in my mind, stealing my ability to breathe.

The shambling corpse came forward, its glowing eyes fixed on me.

What did it want?

"Back off, *fiend.*"

Ashlyn—who had run up close, though I hadn't seen her do so—held up her hand, her face fixed in a hard-set glare. A blast of lightning shot from her palm and struck the undead monster. The raw power crackled over the body, the goo of its bizarre flesh falling off its skeletal body and hitting the ground with an odd *gloop* sound.

"Are you okay, Gray?" Ashlyn ran to my side. When the corpse continued to stumble forward, she half-stepped over me, shielding me from the monster. "*Don't worry.* I'll handle this."

She evoked another blast of lightning, this one a bit brighter than before. Ashlyn was already making improvements in her magic, and we had only just begun schooling.

I needed to be more like her.

Ashlyn struck the corpse creature, and more of its outsides splashed to the ground. But that only slowed its pace. With another groan, this one bordering on *enraged*, the monster flung itself at Ashlyn. The corpse crashed into her, and they both tumbled to the ground. Ash from the fire puffed into the air like a black fog.

Ecrib came crashing forward. Typhoon dragons weren't the most graceful mystical creatures when on land, so Ecrib ran like a lumbering adolescent elephant, the fins on his legs practically getting in his way. Then Ecrib crunched his fangs down on the corpse and tossed it off of his arcanist.

Ashlyn leapt back to her feet, just as shaken as I was. She almost couldn't get her footing. Her dragon eldrin stayed close to her, offering his shoulder to help steady her footing.

The monster got back up, its seaweed insides spilling across the ground.

Twain ran into my lap, half-startling me. I flinched, my heart pounding, but I settled once I realized my eldrin was close.

"What're you doing?" Twain yelled. "*Get up!* We have to do something."

"R-Right."

I closed my eyes and searched for nearby threads of magic. What could Twain transform into? It was difficult to sense things. Everyone was so far away.

And the corpse...

It was magical, but...

Its thread of magic wasn't right. It wasn't like all the others' threads, which were solid and led to a source. This creature had magic that seemed to come from... nowhere? When I tried to tug the thread—so that Twain could transform into it—it was like tugging on a rope that had been cut.

Nothing happened. There was no "source" for Twain to assume the shape of.

What was going on?

Instead of dwelling on that, I focused on Ecrib.

Twain bubbled, and his orange fur shifted into blue scales. He meowed as his skull contorted into a dragon-like shape. I managed to push him off my lap before he swelled up into his new giant size. But Twain was tired. He wouldn't be able to maintain his typhoon dragon shape for long.

I held up my hand and evoked lightning. The blast of power hit the corpse's leg and the femur cracked. Then the monster's leg broke, and it toppled over. Once on the ground, it moaned and crawled forward, digging its bone claws into the blackened dirt.

It headed toward me, its glowing eyes flickering.

What was this?

I finally managed to stand. "Crush its skull," I commanded Twain.

With a slight frown, Twain lunged. In his new typhoon dragon form, he managed to bite down on the head of the monster and crush the creature's dome. The moment the skull *cracked* open, a scream and a sigh exploded out of its body.

The monster's mouth fell open, its body went completely limp, and the glow of its frightening eyes vanished.

Then the corpse's body melted away. The bones. The seaweed. Everything. It all turned into a bluish-white goop that liquefied faster than ice caught in a bonfire. Wisps of steam sailed off into the air, leaving nothing behind.

The corpse had just... vanished.

Twain shook and then reverted back to his orange kitten form. His sapphire scales disappeared as he shrank down. Then he shook out his whole body and turned to me with his eyes narrowed.

"I didn't like that *at all*," he said. "Do you know what that tasted like? Of course you don't. *You* weren't the one to get a mouthful of grave-creature." Twain rubbed at his tongue with one of his front paws. "Next time," he said between rubs, "I'm ordering *you* to shove death down your throat, got it?"

I just stood there, my shoulder bleeding, the pain intense. I wanted to joke around with Twain, but I found it difficult to breathe. Something still wasn't right. Although the monster had disappeared, I still felt like it was nearby. The presence of the monster lingered in the air.

Ashlyn shook her head. Her eldrin gently bumped her with his snout. She rubbed Ecrib's horns, and it seemed to soothe her.

"Thank you," she whispered to her dragon.

Ecrib snorted as he nodded once.

Twain walked over to me, his nose in the air, his ears laid back. When he reached my feet, his fur was puffed out. He looked like an angry potato. "Did you hear what I said?" Then Twain tilted his head. His two-colored eyes landed on my injury. "Gray? Are you still bleeding?"

I kept my right hand pressed over the injury, but blood still flowed out from between my fingers. After gulping down some air, I managed to shake my head. "Something is still nearby," I whispered. "We need to find it."

"Are you okay?"

"We need to find it," I repeated.

I ran my left hand through my hair as I forced myself to walk forward. The trees in the area were already warped from the occult ore soaking through the ground, but it seemed the farther I went along, the more they became twisted and saggy. The trunks drooped, and the leaves hung heavily on the branches.

It was like they were dying.

Water soaked the earth beneath my feet. I walked through puddles and patches of mud, my footing unsteady. Why was there so much water here? We weren't close to the river, and I hadn't seen a pond or a lake.

"Gray? Gray!"

Ashlyn and Ecrib rushed to my side, Twain in Ashlyn's arms. She handed me my eldrin, but I refused to remove my right hand from my shoulder. Instead, I took Twain with my other arm, a little awkward, but still. Twain snuggled against my chest and quietly purred.

"What's going on?" Ashlyn asked.

I shook my head. "I don't know. But something is nearby."

"How can you tell? I don't sense anything." She turned to her dragon. "Do you feel it?"

Ecrib scoffed. "The nature of magic isn't something I'm familiar with, but as a typhoon dragon, I understand water. And the water here is salted, like the ocean. Furthermore, the water doesn't smell of algae or seagrass."

"What does that mean?" Twain asked.

"It means the water came from the Midnight Depths."

When it was obvious that Twain didn't know what that meant, Ashlyn sighed.

"The *Midnight Depths* are the places in the ocean that are so deep, the light never reaches there." Ashlyn straightened her blonde hair. "No plants grow when there's no light. Ecrib is saying this water came from the deepest part of the ocean."

Twain sarcastically glanced around the forest. Then he narrowed his eyes. "And what delivery service does this area use? Because I want in."

"This is serious," Ecrib growled, his scales flared.

Twain hid in my arms. "Well, I was *kinda* serious," he muttered. "How did water from the Midnight Depths get all the way *here?*"

I ignored his question. Instead, I stepped forward, determined to find the source of my anxiety. Something was here. I just had to find it. The problem was—I didn't know what I was looking for. Another corpse? More ocean water?

Something.

I leaned over, scanning the water-soaked ground as I went. Ashlyn and the typhoon dragon followed close behind, neither saying a word. I appreciated their presence, considering my mounting levels of dread.

Then I spotted it.

A small speck of silver at the base of a rotted tree. The branches hung so low, they created a curtain that almost blocked my view of the shimmering silver.

I rushed through the swamp-like environment, hurrying as fast as my legs would take me. The mud got so thick near the dead tree that when I lifted my right foot, my boot was left behind. I didn't care. I kept trudging forward until I eventually lost my left boot. Who needed boots, anyway?

"This place is scaring me," Twain whispered. He snuggled close to me, his eyes wide.

After taking a deep breath, I pushed some of the branches aside and stepped closer to the trunk. The silver glittered, even though no light was shining here. The afternoon sun couldn't pierce through the thick canopy of leaves.

With slow steps, I made my way over. Then I knelt next to the strange object.

It was the size of my pinkie and half-buried in the mud. The silver had lines across it, like it had once been a part of a large object with a picture etched across it. Was this a puzzle piece?

No.

I set Twain down next to me. He arched his back and practically hissed at the swamp around us.

With my breath held, I reached for the sliver of silver. Right before I touched it, I jerked my hand away. The object had *rizzel* magic on it. I recognized the tendrils of magic. As a mimic arcanist, my innate ability was to sense magic, after all—I trusted my assessment more than any book or professor at Astra Academy.

This was a fragment from the Gates of Crossing.

But not *any* gate.

This was the gate used to open a pathway to the abyssal hells.

When I had destroyed the gate, pieces of it had gone shooting off in all directions. They had shot off with such force, they had broken through the walls of the Academy. And they had traveled *far*. At least, from what I could remember.

This realization shook me. I stood, my heart hammering. I removed my right hand from my shoulder. My injury... it was still bleeding. Arcanists healed quickly due to the magic flowing through their body. Why wasn't I healing now? Was it because that corpse had come stumbling out of the abyssal hells?

I turned on my heel, my eyes on the water all around the tree.

This ocean water...

It was from the abyssal hells, too.

The fragment was somehow summoning it all here with rizzel teleportation magic.

Ashlyn and Ecrib pushed aside the low-hanging branches and walked over to me. They had moved slowly enough that Ashlyn had managed to keep her boots.

"What's going on?" she asked.

I pointed to the glittering bit of silver. "That's a fragment from the Gates of Crossing. Not a normal gate. It's from the gate that led to the abyssal hells."

Ashlyn's eyes went wide, her eyebrows shooting to her hairline. Her eldrin flashed his fangs and flared his scales for a second time. With a glare, he stared down the tiny metal fragment. Twain leaned against my leg and stared up at me with a frown.

"You're sure?" he asked.

"Very," I muttered.

I wasn't wrong. I knew. And if we didn't remove the fragment, more disgusting creatures would show up in this area.

Some perhaps bigger and more powerful than the shambling corpse.

# CHAPTER 10

## GATE FRAGMENTS

"We need to take this gate fragment to Professor Helmith," I said.

Ashlyn glanced at the small, silver object and then back to me. "You want someone to *touch* that thing? That's a terrible idea. What if it teleports us to the abyssal hells?"

"We can't leave it here. What if some random person touches it? They have no idea how dangerous it is."

Ecrib snorted and then shook his head. "The professors—or some other master arcanists—can handle this. We don't need to do anything."

Twain, who hadn't moved since I had set him down in the swamp waters, glanced up at Ecrib with a smile. In a tone bordering on a condescending purr, he said, "Aww! Is the big, powerful dragon scared of the little silver piece?"

"Quiet, *kitten*." The typhoon dragon flashed his fangs and growled at Twain, but he didn't move any closer. That would've put him near the gate fragment.

Arguing was pointless. Either we were going to risk the danger and pick up the fragment, or we were going to be cowards and wait until someone else handled the problem. Both were viable choices, but for some reason—it was irrational, but still—I felt responsible for the gate fragment's presence.

It wouldn't have been out here if it hadn't been for me.

Well, technically, it had been Professor Zahn's fault. He was the one who had built the gate to get into the abyssal hells... But still. *I* was the one who had exploded it.

I grabbed the hem of my robe and ripped off a small line of fabric. The others watched me in silence as I created a tiny hammock and then used it to cradle the silver sliver of gate. Without ever touching the fragment myself, I wrapped it in the cloth and then lifted it from the water. With quick movements, I tied the cloth in a knot and held the very top with just my pointer finger and thumb.

Although I couldn't see it, I *felt* the gate piece as though it were a burning piece of coal radiating heat. Something about this object disturbed me. Probably the *abyssal hells* part, but I couldn't be any more specific than that.

"Okay, nothing happened," I said with a forced smile. "Step one of my master plan worked. Let's go take this to Professor Helmith."

"We should probably take it to Captain Leon." Ashlyn eyed the cloth. "And you're sure that'll be okay? You're not going to drop it?"

I glanced at the blood on my shoulder. The injury still stung. "I think I'll be fine." Then I shrugged, and pain shot through my arm. After I grimaced, I returned my attention to Ashlyn. "I trust Professor Helmith. And she knows lots about magic. I'd rather give it to her."

Ashlyn didn't offer any more protests. We walked away from the swamp around the tree as a group. Twain didn't trudge from the water, though. As soon as Ecrib turned around, my mimic jumped onto the typhoon dragon's tail. Ecrib growled, but Twain just clung to the scaled tail, his claws practically digging into the dragon's flesh.

"I hate the water," he said with a mew.

Ecrib snorted. Without another word, he stomped forward, carrying Twain until we were out of the swampy mess. Then he shook his finned tail and flung Twain onto a nearby patch of grass. "I'm not your horse," Ecrib muttered.

With all the grace of a baby rabbit, Twain hopped to his feet. He walked off as though he owned this whole forest, his nose in the air, his ears rested back against his head.

I walked after him, trying to keep my focus on the gate fragment. The cloth wasn't teleporting away... That was a good sign.

"Gray."

I stopped and turned. Ashlyn stood close. She reached into a pouch on her belt and withdrew white bandages. Then she motioned for me to turn. I did as she silently instructed, wondering if she knew anything about medicine.

"I packed extra," she said as she tugged at the collar of my shirt and robes. With some effort, Ashlyn managed to expose most of my injury. "Lift this arm."

"Good thing you came prepared," I said. I kept the fragment held in my other hand as I lifted my arm.

"*Ha, ha.*" Ashlyn rolled her eyes. "Your sarcasm gets old sometimes."

"I wasn't being sarcastic. I'm really glad you packed extra. Thank you."

Ashlyn wrapped her bandages around my shoulder, but she kept her eyes narrowed in suspicion. When she tightened the bindings, I flinched. She frowned and loosened everything. "You're welcome."

As Ashlyn delicately finished the wrapping, I wondered if I should tell her she was beautiful. She was, obviously. Even after fighting a monster—with mud splashed on her white pants, and her blonde hair tangled in her ponytail—she still had this youthful confidence and athletic poise. But was now the right time? Would she think I was being sarcastic again?

Ashlyn stepped away from me. "Done. You can put your arm down."

I did so.

And the moment to compliment her was gone. I turned away, cursing myself for not just *going for it.*

"Are you okay?" she asked.

I rotated my shoulder. "Yeah. Why?"

"Your face is red."

I huffed and hurried to catch up with Twain and Ecrib. "It's just hot out here, and I'm tired. We should get back to Professor Helmith. C'mon."

Ashlyn easily kept my pace as we hurried back to our camp spot.

The field for our campsite had been completely transformed.

Five tents had been erected while we had been gone, all positioned in a circle around a large firepit. Sticks, Leon's faithful cerberus, gathered wood for the fire like it was a game. The giant, three-headed dog bounded from the campsite, into the woods, and then returned with two logs and a mouthful of twigs.

Sticks then dropped everything off next to the stone firepit, wagged his tail, counted all the logs in the pile, and then bounded away again. It was as if the dog lived for this task.

Leon knelt next to the fire pit, slowly arranging the stones in a perfect circle. He even went out of his way to make a spit for roasting meat and vegetables. Everything was in its place. Everything had a place. The man was so focused on his work, he didn't even notice me or Ashlyn as we exited the trees.

The tents kept my attention as I walked toward the firepit.

Two of the tents were black, two of the tents were dark brown, and one tent had a white tarp over the top. They were grouped together according to color, and each one was large enough to comfortably fit eight people. A pole kept the middle of the tent propped up, and I wondered who had gone through the effort of hammering each pole into the ground.

Ecrib stomped into camp, but slowed his pace when he spotted Sticks bounding away into the trees. Twain walked over and watched the cerberus as well, his ears straight up.

Before I could call out for Professor Helmith, she emerged from the tent with the white tarp. She smiled when she spotted me, her lavender eyes bright with the afternoon sunlight. But then her expression hardened.

"Gray?" she asked. "What's wrong?"

I hurried over to her, still holding the cloth with the fragment in two fingers. "Professor Helmith—something terrible has happened. We were out gathering the ore and I found *this*. It's a piece from one of the Gates of

Crossing. The one Zahn created." With a quick thrust, I handed over the fragment.

Professor Helmith took the cloth in her palm and undid my knot. The silver fragment glittered in the light, but the cloth around it was wet with fresh ocean water. Somehow, the little fragment was moving things from the abyssal hells to this location.

But how?

"I see," Helmith whispered.

I nodded once. "There was a corpse out in the woods. Ashlyn and I fought it and then it just disappeared." I spoke so quickly, I practically tripped over my words in my haste to speak. "It was trying to get me. Specifically. It lunged, and we fought it, and it cut my shoulder. Right here. Ashlyn bandaged it because it wouldn't stop bleeding, and—"

"Everything will be okay," Professor Helmith said, cutting me off. She wrapped the fragment back in the cloth and smiled. "You're safe now. Thank you for bringing this to my attention. I'll take it to the headmaster straight away, and we'll get this all sorted."

"Really?" I stood a little taller. "You're not... worried?"

"I can be worried and still think everything will turn out all right." Helmith smiled a little wider. With a gentle motion, she brushed some of her silky, black hair behind her ear. "Please don't fret. You've been through a lot, and the last thing you should do is dwell on this."

"The gate fragment is dangerous, though."

"The arcanists of Astra Academy will handle it. All you need to do is focus on your magic and studies. We're here to learn, remember?"

Professor Helmith closed her hand around the cloth and then tucked her hand into the pocket of her feathery, white dress. I wished she wouldn't hold it so tightly. What if something happened to her? She had said not to fret, but her disregard for the danger was causing me more panic than before.

"There's no need to cause a panic," she said.

I shook my head. "I won't."

But what if a Death Lord from the abyssal hells showed up here? Who was going to handle that? But I didn't voice any of those concerns. No Death Lords would be showing up here.

Definitely not.

Definitely.

"Did you find any occult ore?" Helmith asked, drawing me out of my dark thoughts.

"Yeah," I said.

Ashlyn nodded once. "We found some before the corpse attacked."

"Were you the two to use the fire?"

With a grimace, I nodded. "Uh. Yes. Sorry about that."

Helmith shook her head—somehow gracefully, like her hair was a flutter of black butterflies. "This is an opportunity to learn, actually. But first we need to wait for the others. Give your ore to Leon, and then have a seat by the firepit. I'll take this fragment to the Academy straight away, and when I return, we'll learn all about *cultivating the land*."

I wasn't sure what she meant by that, but I was excited enough that some of my anxiety bled away. If Professor Helmith was confident the gate fragment wasn't a problem, it probably wasn't.

I hoped.

Ashlyn and I bowed our heads once before turning away from Helmith. As we walked over to the firepit, I took the three pieces of ore I had gathered out of my pocket and slipped them into Ashlyn's belt pack as slyly as I could manage.

She didn't seem to notice. Her eyes remained focused on the ground in front of her. The intensity of her stare practically drilled a hole in the dirt. What was she thinking about?

When we arrived at the firepit, Captain Leon stood straight. He wiped sweat from his tanned skin and then combed his white hair back with his fingers.

"Are you two okay?" His eyes went to the blood on my shoulder. Before I could respond, he leapt over the stone firepit and stood in front of me. "What happened? How were you injured?"

"Ashlyn and I ran into some difficulties, but we told Professor Helmith all about it, and she said she would handle everything." I shrugged, the pain less than before. "I'm an arcanist, remember? I'll heal up. Nothing is wrong here."

My calm act must've been enough, because Leon stroked his beard as he took a step backward. He examined me for only half a second before sighing. "Very well. And the occult ore?"

Ashlyn reached into her pouch and withdrew four pieces of ore, her eyes wide. She shot me a quick glance.

"Very good!" Leon took the four ore. "And you found this so quickly. No one else has even returned yet." He chuckled as he pocketed the magical material. "Ashlyn, my star student, you are the one who everyone will look to when they're measuring themselves."

She said nothing.

When Captain Leon turned to me, I just shrugged again. "Sorry. I didn't find any."

"Really? That's... strange." Leon glared. "I'll let it slide, since you obviously found yourself in a bit of a scuffle, but in the future, you should take these tasks seriously, young man. Life will always be filled with unexpected hardship, and you can't allow that to stop you from achieving your goals."

"I understand."

When I said nothing else, Leon just frowned. He turned on his heel and returned to his work with the firepit. With each piece he placed, he glanced back at me, as though he wanted to say more—or berate me for not taking his *wise words* more seriously.

"Captain Leon?" Professor Helmith called out.

"Hm?" He stopped his work, turned, and headed over to her. "Yes, Rylee?"

"I need to discuss something important with you. It'll be just a moment."

Leon left us alone, and I suspected he would soon know about the corpse as well.

Four tree trunks had been placed around the pit. I took a seat on the closet one, and Ashlyn sat next to me. Our eldrin stood near the far trees, watching Sticks but never helping.

"Why did you give me your ore?" Ashlyn whispered. She kept her gaze on her typhoon dragon, away from me.

In an equally quiet voice, I said, "You bandaged me up. I thought it was only fair."

"I didn't need your help."

"Finding the most ore was a competition slapped onto a lesson to motivate us to try harder," I muttered. "We both know you don't need any help in the motivation category. I just wanted to be nice."

Ashlyn didn't reply to that.

She didn't even look at me.

Was she mad? Because I had given her ore? Why? It didn't make any sense. I had thought she would've been happy. But perhaps I didn't know women that well.

The branches of nearby trees rustled.

I stood from the tree trunk, hoping to catch sight of my brother. Professor Helmith had said not to cause a panic, but I had to tell him what was happening. I never kept anything from Sorin, after all. And I could trust him to keep it secret.

# CHAPTER 11

## MANIPULATING RESULTS

As the sun set, the others gradually returned from their ore hunt. The only ones missing were Raaza, Nini, and my brother, Sorin. Ashlyn, Phila, and Exie all sat together—a group of girls on one log, their eldrin around their feet.

I sat alone on my log, my mimic asleep on my lap.

Knovak *also* sat alone, most likely because he wanted to avoid the fleas infesting lowborn arcanists. I didn't know that, though. I just liked to imagine that was his justification.

Nasbit sat away from us, but I suspected it was so he could find some quiet.

Captain Leon tended the flames in the firepit with his cerberus. If an ember ever escaped, he snuffed it immediately with a wave of his hand. Cerberus arcanists could manipulate flames, and as I watched him expertly use his magic, I was tempted to have Twain transform so I could try the same thing.

Sticks, his cerberus, was much more playful. The massive three-headed dog scooted close to the firepit and sniffed at the flames. Whenever a spark flew out, the three heads tried to snap it out of the air.

"Listen up, everyone—every arcanist can manipulate *something,*"

Captain Leon said as he wandered around the stone pit. "Manipulation is the arcanist's ability to influence something in the world around them. Sea serpents manipulate the tide, cerberus arcanists manipulate fire…"

Nasbit sat the farthest from the firepit, his stone golem standing next to his log bench. He read a book while we waited for the final three students to return.

It was strange. Nasbit was so quiet, he was practically an unmoving golem himself. Under the light of the fire, his brown hair seemed redder, and his dark eyes appeared watery. He sweated a lot, which was odd. He kept wiping his forehead and puffy cheeks, his sweat actually sliding around the grooves of his arcanist mark that were etched into his flesh.

It seemed to irritate him.

"Are you listening?" Leon snapped, turning his attention to Nasbit.

The portly boy just nodded. He never removed his eyes from his book. "You were speaking about magical manipulation. You were telling us arcanists can all do it, and that each is different depending on their eldrin. Elementary information—I learned it years ago."

Captain Leon frowned. "You're a first-year student."

Nasbit hefted his book a bit. "*Anyone with the will to read is a student of life.* That's a direct quote from the Scholar King Ovantain, my personal hero." He gave Leon a smug smile before returning his attention to the pages. "I was a first-year student when I was *four*. Now I'm in my eleventh year of study, and I'm ready for more challenging concepts."

"Oh, yeah?" Leon straightened his belt, his frown deepening. "What do stone golems manipulate?"

"The type of stone their golems originate from," Nasbit answered matter-of-factly. He motioned to his eldrin, though he kept his attention on his book. "Brak is a sandstone golem. So I can manipulate *sandstone* as though it were putty."

"And do you have any sandstone on you?"

Nasbit hesitated. Then he slowly closed his book and reached into the pocket of his trousers. He held up a bit of golden sandstone. It practically sparkled in the light of the fire.

"This is the perfect time to practice your manipulation." Leon pointed to the rock. "Go on. Since we're waiting for the last three anyway. Let's all go around and see what you brand-new arcanists can do."

Nasbit sighed. He furrowed his brow and concentrated deeply on the palm-sized piece of rock in his hand. It was already a misshapen stone—lumpy and distorted. If I had to guess, I would've said that Nasbit had already manipulated it.

After a few seconds of deep breathing, Nasbit managed to squish the rock in his hand. True to his word, the hard stone shifted as though crafting putty. Practically a goo in his magical hands. With a proud smile, Nasbit held it up for everyone to see.

"There," he said after a long breath. "I did it!"

Captain Leon clapped and nodded his head. "Very good."

While everyone was paying attention, no one else applauded or heaped praise. I wished my brother were here. Sorin would've given Nasbit all the clapping he could ever want.

"This is actually how I gathered my two pieces of occult ore." Nasbit lowered his hand and cradled his sandstone. "I shaped this rock into a little shovel and dug the ore out of the ground."

"Excellent work. You have a special talent for academic work. Real self-guided, aren't you?"

Nasbit straightened his posture. "I pride myself on my discipline. My aunt said I'm a little *too* studious, and that I'm never going to get married unless I stop reading all the time, but I think being true to one's self is—"

"Okay, okay." Leon waved away the comment. "We don't need to hear *everything*. I get enough of that from a certain rizzel arcanist." Then Leon turned to Phila. "You there. Lass. You have a coatl, correct? What can you manipulate?"

"Me?" Phila pointed to herself. Her eyes grew large. "Uh. Well. I can evoke wind. I know that. And... I know I can manipulate *something*."

Leon ran a hand down his face.

His cerberus snickered.

"Okay," Leon said, more to himself than anyone else. "So this is how it's going to be..." After a deep breath, he smiled and increased his volume. "Listen. Coatl arcanists manipulate vegetation. Plants. Vines. Ferns. They can force growth, move them around as though puppets—even rend them apart."

Her coatl, Tenoch, nodded his snake-like head. "Yes. Yes! My father, Lord Coatl of the Jungle, manipulated the vegetation to hide his nesting grounds. He even became so powerful, he could move the *redstone trees* deep in the jungle's heart. They were thought to be *impossible* to move."

"You never told me that," Phila said as she petted her coatl eldrin.

The coatl fluffed the parrot-colored feathers on his majestic wings. "Yes, but dramatically revealing my lineage seemed appropriate." He spread his wings. "For greatest impact."

Phila giggled as she smoothed the feathers on the winged snake. "I agree. Dramatic flair is important."

"*Enough,*" Leon barked. He motioned to the blue grass on the other side of the log bench. "Why don't you try manipulating that?"

The area around us was still tainted by the occult ore seeping up through the ground. The strange colors of all the plant life made me wonder if magic would work properly on them. I supposed I was about to find out.

For a long—and painfully awkward—moment, Phila just stared at him. Then she turned her attention to the grass. Her coatl did the same. "Tenoch?" she asked. "Can you manipulate it?"

The coatl slithered over and sniffed at the blue blades of grass. After a few seconds of concentration, the grass grew a few inches taller. And not just a small patch of grass—but the whole patch around the log bench. The grass sprang up, damn near like weeds, threatening to swallow their whole bench.

Exie gagged and leapt away from the log. "Disgusting. I don't want to sit in *grass.*"

Her erlking fairy flew away to join her. Then they both took a seat on *my* log, of all places. To her credit, she sat at the very opposite end from where I was, but still. This wasn't an ideal situation.

Ashlyn didn't move from her seat. She just ran her hand over the grass and nodded. "Good work, *Tenoch.*" She shot Phila a glower. "If only your arcanist had done that..."

Captain Leon pointed to Phila. "*You* manipulate the vegetation."

"Ah. I see." Phila held her hand out. After a short moment, she shook her head. "Perhaps you should return to me after a little bit. I need to warm up."

Sticks wagged his tail. Then one of his heads turned to face her. "You didn't bring back any occult ore. Was it because you weren't confident with your magic?"

"Well, I was practicing my evocation, but creating wind didn't help with the ore at all." Phila brushed back some of her strawberry-blonde hair. With a frown, she added, "And wasn't it more important to practice magic than gather rocks from the ground? I believe that was what Captain Leon said."

After a long and deep sigh, Leon placed his hands on his hips. "Ya know, back when the Academy started, students were so eager to practice their magic, we had to force them to take breaks."

"How dreadful," Phila said.

"Look... Just practice your magic, all right? I'll get back to you." Leon glanced over at Ashlyn and grinned. "You already know what you manipulate, don't you?"

"Water," Ashlyn replied—quick, precise. She had known he would ask, and she had long since prepared her answer.

"And you've done it? You've manipulated water already?"

"I used it to help put out the fires Gray started earlier today. That was how I gathered so much ore."

"Perfect. Just as you were supposed to." Leon slowly turned his attention to me, once again frowning. "And burning the area to find ore... That was a good idea. I'm surprised you didn't find any."

I shrugged. "All the flames caused me to panic. Good thing Ashlyn was there with her water manipulation." I offered her a sly smile. She didn't respond.

"Yes. Very true." Leon crossed his arms. "That's why she came back with four ore. The most so far."

Knovak scooted to the edge of his log and lifted his hand. His giant hat—pointed and tall—seemed warm, considering he was so close to the fire, but the man refused to remove it. For some reason.

Captain Leon glanced over. "Yes, Knovak?"

"You didn't ask me about *my* manipulation. You basically skipped right over me." He pointed to Nasbit, then to his log, then to the log with Ashlyn and Phila. "Don't you want to instruct me on how to use unicorn magic?"

Starling, his unicorn foal, stood and swished his tail. The horn glittered no matter the time of day, or if there was even sunlight, but next to the fire, it practically glowed with inner power.

"Well..." Leon groaned as he walked around the firepit. "Why don't you just wait until we get back to the Academy? Hm?"

Knovak stood from his seat, his lips pursed. "Is it because my eldrin is the weakest of all the arcanists' here? Is that it? You don't think my manipulation is worthwhile?" His voice got louder with each word, and his face reddened slightly.

"Hmpf!" his unicorn chimed in.

"Quiet down," Leon barked. He pointed at Knovak. "It has nothing to do with that, *boy*. It has everything to do with the fact that unicorns manipulate *emotions*, basically."

Knovak lifted both his eyebrows. "Really? So I can force people to cower? Or force them to feel guilt for their actions? Or shame them with overwhelming embarrassment?"

"Uh. No. Unicorns are creatures that change their own dark emotions into *good feelings*. Confidence. Courage. Determination. It's not... *easy*... to teach. Out in the woods." Captain Leon ended on a weak note, like he wasn't even sure how to explain the problem.

But I understood.

How was Knovak supposed to practice his magical manipulation if all he did was change his own mood into something positive? That was pretty weak. And difficult to quantify.

"Oh," Knovak said. He slowly sat back down on his log. "Yes. I see."

"Unicorn arcanists make great knights," Nasbit interjected. He nodded once. "Since they force themselves to stay the path, no matter the obstacles."

"Wow. Great."

Knovak no longer seemed like he wanted to participate. He tugged the brim of his hat to cover most of his face.

Nasbit sheepishly returned to his book, a slight frown on his face. Had he brought up the knights to make Knovak feel better? That was kind of him, even if it hadn't worked.

Everyone was quiet after that.

The crackle of our campfire was our only entertainment. In moments like this, I missed Sorin's poetry. I almost laughed at the thought.

The universe had won.

I missed Sorin's terrible rhymes.

What was next? I'd start missing the smell of my father's candles?

"I already know what *I* manipulate," Exie proclaimed, shattering the silence with her haughty tone. She stood, and her erlking fairy fluttered up to fly around her head. "Erlkings manipulate and evoke the same thing, basically. *Light*. That's how we create illusions. We change the light around."

Exie waved her delicate hand.

The log we now shared shimmered and then became a proper stone bench. It *wasn't* stone, but now it *looked* like stone. It even had armrests and a backrest. None of that would work, since it wasn't real, but it looked convincing enough.

"See?" she said. Then she tossed some of her chestnut hair over her shoulder. "Brilliant, I would say."

"How many pieces of ore did you bring back?" Sticks asked. The cerberus huffed out some fire. "Did you use your magic to help?"

"I brought back two pieces, thank you very much." Exie crossed her arms over her chest and then carefully sat down on the "stone" log. After tucking one ankle behind the other, she added, "This whole area is confusing, and dirty, and I didn't want to stomp around in the mud. After I found two lying around in the grass, I practiced my magic away from the others. I don't want to win the competition—I just want this whole camping trip to be over as quickly as possible."

Sticks tilted one of his heads. "Finding two pieces is impressive."

Exie smiled. "Thank you."

Very impressive—for someone who didn't want to get dirty. It made me wonder how she had found the ore. And whether or not she'd had help.

The rustling of grass and the snap of twigs drew everyone's attention. Leon walked around the fire until he had a clear view of the people approaching. Fortunately, it was just Nini and Sorin. The two of them hurried over, my brother offering me a wave as they approached.

I half-waved back, wondering why he was so *boisterous*, even when he wasn't making any noise.

My brother was just larger than most, and it was painfully obvious when he entered camp. He hopped over Knovak's log and then took a seat next to him. Sorin took up way more space than Knovak. I suspected, if Sorin focused on his physical training, he'd be twice the size of the others.

Sorin patted the log next to him, and Nini hurried to take a seat at his side.

Nini was half-human, half-laundry-basket. She had so many layers of clothing.

So many.

Was she wearing more than she had been when I had last seen her? Had she come back to camp and put on another coat? Her long coat was dirty and covered in sap and leaves, but she wore a smile brighter than I had seen before, so I figured everything must've gone well for them. Her reaper floated over to the firepit without making a sound. Even the small chain that hung from its cloak didn't rattle as much.

Waste's scythe was creepy, but he kept it behind his cloak, out of view. Nice of him.

"Hey, everyone," Sorin said, all smiles and grins. He reached into his pocket and withdrew two reddish-silvery ore. They glittered in the campfire light. "Look what I have!" He offered the ore to Captain Leon. "So, do I have the most?"

The captain shook his head. "Ashlyn is the one to beat, currently. She gathered four pieces of ore."

"Not Gray? Really?"

"No. Gray didn't turn in *any* ore." Leon glanced over at Nini. "Did you find some?"

Nini adjusted her glasses on her nose before reaching into her coat and pulling out three additional ore. "I found a few pieces. S-Sorry it wasn't the most. I think we got lost." She smoothed her red hair and even removed a broken twig from her locks.

"You don't need to worry." Captain Leon softened his words. "You and Sorin have been doing an excellent job. Unlike most here, I've seen your magic manipulation at work, and I know you've been practicing hard."

"I'm a natural at manipulating the shadows." Sorin waved his hand, and the darkness around his log reached upward, little shadow tendrils grasping for the air. "Thurin says I'm going to make a great knightmare arcanist."

His knightmare, Thurin, shifted through the shadows at his feet. He was just a puddle of darkness unless he lifted from the shadows, even when he spoke. "You've made great progress already, my arcanist."

When Leon glanced at Nini, the two of them just shared a short stare.

Reaper arcanists manipulated blood.

No one wanted to see that happen. Not here, anyway. Not on a camping trip.

When another set of footfalls caught everyone's attention, I stiffened. Raaza returned to the group alone, his expression hard and his gaze distant. He just stared at his boots the whole time he walked over to us. His kitsune trotted by his side, her feet flashing with fake flames. Nightfall was almost upon us, and her steps blazed like stars.

As Raaza approached the firepit, he reached into his pocket and hesitated. "Who has the most ore?" he asked. He looked up and glanced between us all.

Sorin chuckled. "It's Ashlyn."

"How many does she have?"

"Four."

After a short moment of hesitation, Raaza withdrew a pile of ore from his pocket. "Lucky me. I gathered *five*." He presented the shimmering ore to Leon. In the light of the camp fire, it practically glistened. "That makes *me* the winner."

His kitsune fox danced around his feet, her red fur lustrous. "Hurray for my arcanist! Celebrations all around."

Captain Leon took the ore and shoved it into his pouch, alongside the other ore we had all gathered. "Congratulations, young man. I'm glad to see you took my task seriously. Your prize." He handed over a small bracelet made of thin gold chains. It was delicate, but beautiful.

"What is it?"

"A trinket imbued with salamander magic. You can't be burned by non-magical means, and you'll always be warm, even in the coldest of storms. You've earned it, young man."

Raaza slipped the bracelet onto his left wrist. Then he shoved the sleeve of his robe over it. "Thank you."

Leon clapped his hands together and pointed to the fire. "Whelp, I'm starved. It's time to teach you all how you eat while camping."

Several groans were his only answer.

Raaza took a seat next to me on the illusioned log. As though she wanted nothing to do with us, Exie shifted slightly, giving us her back. That was fine. We didn't need to talk to her.

"Congrats," I said to Raaza.

Twain yawned in my lap. "Yeah. Woo. You did it."

Miko hopped onto the log and swished her fox tail. She giggled.

"I should thank *you*, Gray," Raaza whispered. He smirked as he said, "I only found enough ore to win because I took your advice."

I lifted an eyebrow. "What advice?"

"The advice you gave me on the boat. I practiced a bit more with my fox fire. I used it to trick the captain. I only found three ore. But now he thinks there's five." Raaza held his hand out, and a puff of fox fire appeared. Then it transformed into a round little piece of ore. He had learned to create something *other* than coins, it seemed.

I narrowed my gaze. "Why are you telling me this? A good con artist doesn't reveal his secrets. Aren't you worried I'll say something to Leon?"

Raaza met my gaze with a cold stare. "Will you?"

"Heh." I laced my fingers together and placed both my hands on top of my head. "Just seems bold of you to tell me without knowing whether or not I would. Is *bold* the right word? Maybe I'm thinking of *foolish*."

"Or maybe... you're the type of man who likes to keep his options open." Raaza closed his hand, and the fake ore vanished. His fox fire wasn't real, even if the object seemed real for a short while. "I think you value having me indebted to you more than the praise you would receive for turning me in."

He wasn't wrong...

But I hated it when people guessed my motives or actions. It bothered me on a deeper level that was difficult to explain. I was tempted to snitch on him—explain everything to Leon—just to prove Raaza wrong.

"*Who wants meat?*" Leon practically sang as he walked back over to the fire. He carried a platter piled high with chicken, beef, goat, and pig.

Probably some rabbit, too, but it was difficult to see under the mess of flesh.

I'd deal with the Raaza situation later.

First, I would eat. Then I would talk to Sorin about the gate fragment. If I had any more time—or gave a damn—I'd contemplate Raaza and his deception.

# CHAPTER 12

## THE FIVE LAYERS OF THE ABYSSAL HELLS

Congratulations to Captain Leon.

I had never consumed so much meat that I regretted not having vegetables. Tonight was the first time. My belly threatened to burst at any moment. There was so much food in my gut, my lungs struggled to find their place in my torso.

Captain Leon said this was "camping food," but it felt more like an old-fashioned street feast to me. On the Isle of Haylin, we sometimes celebrated minor events with a street feast. Everyone brought raw food, and fires and spits were set up to cook it all for those who attended. Those days were filled with merriment.

I supposed camping was filled with merriment as well.

Sorin held a drumstick aloft as he said, in poetic fashion, *"From the spit and to the grill, roasting meat is quite the thrill."*

Nini clapped in time with his words, almost creating a song. And while I had missed his rhymes before, I quickly remembered why I thought Sorin should stop. The others gave him sideways glances and muttered things under their breath too quiet to hear.

*"Cooking and camping, a perfect pair!"* Sorin gestured to everyone. *"Memories made that we'll always share."*

No one said anything. Nini clapped louder once my brother was finished. The only other person to react was Captain Leon, of all people. He stood and also offered a bit of applause. "Excellent! Sorin, you're a natural. Back in my day, we would tell stories and sing songs. This is even better. Fireside entertainment."

Sticks wagged his tail, and all three of his heads nodded along with the statement.

Sorin bowed and then took a seat back on the log. "I've been practicing a lot. You can thank my brother for my performance."

When the others all turned to stare at me, I shielded my gaze by rubbing at my eyes. I didn't want to be associated with this. Why did Sorin always rope me into his childish antics?

Twain rolled around on my lap, his belly distended. He burped and then twitched his long ears. "Oh. Carry me, Gray. I'll never make it back to our tent in my condition."

For some reason, his statements caught Exie's attention. She shifted on our log, finally turning to face me. With a sneer, she stared down at Twain. "You know, you would be a cute eldrin if you tried even a little bit."

Twain twitched his whiskers. "Hey! What're you trying to say?" He belched a second time, punctuating his questioning with a waft of foul-smelling meat.

"I'm saying you should act *cuter*." Exie narrowed her eyes into a glower. Somehow, she was still beautiful, even when irritated—even when bothering my eldrin. "Perhaps say adorable phrases—and stop *burping*. More people will like you. They'll pay more attention."

Twain batted his little kitten eyelashes. "I'm sworry! All the itty-bitty pieces of meat make me want to poopsie-doopsie."

I snorted back a laugh.

Exie didn't find it funny. At all.

She huffed as she stood from the log. Without another word, she stormed over to Ashlyn and Phila. Despite the fact that their log was covered in blue grass, she took a seat with them, her cheeks red.

"Hehe," Twain said as he curled up in my lap.

"I hear people get sent to the deepest layers of the abyssal hells for less than that," I muttered, equally sarcastic.

"Eh. It was funny." Twain opened one cat-like eye and stared up at me.

"Write that on my tombstone, okay? That's my motto from now on."

"I'm not writing anything on your tombstone because if you're dead, I'm also dead." I scooped Twain up into my arms and then stood from the log. "C'mon. You've had enough to eat, we've definitely not made any friends, and I need to tell Sorin all about what we saw."

Raaza shot me an odd glance after the last part of my statement. He didn't ask what I meant, though. Which was good—because I wasn't going to tell him.

I walked around the firepit and headed for Sorin. My brother spotted me right away. In the blink of an eye, he was on his feet and smiling. He motioned to his spot on the log—right between Knovak and Nini. "Did you want to sit here, Gray? I can always sit on the dirt."

"Actually, I'm full." I motioned to one of the tents with a tilt of my head. "I was hoping I could speak with you before I hit the sack. It'll be quick."

Sorin leaned in closer to me. In a whisper, he said, "I know you think I should stop with the rhymes and stuff. Do we really need to talk about it again?"

"That's not what I want to talk about," I replied, my voice equally quiet. "Please. It's important."

Although I hadn't told him the topic, Sorin hardened his expression and nodded once. Together, we turned away from the campfire.

Captain Leon spotted us going. He whirled on his heel and then gestured to the dark brown tents. "Those ones over there are for the boys. Your belongings are already inside. Get plenty of sleep. Tomorrow we'll start construction and further your magical knowledge."

We waved to acknowledge his statements and then quickly headed for the tents. It was dark, and once we were away from the fire, it felt as though we had stepped into a shadowy void.

"I can see in the dark," Sorin whispered.

"Good ol' knightmare magic." I held Twain close. I wished mimic arcanists had more abilities than the ones I stole from others.

"The stronger the mystical creature, the more innate abilities they grant their arcanist. That's what I've learned, anyway. Knightmares are fairly strong, so one of my innate abilities is to see through *shadows*." Sorin flared his hands out when he said the last word.

"Uh-huh. I know. We're in the same classes, remember?"

Sorin exhaled and then shrugged. "It's okay if you're jealous."

"I'm *very* jealous. As soon as Twain isn't a bloated meat wagon, I'm going to have him transform into a knightmare."

We entered the tent together, laughing as we threw back the flap. Sorin always made me feel at ease. The benefit of being twins, I supposed. Nothing was ever really wrong between us. We argued sometimes, and disagreed on a lot, but no one had my back like Sorin did.

Our tents were impressive on the inside. They were rectangular and spacious.

Five feet by six feet with cloth walls that were at least five feet high themselves—and a pole in the center that held the roof up even higher than that, so we didn't have to duck to move around. We had three cots in the tent, with a rug across the grass and dirt. Everything was elevated off the ground, including a little table that held our backpacks and supplies.

A single glowstone, placed inside a glass bottle and tied to the pole of the tent, kept the inside illuminated.

It felt cozy.

The moment Sorin closed the tent flap, I grabbed his bicep.

"Remember the Gate of Crossing that Professor Zahn made?" I asked, my voice low, but my words fast. "The one that teleported people to the abyssal hells? The one I exploded?"

Sorin's eyes widened. "Is this... a serious question? Because I'll never forget that. A *Death Lord* walked out of that gate."

"I found a fragment of that very gate out in the woods." I pulled Sorin closer. "Ashlyn and I fought a... a *corpse*. Or something. Water from the deepest part of the ocean was everywhere around the gate fragment. Ashlyn thinks the piece of gate was somehow teleporting *things* from the abyssal hells and throwing them around the nearby area."

Professor Helmith had asked me not to start a panic, so I had waited to tell Sorin, but now that I was voicing everything, my fear seeped into my tone. What if things really were being teleported here? What were we going to do about it? Helmith hadn't been frightened, and she had sounded confident that the headmaster would know what to do, but I wasn't convinced.

The headmaster hadn't known about Professor Zahn's plan, after all.

That man had worked on the gate in secret for years without anyone suspecting anything. Would the headmaster really know what was best here if he couldn't figure out the gate's true purpose when it had been right in front of him?

Sorin placed a hand on my shoulder. "Hey. We're becoming arcanists now, right? We have magic and power. We can solve this. And I'll be with you every step of way. There's no need to worry."

He spoke in a calming tone, but my dread was as constant as my heartbeat nowadays.

Twain shifted in my arms. Then his ears twitched. He turned his attention to the tent flap. "Someone's here," he whispered.

Without saying a word, Sorin grabbed the flap and threw it open.

Nasbit stood on the other side, all color draining from his face the moment he realized he had been caught. Had he been spying on us? He was clearly leaning close to the tent.

With giant, circular eyes, he mumbled out, "O-Oh, well, uh, you see, I couldn't find my things in the other tent, so I thought, um, maybe they were here?"

I snapped my attention to the backpacks on the little table. One was mine. The other... It wasn't Sorin's, and it was stuffed to the brim with tomes and paper. Nasbit's.

"Did you hear anything?" I asked as I returned my attention to him.

Nasbit stared at me for a prolonged moment. Somehow, despite the fact that he was silent, he admitted everything. He had heard all about the gate fragment and my theories on the matter.

I grabbed his robes and pulled him into the tent. Sorin shut the flap, and we all huddled close to the wooden pole in the middle of the tent. It was already getting crowded with just three people and a kitten. Good thing Brak wasn't here. We couldn't handle the stone golem's presence, no matter how we arranged ourselves.

"Don't tell anyone what you just heard," I stated. "We're trying to avoid causing a panic."

Nasbit nodded. Then he slowed his nodding and started shaking his head. "Wouldn't it reassure people to know what's going on?"

"What *is* going on?" I asked him.

He just shrugged. "Um. You think things are coming out of the abyssal hells?"

"But I don't know that. It's just a guess. And even if I *did* know that for sure, I don't know what's in the abyssal hells other than freakish monsters, Death Lords, and souls, so I wouldn't be able to explain what the danger level is here."

"You... don't know what's in the abyssal hells?" Nasbit nervously chuckled. "Uh. I can help you with your, um... lack of knowledge."

"You can?" Sorin asked.

I let go of Nasbit's robes. "How?"

Nasbit pointed to his backpack. "Well, after I heard that Professor Zahn had made a gate into the abyssal hells, I went to the Academy's library and searched for books on the matter. I figured it would be interesting reading, and there was a chance it would come in handy."

I mulled over his words for a bit. "Huh. That's clever."

"Clever?" Nasbit frowned. "I thought it was basic *due diligence*. I mean, if *I* had been the one to see a Death Lord, I would've read every scrap of information they had in the Academy about the man. I find it mildly disturbing you haven't investigated yourself."

"Yeah, okay," Sorin muttered. "We get it. You don't have to be a sass-hole to my brother."

"All right."

Nasbit tried to step around me and Sorin. His larger body, and gut, made it awkward, but he eventually moved around the wooden pole and reached his pack. He rummaged through it until he withdrew a small tome.

"You might not know this, but centuries ago, there was a widespread church dedicated to teaching about the abyssal hells. This was one of their books, written by a scribe." Nasbit opened up to the first chapter. "You can tell by all the fancy penmanship."

Sorin actually leaned in to get a better look at the loops on the letters. "Oh. I'm impressed."

I snatched the tome from Nasbit's hands and shot my brother a glare. "What's with the both of you? This is important." Twain flailed around in my other arm, so I set him down on the cot. "I want to know about everything in the abyssal hells, starting with the most dangerous stuff."

Nasbit glanced at the tent flap and then back to me. "I can give you a quick summary."

"Good—do it."

He held up his hand, his five fingers spread out. "There are five layers to the abyssal hells. According to the scribe who penned that book, *all* souls go to the hells once they've shed their mortal coils. The more dastardly you were in life, the deeper your soul goes."

Sorin crossed his arms over his wide chest, his expression grim.

Nasbit pointed to his pointer finger. "The first layer of the abyssal hells is where souls go to, uh, be reborn, I guess. They somehow return to the world. I read stories where they return as star shards, and other stories say they're reborn as babes. Lots of speculation, but safe to say, the *first abyss* is the kind one. If you were great and gentle and amazing while alive, your soul would go here and somehow return to the world."

"Okay," I muttered.

"The *second abyss* is the next layer, and they say it's a labyrinth built from bone and meant to keep people from gaining access to the scariest parts of the abyssal hells. It's also a place where mystical creatures are born. Scary creatures. The kind born from tortured souls and anguish." Nasbit frowned as he motioned to his middle finger. "I skimmed most of that chapter."

Sorin and I exchanged a quick glance, but otherwise said nothing.

"The *third abyss* is where all the Death Lords dwell," Nasbit stated as he pointed to his third finger. "Lost souls gather here. *Lost* in the metaphorical sense. The souls of blackhearts and scum descend to this layer, and then the Death Lords greet them and graft their souls to the abyssal dragons to empower their eldrin."

"Those were the stories I heard when I was younger," Sorin said. "Death Lords would torture souls by flaying them. Or something." He glanced over at me. "I always thought it was weird, because how do you *flay* a soul? They don't have flesh."

I didn't reply.

I could still picture the abyssal dragon stepping out of the gate. The dragon's wings... They had been translucent and wicked, and made of a hundred faces and ghostly bodies—like souls had been stitched together to create a limb for the monster.

I supposed that part of the story was true, then.

"According to the book," Nasbit continued, oblivious to my anxiousness, "the Death Lords want to control every layer of the abyssal hells, but once the hells were sealed, they couldn't seem to travel between them."

"The Death Lords don't want to enter the land of the living?" Sorin asked.

"Oh, they do." Nasbit frowned. "But, uh, back thousands of years ago, they couldn't take over the land because not only were the gates sealed, but there were arcanists around who could stop them. *God-arcanists*. And other such things... that no longer exist. Because they all died."

"Perfect," I quipped. "Just what I wanted to hear."

"The *fourth abyss*," Nasbit said, ignoring my comment and pointing to his pinkie, "is where the elder-creatures dwell." He narrowed his eyes. "You two know how mystical creatures grow, right?"

Twain rolled around on the cot, his ears twitching. "Everyone knows that, *rock boy*. Mystical creatures bond with humans so that we can nibble on their souls."

"It sounds creepy when you say it that way," I said.

Twain frowned. "It doesn't kill the human—just like a little paper cut wouldn't kill someone. We only take tiny bits of the soul! Similar to droplets of blood."

"It still sounds creepy."

"That's not *my* fault. I didn't make the rules."

Nasbit waved his hand, interrupting us. "Okay. Yes. That's right." He sighed. "And that's important to keep in mind when you learn about the *fourth abyss*. You see, the elder-creatures down there eat the souls that descend to their level. And because they're *consuming* whole souls—"

"They grow big and powerful without ever needing to bond with anyone," I interjected, my words soaked in realization and awe.

Sorin rubbed at the back of his neck. "We don't want to hear about the *fifth abyss*, do we?"

Deafening silence was our only answer. Nasbit paled even further. Would he tell us? Part of me didn't want to know.

Nasbit pointed to his thumb.

"The *fifth abyss*... is something far worse than the others."

# CHAPTER 13

## THE FIFTH ABYSS

"What's in the fifth abyss?" I asked, my mouth dry.

Nasbit nervously chuckled as he said, "They say magic comes from the soul. Well, according to this book, the fifth abyss is a place where souls are destroyed—it's the source of all corrupted magic. The book describes it as an oblivion. Anyone or anything that goes there is gone forever."

I didn't like that at all.

If I had heard this a few months ago, I would've ignored it as fantasy and superstition. Younger me hadn't believed the abyssal hells was a *real* place, so why would I have paid attention to all the childish fairy tales surrounding it? Now that I knew the truth, I cursed under my breath.

I should've paid more attention to those tales.

An icy chill crept over me. I shivered and rubbed my arms.

"They describe the fifth abyss like a unique location." Nasbit patted my shoulder and forced an awkward half-smile. "Like a whirlpool in the ocean. You don't need to be afraid of it. And no one can teleport it anywhere. You need to go to it, if that makes sense."

"But *Death Lords* can still be teleported places," I growled. I jerked away from Nasbit's touch. He was trying to cheer me up, but he was doing a poor job of it. "Just don't tell anyone about this, all right? Not until Professor Helmith tells everyone."

"Uh, all right."

Then Nasbit went quiet. My brother glanced between us, his brow furrowing. The dark puddle around his feet moved across the rug like only a shadow could. Sorin's knightmare spoke in a deep and worrisome tone. "My arcanist—perhaps it would be best to scour the library for stories about the abyssal hells being sealed? We can learn more about combating the threat. Once we return to Astra Academy, of course."

Sorin glanced down at the darkness. "Yeah, Thurin. That's a good idea."

"My idea, technically," Nasbit whispered.

"Once the camping trip is over, that's what we'll do." I glanced over at my cot and frowned. "Until then... I'm going to get some sleep. We can talk more about everything tomorrow. Once we're all rested."

Captain Leon stayed up with the others long into the evening.

Tent walls didn't do much to block out the sounds of talking and laughing. I tried not to think about anything—I wanted to drift off into a quiet slumber—but sleep never came.

Twain didn't have any trouble. All that meat in his belly had been like a sleeping draught. Even if I shook him, Twain wouldn't wake.

But what was I to do?

Professor Helmith was an ethereal whelk arcanist. She could put people to sleep with her augmentation. I was tempted to ask her to help me, but I also didn't want to venture out of the tent. Instead, I held my blankets close and stared at the tent wall, hoping fatigue would eventually get me.

Our glowstone had been wrapped in cloth, shrouding the inside of the tent in the thick darkness of night.

Once it grew quieter, Nasbit and Sorin returned to the tent to sleep. They settled into their cots, and within a few minutes, Nasbit's breathing was shallow and even. But not Sorin's. As the minutes passed, I knew he was just as awake as I was.

"Brother?" I whispered.

"Hm?" Sorin replied.

"What're you thinking about?"

The stillness of the night brought an eerie silence. I had thought I would hear more insects and owls and wilderness, but the world around us seemed dead.

"What layer of the abyssal hells do you think Mom went to?" Sorin asked, his voice soft and slow.

The question caught me off guard. A lump formed in my throat like a ball of wet dough. Despite my anxiety, I forced myself to speak. "Our mother went to the first abyss, obviously."

Our mother had died giving birth to us, and Sorin blamed himself specifically for her death.

I couldn't let him think she was suffering. He didn't deserve to drag this weight around.

"What if she went deeper than that?" Sorin rolled to his side, his cot straining under his size. "What if she went to the fifth abyss?"

"She didn't. Trust me. All the stories of our mother are bright and positive. She was kind."

"Everyone talks about the dead as though they were great."

That was true. But still. "Just drop it, okay? It's stupid to think about. You're just making yourself sad for absolutely no reason."

"Hm." Sorin shifted his weight and sighed. "Hey, Gray... What do you think would happen if a soul was taken *out* of the abyssal hells? Would that person come back to life?"

"I don't know," I muttered. "But I don't think you should worry about it. The goal is to keep all the gates closed, remember?"

"Right..."

I wanted to change the subject. Anything was better than this. It was like having a splinter in my heart. Most times, I felt no pain, but whenever Sorin mentioned our mother, a sharp agony shot through my chest.

"Did you have fun finding occult ore?" I asked.

Sorin sighed. "It was fine. I gave some of my ore to Exie, since she didn't want to look around in the mud."

All my sadness vanished. Instead, it was replaced with mild disgust and disappointment. "Seriously?" I asked, probably louder than I should've been. "Why?"

"She asked for some. I wanted to help her."

"Exie is just taking advantage of you. Sorin—you can't let people do that." I rolled all the way over and glared at him through the darkness. "You should've focused on finding the most ore and winning."

"Really? I figured *you* were going to win." Sorin stretched, his cot once again protesting. "You and Ashlyn were so energized to go out and find ore. I mean, I thought trying to compete against you two was impossible."

I didn't say anything.

My brother must've sensed my reticence. "Why didn't you find any ore, Gray? That's not like you."

"I…" The irony of the situation wasn't lost on me. I almost laughed at myself. "I gave it to Ashlyn."

Sorin snorted and chuckled. The irony wasn't lost on him, either.

"My uncles say boys do stupid things for girls all the time," Nasbit whispered from the darkness, his voice startling me. I hadn't realized Nasbit had woken up. How long had he been listening?

"I was *thanking* Ashlyn," I stated. "My situation is different. She helped me out, so I helped her back. It was a chain of reciprocity."

Sorin rolled to his other side, still chuckling. "Uh-huh. Well, think of this way. Someone always has to *start* helping someone for a chain to begin."

"That's a fair point," Nasbit whispered, just interjecting himself into the conversation.

I sighed. "If Exie never helps you out, how will that make you feel? Going out of your way for people who don't care about you makes you a dullard."

Sorin stopped his chortling and went silent for a long moment. Then he whispered, "It was my choice to help Exie. I'll never feel ashamed of that, no matter what you say. I think she'll return the favor, and we can be good friends—and only *her* choices can prove me wrong."

"Maybe," I replied.

Nasbit rustled his blankets. "Sorin makes lots of good points, really."

"Honestly, Gray, you're afraid a lot, lately." Sorin exhaled. "I wish you'd stop thinking everyone is out to get us."

I didn't say anything in response. Perhaps he was right.

In the morning, we woke with the sun, got dressed in our tents, and then wandered out into the sunlight. Unlike at the Academy, where we had glorious pipes and water, our camping spot had a cold river. And that was about it.

I had bathed in icy water many times, but some of the others weren't having it. Over half our class had opted not to bathe in the river, and it smelled like it.

Professor Helmith waited for us by the cold firepit. Her long black hair waved through the morning winds like a fluttering raven's wing. Her long white dress imitated a dove, and all I could think of was the feathery glory of birds.

"Good morning," Helmith said as we gathered near the log benches. She was chipper and smiled widely. "You'll be happy to know that the people of Red Cape have brought gifts for the arcanists who will be helping build them a school."

"What kind of gifts?" Exie asked.

She was one of the arcanists who refused to touch the river. Despite that, her shoulder-length chestnut hair was pulled back into an intricate ponytail-and-braid combo. I wondered how long she had spent on it.

Professor Helmith delicately laced her fingers together. "You can't have the gifts until the school is complete, I'm afraid." She motioned to the ground.

The grass was green.

No longer blue or strange. Just vibrant emerald.

"Once the occult ore is taken from an area, it returns to its normal luster." Helmith smiled bright enough to rival the sun. "Now that you've all helped clear the area, we'll be going up the hill over there and constructing a school. Captain Leon and Professor Jenkins are already at the hill with all the wood and fastenings you'll need."

Nasbit gestured to his stone golem. "Brak can do most of the heavy lifting," Nasbit said.

Out of all the eldrin, it was the biggest and sturdiest. That wouldn't last forever. Ashlyn's typhoon dragon would one day be large enough to capsize a whole three-masted ship, but since everyone had little baby eldrin, the golem won out on size.

His stone golem lifted its rock arms as though flexing. Brak said nothing.

"I appreciate Brak's willingness," Helmith said. "But there are two things I want to focus on today. The first is the reason we're doing this. Headmaster Venrover wants to instill a sense of community and growth within you all. It's important, as arcanists, that we help the people and the land. It's a sacred duty that those with power all share."

I nodded with her words, though I wondered to what extent we needed to help.

Sorin listened with all his focus. He seemed utterly transfixed by the idea. Nini stood between me and him, and she glanced between us, as though noting our responses. When she caught me staring, she half-chuckled.

Her reaper silently floated around us, his robes rustling like a ghost.

"The second thing we should focus on is *cultivating the land.*" Professor Helmith motioned to the area around us, and then pointed to the far hill where we would set up the school. "The occult ore can be used to create runes on arcanists, permanently adding to their magic and power. The ore can also do that to the land."

Nasbit energetically nodded along with her words. "This is the kind of lesson I've been waiting for," he whispered, more to himself than anyone else.

"Arcanists can enchant the ground, the vegetation, and even the currents in the air." Helmith closed her eyes as a slight breeze rushed by. Her inky hair flowed behind her like silk. When she opened her eyes, she glanced between us. "My father spoke at great lengths about how arcanists should *build* toward something. A home. A community. A nation. Today, we're going to show you how to do that."

"Her father?" Raaza asked under his breath.

Nasbit practically twirled around to face him. "You don't know?

Professor Helmith's father is the *Warlord of Magic!* He fought in the God-Arcanists War and even helped build Astra Academy."

Raaza crossed his arms. "The Warlord of Magic? Isn't that Volke Savan?"

"It's pronounced like *volk* and yes. That's him. He's a legend."

"Hm. Interesting."

Nasbit smiled wider. "And Professor Helmith's husband, Kristof Helmith, is a mystic guardian—one of the first to graduate the Academy—and he even helped establish some of the *farthest* Gates of Crossing!"

Sorin leaned over to me and frowned. "Uh-oh, Gray. I'm so sorry."

"Why are you apologizing?" I snapped.

"It's just sad that you would have to compete with all these amazing men for the attention of your honeysuckle."

I wanted to punch my brother in the throat. My face went red both from embarrassment and frustration. A few others—only the ones nearby who could hear—snickered. Why did Sorin *insist* on calling Professor Helmith my honeysuckle?

She wasn't!

I just admired her. Nothing more.

"Please quiet down," Professor Helmith said. She reached into the pocket of her dress and withdrew the glittering silver gate fragment. With her bare hand!

"P-Professor?" I asked as I half-stepped forward.

She smiled. "It's all right, Gray. Last night, I spoke with the headmaster. This piece is okay to touch." Professor Helmith held it up to show everyone. "However, I have reason to believe there might be more pieces like this one nearby. Can everyone see?"

"What is it?" Raaza asked, his tone all business.

"A fragment from a broken Gate of Crossing. It's imperative we retrieve them, so anyone who finds one needs to bring it to me straight away, understood? But please avoid touching them directly. They might be dangerous, and we can't leave them near a mortal village."

Everyone nodded.

I calmed down a bit as she tucked the fragment back into her pocket. She hadn't told the class where the gate led to, which I found interesting, but perhaps they didn't need to know. Nasbit, Sorin, and Ashlyn all casually glanced over at me, since we were all in on the secret.

Hopefully, any other fragments we stumbled across wouldn't have any monsters around them, but I had a terrible feeling that wouldn't be the case.

# CHAPTER 14

## CULTIVATING THE LAND

T he new schoolhouse would sit atop the tallest hill in the area. From the peak of the hill, it was easy to spot Red Cape. The small collection of houses sat next to the ocean, their small docks poking out into the water.

A small forest surrounded the hill, but paths were littered throughout the area. One path led to a logging operation. One led to distant waterfalls. Another led to a small shack. Clearly, Red Cape wanted to expand, but they were taking their sweet time about it.

We just had to build this school for them.

Unfortunately, building a school wasn't really in my wheelhouse.

Thankfully, Captain Leon and Professor Jenkins made this much easier. Although, it was odd calling her *Professor Jenkins*. She was just *Piper* to me, ever since the first day I had arrived at the Academy.

Piper stood around the construction site, her weight mostly on her back foot, one hand on her waist. She had dark rings under her eyes, as though she hadn't slept in days. Her long, black hair reminded me of Professor Helmith's, but Piper's always had some element of *bedhead* going on.

Her eldrin, the rizzel named Reevy, stood by her feet, his white ferret body hard to miss. He had little silver stripes across his fur that practically glistened. He, too, appeared tired. His eyes didn't blink in time with one another, and sometimes they weren't open at all.

The little rizzel swayed on his feet until he eventually curled up into a ball to sleep.

Piper used her magic to teleport the heaviest objects into place. The support beam for the school, the bricks for the outer wall—everything that would've taken hours to haul, it was just *poofed* into place with a puff of glitter.

Captain Leon and his cerberus had fire under control. We would lay bricks, and he would use his magic to heat the sealants into place. I wasn't sure what it was called. Mortar? Cement? Something similar to those. Like I said, constructing a school wasn't in my wheelhouse. I just did whatever they told me to do.

As everyone set down wooden beams, or helped hammer in nails or cut slots for windows, Professor Helmith would take individuals one by one and instruct them on how to use their magic to cultivate the land.

I worried about my lesson.

It was obvious what everyone else would do. They all had specific magics. Ashlyn would obviously use her typhoon dragon magic to alter the water. Phila could make it so plants could grow faster in the area.

Even Sorin could make it so the darkness was less intense, and Exie could make light even brighter.

But I was a mimic arcanist. I had no magic of my own. I just borrowed abilities from others. What was *I* going to do?

The half-formed schoolhouse would eventually be two stories and twenty feet long. It seemed rather large for the small town of Red Cape. But what did I know?

Phila stood next to a long plank of wood. She held a hammer in one hand, and a nail in the other. Her coatl slithered around her feet, glancing at the wood and then up at his arcanist. They both wore confusion across their faces blatant enough to see from the sky.

"Piper?" Phila called out. "I thought this board was being used for the eastern wall? But it's not the same size as the others."

Piper ran a hand down her face. Her tanned skin seemed healthy in the sunlight, but she squinted as though it hurt her. "Just use a different board. I'm sure we'll find out what that one is for once we near the end."

"Captain Leon said if we don't do everything in the proper order, we could cause a cascade of problems."

"Listen. Just use another board. It's too early in the morning to be fretting about this."

Phila gazed upward at the sun hanging overhead. "But... it's well past noon?"

Piper shot her a glare. "Who's the professor here? You or me? Just use another board."

"*Yeah*," Reevy chimed in, his cute voice a bit groggy since he just woke up. "Whatever my arcanist said." He jutted his little rizzel thumb up at Piper and then crossed his forearms.

While they discussed which board was best, I walked around the south side of the school. Twain kept pace, hopping along with kitten spunk. Some of our class—mostly Exie and Ashlyn—were focused on constructing furniture. They made desks, benches, and tables. Ecrib made most of the heavy lifting easy, since he was a powerful dragon, even as a hatchling.

To my fascination, Exie used her illusions to make "marks" on the wood for where to place the nails. She stood next to the latest desk they were working on and carefully measured all the points for nails before creating little marks. Ashlyn then hammered the nails in one at a time. She took a moment to wipe sweat from her brow as I wandered by.

"Where are you going?" Ashlyn asked.

"To help Sorin," I replied.

She eyed me for a second before holding up a hand. "Gray, wait."

Twain and I stopped.

Exie glanced up from her work and frowned. "Uh, really? You said we could take a break once this was done. And in case you didn't notice, *it's not done.*"

"It'll take only a minute," Ashlyn said to her. Then she hurried to my side. "Gray. Listen. I just wanted to thank you."

"For what?" I asked.

"For the ore you gave me. I didn't want you to help me, but after I thought it over, I realized you were just being nice because I helped you with your injury." She motioned to my shoulder. "Is it feeling better, by the way?"

I grabbed my shoulder and then rotated it. "Yeah. It's just healing slower than I'd like." And slower than normal. It wasn't a regular wound. But I didn't want to bother her with my concerns.

"Well... That's all." Ashlyn shrugged. "Thank you. But don't help me again."

"Sure. I've learned my lesson," I sarcastically added. Then I tipped an imaginary hat and started to turn, but Ashlyn once again held up her hand.

"I won't improve my magic or skills if you help me like that," she quickly stated. "*That's all.* I don't want to win by relying on others. That's not how my family does things, okay? My brother *never* relied on anyone's help when he went through the Academy."

Her brother?

I had heard about him before from Nasbit. Apparently, Ashlyn was in some sort of competition with her sibling. Although, her brother had already gone through the Academy, it seemed. Which meant she was just trying to beat his school record, like some sort of scoreboard.

"Okay," I said. "Calm down. I won't do anything to ruin all your skill and magic growth." I couldn't keep my sardonic tone from my words. "But don't complain when I start being *extra* motivated at these classes. I have to keep you on your toes, apparently. That's the only form of *thank you* that you'll accept."

"Ya know, if that corpse hadn't jumped out of nowhere, Gray and I probably could've found a bunch more ore," Twain chimed in. He rubbed against the side of my leg as he added, "The fire method worked the best. You saw. You got lucky when Gray didn't win immediately."

"Yeah, and if I hadn't been busy putting out your flames, maybe I could've found a bunch myself," Ashlyn snapped.

Twain twitched his whiskers. "Hm. I acknowledge your point."

"Let's calm down." I held up my hands and shrugged. "Everything is fine. I'm fine. You're fine. We understand each other—I accept your thanks—and we can go on with our lives." I scooped up Twain and cradled him against my chest, his paws in the air. "Have fun making furniture."

Then I left.

Ashlyn watched me the entire trek over to my brother. Her scrunched eyebrows told me she wanted to say something else, but couldn't manage to get the words out. I wondered why. But perhaps we'd discuss it later, when she wasn't worried about falling behind the shadow of her brother's progress.

I thanked the good stars Sorin was so agreeable.

With a smile, I headed over to his portion of the wall. He was cutting a few boards to allow for window slots. His knightmare, the empty suit of plate armor, stood next to him, holding the sawing table steady. Tendrils made of darkness secured everything in place as well, as though black ropes had tied this portion of the school down.

Nini stood nearby.

She held the measurements of the window in hand, her red hair swirling in the bluster of the afternoon wind. Her reaper, Waste, was also bothered by the breeze. His cloak fluttered to the side, revealing his gold chains. They clattered louder than normal.

Their empty eldrin were an interesting sight. The suit of armor devoid of a human, and the cloak and scythe, just floating around, as though worn by an invisible person.

It was like they were ghosts.

Nini pushed her glasses up further onto her nose as I approached. "Oh. Hello, Gray."

"Hello." I motioned to the half-constructed window. "Need help?"

She nodded. "Oh. Maybe you can have Twain transform into Brak so we can have the strength of a stone golem to help."

I patted Twain's head. "He can't hold the shape for very long, actually. He's already tired."

Twain yawned. "I'll be back to full strength after a little catnap." He closed his two-toned eyes and purred in my arms.

"You could help me decipher these instructions." Sorin pointed to the book on the ground. The pages flipped over at a rapid rate each time the wind blew by. Whatever page he was on was long gone.

I knelt and picked up the book. "Sure." I wasn't entirely sure how this would help us become better arcanists, but the faster we built the schoolhouse, the faster we could get on with everything else.

It took us thirteen days to construct the building. Everything went so much faster with teleportation and large mystical creatures to do the hauling. I thought it would've taken us more than a month, but by the seventh day, the whole building had taken shape. After that, we focused on all the details.

Captain Leon said the biggest struggle with new construction was exposure to the elements. No one wanted the structural wood and material pelted with wind and rain, so constructing the building as fast as possible was always the goal.

At night, we cooked meat and vegetables over a camp fire. Captain Leon taught us a few songs—that Sorin then improved upon—and occasionally fireflies danced around in the sky with the stars.

Then we slept in our cramped tents.

It wasn't bad, actually. We got to practice our magic every day, and life seemed simpler—even easier. It was like this trip had specifically been designed to help everyone recover after what had happened with Professor Zahn.

I appreciated that.

In the morning, we did it all over again. And while some people got used to the cold river water baths, Exie refused. Absolutely. I thought she would've started to smell, but each day she just stank of perfume. Apparently, she had dragged along a whole bottle of the stuff.

It smelled of dried flowers. Especially lilac.

At one point, Raaza called her *Ex-Lac*, but that didn't go well.

I avoided her. My nose demanded it.

During the entire time we built the schoolhouse, however, Professor Helmith never called me or Nini out to learn about cultivating the land.

On the last day of construction, while Captain Leon and Raaza were finishing the roof, the rest of us painted the inside and outside of the building. It was easy work, but boring. My mind wandered as I walked around the inside of the newly constructed building.

Sorin and Nini worked with me. Nini's layers of outfit made her work more difficult than it needed to be. Her long sleeves kept accidentally getting dunked into the white paint, which then dripped everywhere, including onto Nini's front. Flustered, she stopped her work to clean everything up.

I thought this would repeat forever, but Waste floated over to her, the empty cloak and scythe, and slowly wrapped himself around her. Reaper arcanists could merge to become a single being, and once Waste was on her shoulders, the scythe at her back, Nini had all of his strength and skill added to her own.

Waste helped her dexterity and fine motor control. Together, they picked up the brush and worked in clean and efficient patterns.

"Oh, wow," Sorin said, watching from afar. "Thurin, you think we can do that?"

"I doubt it, my arcanist," Thurin muttered from the shadows.

"Why not?"

"My armor is thicker and more intrusive than a reaper's cloak. I suggest you manipulate the darkness to help you paint if you want to use magic to make this work better."

Someone opened the front door of the school. I stopped my painting and glanced over. Exie walked in, her hair pulled back in a loose braid, her blue dress spotless, even though everyone else had paint or mud stains. Somehow, despite not even bathing, she had the radiance of a princess attending a gala.

If Exie put half as much effort into life as she did her appearance, she would've solved world hunger. I was almost in awe of her sheer dedication.

With a smile, and her erlking fairy fluttering behind her, Exie strode straight over to my brother. Her dress swayed with each step, somehow thin enough to see her figure, but long enough to be considered extremely modest.

But her perfume was noticeable, even from across the room, ruining her sultry entrance. Twain made a silent gagging gesture and then mock-dunked his own head into the bucket of paint. I tried not to laugh, which just resulted in me snickering under my breath.

Sorin shot me a glare.

He knew what I was doing. With a sigh, I stopped.

"Sorin?" Exie asked once she had reached his side. "Do you have a moment, darling?"

Had she just called him *darling?* This was getting weird. Or interesting? It piqued my interest, to say the least.

Sorin hesitantly lowered his paint brush and lifted his eyebrows. "Uh, yeah, I have a moment. Something wrong?"

Exie's erlking, Rex, flapped his beautiful feathered wings. "Nothing's wrong. You're just tall enough to help with certain finishing touches." The fairy flew circles around Sorin's tall frame. "Help us! We definitely need someone like you."

Rex tugged at the sleeve of Sorin's shirt. He was so small, his pulling barely moved Sorin's outfit.

"Yes, please," Exie said with a smile. "It would help out so much."

Sorin set his brush down into the paint can. "Uh, sure." He gave me and Nini a half-shrug before following Exie to the front door. "This won't take too long, right? I want to help finish what we started here."

"It won't take too long at all. I promise."

Then they left. I had to admit, she wasn't *impolite* to my brother. Exie had been perfectly reasonable and respectful. I supposed it could've gone worse.

It was late in the day, the sun setting in the far distance. The orange of the sky had a calming presence. The air smelled fresh and crisp. I returned to painting, wondering when Sorin would return.

Nini and Waste unmerged. The tattered cloak slid off of Nini's shoulders, and the rusted scythe twirled around.

But they didn't say anything. Nini worked in utter silence, and her eldrin just "watched," though it was difficult to tell since the reaper didn't have a face. Or eyes. Just an empty piece of clothing.

The door opened again.

"Finally," I said, turning on my heel. "Let me guess, Exie needed—" I stopped myself short.

Professor Helmith stood at the door.

She wore a dress as black as her hair. And she was barefoot. A small anklet clinked softly whenever she walked. I was surprised she would opt to leave her boots behind, considering all the twigs and rocks around, but she didn't care.

"Gray, Nini," Professor Helmith said. "Care to join me for your cultivating lesson? We'll be done before it's time to gather round the campfire."

Nini didn't voice an acceptance. She merely nodded, fixed her paint-stained coat, and then hurried toward the professor. Her reaper floated silently behind her, like a second shadow.

I grabbed Twain and went as well. "All right."

Even if I couldn't cultivate like the others, I wanted to spend more time with Professor Helmith. She had taught me so much when I had been younger, and I missed those lessons. Perhaps I could ask her a few questions about the abyssal hells.

Professor Helmith smiled as Nini and I approached. Helmith's purple eyes were more conspicuous in the sunset. They practically glowed, matching the tattoos on her arms, which sparkled with inner power.

"I'm sorry the two of you had to wait so long for your lesson," Professor Helmith said. She walked out of the school and then motioned to the shabby road down the hill. "But the two of you have magics that make this process difficult."

Nini tucked some of her thin hair behind her ear. "Uh, do you think a reaper arcanist can even do this? Cultivate the land, I mean. None of my magics... are helpful."

Helmith shook her head. "You don't give yourself enough credit. Building and improving can come from anywhere, even a reaper."

"We are born from death," Waste said, his hollow voice ominous.

"I'm aware." The professor walked with us across the dirt, and then the grass, and toward the small forest where I had found the gate fragment. "But magic itself is a creation. You'll see."

"But *how* are we going to help the people of Red Cape?" Nini asked.

Professor Helmith pointed to a worn path shrouded in shadows. The trail was thin, and mostly hidden behind shrubs and weeds. "I've found a place where your magic will benefit the residents the most."

"Where?" I asked.

The professor smiled at me. In a singsong voice, she replied, "The graveyard."

# CHAPTER 15

## GRAVEYARD WOES

The walk to Red Cape's graveyard was a cold one.

Twain shuddered in my arms, his eyes wide the entire trek. Professor Helmith walked ahead, guiding us like she had visited this graveyard hundreds of times before. Her presence calmed me. Although I didn't like the thought of hanging around corpses—not after all that talk about the abyssal hells—knowing she was here made things easier for me.

But not for Nini.

Anytime a twig broke or a leaf rustled overhead, Nini caught her breath. She practically jumped into me a couple of times. Why was she so jumpy?

Her reaper hovered closer than normal.

Thankfully, it didn't take long before we reached a wrought-iron fence. Small statues and tombstones littered a tiny plot of land designated for the dead just beyond the main gate. How many people were buried here? Ten? Twelve? That didn't seem like many. But it was dark here. Darker than I'd like.

Professor Helmith held up her hand, and an orb of light burst forth from her palm. It floated just above her grasp, illuminating the area. Once the shine of her magic reached the far end of the graveyard, I saw the plot went farther than I had originally thought.

Much farther.

There were probably hundreds of graves.

"Ushi, reveal yourself," Helmith said.

Fragments of light coalesced into a solid form. The shine became a floating sea snail, complete with a spiral shell. Small tentacles, like an octopus inhabited the shell, hung below the ghostly snail.

Ushi.

This was the professor's eldrin. An ethereal whelk.

I had met Ushi once before, but it had been brief. She was just as beautiful now as she had been then. Her shell sparkled with an iridescent sheen. Her little eyestalks poked out from the shell as well, giving her a cuter than average appearance.

"My arcanist?" Ushi asked, her voice just as singsong as Helmith's. "The darkness here... It doesn't feel right."

"Everything will be okay," Professor Helmith stated with confidence. "Help me light the way. It's time these arcanists learned about cultivation."

"Of course! It would be my pleasure."

The head-sized snail wiggled her tentacles. Another mote of light appeared, this one hovering above the whelk's shell. With two lights, the graveyard didn't seem so haunting.

Helmith pushed open the gate, and we all walked inside.

A chill ran down my spine as I entered. It was the same type of icy feeling I'd had when Ashlyn and I had discovered the gate fragment. Was another one here? It made me worry.

"When cultivating the land, picking the physical location for your magic is extremely important." Helmith motioned to the long pathway that led deeper into the graveyard. "We should find a good spot first."

I glanced around, eyeing the moss-covered tombstones and cracked statues. This place didn't have a keeper, that was for sure. "Are you sure our magic is needed here? It doesn't look like the citizens of Red Cape come here often."

"Graveyards are sacred places. While not the center of a town, they hold importance to many."

Nini smoothed her red hair. Then she straightened her coat. She couldn't stop fidgeting. Whenever her gaze landed on a grave, she immediately turned away and opted to stare at her boots as though they were the most fascinating thing to ever exist.

Professor Helmith turned her attention to the nearest grave. Weeds grew across the top, and moss dotted the base of the tombstone. She frowned as she stared, her brow furrowed.

"Let's see," she muttered. "Would you two mind helping Red Cape a bit? Perhaps if you tended to the weeds, this place would seem more *sacred* and less..."

"Sad?" I quipped.

Helmith nodded once. "While you two tend to the graves, I'll find the perfect spot to show you the importance of cultivation."

"All right."

Although I didn't want to, I owed Professor Helmith so much, I'd probably clean the whole damn Academy if she asked me. She had done so many things for me, that even de-weeding a few graves was hardly a big request.

With a smile returning to her face, Professor Helmith wandered deeper into the graveyard. She left her ethereal whelk behind to give us light, which I appreciated. Ushi floated around us, her orb of light brightening the area.

Several seconds passed before I walked over to the nearest grave. Twain twitched his large ears. He said nothing as I set him on the grass. Should we use our hands? Or perhaps Waste could use his scythe...

Nini practically hugged herself, her attention still on the ground. "I don't like graveyards," she whispered.

"No one actually *likes* them," I said. "Even if they're considered sacred."

"I don't even consider them sacred. They're simply awful."

I turned to her, one eyebrow lifted. "Oh?" Anxiety plagued me. Something was off about *this* graveyard, but I suspected Nini didn't mean that.

But she didn't elaborate. Nini stood as still as the wrought-iron fence, and perhaps just as cold. Her reaper said nothing, either.

I sighed. "If you're that uncomfortable, I'll handle everything." I knelt and grabbed the weeds with my bare hands. After I yanked a few from the ground, I glanced over at Twain. My eldrin stared back at me and then frowned. He didn't want to pick weeds, either.

"Uh, Gray?" Nini whispered.

I almost didn't hear her. With as much speed as I could put into my work, I yanked out the weeds covering the grave. "Yeah?" I replied between pulls.

"I'm sorry. Let me help."

She knelt beside me and plucked a few weeds from the ground. Her hands shook whenever she glanced at the tombstone, but she didn't stop. Once we had cleared one grave, we went to the next, and I wondered why Waste was just waiting by the gate.

"Gray," Nini said again.

"Yeah?"

We knelt over the grave and pulled the weeds right out of the dark soil. If we did this by hand, we'd be here all night. We had to think of a faster way.

"Do you think Sorin likes Exie?" Nini pushed her glasses up her nose. "She's very beautiful. And her family is so wealthy." She met my gaze with a frown. "I-I don't know if you two talk about things like that..."

"Aren't you and Sorin *together*?" I asked, emphasizing the word.

They always ran off as a couple, doing all assignments and tasks as though they were tethered at the hip. In my brief imaginings of their adventures, I had figured their mouths had been locked against each other's the moment no one had been looking.

Nini's red cheeks told a different story, though.

"Ever since..." She lowered her voice to a volume barely audible. "My brother died... I've been really afraid."

"Afraid of what?"

"The people of my island say I'm cursed. So... when Sorin said he wanted us to be sweethearts, I told him I needed more time."

"Time for what?" Twain asked, interjecting himself into the conversation. He sounded just as demanding and indignant as I was.

"You know what I've done," Nini whispered. "And I'm a reaper arcanist. Reapers are considered ill omens. What if something happens to Sorin because he's with me?"

*You know what I've done.*

She had accidentally killed her brother. That was the only reason Waste had bonded to her—reapers only bonded to individuals who had killed a family member. But that didn't mean she was cursed. One bad event didn't define her.

"You're not cursed," I stated.

"You don't know that."

I met her gaze. In a flat and hard tone, I said, "You bring a lot of happiness to Sorin." Then I glanced away and yanked out another weed. "And I'm pretty sure my brother is a *one lady* kind of guy. He doesn't have eyes for Exie." At least, I hoped he didn't.

That statement seemed to ease some of Nini's anxieties. She still refused to glance at the tombstones, but she seemed far happier than before. She tugged a dandelion flower free from a weed and grazed her fingers across the yellow petals, her thoughts clearly on distant things.

After another short sigh, I glowered at Twain. "How do you feel about becoming a reaper?"

"To reap the weeds?" Twain tilted his kitten head. "Seems dull."

I narrowed my eyes into a sarcastic glare.

Twain huffed. "*Fine.* I'll help. But know that it's only under protest."

With a smirk, I closed my eyes and searched for the thread of magic that led back to Waste. I felt Ushi's first, and surprised myself when I realized I was starting to sense more about each creature from their specific thread. Ushi was... female. Old. Near the peak of her magical power. I hadn't been able to glean those kinds of details before.

Then I felt Waste's thread. He was weak. Young. But eager. Something about the reaper's magic made him seem thirsty.

And then...

I felt three more threads.

That was strange. There weren't supposed to be any other arcanists around us. Perhaps these were unbonded creatures? Baby mystical creatures born around Red Cape? But when I focused on these threads, my heart sank into the pit of my stomach.

Their threads didn't lead anywhere.

It was like with the corpse near the gate fragment. That meant there were abyssal monsters nearby—more corpses or fiends haunting this very graveyard.

Shaken, I got to my feet and wildly glanced around. Ushi's light kept the darkness at bay, but I couldn't see anything beyond the bubble of illumination she had created. I didn't see the foul creatures near us, which meant they were hiding in the dark, just out of view.

"Gray?" Twain asked. "What's wrong?"

I ran a hand down my face, clearing away cold sweat. "There's a gate fragment nearby."

A low moan echoed from the darkest corner of the graveyard. A groan issued from the opposite corner. They were moving closer.

"*Professor Helmith!*" I shouted.

The light of her magic... where was it? I didn't see even a glint at the far end of the graveyard.

Had something happened to her?

# CHAPTER 16

## TESTING A THEORY

"**I**s something here?" Nini asked, her eyes wide. "I hope it isn't highwaymen."

"It's monsters," I said through gritted teeth.

They stalked through the gloom, creeping toward us. Ushi hovered closer, her light warm and comforting. But that didn't stop the fiends. When they moved, it sounded as though they were sloshing through a swamp, and their moans grew hungry and harsh. Once they were closer, the silhouette of their grotesque forms took shape.

What were these things?

More corpses? Or something else?

"My arcanist will return shortly," Ushi whispered. "You students should run. I will stay to slow them."

And while I thought the floating whelk was brave for volunteering herself, all my thoughts immediately went to my guilt. The gate fragment was here because of *me*. What if Professor Helmith was harmed? And what if she was harmed because I didn't stay and fight alongside her? What kind of arcanist would I be?

The air was thick with the smell of decay and damp earth. My heart beat fast.

"I'm staying," Nini stated, her voice somehow stern but quavering.

Her reaper wrapped his cloak around her. The two merged into a singular being—a young girl with bloodred hair wearing a tattered cloak and holding a scythe. While fused with Waste, she was stronger and actually skilled with her weapon. If Nini had been alone, I doubted she would've known what to do with a scythe—or could've even hefted it for a swing.

"Reapers are lords of the graveyard, after all," Nini and Waste said as one, their voice intertwined.

"*Twain*," I shouted. "Let's handle this."

"Of course!" Twain called back, his back arched.

I felt the thread of Waste's magic and tugged on it. Twain bubbled and shifted, his orange fur shimmering before forming into the frayed edges of a reaper cloak. A scythe identical to Waste's appeared out of Twain's changing body, and within a matter of seconds, my mimic was now a reaper.

Then Twain wrapped his cloak body around my shoulders.

Cold—almost malevolent—power rushed through my body. The hood of the cloak fitted over my head, and my fingers slid around the long handle of the scythe with new purpose. Nini had once said she felt capable when merged with Waste, and I fully understood why.

"Let's do this," Twain and I said at the same time, our voices just as laced together as Nini's and Waste's.

The monsters that shambled out of the darkness were just like the corpse I had seen before. Waterlogged bodies tangled in seaweed and twisted by some sort of fell magic. They were half-rotted humans with bloated skin that fell off in chunks, and bone hands with fingers that sharpened into razors.

They moved and operated as if they were mystical creatures, but for some reason, my mimic magic couldn't identify the source of their power. I decided to ignore that. I focused instead on their skulls, and the soggy bits of skin hanging over the eye sockets.

Nini lowered her scythe and then cut her forearm with the rusty blade. Her weapon sliced through the sleeve of her coat and straight into her skin, drawing a line of scarlet blood. With her jaw clenched, she ran her palm over the blood and then *threw* it at the monster closest to her.

She manipulated the glob of blood midair. It hardened like a small knife—or perhaps a nail—and flew through the body of the corpse.

The monster groaned and held out its clawed hands. The hole in its body didn't bleed. The corpse didn't even react. Could it even feel pain?

Nini took a shaky step backward. Then she held up her hand.

Reaper arcanists manipulated blood, but they evoked terror. Most mystical creatures and arcanists, when caught in the haunting terror, would see visions that terrified them. But when Nini used her magic on the corpse...

Again, nothing happened.

It didn't scream, or yell, or even cower. It quickened its steps and lunged for Nini. With its bone claws, it slashed at her body, trying to rend her into pieces. She stepped backward, not fast enough to counterattack.

Instead, I slashed with my scythe.

The blade slammed into the monster's chest, knocking it off course. Its bone claws didn't cut Nini. It stumbled to the side, my weapon in its rib cage, its mouth open and gurgling out screeches.

The second corpse leapt for me.

Nini, having regained her balance, swung with her scythe. Waste's expert skill helped her. She didn't aim for the torso—she went for the neck. With deadly grace, she swung at an upward angle, slicing through the monster's neck and even part of its jaw. Bits of flesh—and some brackish water—splattered across the nearby tombstone.

Was it dead?

The monster hit the ground and stopped moving.

The other corpse pulled itself free from my blade. Then it slashed with its bone claws. Fortunately, I was much faster when merged with a reaper. Twain and I effortlessly dodged aside. I swung again, slicing off its arm. The monster yelled, its mouth wide, its tongue fat and blue with ocean water.

Another figure emerged from the darkness.

Professor Helmith.

She came up behind the one-armed corpse and grazed her fingers across its bloated skin. The next moment, the monster collapsed to the ground. Water gushed from its mouth, as though the corpse was vomiting, but then it didn't move.

I hesitatingly took a step backward. "Professor?" Twain and I asked together.

Professor Helmith stepped over the corpse she had incapacitated. "Yes. I'm here."

Her left arm bled. There was just a small scratch—like a bone claw had swiped her—so it wasn't life-threatening, but the sight still rattled me. Twain and I unmerged. The cloak slid from my shoulders, and the scythe floated out of my hands. In the next instant, I was weaker and slower, but more *myself*.

Twain transformed back into his kitten-mimic self. The cloak fell to the ground, practically in the mud, and then twisted into the shape of a kitten. The orange fur sprouted out of the fabric until everything shimmered and Twain was once again the large-eared cat I knew him as.

Nini and Waste also unmerged.

With wide eyes, Nini ran to my side. She stared at the professor and frowned. "You're hurt..."

"I'm all right." Helmith placed her hand over the injury and forced a smile. "I had to fight a monster of my own. Are you two uninjured?"

"We're fine. I think... I think I killed mine." Nini glanced over at where the body had been. It was gone. No flesh. No bones. "W-Wait a minute. Where did it go?"

When Waste floated over, the chain in his cloak rattled. Before this evening, the chain had only been three links long. Now there were four.

"It's dead," Waste said, his voice cold and ominous. "And it was once an arcanist. Reapers gain permanent strength from the arcanists they slay. With each kill, another link." Each link in the chain had a name etched into it. But the new link...

Had no name.

Waste's scythe, once rusted, shone brighter in Ushi's light. He was more powerful now that the corpse was disposed of.

"We need to find the gate fragment," I said, my mind wheeling as I tried to process all this new information.

Professor Helmith lifted a small, silver fragment the size of her pointer finger. It was almost as thin as a needle, but it sparkled with magic all the same. "I found it." Then she shook her head. "And you both must forgive me. I wanted to teach you techniques of cultivation... but I also wanted to test a theory."

Nini touched Waste's chain, her attention half on her eldrin, and half on the conversation. "Theory?" she whispered.

"I think these gate fragments are activated by Gray's presence."

I caught my breath.

We didn't need to discuss this any further. She was right. I knew the moment she spoke the words. All Gates of Crossing needed objects and things to help them determine the location they would open to. When Professor Zahn had made his gate to the abyssal hells, he had needed the souls of older twins.

And I had been the last one Zahn had wanted to gather.

"Damn," I whispered, my gaze falling to the ground. I ran a hand through my hair, uncertain of what to say. "Why didn't you tell me?"

"I should've at least mentioned it," Professor Helmith said with a sigh. "But you had been so unnerved when handing me the last fragment, I didn't want to disturb you. And I didn't think three of these... things... would enter our world. Forgive me. I should've either better protected you, or better prepared you for the reality."

Her apology left me nervous. I rubbed the back of my neck and half-shrugged. "No. It's fine. You warned us before there might be more fragments about." Helmith had protected me for years before I had enrolled at the Academy. She didn't need to do that forever.

I wanted to prove to her I was capable.

"How were you injured?" Nini asked the professor.

"A creature came out of the darkness." Helmith pointed to the far end of the graveyard. "Right where this fragment rested in the grass." She turned back to us. "I see you both are getting used to your magics. I'm sorry you had to learn in such a stressful way."

Nini shook her head. When her glasses slid down her nose, she pushed them back up again. "It's okay. I... I just didn't know I was killing someone." She pointed to the chain hanging from Waste's cloak. "What does this mean?"

"It means that bits of the abyssal hells are leaking into the world. These lost souls clearly took hold in nearby bodies." Helmith turned on her heel.

The corpse she had touched was still on the ground.

"Why is this one still here?" I asked, lifting an eyebrow. All the other corpses had vanished once they had been "re-dead."

"I put him to sleep," Helmith replied matter-of-factly. She gripped her injured arm a bit tighter. "As an ethereal whelk arcanist, I can evoke light, manipulate dreams... and augment people's wakefulness." She genuinely smiled as she said, "*Augmentation* is your next big lesson once we head back to Astra Academy. Augmentation is where you alter something already in existence with your magic."

"Altering people's wakefulness..." Nini glanced down at the bloated body. More water gushed from its mouth. "This was an odd way to learn about ethereal whelk powers."

"I'm a professor first and foremost. I'm always looking for ways to incorporate *learning* into our activities."

For some reason, I imagined Professor Helmith giving a lecture in the middle of a murder scene. It would be hilarious to hear her talk about the effectiveness of certain evocation in the terms of *best murder weapon*, but I kept all that sarcastic commentary to myself.

Twain nuzzled the side of my leg. When I glanced down at him, he frowned. "Pick me up," he whined. "It's muddy here. I'm getting dirty."

I scooped him into my arms. His orange fur was spotted with dirt. I patted most of it away. Twain just laid his ears back against his head, his eyes narrowed in irritation.

The evening winds rushed by, sweeping away the smell of rot. Everything was crisp again, even though a waterlogged corpse was still in our midst. I inched away from it, frowning. Where was Sorin? I would've felt better if my brother were here.

Clouds moved across the sky, blocking the rising moon and glorious stars.

Ushi's light was all we had.

Waste floated over the body, his scythe silently twirling through the air. "And what shall we do about this monster? Kill it? If yes, I can grow stronger. Nini and I need that."

Professor Helmith stared at the corpse for several minutes. No one spoke, even as the winds grew chillier.

"It's not the soul's fault for being here," she whispered. "I wonder what my father would do in this situation..." When we remained quiet, Helmith closed her eyes and muttered, "*Vigilance. Without it, we allow our enemies to have the advantage.*"

"What was that?" I asked.

Professor Helmith shook her head. "Advice from my father." She turned to Waste. "You may destroy it."

Waste didn't hesitate. He slammed his scythe down on the sleeping corpse, slicing into the chest. Water gushed from the injury, splashing onto the ground. The monster moaned, but then dissolved, like the other.

Waste gained another link on his chain. He was up to five.

This one also didn't have a name.

"Now that I know your presence is causing the fragments to activate, I think it would be best if we ended the camping trip early." Professor Helmith patted her floating ethereal whelk and then pointed to the wrought-iron gates. "Come. We should get back to the others—and I should secure this gate fragment as soon as possible."

# CHAPTER 17

## TYPHOON DRAGONS AND WATERFALLS

T he campfire raged before us. The plan was to rest for the night and then leave in the morning. We had already finished the schoolhouse, and while spending peaceful days out in the wilderness had been fun for a while, I had to admit I was ready to return to Astra Academy.

Captain Leon walked around the blazing fire. He reached his hand into the flames—unharmed, thanks to cerberus magic—and then withdrew an iron pan. Any normal person would've been burned and charred ten times over, but Leon just smiled as he showed off his blackened hunk of meat in the pan.

"Ya see, the *inside* is quite juicy when you flash-fire it like this." Leon brought the pan close to his nose and inhaled deeply. "Ah, yes. Perfection. Are you all taking notes? This might not be on an exam, but it's a real-life lesson."

"That meat is deader than the corpses we tore up in the graveyard," Twain quipped, his sarcasm in full force.

I chuckled as I waited for Leon to pass out the crispy dinner to everyone.

I sat next to Sorin and Nini on the far log, my mind half on the gate fragments and half on our dinner. Twain stretched himself out on my lap, his little claws poking out of his digits and then sheathing themselves after.

The smell of burning wood, and the crackle of flames, had become soothing.

Nasbit, Exie, and Phila sat at the farthest log from us. Raaza and Knovak sat next to them, and Ashlyn occupied her own log, her dragon whispering things straight into her ears. As Captain Leon passed out the meat, I realized both Piper and Professor Helmith were absent. Had they quickly returned to the Academy to drop off the gate fragment? Piper could teleport with her rizzel magic.

That was probably what had happened.

When I glanced over at Ashlyn a second time, her bright blue eyes met mine. We stared at each other for a prolonged moment, neither of us looking away. She lifted an eyebrow, and I knew she wanted to talk.

I set Twain down on the ground and then stood from my log. After nudging my brother, I said, "I'm going to grab some water. Want any?"

He shook his head. "Nah." Then he smiled at Nini. "So, I think I wrote a pretty inspiring ballad about our time constructing the schoolhouse."

Nini smiled and nodded along with his words, clearly content to just listen.

While they were distracted, I casually ambled over to Ashlyn. She watched me as I approached, and I offered her my own lifted eyebrow.

"Tonight is our last night here," Ashlyn whispered when I was close enough. The crackle of the flames was louder than her voice, but I still managed to hear everything.

I shrugged as I slowly made my way behind her log.

"There are waterfalls nearby with magical properties." Ashlyn glanced over her shoulder and concluded with, "I'm going to go see them."

She said nothing else. I continued my inconspicuous walk over to our water barrel, wondering why she would be interested in a silly little waterfall. Then I turned my attention to her dragon. Typhoon dragons were the kings of water. Perhaps the thought of finding a magical waterfall intrigued Ecrib.

Whatever the reason, she was obviously inviting me to take part in her extracurricular activities. But why?

If I had to come up with a reason, perhaps I was invited to take the fall if we were caught. Was that Ashlyn's plan? I had given her my occult ore, after all. She might have thought I would do something *nice* for her in the future.

After I had filled a cup with water, I wandered back over to my brother, the dancing flames a beautiful backdrop to my odd thoughts.

What if the waterfalls were substantially magical? They were so famous, some of the others had heard of them before we had even arrived. I wanted to experience that.

On the other hand, the gate fragments were activated by my presence...

It could be risky.

I sat on the log and smiled as Sorin continued talking about his ballad.

After a few moments, I made my decision. I would go with Ashlyn.

Night came faster than I had expected. Everyone had eaten themselves into a coma, and by the time the moon was high in the sky, I heard their snores more clearly than I heard my own thoughts.

Nasbit especially. He practically spoke in his sleep. As I slid out of my cot, he snorted, and I almost panicked. Fortunately, he just rolled over and returned to his deep breathing.

My eldrin sat by my feet, watching as I slid off my cot. Twain smiled, never making a sound.

My brother remained asleep, even as I dressed and walked around the support pole in the middle of the tent. I felt bad that I hadn't told him my plan, but I already knew what he would have said. Sorin disapproved of any and all rule breaking. He wouldn't have stopped me from going, but he would have frowned and complained, and probably given me some sort of poem about how only villains sneak out of their tent at night.

The sad thing was—Sorin's guilt trips usually worked.

Which was why I couldn't tell him.

As I grabbed Twain off the end of my cot, the darkness intensified under my feet.

"Damn," I muttered under my breath.

I had forgotten knightmares never slept.

"Going somewhere?" Thurin whispered.

"Don't wake my brother," I said, my voice equally quiet. "He doesn't need to fret about any of this. But if he *does* wake up, tell him I just went out to bathe really quick."

"That..." Thurin sighed. "Is clearly a lie."

I waved away his comment. "It's only *half* a lie. I'll be right back."

"Hm."

Thankfully, Thurin didn't stop me. I walked over his shadow puddle and exited the tent with a confident smile. The firepit was cold, the other tents quiet, and everything was as it should have been. My heart beat a little faster as excitement entered my system.

Now for magical waterfalls.

I spotted Ashlyn's dragon over by a cluster of trees. He was far too large to hide. With quiet steps, I hustled over, Twain held tightly in my arms. My eldrin's ears twitched to face every sound in the distance, but nothing indicated any of the other arcanists had awoken.

The moonlight guided my way until I came to the trees.

Ashlyn stepped out from behind the trunk of a large oak, her blonde hair tied in a messy bun. She wore thin pants and a long tunic—not her usual adventuring gear. She seemed comfortable.

"Nice outfit," I said. "Not too formal. Not too casual. Just the right amount of classy for a delinquent sneaking out of her tent."

Ashlyn tried to restrain a smile, but a corner of her lip twitched upward, escaping her control. After rolling her eyes, she asked, "Why are you like this?"

I shrugged. "I'm the smaller twin. I didn't get as many nutrients."

"Hmpf!" someone huffed from a few trees over.

Both Ashlyn and I tensed as we whirled to face the speaker. A unicorn foal pranced out from behind a trunk. Starling. His white coat glistened in the moonlight, and his horn sparkled with the intensity of the brightest star. When he swished his mane, he did so with his snout up.

"Here you are," he whispered. "My arcanist? Do you see this?"

Knovak also stepped around the trunk of the tree. He wore a pair of muddy boots, long trousers, a black silk tunic, and his large-brimmed hat.

Why the hat? There wasn't any light to block from his eyes. Yet still—he wore it. Unironically.

"I knew something was going on," Knovak muttered. "The two of you... are going to see those waterfalls, aren't you?" His dark eyes narrowed into a glare before we could even voice a reply. "*I* was the one who told Phila about those waterfalls. If anyone should see them, it's me."

Ashlyn and I stared at him for a long moment.

I waved him toward the river. "By all means. Go on."

Knovak gestured to me, and then Ashlyn. "We're *all* going." He stomped over, practically huffing all the way over. "So no one goes back and tells the captain. Or Professor Helmith." He shot me another glare. "I know how much you *love* talking to her about everything."

Ashlyn didn't reply.

I held back a chuckle. He was afraid we would rat on him? What a bizarre man. I didn't have a real good bead on Knovak, it seemed. I had thought he would have been giddy to go to the waterfalls, but he seemed more indignant than anything.

Was he upset because we hadn't invited him to go?

I shook my head.

That was silly.

Starling pranced over, his snout still held high. He said nothing as he followed his arcanist toward the water. Ashlyn shrugged and then pointed at her dragon. Ecrib carefully crept through the undergrowth, obviously trying to limit the amount of sound he made.

With Twain in my arms, I watched our rear.

The tranquility of the night helped to relax me. Twain even purred as we walked through moonlight pillars shining through the tree canopy. Ashlyn glanced over her shoulder a few times, and each time, I gave her a different look. First a shrug, then a lifted eyebrow. By the third time, she was just chortling to herself.

It felt like a game we were playing, though I had to admit, I didn't really understand what we were doing.

Knovak practically stomped the entire way to the waterfalls. When we drew near, the crash of water rang over the small forest, and mist hung on the air. My hair was damp by the time we spotted the falls off in the distance.

I caught my breath once I had a good look.

Three waterfalls—perhaps ten feet high—all cascaded into the same river. Rocks separated them, but they were each distinct. The middle one was wider, the far waterfall crashed onto a boulder and then splashed to the side into the river, and the one closest to us had a small cave behind it.

The mist...

It smelled sweet. Not like normal water at all.

And even in the moonlight, the falls created small, multicolored rainbows that spanned the rushing waters.

This place was far more beautiful than I would've expected.

"Wow," Starling said as he clopped over to the riverbank. "How wonderful. My arcanist? Are you seeing this?"

Knovak walked over to his eldrin and patted Starling on the neck. "It's gorgeous."

"Ecrib," Ashlyn said as she turned to her dragon. Then she pointed to the river. "Check it out. Let us know if it really is magical."

Ecrib snorted as he hurried into the water. The typhoon dragon slid into the river, his movement becoming a lot smoother the moment he could swim. His blue scales—already shimmering from the moonlight—glittered brighter than ever before. The dragon lapped up some of the water and then turned to face Ashlyn.

The sparkle of his scales...

Ashlyn smiled widely. "It *is* magical, isn't it?"

Ecrib nodded.

With a giddy laugh, Ashlyn kicked off her boots and then pulled her blonde hair out of her bun. Then she shot me a playful look. "Well? Are you gonna swim or not?"

I grabbed my tunic, ready to rip it off and show her how well we islanders swam, but I hesitated before anything happened. I had scars on my body. I wasn't like Ashlyn, who seemed perfect in all regards. Beautiful skin. Luscious hair. Eyes that had stolen their color from sapphires.

Arcanists weren't supposed to scar.

They only had scars if they'd had them *before* they gained magic.

I tugged at the bottom of my tunic. In an awkward tone, I asked, "So, Ashlyn. How do you feel about men with scars? Like *battle* scars. Awesome, right?"

She walked over to the edge of the river and then glanced back at me. "Oh, yes. Nothing is as manly as scars."

I couldn't take off my tunic fast enough.

I wasn't as large as my brother, but I wasn't a slouch, either. Although, I immediately recognized how ridiculous this was. I seriously doubted Ashlyn had invited me out to see the waterfalls to get my shirt off.

But I liked to imagine that had been the reason.

After kicking off my own boots, I hurried to join her near the water's edge. Knovak watched as both Ashlyn and I stepped into the freezing river, still fully dressed, though I wasn't going to comment on that part. I shivered as I got in up to my knees. Twain huffed and spat and muttered irritations. No way *he* would get near the water.

"Just because the water is *magical* doesn't mean it's *good*," Knovak said as he crept closer to the river's edge. "What if you get an ailment? Or worse?"

I sucked in air through my teeth once the water had reached the top of my legs. Ashlyn exhaled, but genuinely laughed afterward as she sank to her shoulders. Ecrib swam to her side, and the fins on his back resembled a whole gang of tiny sharks.

She patted his head, and the two of them swam toward the waterfalls.

I glanced back at Twain. "C'mon. Join me."

His ears drooped. Then he pounded the dirt with a forepaw. "Fine. But you owe me. At some point, you need to get me a fish. *A whole fish.* That I get to eat all by myself."

"Fine, fine. Just get over here."

Twain walked to the edge of the water, his orange fur puffing out as the mists of the falls washed over him. Before he could complain about his fur, I focused on the mystical creatures in the area, and I tugged the thread of magic that led to Ashlyn's typhoon dragon. Although Twain could only maintain a stolen shape for a few minutes, that would be enough to bathe in the magical falls.

In a matter of moments, Twain's body bubbled and shifted. His tiny cat body exploded outward until he was the size of Ashlyn's typhoon dragon. Twain grew blue scales, fins, and even razor-sharp claws. My arcanist mark rearranged itself on my forehead until Twain finished transforming.

"Heh," Twain said, his voice deeper and more menacing. "Let's get us some magic." He stomped into the water and then swam forward with the same grace as Ecrib.

I grabbed on to Twain and rode with him to the waterfalls. The frigid water caused my fingers to turn blue, but at least they also became numb. Despite the temperature, the tingle of the water invigorated me. Something about this place...

I glanced upward as we neared the three falls. The moonlight rainbows were transfixing.

Ashlyn stared up at them, too. "I'm so glad we did this," she whispered.

The crash of the water almost prevented me from hearing her. Almost. They were small waterfalls, though. They made a constant racket, but it wasn't too much.

My teeth clattered as the cold seeped deep into my bones.

Ashlyn waved her hand, and water from the falls splashed outward. I was hit by her wave and fell off Twain. While I tumbled through the river, I shook my head. *I* was a typhoon dragon arcanist as well! Once I swam to the surface, I spat river water out of my mouth and also swished my hand.

A tiny ripple swept across the water.

Ecrib laughed.

Twain shook his dragon head. "Really?"

I shot him a glare. "*I'm* your arcanist. You're not supposed to judge me."

"*I'm* your eldrin. Stop embarrassing me!"

With gritted teeth, I waved my hand again. This time, the water lifted a few inches before splashing back down.

Ashlyn swam over to me, her fingers equally as blue, her teeth also chattering. Despite all that, she smiled as she neared me. With a gentle touch, she grabbed my arm. Her icy fingers were confident. "You're not doing it right. Evocation is when you force your magic outward. That's what you're doing. But you need to *manipulate* it. Think of the water as your hand."

She grabbed my hand and spread my fingers. Then she placed my palm on the surface of the water.

It was difficult to swim and have her move my arm. We both stood, my feet sinking slightly into the muddy riverbed.

"Here," Ashlyn said. "Now move the water like it is your limb." She leaned against me, keeping her balance by bracing half her weight on my shoulder.

If every class was like this, Astra Academy would be amazing.

With a chuckle—and pushing my thoughts from my mind—I said, "I'll try."

I did as Ashlyn had instructed. I tried to imagine the water as part of me. When I envisioned it moving, I was shocked to see it working. A larger wave of water lifted from the river and splashed over Ecrib. The typhoon dragon practically smiled, though. He enjoyed every moment we could splash around.

"There," Ashlyn whispered. "You did it perfectly."

"Are you two practicing your magic?" Knovak called out from the shore.

To be honest—I had completely, utterly, one hundred percent forgotten Knovak was there.

Ashlyn turned to face him. "Yes. Just our manipulation."

Knovak huffed and rolled his eyes. He stomped down to the edge of the water and crossed his arms. "Did you even notice how Captain Leon didn't want to help me train? Everyone else has a *flashy* manipulation, but since the unicorn arcanist doesn't, I'm just invisible."

I didn't know what he was doing, but Knovak tore off his hat and then threw it to the ground. Then he pulled off his tunic and threw it on top of his hat. Starling trotted over to him and snorted in irritation.

"Well, I can practice my manipulation, too," Knovak said, practically yelling.

He held out both his arms.

For a long while—at least thirty seconds—everyone was silent. The roar of the waterfalls kept the area filled with noise, but otherwise, no one said a word.

"*Did you see it?*" Knovak shouted.

"See what?" I asked.

"I made myself *bolder*." He spoke the last word with the drama of a thespian.

I didn't know if it was because the situation was preposterous, but Ashlyn couldn't stop herself from laughing. She laughed, and then half dunked her head into the water to cover her mouth. Which made me laugh. And Twain. And Ecrib.

I grimaced when I turned to face Knovak, fearing he would take all this laughter as ridicule.

Fortunately, Knovak also seemed to think it was funny. Our laughter grew louder, which caused him to smile, until he was finally laughing alongside us. He slapped his own knee and half-shrugged.

"Did you love that?" Knovak asked.

Starling wasn't laughing, though. The little unicorn drooped his head and frowned.

Knovak pointed to the waterfalls. "I'll prove I'm bolder. Watch this!" He ran to the nearest of the falls and hefted himself onto the rocks. The rushing water was slippery—I knew from a lifetime of experience—but Knovak bravely scaled the rocks regardless.

Mist swirled around him as he ascended higher and higher.

Once he was a good eight feet up, he stopped and glanced over his shoulder.

"Watch this!" Knovak shouted. "I'm going to manipulate myself right into the river!"

With a laugh that bordered on madness, Knovak let go of the rocks and careened into the river below. That madman slapped onto the surface of the water, hitting it like a flat plank of wood. It had to have hurt. By the abyssal hells—it had hurt *me* just watching it.

Knovak sank below the surface afterward.

Starling gasped. "M-My arcanist!"

Without needing a command, Ecrib swam through the waters and went straight for Knovak. The dragon scooped the man up and then carried him to the shore. Knovak shivered the entire time, his manipulated courage obviously at an end.

I slow clapped. "Very brave. Ten out of ten, would watch again."

"Gray?" someone called out. "What're you doing out here?"

# CHAPTER 18

## THE HALLS OF ASTRA ACADEMY

P rofessor Helmith stood on the shore of the river, the moonlight
bathing her in an otherworldly glow. Her black hair shimmered
as she took a hesitant step forward. She frowned. I hated seeing
her frown.

"Gray?" she asked. "You ventured away from camp?"

I sloshed through the water, heading toward the bank. "Uh, well, I can
explain."

"I told you that your presence could activate the gate fragments."
Professor Helmith sighed, her disappointment cutting me deep. "You put
everyone in danger by coming here."

I didn't have a response to that. Sure, I could spin a tale or weave an
excuse, and if anyone other than Helmith had caught me, maybe I
would've, but not with her. I allowed my gaze to fall to the ground.

"I'm sorry," I forced myself to say, though it was barely audible.

Twain splashed his way to the shore and shifted into his kitten form in
order to stand next to me. He, too, bowed his head, like he was also in
trouble. The cold night air whipped across my wet body, creating an icy
sensation that nearly hurt.

Ashlyn and Ecrib also swam to the shore and stepped out.

Professor Helmith gave her the briefest of glances. "Ashlyn, I thought you were also better than this. Your instructions were to stay in your tents."

"Forgive me, Professor." Ashlyn bowed slightly. "Typhoon dragons are attracted to strange and powerful waters and—"

"I'll be issuing you a demerit."

Ashlyn stopped speaking.

Astra Academy had a demerit system to help correct delinquent behavior. Although I had never experienced anything like this, the other arcanists in my class seemed to fear having a demerit on their record.

Even Ashlyn seemed angrier than before.

"Gray—I'll be issuing you two." Helmith sighed. "One for breaking the rules, and one for selfishly disregarding the safety of others."

"Yes, Professor," I muttered.

I wouldn't fight her on this. Helmith was probably being nice to me, given the circumstances.

That was when Starling clopped over to us. Helmith's lifted eyebrows betrayed her surprise. She also stared in quiet disbelief as Knovak emerged from the mists around the waterfall, his silk shirt on his arm, his hat perched on top of his wet head.

"Professor," he said through chattering teeth. "You sh-shouldn't be too hard on them. I w-was the one who urged them to go. I was a-also the one who told them about the w-waterfalls in the first place. I even, uh, mildly threatened them."

His unicorn nodded his head several times. "Yes. It's true. All of it." For some reason, Starling held his head high, as though proud of his declarations.

It wasn't entirely *not* true, but Knovak was definitely taking liberties with the truth. And why? To help me and Ashlyn?

"I see," Professor Helmith muttered. "In that case, you'll take Ashlyn's demerit *and* your demerit." She gave Ashlyn a stern glance. "But you should know better. I've seen you make far better choices in the past."

Ashlyn nodded once. "Yes, Professor."

Without another word, Helmith turned and motioned for everyone to follow. She evoked a ball of light in her hand and headed for the trail away from the water. She didn't look back, and I felt the disappointment radiating off her.

I grabbed my shirt and threw it over my wet skin. Then I scooped up Twain.

Ashlyn waited until Knovak was close before asking, "Why did you say that?"

"I know it's really important to you not to have any b-blemishes on your record," Knovak muttered, his chattering still noticeable. "And my folks won't care, so long as I don't get kicked out."

Ashlyn didn't reply to this.

Like with me, she almost seemed angry, or cold, and I wondered if she thought of *everyone's* help as though it were somehow a mark against her. Like she wasn't competent enough, and needed the aid of others. That was a silly thought, obviously, but she seemed so against any kind of assistance, what else could it be?

"That was nice of you, Knovak," I said.

He fixed his large-brimmed hat tighter over his wet hair. Once Ashlyn had left to follow the professor, Knovak whispered, "I was just doing what you recommended, ya know."

"What do you mean?" I asked.

"I mean... I'm not part of the nobility, but you said I would be treated like one if I *acted* noble. I'm trying that out."

Starling snorted. "Yes. It was good advice. And we're going to be the noblest of all."

I had completely forgotten I had told him that. At the time, it had been to get him out of his depressed slump. For some reason, Knovak had always been concerned with the fact the arcanists from noble families didn't want to associate with him. He came from a *rich* family—the Gentz Merchant House—but that apparently wasn't enough in the eyes of future dukes and cousins of literal royalty.

"You shouldn't care what other people think of you," I said. "But I will admit... That was a nice thing you did for Ashlyn."

Knovak scoffed and offered a weak shrug. "Fantastic. Any more contradictory advice?"

"Let's just get going." I slapped his shoulder and motioned him toward Helmith's light. "You don't want to be left behind, do you?"

In the morning, we left our tents and headed for our ship.

The entire time, we never really saw the citizens of Red Cape. There were a dozen near the dinghies when we arrived, but otherwise, there was no meeting with them, or even a celebration for finishing the schoolhouse. I wondered why, but I pushed it out of my mind.

Perhaps we *would* have celebrated with them if we hadn't found the gate fragments nearby. Now we just needed to get back to the Academy so my presence didn't set any more off. No one wanted corpses around.

It was quiet as everyone piled onto the ship. The loudest thing was Brak as it stomped across the deck, its giant stone golem feet slamming hard, even when it was trying to be delicate.

Professor Helmith, Piper, and Captain Leon muttered things under their breath to one another the whole trip, even as we sailed for the Gates of Crossing that led back to Astra Academy.

Sorin stuck close to me, and so did Nini, but Ashlyn didn't even glance in my direction. She spent her time with Phila and Exie, away from everyone else. Her dragon made sure of it, too. Anyone who got close to their group would have to deal with Ecrib—and that typhoon dragon wasn't in the mood for talking.

Silence was a constant companion on our trek.

That was fine. I didn't like the fact that I had disappointed Professor Helmith so much, so I made a promise to myself to extra behave once we returned to the Academy. It wouldn't be too hard.

I hoped.

Our ship traveled through the Gates of Crossing and emerged on the other side of the teleport in the middle of a grand lake. The water reflected the blue sky with the brilliance of a polished mirror. Our ship sailed over the reflection of clouds, and my mind filled with a sense of wonder and imagination.

Astra Academy sat atop the nearby mountain.

It was a black stone castle. Five additional buildings dotted the other mountaintops, each made of the same dark stone. They were tall and imposing, and a stark contrast to the gray and white of the mountains. Green pine trees added a bit of color to the campus, but nothing was quite as impressive as the treehouse.

The gargantuan redwood tree grew on the east side of the Academy. Its thick branches wrapped around portions of the walls and created walkways for everyone's eldrin. The paths connected to the windows, allowing the larger mystical creatures to come and go without needing to worry about the size of doors.

Ecrib was growing fast. Soon, he wouldn't fit through a normal door. Thankfully, the treehouse had rooms built into the main trunk specifically for eldrin to sleep in. It was a useful system, though Twain rarely wanted to go there. And since he was the size of a kitten, it didn't really matter if he slept on my bed.

Our ship docked, and as a class, we headed for the long stone staircase that led to the Academy's entrance. The grand scale of everything impressed me, but my legs burned by the time we reached the last step. I wished they had built another gate just to take us from the bottom to the entrance—but maybe I was just feeling lazy. My dour mood made everything a little less exciting than before.

"Ah, it's good to be back," Captain Leon said to everyone. "And don't worry. Since the camping trip was cut short, there's no grand prize at the end, but I'll carry over any points and victories to the next outing you have a class."

His cerberus wagged his tail. "It does feel good to be back," the middle head said. "And I love prizes!"

Leon threw open the main door and ushered us through. Without much thought, everyone headed for the courtyard. It was a massive square area in the middle of the Academy that basically acted as the central hub.

The courtyard was surrounded by stone walls on all four sides, each lined with windows and balconies. The greenery in the middle of the yard was so vibrant it felt like summer, even though we were deep into autumn. A small brook also meandered its way through the middle of the courtyard—a beautiful addition to an already gorgeous location.

Sorin glanced around with a smile. "I love this place."

"Me, too," Nini said as she straightened her glasses. "It's so tranquil."

Four statues were positioned in the corners of the courtyard. One was a gold-and-silver globe the size of a small shed. It showed all of Vardin, our world as we knew it. Another was a sundial—equally large. The third was a statue of a seven-pointed star.

The last one...

It was a statue of twisted, upside-down gates. Normally, I would've said the statue of the gates was the most beautiful. They were sparkling gold, and the detailing on the metalwork was apparent, even from halfway across the courtyard.

But the upside-down gates represented the abyssal hells.

Now it was my least favorite statue.

"Do you remember our school motto?" Sorin asked once he noticed me staring at the decorations.

Nasbit coughed and stepped closer to us. Even though Sorin had clearly been speaking to me, Nasbit replied with, "*In Life, Through Time, With Magic, Till Death.*" He pointed to the statues. "That's what each of those mean," Nasbit said matter-of-factly.

"Who do you think wrote the motto?" Sorin ran a hand through his hair and narrowed his eyes. "Do you think that's a job they hand out to anyone? Or... do you have to have connections?"

"There's a book on the Academy's history in the library." Nasbit pointed to a far door as we reached the other side of the courtyard. "I saw it, but I was too busy reading about the God-Arcanists War to read everything about Astra Academy. I'll eventually figure out who wrote the motto, though."

Sorin turned to me. "Aren't you happy to be back, Gray?"

I nodded. "Yeah."

"Are you okay, Gray?" Nini asked, frowning. "You haven't seemed like your normal self."

"He's upset because his honeysuckle is mad at him." Sorin shrugged. "But Gray is overreacting, because everyone knows Professor Helmith will forgive him. They go way back."

I fought the urge to punch my brother in the shoulder. Why did he always call Helmith that? It was starting to eat away at my patience. Even Twain shot my brother a glower, like it was upsetting him, too.

We entered the Academy and headed for the grand staircase that led to the dorms. As everyone headed straight for the steps, Leon stepped in front of Sorin, Nini, and me. He motioned for us to stay behind.

For some reason, Nasbit was trying to stay behind as well, but Leon pointed him away. "I need to speak to these three."

Nasbit weakly nodded and then headed off with his stone golem.

Once we were alone, Captain Leon and his cerberus stood close. Sticks and his three heads gave us each a once-over. Then Leon placed a hand on my shoulder. "So, I, uh, need to apologize to you three."

"Why?" Sorin asked.

"I set up this camping trip to give you three a little vacation. Something easier. Ya see, when I was younger, taking a trip to the woods was my favorite pastime. I thought you all would enjoy it, especially after everything that had happened with the gate and Professor Zahn."

Sorin crossed his arms. "I enjoyed it."

"So did I," Nini added.

"As did I," Thurin said, his voice drifting up from the darkness around Sorin's feet.

Waste twirled his scythe. "I have two new chains for my collection. I would say it was a worthwhile expedition."

My brother glanced over to me.

"It was great," I muttered.

Captain Leon frowned as he stroked his trim, white beard. Then he sighed. "I didn't think you would get into trouble. So, I'm sorry for that."

Sorin waved away the comment. "No need to apologize. No one could've known about that. Thank you for looking out for us."

"Yes, thank you," Thurin chimed in.

With a smile, Captain Leon motioned us back to the hallway. He and Sticks guided us the rest of the way to the staircase. "You all should get some good rest today. Tomorrow your classes will start up again. Regular schedule. And don't worry, most of the professors know of your situation, so you'll be caught up on everything you missed out on."

"Does everyone know now what happened with the Gates of Crossing to the abyssal hells?" I asked. "And not the professors... I mean the other students. Were they informed while we were out camping?"

Leon replied with a curt nod and then said, "Yes. Well. Most were informed what happened, since a portion of the Academy was wrecked. But you don't need to dwell on that. I doubt anyone will mention it."

# CHAPTER 19

## NORMAL SCHOOL LIFE

W hen I walked the halls of Astra Academy, people whispered and pointed.

I was the only mimic arcanist on campus, so it wasn't difficult to spot me in a crowd. The arcanist mark on my forehead was blank, and a dead giveaway to my identity. The second-, third-, fourth-, and fifth-year students all wore different robes to distinguish their area of study, and their year at the academy, and for some reason, there were more of them around than usual.

They were the ones who were more brazen when they singled me out.

"There he is," a third-year muttered. "The arcanist who supposedly fought a Death Lord."

"He's so young," a fourth-year said, louder than the other. "Are mimic arcanists just that strong? I thought mimics were a low tier of creature."

"They're whatever tier they mimic, actually."

First-year students all wore velvet robes of black and blue with silver lining. Our robes were marked with the Academy's symbols—the globe, star, sundial, and upside-down gates.

The second-year students had robes of pure silver.

Third-years had robes of red with silver lining.

Fourth-years had robes of blue with gold lining.

And fifth-years had robes of black with gold lining, stitchwork, and symbols.

Only the first-years had the Academy's four icons. Once a student became a second-year, they had to pick a specialization of study. If they picked the *knights*, they would get a helmet on their robes. If they picked *artificers*, they would get a hammer. *Mystic guardians* would get a compass. *Cultivators* would get a tree with long roots. And *viziers* would get a quill.

It made it easy to identify everyone's year and specialty with a quick glance. And if someone couldn't remember the colors—or they had a hard time seeing the colors—the year of each student was stitched onto the shoulder once they were beyond their first year.

But I tried not to focus on the other students. Instead, I turned my attention to the Academy itself. The high ceilings and blue rugs gave everything a lush feel. The tall windows allowed me to view the vast campus as I headed to class.

The mountains around Astra Academy were nearly as magical as the students. The Nimbus Sea—a mountaintop surrounded by perpetual clouds—remained one of my favorite locations. I stared at the swirling nimbuses, wishing some of my classes took place on the plateau just above the cloud line.

The growing mutters of other arcanists drew down my enjoyment. With my notebook, pencils, and books in my arms, I hurried along. Twain bounded after me, his footfalls silent.

I felt relief the moment Twain and I reached our classroom. I stood before a large oak door. On the front of it was carved the words: CLASS ONE, YEAR ONE.

I pushed open the door. My classroom greeted me with a welcoming warmth that reminded me of home. And that surprised me, because the far back window was open. A treehouse branch was positioned just beyond the sill, to allow for everyone's eldrin to enter.

The room was just as I remembered.

Five large tables stretched across the room, each facing the professor's desk at the front. A chalkboard, covered in a fine dust, hung on the wall. It was cozy. I liked it.

And I immediately took my seat at the table near the front. Professor

Helmith would teach our class for the day. She was the professor in charge of teaching us everything about mystical creatures. It was probably my favorite subject.

Twain jumped onto the table just as I set all my supplies down.

He stretched and then curled himself into a little loaf shape. "Wake me when it's over, okay?"

"Aren't you going to learn any of this?" I asked.

"Do I need to?" Twain twitched his large lynx-like ears. "We'll be together for the rest of our lives. If I need to know the information, *you'll* have it. If we were smart about this, I would study half the classes, and you would study the other half... Half as much studying, but full amount of benefit." Twain tapped his temple with his forepaw.

"Good luck writing notes with your lack of thumbs," I quipped.

Twain lifted his head and glared. "Low blow, Gray. Low blow."

The door opened, cutting off our playful conversation. Sorin and Nini entered together, both wearing their robes and smiles that stretched to their ears. Nini also had a coat, and a shirt, and maybe two vests—she had enough layers to clothe an entire orphanage.

Waste floated in behind her, and I found it ironic that her eldrin was basically *yet another* layer of clothing she could wear.

I snorted back a laugh.

Sorin and Nini both sat at my table and spread out their notebooks and materials. All our eldrin were small, thin, or a puddle of darkness. The whole table was practically empty.

Ashlyn, Exie, Phila, and Nasbit entered next, none of them with their eldrin. They took a seat at the second table closest to the professor's desk, each of them radiant this morning.

Especially Exie.

She must have bathed four times over to wash away the "gunk" of camping, and also all the perfume she had used to cover the scent of our campsite. Her chestnut hair practically sparkled, and while she wore her uniform robes, she had them tied tightly around her narrow waist, giving her an exaggerated hourglass figure.

There was no way that was an accident.

Ashlyn's brilliant blonde hair looked slightly metallic in the glory of the morning light. When she glanced over at me, I thought I would see ice in her eyes, but instead, she offered me a slight smile.

I returned the gesture.

She quickly looked away and took her seat between Exie and Phila.

Phila was probably the oddest one of the trio. She didn't wear her robes fancy, and her strawberry-blonde hair was pulled back in a bun. But when she smiled... it was bright and genuine. She had a face that came alive whenever she grinned.

It reminded me of Sorin.

For that reason—which was illogical—I liked Phila. I knew very little about her, but something about the way she held herself seemed pleasant. Beautiful.

"I think this class is going to be interesting," Nasbit said as he sat on the opposite end of the table from the three girls. "I heard the headmaster has summoned several powerful arcanists to give guest lectures to the students, and one of them might even be Professor Helmith's father."

Nasbit's robes were pulled tight around his round body. Was he cold? Or just trying to hide himself? Either way, he wore his uniform like someone wore a blanket.

"Guest lecturers?" Exie frowned. "*That's* what you're excited about? Naz, darling, you need to straighten out your priorities."

Nasbit opened his notebook. He pointed to a page with a copious number of notes. "W-Well, I'm really excited to fill in a few bits of information I don't have. See, Professor Helmith hasn't gone over several subjects regarding mystical creatures, and I wanted—"

Exie rolled her hand, gesturing for Nasbit to get to the point.

"I'm just excited for specialists," Nasbit lamely ended. He stared down at his notes and sighed.

Knovak and Raaza were the last to enter the room. They didn't enter together. No—the exact opposite. I suspected both of them had reached the door at the same time, and then they awkwardly determined Raaza would go first, and Knovak huffed in afterward.

Raaza wore his robes open and half on his shoulders, as though he would need to throw them off at any second. He rubbed at his scars as he sat at the very back table. Away from everyone. His kitsune hopped along behind him, her flame-feet an interesting sight. Her fire flashed with each step. Small flashes, but still.

"Hey, Knovak," Sorin said with a wave. "Did you manage to find the right notebook?"

"It was hidden under my bed," Knovak stated.

The man didn't know how to do anything halfway. He wore his robes, a silk white shirt, a pair of knee-high trousers, shiny boots, and a black hat. With the pride of three kings, he strode over to the third table and sat.

All alone.

Unlike Raaza, who had a whole table between him and the rest of the class, Knovak took a seat that was semi-close, but still notably away. I almost called him over to our table—since we had so much room—but I decided against it. Perhaps Knovak *wanted* to be alone.

A few minutes later, several eldrin entered through the treehouse entrance. Ecrib, Starling, Rex, and Tenoch entered in a line, as though on parade. Brak was the only mystical creature that took its time. It stomped in last, long after all the other creatures had gone to their arcanists.

Then the classroom door opened again.

Professor Helmith.

She walked in, smiling bright. Her robes were like ours, and I wondered if the color signified she was a professor for first-year students. That would make sense, but I had never asked to confirm.

"Good morning, students," Helmith said in a singsong tone.

Everyone quieted down. Nasbit sat forward, his pencil already poised above his notebook. He looked almost as excited as I was to see our professor.

When Helmith turned to face me, I grimaced. In my heart, I feared she would still be upset. Instead, she maintained her bright smile. Her eyes— lavender, with a mystical quality all their own—told me she was pleased to see me here.

I exhaled in relief.

"I hope everyone is prepared to learn everything they possibly can about mystical creatures."

She walked around her desk, and the clink and chime of her gold anklet faintly echoed in the room. Everyone was so silent.

"I believe you all learned about the four tiers of mystical creatures, correct?" Helmith took a piece of chalk and wrote numbers one through four on the board. "Where one is the weakest creature, and four is the strongest?"

Nasbit raised his hand.

Professor Helmith didn't even turn around. She kept writing as she said, "Yes?"

"Isn't there a fifth tier of creature? God-creatures?"

Helmith nodded once. "There is, but they have all, unfortunately, passed away." She turned to face the room, her long black hair flowing with her movement. "Did you have any other questions?"

"Yes. What about *elder-creatures?*"

The question caught me off guard. Those were the sinister beasts that supposedly lived in the fourth abyss. Nasbit had said they ate the souls of everyone who went there.

"Elder-creatures are said to range," Professor Helmith quickly answered. "Some are the lowest tier, while others are said to be more powerful than dragons."

"So you know about them?" Nasbit wrote some notes down.

"I've never seen one. I've just studied every scrap of material on mystical creatures that I've ever gotten my hands on."

"But dragons are usually tier four..." Nasbit glanced up from his notes. "If some of the elder-creatures are stronger, would they be on par with god-creatures?"

Professor Helmith shook her head. "I apologize. I don't actually know. Most information about them is written like a fairy tale. Some stories have them rending the sky open, and others are simply cautionary allegories about avoiding the abyssal hells altogether."

"Hm. I see..." Nasbit had no other comments. He focused on his notebook as he wrote even *more* notes.

What more was there to write? Why was he so obsessed?

Smiling, Helmith returned to the chalkboard. She wrote the words PROGENY and FABLE and then returned her attention to everyone.

"Today's lesson is about how new mystical creatures come into the world."

"Gross," Exie muttered under her breath.

Professor Helmith held up two fingers. "There are two ways new creatures come into existence. The first is the *progeny* method. As the word suggests, this is when a female creature and a male creature come together to have babies. Either with eggs, or live birth... All mystical creatures that have families—and nesting grounds—are classified as *progeny creatures*."

Everyone in the room glanced around.

I turned to Twain.

My little mimic twitched his ears.

Helmith pointed to Starling. The unicorn perked up and swished his tail. "Unicorns are progeny creatures." Then she gestured to Ecrib. "So are typhoon dragons." Then she pointed to Tenoch. "And coatls."

For a long moment, there was silence.

Professor Helmith nervously chuckled. "Oh. Well. This is interesting. Most classes I teach, the majority of creatures in attendance are progeny creatures. It's rare to see so few. Progeny creatures are the most common."

"What's the other kind?" Exie asked. She pulled her erlking fairy close and practically hugged him.

Her erlking tilted his head and glanced up at her in confusion. "You've never asked me about erlking reproduction."

"Ew," Exie said. "Don't call it *reproduction*. I just want to know if there will be more erlkings, and how."

Professor Helmith held up her hand to interrupt their conversation. "I'm so glad you're curious, Exie. The other classification for mystical creatures is *fable*. That's when a mystical creature comes into existence after a certain set of criteria is met." She gestured to Sorin. "You have a knightmare, yes?"

Sorin stood from his chair. "Oh, I know this." He faced the rest of the class. "A knightmare comes into existence whenever a king or queen—or sole ruler—is killed via assassination or betrayal."

I had heard this before, but I hadn't thought much of it.

Nini raised her hand. Helmith pointed to her.

"Reapers... They come into existence when the blood of a thousand people has been spilled across an acre of land." Nini straightened her glasses. "Which means they're basically born on battlefields. Or at the base of gallows. Or jails."

Professor Helmith clapped her hands together once. "That is

absolutely correct. Both of you. Reapers and knightmares are classic examples of *fable creatures*. They don't breed or produce babies, but the good news is that no matter what happens, they—theoretically—will never go extinct."

Phila raised her hand. When the professor pointed at her, she furrowed her brow. "Are all fable creatures born from... killing? It seems a bloody affair."

"That is a good question. The answer is *no*." Professor Helmith's expression lit up as she asked, "Has anyone here seen a *relickeeper* before?"

Nasbit's hand shot into the air, his fingers spread. Helmith chuckled as she pointed to him. Nasbit slowly lowered his hand and cleared his throat.

"Relickeepers are pseudo-dragons. Their body is made up of broken materials. Wrought-iron, bricks, stone, glass—but shaped as a massive dragon. They are held together by nothing but threads of magic."

Professor Helmith laced her fingers together. "That's correct! Thank you so much, Nasbit. Do you know how one comes into existence?"

"Of course I do," Nasbit said, chortling. He glanced around as though we would all join him, but the rest of the room was dead silent. Nasbit then coughed and said, "Relickeepers are born from hoards. Specifically, a hoard of wealth or valuable martial objects that has been sequestered from the world for exactly one hundred years." Nasbit sighed. "It's actually rather rare, but sometimes pirate treasure turns into a relickeeper. By accident, mind you."

"Yes. Right again, Nasbit. You're quite well-versed in this subject. I can't wait to see your test scores."

"Well, what about erlkings?" Exie interjected. "I wanted to know about my creature first."

Her anger came quick, it seemed.

I glanced over my shoulder and spotted Nasbit scooting closer to her. He whispered something—probably trying to tell her the answer—but she leaned away from him and frowned.

"Erlkings are disturbing creatures, actually," Professor Helmith said, her voice devoid of emotion. In the same monotone, she continued, "They're fable creatures, yes... They're born after a queen fairy consumes the corpse of her former arcanist."

160

# CHAPTER 20

## RUMORS OF A COTILLION

alf the class either sneered or made a gagging noise.

I had to admit, I hadn't expecting that. The reaper fable birth was already a little grim, but the erlking was surrealist nightmare fuel.

Exie slowly unwrapped her arms from Rex. Her eldrin fluttered his wings. "Hey!" he barked. "*I* didn't eat anyone!"

"The queen fairy eats the corpse of her arcanist and then vomits it," Professor Helmith added, like she wanted to really drive this home. Or perhaps disturb Exie, I wasn't certain. "The vomit is what forms into an erlking." Then Helmith's good mood and pleasant tone returned as she said, "Erlkings are considered the strongest of the fairies. They're a tier *three* creature, while all other fairies are tier one or two."

Nasbit made more notes, half-smiling to himself while he worked. If anyone was having a good time, it was him. I sometimes wondered why he was so passionate about schoolwork, but I never remembered to ask him when we were alone.

"Okay, so now that you're all aware of progeny and fable mystical creature births, I want you all to start reading your textbook from page fifty to one hundred." Professor Helmith wrote the information on the board. "Those pages cover the most common mystical creatures. I want you to learn their tiers of power, as well as their reproduction methods. You'll have a test on it next week."

"A test?" Raaza lifted his head a bit. "Already? We just got back from camping."

"There isn't too much information to learn." Helmith turned around and smiled. "And the test will be multiple choice, so even easier. I just want to make sure you're all absorbing some of this information."

No one complained after that. Instead, the room filled with the sound of pages turning. I pulled my book close and casually glanced over the pages. Our bestiary was rather comprehensive, and only two creatures fit on each page. That meant our test would potentially cover a hundred mystical creatures... That didn't seem as easy as Helmith was making it out to be.

But no use complaining.

I didn't want to disappoint her again. If I just buckled down, mastered the test, and showed her I was learning, I was positive Professor Helmith would forget all about my stunt at the waterfalls.

Well, I hoped, at least.

Over an hour of reading, and my eyes hurt.

"Oh," Professor Helmith said, startling half the class. She stood from her desk. "I have a minor announcement. Next week, we'll have a guest speaker. You all know him as the *Warlord of Magic*, but I like to call him *Dad*." She giggled at her own joke.

Nasbit gasped so hard, I thought he might choke on the air.

"By the abyssal hells, it's not *that* exciting," Raaza grumbled, his chin in one hand, his posture slouched.

"He's coming to teach a lesson on *true forms*." Then the professor motioned to the door. "All right. Class dismissed. Remember to continue your reading, and to prepare for a lecture about how all your mystical creatures might one day ascend to their true and rightful form."

She said everything with such joy. I couldn't wait to meet her father. With a title like *Warlord of Magic*, he was probably an imposing man. I could already picture it. Tall. Muscles galore. A beard so thick, it acted as a second shield...

Was I jealous? No. I cursed under my breath. Obviously, I wasn't.

Everyone stood from their seats, leaving their notebooks at their tables, and headed for the door. I followed Sorin to the door, and then he stopped to wait for Nini. She packed up her things, but before she could join us, Raaza walked over to the table.

"Hey, Nini," he said. "Do you have a moment?"

She fidgeted with her notebook, gave Sorin an apologetic glance, and then said, "Yes. What is it?"

"I just wanted to talk to you about your reaper magic."

When the other arcanists in our class went to leave, Sorin and I had to exit into the hall to allow them through. My brother half-shrugged and then pointed down the hall to the bathrooms. I nodded, and together, we headed off.

Twain kept pace, walking directly next to my feet. My brother rotated his arms as we walked together. "Did you know mystical creatures could transform?" he asked.

"I mean, *vaguely.*"

"It sounds amazing."

I nodded once.

"Hey, Gray? Do you mind if I ask for your opinion?" Sorin glanced over at me and lifted an eyebrow. "About personal things."

"What personal things?"

"Well, on a scale of *one* to *obsessed*, how much do you think Nini likes Raaza? I mean, because they normally don't talk, and I was just wondering if maybe there's something to that."

I ran a hand down my face. "Not you, too," I muttered.

"Hm?"

"Never mind." I shook my head. "You said *one to obsessed*? Can I pick negative numbers? Because Nini doesn't care about Raaza. At all. You two need to stop dancing around each other. Just tell her she's not cursed, you want to be sweethearts, and stop asking me silly questions."

"Do you really think that would work?" Sorin asked, hopeful.

"Yes."

Twain nodded along with my reply. "Tell her a cursed woman is your ideal woman."

"No," I muttered. "Don't even imply she's cursed. I can see her thinking it's a confirmation."

Sorin rubbed his chin, clearly pondering the situation. We reached the bathroom without him uttering another word, which was rare. After we had both finished our business, we headed back for our classroom. Sorin remained as silent as the dead.

Astra Academy had a fairly simple schedule. Each day, we studied a single subject, broken into two-hour classes. After the first class session, we had a thirty-minute break, followed by another two hours. Then we had lunch.

After lunch, we repeated the process. Two-hour class. Thirty-minute break. One final two-hour class, and then dinner. The class we had shifted each day. If *Mystical Creatures* was our class today, then we would have *History and Imbuing* tomorrow, the next day we would have *Combat Arts*, all the way through our first year, a general education, curriculum.

Apparently, the classes shifted because some students learned better in the mornings as compared to the evenings, and to make sure everyone had an equal opportunity to absorb the material, the headmaster had the full-day classes rotate.

We studied six days a week, with a single day left over for relaxation or additional studies and clubs. That was fine. I didn't want much time for other things. I had to stay in the Academy, away from the gate fragments, until the headmaster or Professor Helmith could concoct a way to find them.

Second day back, and I had already fallen back into the standard routine.

Today we had Piper for *History and Imbuing*. She was always easy. Mostly because she was tired—or hungover—most classes. Tomorrow we would have *Combat Arts.* I wasn't looking forward to that, even if I liked Captain Leon. And the day after that, we would have *Magical Fundamentals.*

I lifted my head, my brow furrowed.

Professor Zahn had taught *Magical Fundamentals.* But since he betrayed Astra Academy and tried to bring a Death Lord into the realm of the living, obviously he wasn't going to teach anything else. Who would teach that class now that he was gone?

We entered the classroom to find Nini and Raaza chatting together. Since when did Nini get here early to speak with him? I tried not to look worried, so that Sorin wouldn't panic. Everything was fine.

Exie squealed in delight, drawing me out of my thoughts.

Sorin and I glanced over. Exie, Ashlyn, Phila, and Nasbit were all gathered close to one another, everyone standing, except for Exie. She sat on the table, her erlking in her lap.

Exie patted his little head. "That's right. I had a letter waiting for me. I was invited to the *Kross Cotillion!*"

Ashlyn sighed, but said nothing.

"I wonder if *I'll* get an invite," Phila muttered. "I don't see why not. But I suppose my family has little to do with the Kross family..."

"Oh, you'll get an invite." Ashlyn sighed harder than before. "My father did this exact thing when my brother attended Astra Academy."

"If we get an invitation, are we required to attend?" Nasbit laced his fingers together and frowned. "I mean, I don't want to insult your family, or your father, but I hate those kinds of social gatherings."

"You don't have to go if you don't want to, Naz." Ashlyn placed a hand on her hip. "I can always tell my father you were busy studying. He would understand."

Nasbit rubbed his forehead with the back of his arm. "Perfect. Cotillions are the worst."

"What is a *cotillion?*" I asked as I approached their little clique.

Exie threw back some of her beautiful brown hair. "A cotillion is a party to celebrate debutants. Basically, it's for people who have just come of age, and want to mingle with powerful arcanists and make social connections and network." She giggled before adding, "And it's where all the young and single arcanists go to flirt."

Ashlyn exhaled. "Exie…"

"Cotillions are the worst," Nasbit said, glancing in my direction. "Don't worry. You won't be missing anything."

"I want to go," I said. "Where do I go to find my invitation?"

The silence after my question could've suffocated a small child. Phila and Nasbit glanced to Ashlyn. She avoided looking me in the eye. Exie snickered, breaking the quiet that had settled between us.

"Oh, I'm so sorry, Gray." Exie dismissively waved her hand. "The Kross Cotillion is for established families. You know how it is. Nobility. Royalty. Government officials. There simply isn't enough room, amazing food, and beautiful music to invite *just anyone*."

"*Exie*," Ashlyn hissed under her breath.

The two girls stared at each other for a long while, obviously having some sort of silent conversation between them. Once their deadlock was over, Exie slowly returned her attention to me.

"Archduke Kross—Ashlyn's father—is rather picky about who he invites. That's the truth. I figured you should hear it now, rather than get your hopes up." Exie patted her eldrin's head again.

The little fairy stared forward with eyes narrowed in irritation. He folded his little arms, obviously displeased with being treated as a cat. Rex didn't say anything, though. He remained in Exie's lap, even when she messed up his hair with her gentle strokes.

Knovak and his unicorn entered the classroom right before Piper and her rizzel. Now that everyone was here, I figured class would begin soon.

I glanced over at Ashlyn. "Well, I'm sure the daughter of an archduke could invite anyone she wants to her daddy's little get-together. But, hey, what do I know? I'm just the son of a tallow chandler."

I didn't really see her reaction to my statement. I turned on my heel after the last word and took a seat at my table. Raaza returned to his place at the back of the room. Nini and Sorin sat around me, but I didn't really bother giving them much of my attention.

A deep-seated irritation burned in my chest. I knew it was petty. What did it matter if I wasn't invited? It wasn't my stupid party. But still. The thought that I wasn't invited because I wasn't important enough sat awkwardly in my thoughts.

What was I supposed to do about it, though? If Archduke Kross didn't want me there, there was no way around that.

Piper took a seat at the professor's desk. Her long black hair shimmered like oil as she combed her fingers through it. Then her hand got caught on a tangle, and she struggled to free herself from her own locks.

Her rizzel, Reevy, watched the whole thing with a neutral expression, like he both couldn't believe, and utterly believed, this was happening.

"Good morning, class," Piper said as she jerked her hand free of her hair. She rubbed her face and leaned heavily onto her desk. She had bags under her eyes again. "So, I want you all to open your textbooks to page three sixty-four."

Everyone did so, though at varying speeds. Nasbit was the first to get to the location. He glanced at the page and smiled. Then he raised his hand.

Piper halfheartedly motioned in his direction.

"Are we going to learn about the God-Arcanists War now?" he asked.

"Nasbit Dodger... I have a rule in my class. If you ask the question more than three times, you get a demerit. And since this is the *tenth* time you've asked that, I think it's time you received one."

"W-What?" All the color drained from Nasbit's face. He stared at her in such shock, it was like he had just learned she had betrayed him to the enemy. His stone golem stood a little straighter, clearly agitated by its arcanist's distress.

Reevy chuckled. The little rizzel clapped his forepaws together. "That one never fails to amuse me."

Piper also laughed. Then she sighed and leaned back in her seat. "Calm down. You're not getting a demerit."

While some of the others in the class giggled at that reveal, Nasbit just frowned. The stone golem turned to face the others, and everyone quieted themselves.

"You aren't excited to teach that subject?" Nasbit asked.

"I'm excited," Piper muttered. "But history is typically taught in order for a reason. It's logical. It flows. And sometimes the actions that nations —or long-lived arcanists—take is entirely dependent on the era they lived through previously."

While Nasbit had been grumpy before, halfway through Piper's speech, he started taking notes. When she finished, he smiled and nodded. "Oh, I agree. I just really want to learn about all the god-arcanists and what happened to the remains of the apoch dragon. My uncles have been trying to get their hands on some of the remains so they can make powerful magical items."

Piper groaned. She rubbed her temple and just shook her head. "Look. We're not going to get there today. Just... read quietly. After that... I'll talk to you all about making magical items."

No one argued.

Piper's rizzel curled himself up into a tight circle and closed his eyes. His white and silvery fur sparkled as the sunlight trickled into the room from the back window. He seemed comfy.

I glanced down at my book and allowed my own eyes to flutter into the half-lidded position.

History wasn't my favorite subject...

I closed my eyes.

A second later, it felt as though gravity had increased on my head. I jerked awake, having almost collapsed forward onto the desk with fatigue. Twain stared at me with his two-toned eyes, his whiskers twitching.

"You need to wake up," he whispered.

"Huh?"

The people in the class were talking. Had I really been sleeping?

"That's right," Piper said. "We're going to have a quiz. Everyone grab a pen and shut your notebooks."

# Chapter 21

## Running

Piper passed out small pieces of parchment to each student. Sorin and Nini took theirs with some hesitation. I smiled as Piper handed me one. While I probably didn't know the subject matter necessary for this, I could fake my way through a lot of things. It probably wasn't a talent I should be proud of, but in moments like this, it came in handy.

"Were you sleeping through the whole class?" Twain hissed under his breath.

I shrugged. "It'll be fine."

"Hm! Or maybe you'll fail." Twain stepped close and narrowed his kitten eyes. "How about I walk around the class, glance at people's answers, and then report back to you?"

"Wow," I sarcastically muttered. "The way you pitched that idea... It almost *didn't* sound like cheating. Way to go."

Twain huffed and stepped away from me. Before I could give him an honest answer, he leapt off the table and hurried under my bench. If I yelled at him now, I'd draw attention to his sneaky ways, and I didn't want that.

Instead, I focused on trying to wake myself. I rubbed my eyes, slapped my own cheeks, and then sat a little straighter.

"You can turn over your quizzes and begin," Piper said as she returned to the desk at the front of the room.

The soft sounds of paper rustling filled the room. I turned over my quiz and read the first question. It was:

*On which coast is the city, New Fortuna, located?*

1. *The Pineapple Coast*
2. *The Veridian Coast*
3. *The Crimson Coast*
4. *The Maple Coast*

This seemed like an odd question for Piper to ask. Fortunately, I knew the location of New Fortuna. Everyone who lived on any of the isles knew about the grand city created by the world serpent arcanist. New Fortuna was just a few miles west of Old Fortuna, and stretched a good distance down the Veridian Coast.

I circled *B* and confidently went to the next question. I would effortlessly pass this quiz, it seemed. The next one read:

*Which was the second mystical creature the famous guildmaster arcanist, Deen Strenos, bonded with?*

1. *Atlas Turtle*
2. *Phoenix*
3. *King Basilisk*
4. *Bunyip*

Whelp.

That was a short-lived burst of confidence. It seemed my knowledge streak was over.

I had absolutely no idea who *Deen Strenos* was, but he sounded important. Out of all the options, I supposed *atlas turtle* was a good choice. They were giant turtles that swam through the ocean. Their shells were covered in dirt that allowed vegetation to grow. Some atlas turtles were so large, buildings could be constructed on them.

They were little living islands.

Phoenixes were nice, but rare.

King basilisks... They were killing machines. Why would a guildmaster bond with *that*?

And bunyips were swamp creatures.

I was semi-confident with A. It seemed logical.

Twain leapt back onto the table. He trotted over to me and curled up next to my quiz parchment. In a quiet voice, barely a whisper, he asked, "Which question are you on?"

"Get out of here," I replied in an equally hushed tone. If Professor Helmith heard I cheated on a quiz... I refused to even imagine it.

Twain glanced at my quiz. "Question two? Okay. Three people picked *A*. Two people picked *B*. Two others picked *C*. And Nasbit wrote an essay off in the margin."

I almost laughed aloud. I hoped Nasbit never changed. But with a huffed chuckle, I said, "I don't want to hear it."

"Nasbit wrote about how Deen Strenos first bonded with a white will-o-wisp, and how he served in the Lamplighters Guild for several years before assuming the position of guildmaster."

"*What's wrong with you?*"

I gripped my pencil tight. Even if I wanted to cheat, this was all useless information. But I didn't. This wasn't worth it. And I seriously didn't want any more demerits. At three, I would be sent to the Academy's counselor.

"Hey," Twain said in a harsh whisper. "You should be grateful. I was trying to be helpful."

Reevy thumped his little ferret foot on the front desk. When I glanced up, I realized Reevy was glaring at me. His dark eyes were hard and discerning, as if he already knew what Twain and I were doing.

"I would be absolutely delighted if I managed to catch a *cheater*," Reevy growled.

That last word drew Piper's attention. She glanced in my direction and frowned. "I hate cheaters."

Both of them had a harshly serious demeanor. That was... completely unlike them.

"No cheaters here," I said with a chuckle.

At least, I was *trying* not to be a cheater. I shot Twain a glare, and my eldrin drooped his head. With his ears low, he just collapsed onto the table, his eyes downcast. While I felt for him, I just rolled my eyes and continued.

Third day back at Astra Academy, and it was *Combat Arts*. In the morning, we had actually studied different forms of fighting arts, from fists to pistols. For the afternoon session of our class, we were supposed to meet out in the training field. But first, we needed lunch.

The dining hall buzzed with excitement as I entered.

Sorin and Nini had left the classroom long before me. Fortunately, I spotted their table at the other end of the room.

Twain was still upset with me, however. I held him in my arms, but his body just dangled like a rag doll. When other students walked by, they gave me odd glances. He had been acting this way ever since the quiz.

It had gone well. I suspected I had answered the majority of the questions correctly. And I was never accused of cheating, which was great. But Twain's grumpiness brought down my enjoyment.

Astra Academy's dining hall was large enough to fit a small village within. Despite that, the volume increased with each laugh, shout, and exclamation. The whole room was oval shaped, and I kept to the outsides to avoid most of the other students and their eldrin.

Large pegasi and sea serpents were crowded around a single table. Due to their size, I suspected the mystical creatures all had higher-year arcanists. Eldrin grew in size and magical power the longer they were bonded. If they weren't bonded, they didn't grow, so any adult-looking creature had to have been bonded for a while. Simple logic.

The dining hall had a central table with all the food. Today, for some reason, the selection for lunch was made up of pastas and soups. The fragrant broth filled my nostrils and ignited my hunger.

I walked away from the wall, navigated my way to the serving table, and spotted something of interest.

"Twain," I playfully said. "I see some fish soup."

"Hm," he muttered.

I held him higher on my chest. His small kitten body was easy to manhandle. I wiggled his forearms up and down, as though playing an invisible drum.

"C'mon, Twain. You love fish soup. Let's get some and enjoy it."

Twain's ears lay back flat on his head. He said nothing.

I was about to try something else, but that was when a shadow fell upon me. I glanced over, and then up. At Knovak's pointed red hat. The velvet material and intricate stitching—which included the Academy's symbol—was no doubt expensive. The tip was crooked to the side, and I hated it. A few people pointed in our direction, and for once, they weren't talking about me.

I supposed I was thankful for Knovak in that moment.

His unicorn, Starling, stood at his side at all times. He was one of the most faithful eldrin at the whole Academy.

"Did you hear?" Knovak asked.

Twain perked his ears. "Hear what?"

"About the cotillion."

I nodded once. "Yeah. It's some shindig put on by Archduke Kross, apparently."

"Some *shindig*?" Knovak repeated in contempt. "Do you hear yourself? It's a grand party! All the most important arcanists from the local region will be there." He grabbed my arm and pulled me close. "Everyone in our class is going. Except for us."

"Why are you accosting me?" I sarcastically asked. I pulled my arm from his grasp. "And I'm pretty sure Sorin isn't going. And neither is Nini. Or Raaza."

"That's who I meant when I said *us*," Knovak growled. "That's us! None of the lowborn arcanists in our class were invited. Doesn't that upset you?"

"A little."

Twain snorted. "And by that, he means *a lot*."

I glared down at him. He matched my gaze. Then I smiled. "Fine. It bothers me. But I have enough etiquette not to run around the dining hall with a chimney for a hat, shouting about my irritations."

Knovak opened his mouth like he wanted to yell some more, but my words obviously sank in afterward. He swallowed his tirade, and this his shoulders fell. After a moment, he glanced at the serving table and grabbed a bowl.

"Yeah, you're probably right," he said.

I lifted an eyebrow. "Oh, yeah?" Then I set Twain down and grabbed two bowls. We needed all the fish soup we could carry.

"I just thought *I* would've gotten an invitation." His anger was returning as he glanced over. "I mean, I helped Ashlyn, and I did what you said—I tried being noble. And I come from a wealthy family, and I'm an arcanist, and despite your bluster about how I have no etiquette, I actually took two years' worth of manners classes!"

"Use your indoor voice," I quipped.

Knovak huffed as he scooped himself some pasta with white cheesy sauce. Then he scooped up some meatballs and threw them on top. "Gray, I want to go to that cotillion."

"Okay," I muttered. "And?"

He lowered his voice as he said, "Help me find a way to do it."

I took my fish soup bowls and turned away from him. "I'll give the matter some thought, all right? Just... keep your cool. I have enough problems in my life. I don't also want to be your handler."

Knovak didn't reply to that. Starling clopped his hooves, but Knovak held up a hand, silencing his unicorn before he made any snide remarks.

As Twain and I traveled away from the serving table, my eldrin sniffed the air. "Oh my. Is that salmon?"

"I scooped you so many pieces," I said. "And you can have both bowls. But only on one condition."

"What's that?"

"You have to stop being mad at me."

Twain snickered and smiled. "Ha! Deal. All the soup for me."

Sticks and Captain Leon were out in the training field long before our class. Clouds wafted overhead, creating pools of darkness that sailed over the ground. The sunlight tried its hardest to pierce through, cascading between the clouds as shining pillars.

For our afternoon training, we were out by the track. It was a giant oval road of dirt around a lush field of grass. Large objects were scattered throughout the field, including several brick walls and balls of iron that resembled cannonballs.

As our class stepped onto the field, Captain Leon motioned to everything around us. "So, I didn't want to have to train you all in weapons, as that's Professor Jijo's specialty, but since he still isn't here, I guess we're going to make do." He forced a cough and glanced over at everyone. "So, I'll be helping all of you build muscle. And endurance."

His cerberus bounded around us. The three dog heads sniffed everyone's hair and even some of our eldrin. Exie held her hands over her head, and Raaza's kitsune attempted to hide between his legs.

"Does your eldrin *always* have to crowd us like this?" Raaza growled.

Sticks wagged his tail. "I'm making sure none of you are sick before our training begins. His second head added, "As a cerberus, I can tell if you're in good physical condition."

"I see..."

Captain Leon ran a hand through his white hair. With a sigh, he pointed to the track. "Listen, I know Jijo has a whole lesson based around physical training. I heard a couple times. Years ago. It went like..."

He thought for a long moment. When he returned his attention to us, his eyes were narrowed.

"Training starts at your core." He slammed his fist onto his chest. "Even if you know how to wield a sword, or aim a pistol, or skewer with a lance, it means nothing if your body is too frail to wield them."

Raaza's whole demeanor changed. "Professor Jijo said that?"

"That's right. Jijo is from a region near the Sunset Desert, where they take combat quite seriously. He has trained all his life to perfect his form with many weapons."

"I can't wait to meet him." Raaza picked up his kitsune, still smiling.

"I want you all to run this track ten times," Leon stated. He gestured to the entire track. "It's important to build stamina."

Nasbit raised his hand.

Captain Leon didn't even call on him. Instead, as a pleasant afternoon breeze whistled by, Leon shook his head. "You can go at your own pace. This is more about having the willpower to see it through. We'll do this three times a week, mixed in with some lifting, and some general stretches to keep y'all limber."

The news obviously didn't sit well with Nasbit. He rubbed at his gut. Nasbit was the chubbiest one in the class, and I felt for him. He clearly didn't want to learn the art of combat, even if Raaza was excited enough for the whole class.

But I figured this was the price we all had to pay for general education. Once we became second-year students, we could pick our specialization. Nasbit would likely pick cultivation, or becoming a vizier. I suspected neither of those involved a lot of physical experience.

Exie raised her hand.

"Yes, you, too," Leon said with a groan.

Exie frowned, her face reddening. "*No*. That's not what I was going to ask. I wanted to know about our eldrin. Do *they* need to run around the track?"

"Oh. Sorry about that. I just... Well, never mind." Leon shook his head. "Mystical creatures don't actually benefit much from physical training like this. Actually, if Jijo is to be believed, the more at peace you are, and focused on your growth as a person—your soul and all that—the stronger and healthier your eldrin will be."

"Really?" Nasbit asked, his eyebrows knitted.

"So he says." Leon ended the statement with a weak shrug.

Exie crossed her arms. "So, they don't have to run? Right?"

"They don't." Leon pointed to the middle of the field. "I'll help them practice their own magics there while the rest of you get to running, all right?"

Twain laughed as he leapt from my arms. "Ha! See you later when you're all sweaty and out of breath!" He chortled the whole way across the grass, his orange fur quite distinct in the middle of all that green.

While I wanted to make a sarcastic comment, I knew I'd feel the same way in his position.

The shadow around Sorin's feet shifted and then slid across the ground. It zipped across the grass and chased after Twain. Thurin was such an odd eldrin. Were all knightmares that silent and mysterious?

Nini's reaper floated off, twirling his scythe the whole time. Rex chased the reaper through the air, his fairy wings leaving an illusionary afterimage of his form as he went. He was beautiful, but I could tell he had a haughty demeanor even from all the way on the other side of the track.

Everyone else's eldrin were noisier. Or bigger. Brak and Ecrib stomped the ground so hard they killed the grass with each step. Tenoch slithered behind them, his parrot-colored wings fluttering. Starling galloped after them.

Miko wasn't so bad. She seemed to delight in jumping in the footprints left behind by the stone golem. With fox-like energy, she leapt from one divot to the next, giggling the whole way.

"I shall leave no tracks," she muttered as she went. "No one will ever know I was here."

Leon clapped his hands together and then fiercely rubbed his palms. "All right. Hang your robes over here on this little brick wall, and then off you go. Come on, come on. We don't have all day." He turned and spotted everyone's eldrin.

The many creatures frolicked across the grass as though they had been let loose to play. Even Sticks got in on the action. The cerberus chased Twain, who hid under the stone golem. Tenoch took to the sky and then landed on the golem's head. He coiled himself until he looked like a hat.

Starling ran circles around Ashlyn's typhoon dragon, When the beast swiped with claws, the unicorn laughed and leapt out of the way. Miko got in on the game and flashed fake fire around, obviously irritating Ecrib. Lightning crackled around Ecrib's fangs as he growled.

"Whoa, there!" Leon jogged toward them. "None of that! We need to be organized."

Ashlyn tossed off her robes and stepped onto the dirt track. Because Combat Arts often involved a lot of physical activities, everyone changed their clothing under their robes before attending class. Trousers. Loose tunics. And after this, everyone would head to the showers.

And while Ashlyn looked good in nearly everything she wore, I did think she was at her peak when clothed in lighter, but practical, outfits. Her lean, athletic build was more apparent then.

Ashlyn shot me a glance over her shoulder. "Think you're suited for this, Gray?"

"Running? Pfft. I'll be fine."

"Then how about we make this interesting?"

I tossed my robes on the waist-high brick wall as well. "How so?"

"I say we have a race." She flashed me a smirk. "How about it? Or are you afraid you'll lose?"

# CHAPTER 22

## TEN LAPS

T chuckled at her challenge.

Then it struck me. I had been having a great day so far, even if I had fallen asleep in class for a short period of time. There had been no dread. No worries about the gate fragments. And even now, as we were about to start a race—just for the fun of it—I felt a sense of excitement and contentment.

Perhaps all the *abyssal hells* nonsense could be put behind me.

"What's with that lopsided grin?" Exie asked as she crossed her arms.

"Oh, nothing." I waved away the comment. "And this race... It doesn't seem fair."

Ashlyn lifted a perfect eyebrow. "Not fair? Heh. I can't wait to hear this explanation."

"Neither can I," Sorin said.

He walked with me across the dirt track. I stopped at the metal pole markers that jutted out of the ground on either side of the track—clearly the starting point. Ashlyn stood near the opposite pole, eyeing me and my brother.

Sorin's tunic barely fit him, and I wondered if the stitchwork would hold out through ten loops around this track. What was he eating? Had he gotten larger somehow? And why did he have to stand next to me? His height and bulk were more noticeable when he stood directly at my side.

But I didn't mention it. I glanced back over at Ashlyn. "Didn't you grow up in a palatial home? I bet it had its own track, and you had a score of trainers who helped prepare you for moments like this."

My simple question and statement clearly struck a nerve. Ashlyn tensed; her playfulness replaced with a neutral expression that betrayed the truth of my words.

Exie stepped forward, one finger up. She didn't wear trousers often, but it didn't matter. She could've been clothed in the guts of a dead octopus and she still would've looked great. The belt around Exie's waist was cinched tight, making the bottom half of her tunic flare a bit, like a little skirt. She wasn't athletic, that much was obvious. If this were a race with *all* of us, I imagined she would be among the last of the class to finish.

"Uh, you don't know what you're talking about," Exie said matter-of-factly. "The Kross Compound doesn't have *a track*." Exie lowered her finger and crossed her arms over her chest. "They have a beautiful garden with a winding trail, but it's not really for running. It only goes a mile and a half."

Ashlyn's expression hardened into ice. She glared at Exie, who obviously didn't understand. Exie huffed and shrugged her shoulders.

I scoffed. "Well, poor lil ol' me grew up in a shack filled with candle wax, remember? I didn't have anywhere to run." I added a sarcastic sigh at the end of my comment, but this only seemed to anger Exie.

Phila, somehow oblivious to my sardonic tone, touched a hand to her cheek and whispered, "Oh, those poor islanders..."

Ignoring her, I said in a serious voice, "Look, running isn't my forte. Just ask the unicorn. And I don't make a habit of jumping into competitions when I know my competitors have leagues of advantages and training."

Ashlyn threw back some of her golden hair. "You know, you could've saved everyone's time and just said you're scared. You didn't have to dance around that with some fancy words and excuses."

That was far more aggressive than usual. Why? Did she need to prove she was faster than me for some reason?

We stared at each other for a split second, her eyebrows knitting as though she were sorry this situation even existed.

Nasbit stepped forward. Although he was a portly individual, his tunic wasn't straining to maintain its form, unlike Sorin's. Nasbit had a perfectly tailored tunic that fit his wider frame.

"Ashlyn," Nasbit muttered. "Please. We shouldn't have a race."

"Naz, this doesn't concern you."

"But it *does*." He rubbed his knuckles. "Don't you remember what happened at the Summer Palace? Your father made us all race and..."

But Nasbit didn't finish. He gazed at the dirt, his lips pursed.

Ashlyn shook her head. "Fine." She turned away from us all. "Let's just... do our running." She took off down the dirt track, not even bothering to speak to anyone else.

Exie followed after her, but while Ashlyn's pace was set to *run*, Exie merely jogged. Or maybe *fast walked* was the better description.

"Well, we don't have to make it an official race," Raaza stated as he dashed past me. "But we can still race." He took off toward Ashlyn, gaining on her.

Everyone else meandered onto the track. I stuck close to my brother, and Nini jogged on the other side of him. Our pace could only be described as *leisurely*. We stayed as a group for one full loop, but at that point, Nini started slowing down. While she had removed her Academy robes, she *hadn't* removed her coat, her undershirt, or any of the other layers I couldn't see.

It was clearly affecting her performance.

When she slowed, Sorin gave me a sideways glance. We were twins. I could tell when he was silently apologizing to me. I gave him a small nod, and he fell behind so he could stay close to Nini.

On the second loop, Ashlyn lapped me. She shot me a glare, but I just replied with a grin. This caused her to huff out a laugh. For a short while, she slowed her pace and stayed near me, but her breathing was heavy. It was difficult to speak.

When Raaza came up on her, she abandoned staying near me and instead sprinted ahead. Raaza shot by, and I gave him a sarcastic salute.

Halfway to the third loop, I came close to lapping Nasbit. The man only jogged occasionally, and instead opted to walk most of our assignment. As I neared him, Nasbit stepped to the side, like I would trample over him if he wasn't at least three feet away.

I slowed to a brisk walk. "Hey," I said between huffed breaths. "Are you okay?"

Nasbit exhaled and waved me away. "I'm fine."

"What happened at the Summer Palace?" I asked. I had been deeply curious about it ever since he mentioned the location.

Nasbit eyed me, and then motioned to everyone else on the track. "You're going to fall behind if you don't run ahead."

"I'm more curious about what happened than I am excited to finish this exercise."

After a short sigh, Nasbit lowered his voice and said, "Ashlyn's father had us all race. This was before Ashlyn and I were arcanists. He made us run some ridiculous loop around the palace's courtyard. Everyone else was so fast, they finished long before I reached the halfway point."

Nasbit slowed his walking. He tucked his hands into his trouser pockets, not even bothering to look like he was trying to complete this task with any sort of speed.

I jogged in place next to him. "Who won?"

"Ashlyn's brother, *of course*." Nasbit glowered at me. "But that's not the worst part. I didn't care who had won. I just wanted to stop. But Ashlyn's father made me run the rest of the way. Everyone else just stood around and watched as I struggled to complete the loop. It was so embarrassing." With another sigh, Nasbit stopped talking.

Now I understood why Nasbit would also be reluctant to go to a cotillion hosted by Ashlyn's father. His words had been so miserable-sounding that I wondered if something else had happened he was just too embarrassed to bring up with me.

But I wasn't sure how to fix his problem.

Instead, I patted him on the shoulder. "Hang in there."

Nasbit gave me a confused glance as I jogged ahead. Then I pushed myself faster, trying to prevent Ashlyn and Raaza from lapping me a second time. Fortunately, a group of clouds passed over the track, keeping me safe from the harsh rays of the sun. My insides still burned from the strain, though. The front of my legs, especially.

I thought I would have even more loops to just wander in my

thoughts and mull everything over, but someone came running up behind me.

"Gray!"

I glanced over my shoulder. Knovak hurried to my side and then slowed. Unlike everyone else—except Nasbit, who was walking—Knovak wasn't breathing hard at all.

Out of everyone here, he was the only student wearing a white silk tunic and crisp black pants. At least he wasn't wearing a ridiculous hat. Where did this man get his fashion sense from?

"There you are," Knovak said, his words clear even while moving at a fast clip. "Have you thought of some way we might get invited to the cotillion?"

I shook my head, my breathing harder than before, my underarms sweating enough to soak my tunic.

"I think I might've found a way."

"Okay," I said between deep breaths.

"You see, I found out that everyone's invitation allows them to bring a guest."

"Uh-huh," I huffed.

"The problem, of course, is that even if Ashlyn, Exie, Phila, and Nasbit all invited another person in our class, that would leave us with one extra person who was completely excluded from the event."

That was true. Our class had nine students, and only four of them had received invitations.

I glanced over at Knovak. He ran just fine, his face scrunched in deep contemplation. How had he uttered an entire paragraph's worth of information without gulping down air? No one could run and pontificate at the same time. Right?

"How are you—" I gulped down another breath, "—talking so well?"

"Ha!" Knovak smiled and laughed to himself. "Now is my moment to revel in my unicorn magic." He smirked as he jogged, his arms proudly swishing back in forth in time with his gait. "I finally have something to lord over everyone else. You see, unicorns have an innate ability to regain stamina nearly three times as fast as normal individuals. I barely feel this run. I could jog like this all day and hardly get winded."

Ah. I finally understood why unicorn arcanists made such great knights. With three times the stamina, it would be no trouble to charge into battle with heavy armor and weapons. Some historic battles had been lost because one army became fatigued, but that wouldn't happen if they had unicorns and their arcanists on their side.

Wait a minute.

I closed my eyes and felt for Starling's thread of magic. The moment I had it, I tugged. Unicorn magic flowed into me. My forehead burned as my arcanist mark shifted to allow for the unicorn image to be intertwined with my star.

Twain, who was in the arms of Brak, bubbled and shifted into a unicorn foal, nearly five times larger than he was before. The stone golem tilted its sandstone head in confusion.

With the power of the unicorn, I understood what Knovak meant. The burn in my muscles lessened, and my breathing eventually became shallower as I rounded the bend into the fifth loop. I wasn't tired at all.

"This is amazing," I said, no longer needing to huff and puff.

Knovak glared at my arcanist mark and deeply frowned. "You just couldn't let me have this, huh? This *one time* I have the upper hand, and you have to show me up."

"How am I showing you up? We're running at the same speed." I motioned to the track, then to us.

"I was enjoying having an advantage no one else had," Knovak muttered, his eyes narrowed. "Now I have to share it with *you*. The mimic arcanist. I can't just have one thing better than everyone else?"

"Heh. You're always going to have share your magic with me. Get used to it."

Knovak didn't answer. Still, I made another mental note to keep track of everyone's abilities. All of their skills were technically *my* skills as well, but they wouldn't do me any good if I forgot to use them.

For the rest of the laps, Knovak and I stayed at the same speed. He was grumpy the whole damn time, though. I really didn't understand the man. Why was he so upset? I pushed it from my mind.

I'd make it up to him by finding a way for us to attend the cotillion.

At least, I hoped.

# CHAPTER 23

## FATHER, ARCANIST, WARLORD

Once I finished the ten laps around the track, I walked onto the grass to find Twain.

Ashlyn had finished first, and Raaza second, but it had been close at the end. Knovak and I were three and four, and everyone else still had a lap or two to go.

Twain had maintained his unicorn shape for longer than ten minutes, which was amazing. I spotted him playing with Ecrib in the middle of the field, but right as I was about to congratulate him—this was the longest he had been transformed—he shimmered and shifted. His white unicorn coat puffed out into orange fur, and his body shrank down to a kitten.

Captain Leon motioned to the eldrin to get into a line. "Twain," he barked. "If you're not transformed, you can't practice your evocation."

"Uh, I need a little catnap first," he muttered.

"Well... All right. Join us once you're ready." Leon returned to his instruction of the mystical creatures while the rest of our class finished their run.

I rushed over and scooped Twain into my arms. "Twain, you're the best!"

He puffed out his little chest. "Yeah," he said. Then Twain glanced up at me. "For what, though?"

"You stayed transformed for so long."

"Oh, yeah. I did, didn't I?" Twain purred, his pupils dilating into huge circles. "I'm going to be an amazing mimic. The best ever."

With a chuckle, I patted his head. As I turned around, I almost slammed straight into Ashlyn. Where had she come from? Her blue eyes met mine, but she didn't say anything. When I went to step around her, she grabbed my shoulder.

"You were supposed to race me," she said in a harsh whisper.

"Yeah, I got the impression you were trying to force the issue." I held Twain against my chest. "But why?"

"Heh, now that I can be a unicorn for several minutes, you have no chance of winning," Twain chimed in. "My arcanist will run circles around you. For about ten minutes. Give or take."

Ashlyn stepped closer. "We were supposed to race, and I was counting on you saying something along the lines of *What's the prize?* That way, I could say the prize is an invite to the cotillion, and then I would intentionally lose." She narrowed her eyes. "But since you messed that up by getting defensive about being a candlemaker's son, it looks like I *can't* get you an invite."

Oh.

I hadn't realized she was trying to help me.

"Wait," I whispered. "Knovak told me you could invite someone to the cotillion as your guest. Why not just invite me normally? We don't need a fake race as a preamble."

Ashlyn's face brightened to a shade of pink. She released my shoulder and stepped away from me in one quick motion.

"I can't just invite you as my guest. That wouldn't be..." She turned away from me, her shoulders tense. "You don't know anything about noble families, do you? Look—forget I even said anything. This is ridiculous." She stormed off the field.

Ecrib growled and then leapt after her, his dragon tail swishing behind him as he walked. The beast glanced back at me and narrowed his eyes before snorting a small crackle of lightning and then looking away.

"I would say that interaction went... poorly," Twain muttered.

"I just don't get her." I patted Twain's head. "Would the noble families ridicule her if she invited me or something? But if that is the case, why would inviting me because of a lost bet be any better?"

"Women—they're a mystery."

Speaking of mysteries.

Professor Helmith emerged from Astra Academy and walked down the stone steps to the training field. The afternoon winds toyed with her long hair, swirling it together as she made her way in our direction.

I hadn't been paying attention to anything but her, so when Sorin jabbed me with his elbow, it elicited a shocked grunt.

"Huh?" I asked.

Sorin's tunic—still holding together, even if strained across his shoulders—was soaked with his sweat. He tugged at the damp fabric as he asked, "Do you know what Professor Helmith is doing here?" He grinned. "I bet she's coming to check up on you."

"Stop," I growled under my breath. "I'm sure she's here to speak to Leon."

"I don't know. She does favor you a little."

"She helped me a lot. We have a special connection."

Sorin just stared at me with his dopey grin. I rubbed my eyes, trying not to exhale in irritation. Why did he have to keep poking me like this?

Professor Helmith reached the edge of the field and stopped. She was barefoot, and her toes curled and uncurled. Helmith refused to step on the grass.

"Gray?" she called out, her attention locked on me. "Can you come here?"

"Told you," Sorin whispered.

"Quiet, *you*." I walked away from my brother, frowning.

But...

I was elated Helmith wanted to speak to me. I did enjoy her company, and any excuse to take a break from class was welcome. As I neared her, she smiled, and it was enough to remove all my anxiety and irritation.

The clouds drifted overhead, bathing us in a beam of fresh sunlight.

I took a deep breath as I came to a stop in front of her. "You wanted to see me?"

"My dad has arrived at the Academy earlier than expected." Helmith placed a hand on my shoulder and motioned to the steps. "I was hoping you could come with me to see him. We need to test something regarding the gate fragments."

Test something?

Dread returned to my thoughts. I really didn't want to deal with corpses and Death Lords. But here we were. Could I get out of this? Probably not.

"Rylee?" Captain Leon shouted. He jogged across the field, his white hair sparkling in the dappled light. "What's going on?"

"I need Gray for a moment." She smiled. "You don't have to be worried about me or the students all the time, Leon."

He slowed his pace and stopped in front of us. Then he folded his arms. "Yeah, well, I don't want a repeat of what happened before, that's all." He narrowed his eyes. "I need to remain vigilant. I'm still frustrated a doppelgänger pulled one over on me."

"It's just me," Professor Helmith said. "And Gray will be back soon. We're going to speak with my dad and the headmaster. It won't be long."

"All right." Leon nodded to Helmith and then to me. "Stay safe, though."

"I will."

Then the captain jogged back to my class. I wanted to join them, but at the same time, I was curious to meet Professor Helmith's father. Nasbit had made the man out to be a living legend. Was he, though? I would have to see for myself.

Helmith walked up the stone stairs that led to the Academy. I followed her, Twain in my arms. We entered the main castle and wandered the halls. Helmith walked with purpose toward a specific destination.

"What kind of man is your father?" I asked. "He's known as the *Warlord of Magic*, right?"

Was he a monster of a man, towering over everyone with an imposing silhouette? That was my first impression, but after Nasbit's burst of excitement, I wondered if I was incorrect. Perhaps this "warlord" was someone similar to Nasbit. Well versed in knowledge. Always willing to pontificate. Perhaps a librarian who loved over-the-top titles.

"It's hard to describe my dad." Helmith placed her hand on a door that led to the Academy's basement. "I think everyone struggles to quantify their own parents. Don't you think? Your eyes are clouded by the fog of childhood."

"W-What do you mean?" I asked.

Professor Helmith pushed open the door and hurried down the stairs, heading straight for the foundation floors. "I mean children often misjudge their parents. When we're young, our parents are strict, which can be frustrating. When we become older, our parents try to impart lessons, which can sometimes come across as condescending. Only once we're wise do we see our parents as people who sacrificed to give us life. Such a special gift you can only be given once."

I walked with her, our footfalls echoing in the stairwell. With each beat of my heart, I felt a twinge of guilt. For the most part, I had never appreciated my father or stepmother for the exact reasons Helmith articulated. Did she know? Was she trying to subtly say something to me?

"And there are examples of the opposite," Professor Helmith said as we traveled. "People who revere their parents so much that it's difficult for them to see their faults. Their parents protected and cared for them— what flaws could they really have?"

"Yeah..."

Twain glanced between me and Professor Helmith. The stairwell was lit with glowstones built into the walls and ceiling, and the soft illumination made it feel like night even though it was still the middle of the day.

Helmith's glowing pink and blue tattoo runes added to the color of our trip. She sparkled with powerful magic.

"I think I may be in the latter category of children. The ones who see nothing but good in their parents." Helmith chuckled to herself. "For a long time, I thought my mom and dad could do no wrong. It wasn't until I was an adult that I realized they're both people, like me, and not infallible beings of virtue."

"So... you admire your father?" I asked.

She nodded. "Very much so. That's why I had to summon him here. You see, my dad carries with him a blade that cuts through any and all magic. While there were closer arcanists who might be able to help, I don't trust them like I do Dad."

That sounded amazing. And as we reached the bottom of the steps, I caught my breath. "Wait. Did you ask him here so he could destroy the gate fragments?"

Professor Helmith turned to me. "Yes. I hope he can help. Then perhaps we'll have a solution to this problem, and you won't have to worry so much."

We stood in front of a long hall with a series of doors. The "basement" of Astra Academy wasn't really a basement—it was just a series of floors built into and around the mountain. Because they were below the front entrance, everyone loved to simply refer to all the foundation floors as a singular *basement*.

This was the area of the Academy where magical items were created.

It was also the part of the Academy where I had fought Death Lord Deimos. Which was why I wasn't very enthusiastic to be here. Twain's presence in my arms helped. He purred and twitched his large lynx-style ears. I suspected he knew I wanted the comfort.

The Death Lord wasn't here, though. All my fretting was foolish.

Professor Helmith walked to the very last door and pushed it open.

Once inside, I spotted two individuals. Headmaster Venrover, and a man I had never seen before. Additionally, the headmaster's eldrin, a beautiful golden sphinx, was also in the room.

Headmaster Venrover stood tall, his lithe body not one of a warrior. He held himself with the demeanor of an erudite noble. He wore a blue vest, a white shirt, and black trousers, each one with a small insignia of the Academy somewhere on it. His boots, perfectly polished, glittered from the light cascading into the room from the far window.

This part of the Academy—a floor built straight into the side of the mountain—overlooked a distant valley. The breathtaking sky was almost a shock to see after all the stairs Professor Helmith and I had gone down.

Headmaster Venrover tucked some of his long black hair behind his ear. "Ah. Gray Lexly. I'm so glad you could join us. Many apologies for the interruption to your class, but this is an important matter."

His sphinx walked around his legs, her padded feet quiet. She had a lioness's body, the wings of an eagle and the head of a human woman. "Welcome, Gray," she said, her voice hauntingly beautiful. She spoke with a deep and knowing tone. Her golden fur shimmered as she took a seat next to her arcanist, her wings tucked close to her body.

"Hello," I said, offering both of them a quick bow of my head.

"It's so good to see you, Dad," Helmith said as she hurried over to the other man in the room. She threw her arms around him in a tight embrace that he returned completely.

The Warlord of Magic wasn't anything like I had expected.

# CHAPTER 24

## ABYSSAL TRIDENT

"Rylee," the Warlord of Magic said. He hugged her for a short moment and then released her. "How're you doing? Is everything okay? Your letter wasn't very descriptive." He grazed his knuckles across her cheek, his expression soft.

The man stood taller than anyone in the room—perhaps even taller than my brother, but they weren't side by side for a good comparison. His black hair was short, but messy, as though styled by the winds of adventure itself.

His arcanist mark... it glowed white. A bright, mystical glow that was difficult to describe. It wouldn't light up a room, but the faint pulse of power was unmissable. His seven-pointed star was laced with a cape and a sword.

A knightmare arcanist.

Just like Sorin.

He was muscled, but not bulky, and he stood with such confidence and balance that I knew he was a warrior of the highest order. A sword in an ebony sheath was tied at his side, and a kite shield as dark as midnight hung on his back.

The Warlord of Magic wore a plain outfit just as dark as his weaponry, but the most impressive part was the many tattoo runes that sparkled across his skin. He had a black mark on one forearm, a red one on the other, and a blue swirl along the side of his neck. When he turned to face me, I noticed one of his eyes was also marked with a rune—it shone with a gentle gold. His other eye was nothing interesting. As black as everything he clothed himself in.

The man had a color preference, obviously.

"Gray," Professor Helmith said, pulling me out of my musings. "This is my dad, Volke Savan, the Warlord of Magic."

The man chuckled and shook his head. "Only the history books know me as the *Warlord of Magic*. Everyone here can just call me *Volke*. I'd much prefer it."

The shadows around his feet fluttered with the sounds of raven's wings. When I glanced down, I realized all the darkness in the room had a slight haze to the edges, as though moving on its own.

Only the shadow at Sorin's feet ever moved. As I turned in a slow circle, I realized *all* the shadows in this room were moving. The high corners near the ceiling, the ones on the floor, even the slivers of shade cast by the panes fixed into the window...

The darkness here was alive.

"You're a mimic arcanist, Gray?" Volke half-smiled. "They're quite rare. I hope you take good care of your eldrin."

"I received *two* bowls of fish soup for lunch," Twain interjected. "I think it's safe to say I'm living the good life." He burped a little.

I forced a laugh. "Ha. Yeah. I try."

Headmaster Venrover motioned everyone close. "No need to stand so far apart." Once we were near, he motioned to a table by the far wall. "Come. We should observe this together."

As a group of four, we walked over to the massive oak desk. Five gate fragments sat on top of the table, along with a weapon stand with a golden trident. I tensed the moment I spotted it. How had I not seen it before? I had probably been too busy gawking at the warlord.

This was Death Lord Deimos's trident.

He had thrown it at me during the fight. It was the weapon that had left scars across my body.

And here it was. Perched on a stand like it was a decoration to be admired.

"They kept this here?" I asked under my breath, staring at the trident.

The entire weapon was made of a singular material. It was dark gold, but I knew it wasn't just plain metal. Something about the weapon was sinister. I *felt* the magic from where I stood. It was the same eerie sensation I had felt when the Gates of Crossing had opened to the abyssal hells.

The three prongs of the trident were hook-like.

My body hurt just remembering how easily they had sliced through me.

"What am I supposed to be looking at?" Volke asked.

Headmaster Venrover motioned to the five gate fragments. Which was odd. Hadn't we only found two?

He picked one up with his bare hands. "These are slivers of the gate." Then he held the fragment close to my body. Once it was within a few inches, it glittered. The power within was obviously reacting to my presence. "Do you see this?"

Volke nodded. "Can you explain it?"

"Professor Zahn didn't manage to completely finish his infernal gate." Headmaster Venrover pulled the fragment away from me. "It required one more soul. And specifically, it needed the soul of a twin—the older of the two. Since Gray is an older twin, these fragments are activated by his proximity."

Volke folded his arms. "Any older twin will trigger this? You're telling me that if fragments are scattered around, there's a chance someone might stumble across them and unknowingly unleash something horrific on the world?"

"Precisely." Venrover then grabbed a second fragment. "But there's more. You see, Gray and Rylee found two pieces while away from the campus on a camping trip. However, once I had word from Rylee that these shattered remnants of the gate could be dangerous, I found a few here in the Academy that were left after the cleanup."

"Three more?" Volke asked, glancing at all the fragments on the table.

"No. Four more. You see, something interesting happened when I placed two together."

The headmaster held up two fragments. One was larger than the other, perhaps the width of two fingers, and just as long. The other fragment was the size of a thumb. When Venrover placed the two pieces flush up against each other, they glittered again and fused together.

Now it was a fat chunk of the gate, and it pulsed with disgusting yellowish energies before calming down and returning to its normal silvery sheen.

"It's more powerful now," Volke muttered, his expression hardening. When he glanced up to meet Venrover's gaze, he added, "The larger the pieces, the more dangerous it is."

"Correct again." The headmaster sighed as he placed the fragment on the table. "But I'm hoping you can destroy this with that sword of yours. If you can, I would sleep easier at night."

"Hm."

Volke rubbed at his chin, his eyes staring at the floor. I couldn't help but stare for a long while. How had he gotten a rune in his eye? Captain Leon had said people crushed up the occult ore to make the tattoos. Had the Warlord of Magic done that?

I rubbed at my eyelid just thinking about how awful that would be.

"Do you think anyone would be mad if I started yawning?" Twain whispered. He blinked his eyes without any synchronization.

I gently shook him. "Don't be rude," I muttered under my breath. "You're going to make me look bad."

"But being a unicorn for so long was tiring..."

"Draw on the power of your two bowls of fish soup. You need to stay awake for this."

Volke grabbed the hilt of his sword. The weapon crackled with energy as he slid the blade out of its sheath, the aggressive snapping noise echoing throughout the room.

Twain's ears shot up, his eyes wide. "Oh, dang. I'm awake now."

The sword was black—again, the man had a color, and he was using it to its fullest extent. But there was something interesting about the blade. The center of it was marked with a cluster of stars. White stars and green stars. They formed a constellation that resembled a serpent.

"And you want to me to strike the fragment?" Volke asked, his weapon held firmly in his hand.

The headmaster nodded. "Please."

Volke didn't strike with much speed. He lifted his sword, and then carefully brought it down on the fat silvery chunk. The blade effortlessly sliced through it. No force was required on Volke's part.

I had hoped the two pieces would fade away into nothingness, but the fragments remained. They were just... smaller now. As they once were before fusing. Volke took his blade and sliced another into two, but neither lost their magic. They glittered with power, and I felt their eerie aura from where I stood a good ten feet away.

"I'm not destroying them," Volke muttered. "I'm just making more."

"Fascinating." Headmaster Venrover stepped closer to the table. He gently touched the fragments and then rolled two into each other. They fused to create one, just like before. "I believe these bits of the gate are drawing magic from the abyssal hells themselves. It seems we will need a solution to this problem other than your sword."

Professor Helmith placed a hand on Volke's shoulder. "Dad, do you know anyone who might be able to help us? I think eradicating all remnants of this gate should be our top priority. Technically, Zahn is still loose in the world. If he discovers any of these fragments, and then figures out he can still use them, I think terrible things will come of it."

"Let me think on it," Volke muttered. He offered his daughter a smile. "Most people come to me when they want something destroyed. I've never really searched for someone else to do that job."

They shared a chuckle.

Helmith's father seemed... so nice.

Much kinder and more rational than his title suggested.

Then Volke turned his attention to the golden trident. He lifted his sword, the constellation sparkling. "I assume you want me to destroy this, at the very least?"

The headmaster actually stepped between Volke and the trident. "Oh, no. There's no need." He held up a hand. "I want this." He motioned to the shaft of the trident. "It's made of abyssal coral, a material not found anywhere outside the hells themselves. But coral can be grown, as they are often a living aquatic colony. I need to research this, and see if there's a way to produce abyssal coral here."

Volke's gaze hardened. "Adelgis... I don't think that's a good idea."

"We shouldn't allow such a magical phenomenon go to waste." The headmaster motioned Volke away. "I may never get another chance to examine something so rare."

"What does this trident do as a weapon?"

"The trident itself seems to amplify the magic of the wielder, and it disrupts the magic of those it strikes. From what I've gathered, it actually shreds the souls of its victims. With arcanists, it limits their healing, and makes it more difficult to use their magic. For mortals, it drains them of energy."

"Have you touched it?"

The headmaster shook his head. "Oh, no. It's attuned to Death Lord Deimos. Only he can wield it. Anyone else would suffer damage to their very being. But the coral... I could reverse engineer it, I'm certain."

Volke exhaled. "Abyssal coral probably grows by destroying magic, then. Or souls. Maybe a combination of the two. We really should just destroy the weapon."

"We won't know anything about the coral unless we experiment. Trust me. This will bring about something good. Either knowledge, or resources. And those are worth having."

After a short moment of contemplation, Volke sheathed his weapon. In a tone devoid of emotion, he said, "You sound like your father when you talk like that."

The headmaster said nothing. They stared at each other for a strained moment. The headmaster's sphinx stepped closer to him, her hackles raised. She, too, said nothing.

Professor Helmith stepped close to her father. "Oh, would you look at the time? The sun is already tucking itself away behind the mountain peaks."

I glanced at the window. A hint of orange streaked the sky.

Headmaster Venrover shook his head and glanced away. "I apologize. I didn't mean to make things... awkward." He brushed his hand along his sphinx's back, calming her fur. "You must forgive me. No one has mentioned my family in some time."

"What about Cinna?" Volke asked. "I thought you were on good terms with her."

"Oh. Yes. I suppose I am. Her sphinx comes to play often. Just my father, then. I'd rather not think of him."

The two shared a slight smile, and it seemed like all the tension in the room was gone.

I glanced over at the table.

The Warlord of Magic couldn't destroy the gate fragments. We would need to find another way to deal with this situation. Nasbit's words floated into my mind, and I realized I hadn't done my due diligence in the matter.

I would need to go to the library and research every method of magical destruction. Perhaps I could help Professor Helmith discover a way to rid the world of this infernal gate.

Especially since the fragments caused my skin to crawl. I hated being in the same room. But what was more bizarre was the urge to get closer to them. Did they want me to touch them? Or was something on the other side of the broken gate reaching out to me?

I held Twain close. "Professor, can I go back to class now?"

Helmith nodded once. "Yes. Sorry, Gray. Thank you for taking the time to show my dad the effect you have on the fragments."

"No problem." I bowed to everyone and then turned on my heel.

## CHAPTER 25

# THE MAGICAL FUNDAMENTALS PROFESSOR

It was the fourth day back at the Academy after our camping trip.

Today, we would meet our new *Magical Fundamentals* professor. I hoped the class would be interesting. When Zahn had run the class, we had observed star shards falling from the sky, discussed how the Gates of Crossing were made, and discussed all sorts of fascinating subjects and phenomenon.

Zahn was also a lunatic who had tried to kill me, but his class had been fun.

I crossed my fingers as I walked the halls of the Academy, praying to the good stars this professor would not want me dead. Twain scampered around my feet, Sorin walked by my side, and Nini walked opposite him, a chipper energy to their steps.

"So, the Warlord of Magic is bonded with a knightmare?" Sorin asked.

With a halfhearted shrug, I replied, "Yeah, but I didn't really see it. His arcanist mark was glowing, and he had a cape and a sword in his star…" I glanced over at my brother, who had a cape and a shield intertwined in his mark.

Sorin rubbed his forehead. "That glowing mark means he has a true form knightmare. I can't wait to see it." He glanced down at his feet. "Right, Thurin? You want to see?"

Thurin's voice rose from the darkness, his tone matter-of-fact. "I have seen the man's knightmare, my arcanist."

"Really? When? Why?"

"Volke Savan was the arcanist who saved me from the depths of a chasm I couldn't escape. He is an honorable warrior, and a proponent of great works of architectural and magical achievement. He took me to the Academy Menagerie when I couldn't find an arcanist to bond with."

Sorin smiled to himself. With a distant look in his eyes, he said, "I should ask Volke which subject to study here at Astra Academy. He sounds amazing. I want to be just like him. *You* should be true form, Thurin."

"Hm."

We reached our classroom and found all the other students already at their self-assigned tables. Which was odd. Since when was everyone excited to get to class so early?

"What's going on?" I said, turning my attention to Ashlyn.

She straightened her robes. "The new professor is arriving today, and Exie is—"

"I met him in the hallway already," Exie interjected. She giggled and waved her hand, her face growing pink. "He's so handsome. And from the *Ren* family. I can't believe how lucky we are."

Oh boy.

Nasbit rolled his eyes, but it was subtle. "It's all Exie was talking about this morning at breakfast. We had to get here early so we could meet him, apparently."

I took my seat with my brother and Nini. Twain leapt onto the table and curled up into his comfortable loaf position. "What makes a human handsome, I wonder?" Twain muttered.

Nini took off her glasses and cleaned them. "I think it has a lot to do with someone's demeanor and personality. Well, and I suppose their muscles. B-But that's not as important as the way they treat people."

"*Handsome* is a subjective term," Nasbit said from the table over. He scooted his chair to the end of the table, closer to ours. "It means different things to different people. Not everyone has to be muscled to be appreciated physically."

"In my opinion, then," Nini mumbled. She poked at her notebook, her gaze down, her hair falling halfway over her face.

Phila sat straighter and smiled. "Oh! I've always found light-colored eyes to be attractive."

"The question was about what makes someone handsome," Sorin chimed in. "Not attractive." Then he held up a finger, and in dramatic fashion stated, "*Handsome is a word often used, to describe a look that's much enthused... A beauty that's only skin-deep, a quality that makes our, uh, well...*" Sorin nervously chuckled. "Let's just say it makes us excited."

I ran a hand down my face, almost embarrassed for my brother.

"Beauty *isn't* skin-deep," Exie said. Her eldrin fluttered around her, the little fairy nodding his head. "All the truly handsome and breathtaking arcanists in the world needed to earn it. They keep their body healthy, they train their magic to accentuate their elegance." Exie leaned back in her chair and smiled. "And our new professor... He's a perfect specimen with his avant-garde tastes and his own unique style."

Exie clearly didn't have enough superlatives to describe this man.

Now I was intrigued.

Then the door opened, and everyone tensed. A man stepped into the room, and *handsome* was definitely not the word I would've used to describe him, though I could see why someone would.

He was tall. Muscled. Free of blemishes. His hair as red as a sunset.

But he had too many quirks that drew my attention in too many directions. Was this the *style* Exie had spoken of? The man had piercings along the entire edge of his ears—at least half a dozen on each ear. They were silver rings, some with gemstones, some without. Why did he have more metal in his ears than a bucket of nails?

He also wore his robe open with a half-buttoned shirt, like he wanted us all to see the flesh of his chest. I could see the man's bellybutton—and his well-defined abs—which had to be a violation of the dress code. He was rather aggressively ostentatious.

To make matters worse, the man had glittering tattoo runes, just like Professor Helmith and her father, but this man needed to *flaunt* them. They adorned his chest, his arms, the back of his hands, and even the side of his neck.

His were red and blue, and each had the curve and spike of fire.

The arcanist mark on his forehead...

It was a seven-pointed star with a spider woven between the points.

The man strode into the room, carrying a small stack of books. He placed them on the front desk and then leaned against the edge to face the class. His eldrin scuttled into the room a moment later, its eight legs *clacking* across the floor.

My skin crawled.

For years, a bizarre spider creature known as a *soul catcher* had invaded my dreams. It had been the doing of Zahn, but now I hated spiders with a tiny passion. Fortunately, the spider that clattered its way into the room wasn't a soul catcher.

This was something different, and far less disturbing.

It was a metal spider that stood three feet tall, with legs that reminded me of a daddy long-legs—the harmless spiders I often found in the corner of a room. This steel creature had spindly legs that were at least eight feet long, but they were bent in such a way as to be compact. The tips of the legs were points, like needles, and threatened to chip the stone floor with each of its steps.

The beast's spider body appeared to be warped metal wrapped around ore, raw gemstones, and other minerals. Jade, diamond, sapphire—the glitter of the precious stones intrigued me. Did the spider have eyes? I couldn't see them, but it had a mouth with fangs made of copper.

"Hello, class!" the redheaded man said as he slammed his stack of books on the desk. "I'm your new *Magical Fundamentals* professor." He lifted both his arms and grinned. "You may call me Professor Ren, and you can refer to my eldrin as Trove."

Nasbit shot his hand into the air. Professor Ren's smile widened as he lowered his arms. His spider click-clacked across the floor until it was behind the front desk, its spindly legs still visible, even if the majority of its body was not.

"Do you have a question?" Professor Ren asked, gesturing to Nasbit.

"Is that a treasure cache spider?"

The professor stared for a long moment, as though processing the question. Finally, he replied, "That's right."

Nasbit half-gasped and half-laughed, as though this was an amazing discovery.

"I take it you want to hear the story of how I found one?" The professor smirked. "It is quite the tale."

I had to admit, I hadn't heard of a *treasure cache spider* before, which meant it was probably extremely rare. Professor Helmith had taught me all about the most common and powerful creatures, so I considered myself rather knowledgeable on the subject of *mystical creatures*.

Before the professor could pontificate further, Raaza lifted his hand.

Professor Ren laughed once. "I haven't even started class, and I'm already drowning in questions..." He pointed to Raaza. "But ask away, I suppose. But keep in mind, we can't talk about me *forever*. We do eventually have to learn." The man combed his hair back, and Exie softly sighed.

"Are treasure cache spiders poisonous?" Raaza narrowed his eyes. "Are they dangerous in any way?"

The professor waited, like he expected more questions. When none came, he asked, "You want to know more about... my eldrin?"

"Yes. Are arcanists like you particularly dangerous? What can you manipulate and evoke?"

Professor Ren frowned. He grabbed one of the books off the pile he had brought and instead of walking it over, or even passing it around, he tossed the book like a disc over to Raaza. Fortunately, Raaza wasn't caught off guard. He snatched the book out of the air and stared at it, one eyebrow raised.

"Listen, we're not here to discuss mystical creatures." Professor Ren grabbed another book and tossed it to Sorin. My brother caught it without issue. "You don't need to worry about Trove. He's just a little nervous."

"He's adorable," Exie chimed in, smiling. She didn't add anything after that, she just fluttered her eyes—not even glancing at the spider.

The professor half-shrugged. "Well, yes. True. But you see, my eldrin—"

"Treasure cache spiders are so rare because they're masters at staying hidden," Nasbit interjected. He turned around in his seat to face Raaza.

"Their Trial of Worth is literally to just find them! That's it. The moment you find one, you've passed their test. They're *that* reclusive and rare."

Raaza huffed and then placed his chin in his hand. "So, they aren't combatants?"

"Oh, well, not really. They're known for keeping a hoard of gemstones and crafting traps. You see, people used to hunt the treasure cache spider back in the day to take everything the spiders had gathered in their nests. The spider traps can be quite lethal, but they don't fight when you find one. They—"

Professor Ren cleared his throat, interrupting Nasbit's explanation. Then he tossed a book at Nasbit, almost hitting the man in the chest. Fortunately, Nasbit managed to catch it, but it wasn't without an exhale of shock.

"This is a supplemental guide to magical fauna and flora."

Professor Ren tossed a book at Nini. Sorin caught it, and then he gently handed it over to her. Nini muttered a quiet thanks.

"My sister wrote this," the professor said, special emphasis on the second word. "We traveled with our family to every corner of the world, bearing witness to the mysteries that have yet to be solved."

No one spoke. Professor Ren glanced around, his smile slowly waning.

"No one?" he asked.

Someone coughed. Then the silence returned.

"You've never heard of my family?" Professor Ren asked.

"I've heard of it," Nasbit stated. "Your father is the Red Wolf, and your mother is the Pirate Slayer." He glanced over to Phila and said in a matter-of-fact tone, "They both fought in the God-Arcanists War."

Phila nodded along with his words but didn't have anything to add to the conversation.

"Aren't you all *impressed?*" Professor Ren placed a hand on his bare chest as he smiled. His teeth were so straight and perfect, he could've been an oil painting. "I'm a living legend. Here in the flesh. You can ask me all sorts of questions about my travels, or about my family."

Several people glanced over at Nasbit. This felt like something he would care about. As far as I was concerned, I didn't have anything to ask our new professor.

"I'm impressed," Nasbit eventually stated. "But, uh, most of my questions are for your parents. I knew the Red Wolf had two children, but their names aren't mentioned in any of the texts I've read. I-I'm sure all your adventures are wonderful, though. You could regale us, if you wanted..."

Raaza sighed loud enough that the whole room heard it.

It clearly wasn't what Professor Ren wanted to hear.

"Well, aren't you all a special bunch," the professor muttered as he folded his arms. "You know what? Let's just get to our studies, shall we? Since you're all so eager to learn new things."

Nasbit's smile returned.

Everyone else exchanged quick glances.

"You see, there are mystical creatures, and there are magical phenomena like star shards and occult ore, but have you ever seen plants or animals that have a slight amount of magic all their own?" Professor Ren tossed me a book. I caught it and set it on the table. "Things like *star moths* and *ghostwood trees* are good examples."

He spoke the words with the confidence of an expert, but with the boredom of someone who had repeated the same thing one too many times. His enthusiasm was long dead.

When he tossed a book to Ashlyn, she caught it with a firm grip. Professor Ren chuckled. "Well, well, well. If it isn't another Kross. Let me guess—you're Ashlyn?"

She nodded once and said nothing.

"The cotillion coming up must be for you." The professor glanced at her dragon. Ecrib sat behind her, away from the table, but his draconic eyes were narrowed in a glare. "No wonder none of you are impressed with my accomplishments and my family. I bet Archduke Kross already came in and bragged about everything he's ever done?"

"My father has never come *here* and done that," Ashlyn said, her tone curt.

"Right, right." The professor waved away her comment. "You definitely take after your parents, though. You're the spitting image of your mother."

Again, Ashlyn remained quiet.

"But as I was saying..." Professor Ren straightened his loose robes.

"These strange fauna and flora have soaked in ambient magic and transcended to become something valuable. Ghostwood produces mist that blankets the area around them. Star moths transform when near corrupted magic. Sounds great, right?"

He tossed a book to Phila. She evoked some of her wind to slow the book before she caught it. Then the professor tossed one to Knovak, and the final book to Exie. She made no attempt to catch it. The book struck her in the shoulder.

"Ow," she said as she rubbed the spot it had hit her.

"Are you okay?" Professor Ren asked.

"O-Oh, of course." Exie offered a fake laugh and a wave of her hand. "Never mind me. I'm just not good at catching anything. Please, proceed."

The professor ran a hand through his red hair, his green eyes rather vibrant. He seemed to mull over the interaction before saying, "Today, I want you all to learn a few things about magical fauna and flora. And I hate tests and quizzes and essays... So we're going to do some hands-on learning."

Everyone in the class brightened at this announcement. Except for Nasbit, who honestly drooped a bit, his posture slumped. Even his golem hung its stone head, as though sad to hear the declaration.

"I went to Astra Academy back in the day," Professor Ren said with a chuckle. "And I *hated* whenever my professors would only teach us from the books. I wanted adventure." He leaned onto his desk, his chest exposed, his strange demeanor honestly baffling me. "Now that I am the professor, we're going to make every class fun. How amazing is that? You all should count yourselves extra lucky."

Twain purred. He glanced over at me, his whiskers twitching. "I like this professor. He has confidence bordering on audacious, kinda like a cat."

"I'm not sure about him yet," I muttered under my breath.

My brother raised his hand. When the professor gestured to him, Sorin smiled. "What kind of adventure?"

"I'm glad you asked." Professor Ren snapped his finger and pointed to the window—the area beyond the treehouse walkway. "I'm going to trap you in a cave, and you're going to use magical wildlife to escape the gauntlet of challenges I've created for you. If you don't find a way out in time, terrible things might happen."

Oh, perfect. Yet another Magical Fundamentals professor out to kill me.

# CHAPTER 26

## MUSHROOMS

"Okay, class dismissed," Professor Ren said. He clapped his hands once and motioned to the door. "When you come back for the afternoon lesson, I'll have the *Gauntlet of Doom* all set up in the cave just beyond the Academy's northern edge."

"Wait, that's it?" Sorin asked with a nervous chuckle. "But you haven't taught us anything yet. You just said that magical plants and animals exist. We know that. Aren't you going to tell us something useful?"

The professor frowned as he picked up another book from his desk. He tapped the cover. "Read this in the meantime. That's why I passed them out." Then Professor Ren glanced at Sorin's arcanist mark. "You're a knightmare arcanist? Ugh. Well, if there's one creature that never finds itself caught in anything, it's a knightmare."

Sorin rubbed his mark. "Really?"

"Of course. They slide through shadows, squeezing through cracks like they are water. And in a cave, with no light to weaken their shadow manipulation? They're quite strong. I might have to give you a different challenge than the others..."

My brother sat a little taller.

Exie quickly raised her hand.

The professor pointed to her. "Yes?"

"Do you think *I* can have a different activity as well? Or perhaps I can do the same challenge as Sorin? I'm quite claustrophobic. The thought of being trapped in a cave…" Exie smoothed her perfect hair. "I would panic."

Professor Ren huffed a sigh and then rolled his eyes. "Ah. You're from the Lolian family, right? Of course you are." He shook his head. "Fine. You can do the same gauntlet as the knightmare arcanist."

Exie glanced over at my brother and smiled. Sorin half-smiled in response, but then turned to me and shrugged.

I couldn't believe this. I shot Exie a glare, and she returned it twofold. Had she really just manipulated her way into having my brother do *this* for her, too? And then she had the audacity to get angry at me for her actions?

Nini raised her hand. "Uh, professor? I'm a reaper arcanist. Perhaps I should also go with the others, because, uh, I can kinda do what knightmares can."

Professor Ren stared at her for a long moment. Then he grabbed a piece of parchment tucked between two books and quickly read down a list. "You're… Nini Wanderlin? I don't recognize your name."

"She's from one of the islands," Exie chimed in. "She bonded with her eldrin here in the Academy's Menagerie—the charity program that the headmaster runs for lowborn individuals."

"Ah, that explains it." The professor set down the paper. "But you don't need to worry, Nini. My gauntlet won't be too easy for someone with your abilities. I know you can move through splatters of blood, but unlike darkness, the cave won't be filled with it."

"O-Oh." Nini ducked her head. "Okay."

"If everyone's done complaining about the assignment, class dismissed." The professor motioned us out.

As everyone stood from their chairs, Professor Ren walked around his desk and petted his gemstone-encrusted spider, his touch delicate. And while I didn't quite like the man's attitude or attire, I noticed the way he soothed his anxious eldrin. The spider relaxed, and its copper fangs clicked in joyful delight.

After lunch, our class went out toward the northern edge of the Academy's campus. Since we were situated on a series of mountain peaks, we had to walk across a bridge to reach our destination. It was a sturdy bridge made of stone and metal, with a flat—and wide—walkway, capable of accommodating both Brak and Ecrib, the biggest mystical creatures in our class... But I still hated it.

The thought of falling bothered me. I couldn't explain it. I walked in the middle of the bridge all the way to the next mountain peak, my gait stiff.

Much to everyone's surprise, Professor Ren and Piper were both waiting for us at a small stone platform located just beyond the bridge. Piper and her rizzel eldrin stood off to the side, while Professor Ren waited with a half-smile in the middle of the platform. His spider was nowhere to be seen.

"Welcome, class," he said.

The earrings that covered his ears glittered in the afternoon light, almost as much as her perfect smile.

Despite the cold mountain winds, the man still wore his robes open, and his shirt half unbuttoned. I was both displeased and impressed. Displeased because why would anyone ogle this, but also impressed because it was as cold as a winter night, yet he never once shivered or complained.

The same couldn't be said of my class, though.

Exie and Phila both huddled close with their eldrin. Phila's coatl was just a snake—a cold-blooded animal with wings—so I doubted that kept her warm. Nasbit stuck close to his golem, but the sandstone creature was devoid of blood, so that definitely wasn't working.

Raaza was the only person who looked like his eldrin was warm, but the tiny fox only had fake flames, so it was all a lie. He kept his arms crossed and shivered along with the rest of us.

Even Nini, who was dressed in extra layers from head to toe, wasn't happy with the chilly weather.

"Professor Jenkins has agreed to help me." Professor Ren motioned to

Piper. He flashed her a grin. "You know, my mother is a rizzel arcanist. They're one of my favorite mystical creatures."

Piper laughed, her cheeks slightly pink. She waved away the comment. "Oh, they're mine, too. Rizzels are adorable."

Her eldrin stood at her feet, his little ferret-like arms crossed. Reevy had a serious expression that made the whole platform a little colder.

"And you can just call me Piper," she said. "Everyone does."

"Piper? That's a nice name. It suits you."

Piper laughed again. Way too much laughing, in my humble opinion. She stepped closer to Professor Ren, her black hair tied back in a ponytail, exposing her slender neck and a beautiful necklace that lay across her exposed collarbones. I hadn't seen that before.

I glanced over at Ashlyn. She met my gaze, and I silently motioned to Ren. Then I shrugged. Ashlyn seemed to understand everything I was asking. She pretend gagged, and I knew she wasn't a fan of our new professor.

I mocked unbuttoning my shirt and lifted an eyebrow.

Ashlyn snorted a quiet chuckle and then half-shook her head. She crossed two of her fingers to form a little X, indicating the professor wasn't her type.

I made a little X as well, indicating he also wasn't my type. That made her genuinely laugh. She covered her mouth to muffle the sound, but it wasn't enough. Half the class glanced over.

"Are you paying attention?" Professor Ren asked.

I whirled on my heel and faced him. I had been glancing in his direction, but I hadn't heard a word the man had said. "I'm paying attention," I said, trying to be casual.

"Then what're we doing?"

"We're about to be teleported," Twain whispered from down by my feet.

"We're about to be teleported," I repeated.

Professor Ren crossed his arms and lifted an eyebrow. "All right. Get over here." He held up his hands to the others. "Wait your turn. Everyone gets their own tunnel in the caves, and as soon as Gray goes, we'll port the next person."

I walked over to stand close to Piper and Professor Ren. Twain stayed by my side, his orange fur moving around in the cold air.

"Are you ready?" the professor asked. "Have you been ported before?"

"Yeah. I'm ready. Let's do this."

"Good. I'm glad you're enthusiastic. The adventure is over as soon as you reach this platform." Professor Ren pointed to the edge of the stone surface, and then to the small walkway down the mountain that led to a cave entrance. "You'll emerge there once you complete all my tasks. Try to be the first out. Understand?"

"Yeah."

Piper walked over and smiled. "I know you're prone to trouble, but try to avoid it this time."

"Oh, I'll try," I quipped.

She placed a hand on my shoulder, and Reevy placed one of his little rizzel hands on Twain's shoulder. Then my body felt like it was being sucked through a tiny hole. My vision went black, but once I blinked, there was silvery glitter everywhere.

The wind stopped.

I stumbled forward and nearly slammed directly into the wall of a cave. Twain popped into existence right next to me, his ears erect. The walls of this cave were mostly smooth, dark stone, which I was thankful for. The stone had a reflective quality, like it was wet, but when I ran my fingers across it, I realized the rocks were dry.

It was colder in here than on the platform. I shivered as I glanced around, surprised I could see. Glowstones littered the area. They were in the rock wall, on the ground, some in piles, others alone. I suspected the professor really didn't want us to be without light.

But there were also spiderwebs. Thick, sparkling spiderwebs, each strand golden and vibrant. I had never seen anything like it. The sticky webs stretched from the cave ceiling to the floor, creating a barrier. A howl of wind echoed from the cave tunnels beyond the web. Behind me, there was nothing but darkness. An unknown tunnel to an unknown destination.

Twain scurried around my feet. "What's the plan?"

"Plan?" I asked.

"Yeah. What're we doing?"

I knelt and grabbed a glowstone. Then I turned my attention to the web. "I think this is the way out." While I wanted to touch the web, I knew I would regret it. These were thicker, stickier webs than any normal spider would create. I would be trapped for certain. "We'll just use some magic to get through this."

"I thought the professor wanted us to use magical plants and animals to get out of here." Twain wiggled his whiskers. "I know you were too busy having a flirty little conversation with Ashlyn, but the professor did say not to have me transform."

"I wasn't flirting," I said with a scoff.

"Uh-huh."

"We were just talking. With our eyes. Everyone does it."

Twain glared at me. "Whatever. We need to figure this out without magic, or else you'll get in trouble. And since you're my arcanist, I can't have your actions reflecting poorly on me."

I glanced at the webbing. Then I lobbed my glowstone straight at it. The webs were so powerful and sticky, they barely moved when struck. The glowstone stuck to the threads and just hung there, suspended in the middle of the spider's web.

"Whelp, I used the magical materials we had," I quipped. "That didn't work. Time to use magical abilities."

Twain narrowed his two-toned eyes at me. "Fine. Just transform me into a rizzel, and we'll teleport ourselves out of the cave. Easy peasy. I'm sure the professor won't be upset *at all*."

I rolled my eyes. Why was everyone so against doing things the easy way? Rather than argue with my own eldrin, I grabbed a glowstone and headed for the darkest part of the cave. Obviously, the trick to this "adventure" was to find something to break the webs.

The cave wasn't complicated, or narrow, which was probably why Professor Ren had picked it. Everything was smooth, and perfectly safe, and I wondered if this cave was used for other classes as well. Even the floor was mostly flat and went straight, with no loose stones or sharp inclines. It was an easy trek, even in the dark.

The cave turned, and the first thing I spotted was glowing mushrooms. They grew on the walls and floor in clusters of a few dozen. They were small, about the size of my fingers, and they came in a wide variety of colors. Most of them were bright blue—the shade of the sky—but some were a bright red, and others were green. The bioluminescence struck me as beautiful. Each color reflected on the wet-looking walls, creating a dazzling array of combinations.

Twain scurried over to a bright blue mushroom and sniffed the cap. "Weird."

"This has to be the solution," I said as I knelt near a cluster of multicolored fungi. "Why else would these be here?"

"What are they?"

"I don't know." I offered him a shrug.

"You were supposed to read the book."

Again, I shrugged. "I read a few chapters, but I didn't have time for all of it. I had to go to the library to get books on the abyssal hells, remember? You were with me when I checked out the books. I didn't have all week to prepare for this. I had half a day."

Twain huffed. "Well, since you don't know what these are, how are we going to use them?"

"We're going to pretend we're field researchers," I playfully said as I plucked a blue mushroom off the ground.

The stem broke the moment I touched it, but the chill of the fungus startled me. I dropped the mushroom, and it hit the stone floor of the cave before shattering into slivers of ice. The entire phenomenon caused my eyebrows to lift to my hairline in surprise.

"Wow!" Twain leapt at some of the snowflake-sized ice slivers. He pounced on one and then another. "This is amazing."

With a lopsided smile, I glanced at the other shrooms. "I get it. I bet the red ones are hot. We could use them to burn the webs."

I reached for a red mushroom and discovered it was warm, just as I had suspected. When I plucked the shroom, it grew hotter and hotter, until I couldn't hold it at all. I dropped the fungus, and it hit the cave floor in a burst of ash and embers.

"Hm." Twain sniffed the burnt spot. "Maybe pick a blue one and a red one at the same time? You know. Squish them together? Keep the red one from getting too hot?"

That wasn't a bad idea.

With a smile, I reached for a blue mushroom, and then for a red one. I was intending to pick them and put them together, but an odd sensation shot through me. A feeling of dread.

Like I had in Red Cape, when around a gate fragment.

Was there one here?

I grabbed the red mushroom, and then went for the blue one, determined to solve this little assignment and speak with Professor Helmith. Unfortunately for me, I reached past the blue shroom and grabbed a silver sliver off the cave floor.

Thankfully, I had found the gate fragment.

Unfortunately, it pulsed with a wicked greenish color, and then melted into my skin.

# CHAPTER 27

## IN MY SKIN

I dropped the second red mushroom and stood. The mushroom exploded into a puff of ash, but I barely saw it. My hands shook as I turned them over and over, examining every inch of my skin.

With panicked movements, I rubbed at my fingers, right where I had touched the fragment. Had I seen that correctly? Had the gate fragment sucked itself into my flesh?

No.

I had to be mistaken.

Headmaster Venrover had picked up a gate fragment with his bare hands, and nothing had happened. Why would something strange happen now? But I already knew the answer. It was because I was an older twin. The fragments reacted to my presence, not the headmaster's.

"Gray?" my eldrin asked. "What happened? You dropped the shroom..."

"Did you see that?" I whispered.

"See what? The shroom? Because I saw how klutzy you were."

"No. The fragment. There was one here. Right here."

Twain hopped over a group of mushrooms and glanced around the nearby area. "Wait, you saw one? Here? Where?"

My eldrin searched around my feet, but when he came up empty handed, he stopped and stared up at me. I knelt again and showed him my hand.

"I touched it," I muttered. "And it went right into my body."

Twain's eyes widened. "That doesn't sound good. Aren't those fragments connected to the abyssal hells? We should speak to Professor Helmith."

"Yeah..." I grabbed a blue mushroom and a red one. When I squished them together, the icy shroom started to melt, but it kept the fiery shroom cool enough to hold. "Let's go."

I ran with the mushrooms back to the spiderwebs. Twain ran by my side, frowning the whole way. Once we arrived at the webs, I tossed the red mushroom at the bottom. The puff of embers, ash, and smoke seemed harmless at first, but a few seconds later, the web caught fire.

Flames licked at the obstacle, quickly consuming the sticky webbing.

"We should just teleport," Twain said. "We don't need to keep doing the assignment if you think something serious is going on."

I rubbed my palms along the sides of my trousers. "I don't know. Maybe I saw things. I didn't even sense the fragment until I was inches from it. I mean, how did it even get in here? I've felt paranoid lately."

Twain tilted his head. "Do you feel different?"

"No."

"Hm... Well, maybe, then... But I'm worried about you."

The two of us watched the fire demolish the spiderwebs. The second I could get through without touching a single thread of webbing, I hurried through the cave, another glowstone in my hand to help light the way.

Twain stuck close. He kept glancing up at me, his concern evident. I tried to focus on the task at hand. Everything was fine. Nothing was wrong. There was no need to be so fearful.

Up until I half-tripped on something I couldn't see. I stumbled, and when I tried to put my weight down on my left foot, I couldn't find the floor. I angled myself to the side and slammed into the wall. As soon as I had my footing, I scooted backward. Twain meowed, his voice echoing throughout the cave. With my heart hammering against my ribs, I glanced around.

"Twain?" I called out.

"Help! I fell into a hole!"

Where was he? No matter where I glanced, I couldn't see him or a hole. I closed my eyes and searched through the nearby threads of magic. I felt Raaza's kitsune, and Ashlyn's dragon, but the instant I sensed Phila's coatl, I tugged on that string of magic. The mark on my forehead burned as it rearranged itself.

"There," I called out. "You can fly now."

The flap of wings sounded throughout the whole cave. Then Twain—in the shape of a winged snake—burst out of the floor. He had flown straight out of the stone as though it weren't there. Was it an illusion? Had Professor Ren set up pit traps to stop us from getting out of the cave?

Twain fluttered his wings, landed next to me, and then coiled his serpent body around one of my legs. "There are holes in the floor, and caterpillars at the bottom of those holes. I think they're making illusions to hide their little nests."

Ah. Another *"learn about magical plants or animals"* lesson. With gritted teeth, I tried to think of a quick solution. Professor Ren probably wanted us to coax the caterpillars from their holes, but I didn't have time for that. If I could just avoid their nests, I'd be able to continue on.

"Wait here," I said.

Twain nodded, and also flicked out his tongue like only a snake could.

I dashed back to the area with the webs. The ground was covered in piles of glowstones. I grabbed an armful of the bright rocks and then headed back toward the area of the cave with holes. Instead of slowly feeling my way through the cave, carefully avoiding the bugs, I threw all the stones forward.

Not only did the glowstones illuminate the cave, but they also either landed on solid rock—a walkway for me to use—or they fell through the illusions and into pits, showing me where *not* to step. Now I had a pathway.

I scooped up Twain. "C'mon."

He grunted something as I leapt from one stone to the next. I picked up a single glowstone as I went, to have light for the remainder of the trek. The cave wasn't long, and we reached the next turn without incident, but I had a feeling there was at least one other obstacle in our way.

And I wasn't wrong.

I stutter-stepped to a halt right before I went straight into a bramble patch. Well, it wasn't a normal bramble patch. The thorned bushes had the metallic sheen of smooth iron, and they were at least three feet in height—too tall to step over, but short enough that I could see afternoon light shining down the tunnel.

We were almost out.

"What are *these*?" Twain asked. "We'll be ripped to shreds if we climb over these."

The thorns on the bramble bushes were the size of my thumbnail, each sharp and curved like fishhooks. It hurt my skin just to look at them.

Maybe they were also illusions?

I slowly reached my hand toward the nearest steel bramble patch.

Once my palm was mere inches from the thorns, the bush moved. *It moved*!

The bush screeched slightly as the metal scraped on metal. It cut me—one of the thorns hooked my palm—and I had to jerk my hand away. That was the second time in this cave I feared for my hand's safety. The pain was intense, but it quickly faded. I stared at the cut, watching my skin knit itself back together thanks to the magic flowing in my veins.

"What was that?" Twain cried, his voice echoing around us.

"That was the bush reminding me I should've read that damn book," I said through gritted teeth as a few scarlet droplets of my blood hit the floor. "Who makes gauntlets like this?"

The professor didn't want us to use our magic to solve this series of obstacles, but I didn't care. I needed to get out of here. I closed my eyes and felt for threads of magic. Professor Ren's spider, Nasbit's golem... Then I felt Piper's rizzel. I tugged that string of magic.

Twain shifted and contorted, his snake body shifting into a ferret with white fur and silver stripes. He squeaked once he was done transforming into a cute little rizzel.

"There," I said with a huff.

"The last time you teleported, it didn't go so well," Twain muttered, his brow furrowed.

"We'll try again."

"In a cave tunnel full of metal thorns and brambles? *Seriously*?"

His comment caused me to hesitate. I glanced at the metallic bushes, my heartrate increasing as I thought about the possibility of teleporting right above them and falling in. Then I glanced at the totality of the bushes. There weren't a lot of them... A few feet of bushes at the most. If I had a short ladder, I could probably get over them.

"I have another idea," I whispered.

"Anything is better than teleporting," Twain whispered back.

I closed my eyes and went straight for Nasbit's golem. When I tugged that thread, my forehead burned, and Twain leapt out of my arms. His tiny body exploded outward into a stone form, the sandstone boulders popping into existence as Twain became a golem.

"There," I said with a sigh. "Now... lie across the brambles. I'll crawl over you and get to the other side." I patted Twain's stone body. "The metal won't hurt you, right? And once I'm over, you can just crawl to me. Everything will be fine."

Twain said nothing.

He stomped over to the brambles and fell forward. He basically slammed into the metal bushes, the cacophony of metal screeching and twisted iron filling the whole cave. I cringed as Twain settled over the bushes, leaving only a few feet of clearance between his back and the ceiling of the cave.

I carefully crawled onto the back of his sandstone legs, and then across his back.

The bushes moved as I scooted across Twain, but they couldn't reach around the golem's body. What were these things? Why would the professor want us to learn about them? I shook the thought from my head as I made my way to the end of the bramble patch. Then I slid off Twain's stone golem head and stumbled forward.

"Okay," I said.

Twain pulled himself forward, the shriek of metal scraping stone worse than fingernails on a chalkboard. I gritted my teeth and tensed as he *scraped* his way over the bushes. Once he was on the other side, he bubbled and shifted, returning to his kitten form.

I scooped him up. "Good job, Twain. You're the hero of this story." Then I dashed for the cave entrance. We had done it—we had come to the end.

"That wasn't too hard," I said as I jogged toward the end.

"I think we didn't handle the last obstacle as intended." Twain twitched his ears. "It seems like maybe we should've found a way to calm the bushes or something..."

"This worked, didn't it? No complaining."

Twain didn't say anything after that.

We dashed out into the daylight, and then went up to the stone platform. Due to my speed, I thought I would be the first one there, but that wasn't the case. Nasbit and Brak were in the middle of the platform, and so were Ashlyn and Ecrib.

Ashlyn's presence wasn't a surprise, but Nasbit?

"You're done already?" I asked as I faced him.

With a deep frown, he replied, "I was the first one here."

"Really? But... how?"

Nasbit held up the professor's book. "The solution to all three problems was clearly outlined within the first fifty pages. It wasn't a difficult adventure once you read the chapters on element-shrooms, mind grubs, and deep blackberries. I'm surprised it's taking the others *this* long for them to return."

"Naz is right," Ashlyn muttered. "If you read the book, this really wasn't that difficult. I feel like the professor just wants to see who was following instructions."

I walked over and set Twain down at my feet. Then I offered my teammates a quick shrug. "Well, I didn't read the book, and I still got out pretty quick. The others will be here soon. Probably."

Professor Ren and Piper stood near the bridge that led back to the Academy. While the professor gave me a thumbs up, Piper spent the whole time chatting at him. Not *with* him. At him. I wondered if Ren even heard half of it.

"—and that's how I met Reevy," Piper said. "Rizzels are quite fickle. Their Trial of Worth is quite easy, but having one as an eldrin can be difficult."

Reevy crossed his little ferret arms. "Yeah, well, it goes both ways, ya know! They never tell us mystical creatures that you can get stuck with a cantankerous mortal as an arcanist. It's just a gamble who comes to impress you for your magic. A terrible, bizarre gamble."

"*Shh,*" Piper hissed.

I jogged over to them, and both professors greeted me with confused smiles.

"Wait with your fellow classmates," Professor Ren said.

"I need to go back to the Academy." I motioned to my hand. "Something's wrong. I have to see the headmaster, or maybe Professor Helmith."

"I think you can wait with the rest of the class. We'll all go in together once they're finished."

Piper and Reevy both glanced over at him. With a tilt of her hand back and forth, Piper said, "Actually, I think you should just allow Gray to go. He has a lot of legitimate problems."

The way she said that made it sound as though I were struggling mentally or physically. Which wasn't entirely true, considering all the outside forces that were determined to get me.

Professor Ren motioned to the bridge. "All right. I'll speak to you later about your performance, I suppose."

I nodded and dashed past them both. In that moment, I didn't really care what my performance was. I just wanted this fragment out of my skin.

I stood around the professors' lounge in the middle of the Academy. The window faced the setting sun, igniting everything with a warm orange glow. The couches, desks, and artwork of gigantic mystical creatures were all bathed in the beauty of a dying day. I sat on the furthest couch from the door, my attention on the painting of a leviathan.

Twain sat in my lap, his ears twitching. "You don't feel different at all?"

I shook my head. "Not yet."

"Maybe you did imagine it."

"Yeah. But what if I didn't?" And how had it gotten there? I still couldn't stop thinking about that.

Professor Helmith and Headmaster Venrover stepped into the room from a side office. The headmaster wore a neutral expression as he walked over, the fingertips of both hands pressed together. "I'm sorry to keep you waiting, Gray."

"Have you determined anything?" I asked. "Do you know if a gate fragment is in me or not?"

"I'm afraid we don't have a method of determining that just yet, but we'll work on it." Headmaster Venrover frowned. "I apologize that you've had so many troubles while you've been here. It feels like Zahn's plot to kill you still lingers."

With a nervous chuckle, I nodded. "Yeah."

"Gray, if you'd rather leave the Academy, and return home to the Isle of Haylin, where you feel safe, I would—"

"No," I interjected. "No," I said again, calmer than before. "I want to stay here."

My home island was a small place. Not just physically, but in terms of education and understanding. My father and stepmother would have me work with the candles, or I would eventually just leave on a ship crew, wandering the seas, looking for a future.

I wanted an education. I wanted to learn all the mysteries of the world. I couldn't do that on the Isle of Haylin.

And where was I most safe? Here, surrounded by expert arcanists? Or on my island, where there was *one* arcanist, and he loved farming more than anything else?

"The Academy might not be safe for you," Professor Helmith stated. "From how you describe the story, I think someone might've placed the gate fragment there for you to find."

"Who, though?" I asked. "Professor Ren?" That man didn't seem like he was concerned with me at all.

Helmith shook her head. "I don't know. But it's something we're going to investigate. Not only for your safety, but the safety of everyone here in the Academy. I just need you to be aware, so that you make appropriate choices."

My gaze fell when she muttered those words. Helmith wanted me to stay out of trouble. I understood.

I glanced down at my palm. Hopefully this wouldn't escalate any further.

"If you are determined to stay here, I'm going to assign a guardian for your safety," the headmaster said in a gentle tone. "Don't worry. He won't intrude on your life in any way. He'll just watch you from afar, and step in if ever there is trouble."

"Who?" I asked. I glanced to Helmith. I wished she could be with me, like she had been in my dreams for years.

Headmaster Venrover motioned to the empty space directly beside him.

A man appeared out of nowhere. There was no teleportation, no rizzel glitter, or pop of air. The man had been invisible. He wore a long black cloak that fell to his ankles with a hood that covered most of his head and obscured the majority of his face.

I had seen this man before.

He was the assassin who guarded the headmaster. A wendigo arcanist —a deadly type of arcanist who ruled over ice and death.

The cloaked man offered me a hesitant bow, but otherwise said nothing. His fingers... they were black. Frostbitten. Disgusting. But before I could comment, he vanished. His invisibility and stealth were nearly perfect. I'd had no idea he was in the room, and even now that I knew, I couldn't detect him at all.

"I trust Fain with my life," Headmaster Venrover stated. "You can trust him with yours. If you ever need help, just call out. Fain will be nearby at all times."

"But not *all* times," Twain said, narrowing his eyes. "Because that would be weird."

I patted his head. "It's fine. Just don't think about the logistics."

"Hmpf! *I'm* your eldrin. You're already protected." Twain puffed his orange fur and practically growled. I had no idea he would be so offended.

The headmaster exhaled. "I apologize. This is the best solution I could think of for the time being. Since you want to stay here at the Academy, and I need time to figure out a way to deal with the gate fragments, extra protection seems like a suitable temporary solution."

I stood from the couch and held Twain against my chest. "I think it's a good solution. Thank you, Headmaster Venrover." I half-bowed to the empty space. "And thank you, too, Fain."

No one replied.

I wondered if the assassin was mute.

Professor Helmith placed a hand on my shoulder and motioned to the door. "Come, Gray. I'll escort you back to your class. I'm eager to hear how you did in your little adventure." She smiled, and her radiance dispelled a lot of my doubt.

"All right," I muttered. But hopefully she wouldn't get too disappointed when she heard how I had solved everything...

## CHAPTER 28

## COTILLION INVITATION

P rofessor Helmith led me through the Academy, and I stayed close by her side. Occasionally, I glanced over my shoulder, half expecting to catch sight of the headmaster's bodyguard. But I never saw anything. No shadow, no movement—I didn't even see the carpet move with his presence.

Either he was really good, or he wasn't here with us.

Twain glanced up at me, his pupils circular. "We should be invisible," he whispered.

I shook my head, but didn't reply to him.

"Have you been enjoying your time here, Gray?" Professor Helmith asked.

"My time at Astra Academy? Yes. Definitely."

"That's good to hear. After your bumpy start, I thought you might dislike it here, but once you told Headmaster Venrover you wanted to stay, I realized I must've misjudged the situation."

We turned down a hall, and then headed for the stairs. I mulled over her comments. For a brief moment, I contemplated telling her that I loved the Academy because of her, specifically, but I kept that to myself. If my brother ever found out, he would never let me forget.

When we arrived at the classroom for my class, Professor Ren was already standing outside the door. His spider, Trove, stood next to him, his extra-long legs clicking across the floor, the metallic body shimmering in the light. Trove was quite beautiful, in a weird and abstract way. Like a pile of jewelry that had decided it needed to escape its owner by assuming a shape.

Professor Ren's eyes went wide when he spotted us. "Rylee? There you are!"

"Roark?" Helmith asked. "Ah. Yes. I remember. Someone told me you would be a professor here. So good to see you again."

She walked over and smiled, but she kept her posture stiff. For some reason, Helmith seemed both excited to see Ren, and not. That made me wonder about their relationship. Who was this guy? If he had hurt Helmith, I would never like him. Never.

"I've wanted to speak with you since I arrived," Professor Ren said.

"Oh?"

"I actually took this position because I knew you were here."

Professor Helmith brushed some of her black hair back. "That's sweet, Roark. It's been so long since we last saw each other... I'm glad you're here."

In an interesting reversal, Professor Ren nervously chuckled. He grabbed the hem of his robes and fidgeted with it, his gaze drifting from the floor to the ceiling before he said. "So, uh, while I have you here... Have you heard about the Kross Cotillion?"

"Oh, yes."

"Perhaps we can catch up there." He stepped closer and smiled his perfect smile. "I'm sure it'll be an amusing event. And I'd love to take you as my guest."

Professor Helmith chuckled. She waved away the comment. "Aren't cotillions for new arcanists and those who aren't married? I'm neither of those, Roark. It would be rather awkward, don't you think?"

A short moment of silence passed between them.

The spider click-clacked around Professor Ren.

"Wait," Ren said. "You're *married*? Since when?"

"For a while now. I changed my last name to match his family's." Professor Helmith lifted an eyebrow. "You were sent an invitation to the wedding, but you never replied."

"Who did you marry?" Professor Ren asked, damn near demanding to know.

"Kristof."

With a roll of his eyes that could be seen from the next nation over, Ren said, "*That* guy? I can't say I'm surprised." He placed his hands on his hips and glared at the wall, never looking at me or Professor Helmith.

"Is something wrong?"

Professor Ren dropped his hands and exhaled. He returned his attention to Helmith and half-smiled. "No. I'm just being dramatic. How about we catch up after the cotillion, then? It would be great to swap stories."

Helmith nodded. "I would like that." Then she gestured to me. "Here's your student back. Thank you for allowing him to come see me. I think everything should be okay from here on out."

I bowed as Professor Helmith turned and wandered back down the hall. Although we hadn't solved the problem of the gate fragments yet, I trusted she would think of something. Professor Helmith was dedicated.

Professor Ren glanced over at me. Then he gave me the once-over. "It seems you get into a lot of trouble."

"Does he ever," Twain quipped.

I held him tighter than before, cutting off some of his air so he had to huff. "It's not that bad," I said. Then I loosened my grip, and my mimic just glared at me.

Professor Ren combed back his red hair. With a smile that could weaken knees, he said, "My advice is to make lots of friends. You would be surprised how easy some problems are when you know the right people."

Which was strange advice, but I pocketed it just in case.

But it also gave me an idea.

"Professor," I muttered. "Are you really going to attend the Kross Cotillion? I mean, you seem... not in the appropriate age range."

Ren slowly lifted an eyebrow. "I'll have to think about it."

"Most of the other established arcanists aren't going to be attending, so I was just wondering. The party is for debutants, apparently."

"That's typically how they go," Professor Ren said with a groan.

"Well, Professor, if you don't end up going, would you mind if *I* had your invitation? I mean, I'm from a no-name family line, and it's been really difficult for me to make connections here at the Academy. I didn't get an invitation, but maybe, if I went to this cotillion, and introduced myself to some more influential people, I might be able to take your advice and make some interesting friends."

The professor chuckled. "Is that right?" Then he shrugged. "Listen, all the invitations are by name only. I can't give you mine." Before I could comment, he held up a finger. "But I like your moxie. If you want, I'll list you as my guest. You can attend then."

His suggestion honestly caught me off guard. "Really? You'd do that?"

Professor Ren flashed another perfect smile. "Of course. I might skip the event, but that doesn't mean you can't get in. And Rylee obviously likes you, so just make sure you tell her *I* let you in." He hardened his expression. "Just don't do anything to hurt my name or reputation, all right?"

"Of course not," I said. "I'd never do that."

Twain slowly lifted his gaze to meet mine. I stared down at him, silently asking that he say nothing. I never *intentionally* got into boatloads of trouble. Trouble just found me.

I headed to dinner without Sorin, which was a bizarre feeling. We had been together our whole lives, but today, I had felt his absence. For some reason, I hadn't seen Sorin or Exie since they were given a special Gauntlet of Doom from Professor Ren.

Nini and I sat together in relative silence as we ate our noodles with sauce for dinner. Her reaper hovered close, "watching" everything we did. Twain snuggled in my lap and occasionally asked for meat chunks.

Halfway through dinner, Nini turned to me.

She stared for a long while.

I stared back, chewing my food. When it became apparent she was too afraid to just ask me her question, I muttered, "Everything okay?"

"You're positive Sorin doesn't like Exie in any way?" Nini frowned. She had barely touched her food. "I mean... Maybe I've been such a fool.

Sorin is so nice, and kind, and wonderful—of course the other girls would want to date him."

I swallowed a mouthful of noodles. "Uh-huh."

"I should've just agreed to be sweethearts when he asked."

"Probably."

Nini pushed her glasses aside and rubbed her eyes. "Don't make fun of me," she whispered. "Please. I just need your help, Gray. I don't want to lose him."

I slurped up another mouthful of food. Once I swallowed, I shook my head. "You don't need to worry. He doesn't like Exie. Whenever you see him next, just tell him you've changed your mind, and everything will be okay."

That seemed to calm her, but she didn't eat her food. She poked her noodles with her utensils and remained unnaturally quiet. My brother's absence was felt the most in moments like this. He always had some fun comment or rhyme to break the tension.

I set Twain on the table and then stood. "Watch my food, okay?"

Twain nodded once and then scooted closer to my bowl. "I'll protect it with my life."

With a forced smile, I walked out of the dining hall and turned down the main hallway. My intent was to head to the dorms and search for Sorin, but that quickly became a moot issue. I spotted Sorin further down the hall, his back against the wall, his attention on a large window directly opposite him.

I jogged over to his side. "Sorin?"

The shadows at his feet shifted as he glanced over. With wide eyes, he pushed away from the wall and smiled. "Gray? Am I glad to see you."

"What's wrong?" I patted his shoulders, still surprised at how muscled he was, but not seeing any injuries or cause for concern. "What're you doing here? We're eating dinner."

"Oh, well, I'm not sure how to tell you or Nini this, but..." My brother sighed. He glanced up at the ceiling like he was struggling to find the right words. He never struggled to find words.

"You can tell me anything," I said, no joking or mirth in my tone. "Just say it."

"Exie asked me to join her at the cotillion."

I waited, but when Sorin didn't finish the story, I asked, "And you said *yes?*"

"Yeah." He didn't even look at me, he just continued to stare at the ceiling. His knightmare fluttered through the shadows in the corner of the hallway, never commenting. I wondered what his eldrin thought of all this.

"Why?" I asked with a long sigh.

"Exie said she wanted to attend the cotillion with someone she trusted, and who would look intimidating because there are people there who would harass her if she was alone." Sorin shrugged and continued before I could speak. "And I already know what you're going to say, but you weren't there when she asked me, okay? We were doing Professor Ren's assignment together, and Exie was distraught about the cotillion, and asked me as a friend to help her."

"Exie asks you for a lot of things," I stated.

"She seemed genuine." Sorin sighed. "But I know this is going to upset Nini. But I told Exie this was just to help her out, and that I was already close with Nini, so Exie understands."

How was it that my brother had landed himself in a boat full of unnecessary drama?

This whole situation made *me* tired, and I wasn't even in it.

I dragged a hand down my face as I mulled over all the details. Then I shook my head. "Look. Just... don't tell Nini, all right?"

"What about when I go to the cotillion?" Sorin frowned.

"You can tell her you're going with me."

"*You're* going, Gray?" Sorin seemed earnestly shocked. "Wow. But... what if Exie tells Nini I'm going with her?"

"Just tell *Exie* not to say anything." I glared at him. "As long as Nini doesn't know you're going with Exie, everything will be fine."

Sorin crossed his arms.

The darkness around us moved, and Thurin finally spoke from the depths of the shadows. "A lie is just a seed of doubt you will plant in everyone who discovers your scheming. Better to be truthful with her. Show Nini that no matter the reality, you won't sacrifice your honor and destroy the trust you've built."

I shook my head. "If you tell Nini you're going to the cotillion with

Exie, no matter the reasoning, she's going to be upset. Like... very upset. Whatever trust you built—" I made an explosion gesture with my hand, "—gone."

My brother sighed. He didn't normally find himself in situations like this. And if Exie genuinely liked him, and wanted to be with him, this would've been a difficult problem, but since I was convinced she just wanted to use him, the choice seemed obvious to me.

"I'm going to tell Nini the truth," Sorin muttered. "I don't want her to worry."

"All right." I motioned toward the dining hall. "Let's get this over with."

We walked into the dining hall as though we were heading for a firing squad. Sorin definitely had the demeanor of someone about to get executed, that was for sure. I patted his arm, trying to reassure him, but I also wanted to point out this was all his fault, and if he had just told Exie *no* literally once, this wouldn't have happened, but I kept that all to myself.

We sat back down at our usual table. Nini glanced up, hopeful and happy. "Sorin, there you are! I was worried."

"Nini," my brother said with an exhale. "I have something to tell you."

# CHAPTER 29

## DREAMS OF THE ABYSS

I held up my hand and cut off my brother before he could speak.

"Exie pleaded with Sorin to be her bodyguard for the cotillion," I said. "And despite the fact he wanted to go with you, he told Exie yes."

Nini's eyes grew wide and glassy. She glanced over at Sorin. My brother nodded once. "It's true. I, uh, I'm sorry. I figured you might be upset, but—"

Nini stood from the table without a word. She didn't touch her bowl of noodles—she just left. Waste hovered behind her, a creepy eldrin that spooked all the other arcanists in the dining hall when he floated by.

"Wow," Twain said. He nibbled a noodle out of my bowl. "That wasn't what I was expecting *at all*. You know reaper arcanists kill people, right? I feel like Sorin's name is going to end up on her chain one day."

"Or Exie's," I darkly quipped.

"I swear it's not like that," Sorin said as he slumped in his seat. "You believe me, right, Gray?"

I shrugged. "Sure. I believe you. But the heart is a fickle thing."

"I'm proud of you, my arcanist," Thurin said from the shadows underneath the table. "It's better that she knows. Now there can be no question about your honesty."

Sorin slid both his hands through his dark hair. *"Sometimes it's easier to tell a lie, to hide the hurt honesty implies..."* He exhaled. *"It's tempting to hide behind a mask, to pretend that everything is just a task... But sooner or later, the truth will out, and then the pain is harder to flout."*

Did he just say *flout*?

My brother was clearly reading a dictionary in his spare time.

"I do think that is all true, philosopher knight," Thurin said. "And I think Nini will realize that as well."

Sorin shook his head. "I guess we'll see. I'll try to make it up to her. Somehow."

Nights were peaceful inside Astra Academy. The larger mystical creatures went to sleep in the treehouse, and then everyone retired to smaller dorm rooms.

I sat on my bed and stared at the far window. Twinkling stars dotted the sky, creating a beautiful blanket that covered the world. Despite the majesty of the evening, my skin crawled. Something felt off, and I rubbed at my fingertips, wondering if it had something to do with the gate fragment.

Twain slept on the nightstand next to my bed, purring whenever he exhaled.

Sorin reclined on his bed next to mine. He had his nose in a book about the abyssal hells, his attention consumed by the information. I suspected he wanted to exit reality as quickly as possible.

Nini still hadn't spoken to him. She had locked herself in the girls' dorm and hadn't exited.

Raaza did push-ups on the stone floor, his kitsune sitting on his back while he did them. For the most part, I ignored his efforts, but occasionally I glanced over to see if he was still at it. The man switched up his exercises, and rarely took breaks.

"You know, you're going to hurt yourself more than improve," Knovak said. He stood at the opposite end of the dorm, casually dressing for the evening. He wore a velvet shirt and a pair of trousers for bed tonight. "You need to allow your body the rest it deserves. Or you need an arcanist with healing to help you overcome the downtime."

Raaza gulped down some air as he finished his fiftieth pushup. With sweat soaking his tunic, he stood. "I didn't ask for your advice."

Knovak gave him a sidelong glance. "Fine. You don't want to listen? Do whatever you want."

Despite Raaza's irritation, the man stopped his workout. He sat on his bed, his kitsune hopping around him. He stroked the fox's fur and smiled.

Once Knovak had prepped his bed, he walked across the dorm, passing both Raaza and Sorin, and went straight to me. Knovak brushed back his short hair, making his unicorn arcanist mark more prominent, before saying, "I have a new plan to attend the cotillion." He kept his voice low and dramatic, and I wondered if he was doing that just because he liked it, or if there was a real purpose.

"What's your plan?" I asked.

"We convince the girls to go *as a group*." Knovak held up a hand, indicating he wanted me to wait. "Listen. Just listen. We tell them it would be beneficial to them, because we can be their hired help or something."

That would've been a fantastic plan. If he had thought of it two days ago. Now it felt completely, and wildly unusable. Exie had already gotten her "hired help."

"Sorin and I already got invites," I muttered.

Knovak placed his hand on his chest. "*What?* Why didn't you tell me?"

"Professor Ren is taking me as his guest, and Exie asked Sorin."

"Exie asked *Sorin?*"

Knovak's shout was loud enough to wake the whole damn Academy. Raaza even stood from his bed in order to glance over in our direction.

My brother buried himself deeper in the book, clearly wishing he could disappear.

Knovak huffed and then crossed his arms. A moment later, he uncrossed his arms and huffed again. "Fine. You know what? New plan. I'll seduce Ashlyn and have her take me to the cotillion."

"*No*," I growled, angrier than I had thought I would be. "You're not *seducing* anybody. Do you even hear yourself?"

"Phila, then. She's pleasant. She'll understand my plight." Knovak leaned in close. "If your *poet* brother can get *Exie* to ask him, I can definitely get Phila. C'mon now."

Raaza walked over to Sorin's bed. "Did Exie really ask you to attend the cotillion with her? If so—congratulations. She's stunning."

My brother shifted in his bed, turning his back to Raaza. He said nothing.

"And you?" Raaza glanced over to me. "Did I hear correctly? Professor Ren asked you?"

I shook my head. "I asked him, actually." I sarcastically swished my hair back and smoothed my sleeping tunic, like I was some suave scoundrel.

Both Raaza and Knovak stared at me with blank expressions, the cogs of their mind turning at unusually slow rates. Finally, Raaza recovered and then scoffed. "That professor has *everyone* under his spell. How does he do it...?"

"Isn't it an ethical violation to court a student?" Knovak shook his head. "How disgraceful."

"Professor Ren isn't actually going to the cotillion." I chuckled. After a long yawn, and a stretch, I said, "He gave me his guest invite because I told him I wanted to attend the celebration. I'm not into the professor."

"Everyone else is," Raaza muttered.

With both my thumbs, I pointed to myself. "Not this guy." Then I pulled my blankets up to my chin and snuggled deep into my mattress.

Raaza and Knovak argued for a long time, discussing something about the cotillion, but I didn't pay attention. I closed my eyes and exhaled, allowing sleep to take hold of my mind. I just wanted this day to be over. Tomorrow, I would feel like my normal self again, I was sure of it.

Dreaming...

I knew when I was dreaming.

For years, Professor Helmith had come to me in my dreams, protecting me from nightmarish creatures. Now, whenever I dreamt, I just knew. It was a strange skill most didn't have, apparently.

But this dream was odd. I sat in class, at my usual table, listening to a professor discuss whatever topic we were in. But I heard none of it. I shook my head, a ringing in my ears. When I glanced to Sorin or Nini, I couldn't really hear them, either.

When I turned my attention to the window, I caught my breath. Both the sun and moon hung in the sky—a sign that the gates to the abyssal hells were open. Was this a nightmare? It didn't feel like it. Glorious afternoon light streamed in through the window, keeping the classroom warm and bright.

The lack of noise unsettled me, though.

"Who are you?" someone asked, their voice directly in my ear.

I flinched and whipped around. The classroom remained silent, even when people spoke. Their mouths moved, but no sound issued forth. Who had spoken? It had been masculine and deep—and filled with confidence.

"Ah. You're the arcanist who thwarted my brother." The voice was dark and laced with an eerie echo. It felt like teeth scraped the shell of my ear as the man said, "This works out perfectly."

With shaky hands, I stood from my chair. The others in the classroom looked at me, their eyebrows knitted, their lips turned down in a frown of concern.

"Who are *you?*" I demanded. I heard my own voice in this dream, but no one else's. It was just me, and this strange, disembodied voice that spoke directly into my ear.

"You know who I am. Anyone who lays their sights on me will never forget."

The haunting tone to his voice revealed more than his words.

Death Lord Deimos.

I shivered as I backed up. I hit one of the tables in the classroom, my whole body freezing. Something about his echoing voice filled me with a deep and unforgiving chill. Even my bones felt cold.

"You're not here," I said, more to myself than to Deimos. "*You're not.* It's just a dream."

"Believe whatever you want to believe."

I scratched at my ear, trying to rid myself of his sinister voice. Nothing I did helped. The others in the classroom stood and huddled around me, everyone worried, even their eldrin. Ecrib placed a dragon claw on my shoulder, and Brak offered me a stony hug.

I felt... trapped.

"Leave me alone," I said through gritted teeth.

"You sealed your fate when you fought against me and destroyed my gate. Now I'll see you suffer. I'll rip your soul apart and graft it straight onto my dragon. There will be no end to your torment."

Deimos spoke his threats in a cold and precise manner, no haste to his words, no anger. It was like a dark promise.

I tried to escape the crowd of people around me, but it was impossible. Everyone in class had gathered close, creating a circle of bodies. I pushed Phila, but then Nasbit was in the way. They wouldn't allow me to escape, suffocating me like only a dream was capable of.

"*Leave me alone!*" I shouted, both at the people and at Death Lord Deimos.

The Death Lord continued to speak to me directly in my ear, even if he had no body or form I could yell at. "My revenge won't just be confined to you. I'll tear your brother apart, your family—everyone you hold dear. Their souls will only empower me, and fuel my return to the realm of the living."

When I tried to leap out of the crowd, Brak grabbed me with its sandstone arms. The stone golem crushed me in a tight embrace, unforgiving boulders smashing my flesh. I was bruised, and no matter how much I struggled, I couldn't escape. Brak squeezed tighter. My bones hurt. They would break.

I couldn't breathe.

"Unless..." Deimos whispered, "you surrender yourself to me. Help me open the gates to the abyssal hells, and I'll spare you—and your loved ones—a thousand lifetimes of torment."

I still couldn't get any air. My heart hammered, and it felt like Deimos's icy grip was squeezing around my heart. Panic set in, but I knew I couldn't allow it to control me.

I had to calm down.

I had to think.

How could I get out of this? *There had to be a way.*

Then I thought of it. I closed my eyes and immediately searched through the dozens of magical threads, quickly sifting through them, like an insane person opening every cupboard and drawer in a kitchen as fast as they could.

Then I found it.

Professor Helmith's ethereal whelk.

I tugged on Ushi's string of magic and became an ethereal whelk arcanist myself. The whelks could manipulate dreams. That was the power I needed. With my heart still hammering, I glanced around and *changed* the environment. I pretended the dream was an extension of my very body and altered everything.

In a flash, I was no longer in the classroom. It had all vanished—the tables, the students, even all their mystical creatures. Instead, I was back on the Isle of Haylin. Although I hadn't meant to transform my dream into my home island, it had been the first thing I thought of when I needed to escape.

I stood at the very edge of Honeysuckle Meadow, the beautiful field of yellow flowers swaying in the island wind. Everything smelled of pollen and salt water, a combination that was more nostalgic than pleasant. The vibrant blue sky calmed me, and the seagulls who floated on the gentle winds were a welcome sight.

I took a deep breath.

Death Lord Deimos's voice was gone.

Everything was okay.

"Gray?"

I jerked awake. With a panicked flail of my arms, I sat up in my bed. My sheets and mattress were soaked with my cold sweat. When I glanced at the window, I realized it was still night.

"Gray?" Twain repeated. "Are you okay?"

I turned my attention to him. He was no longer in his kitten form—he was an ethereal whelk, his shell glittering with an iridescent sheen. The soft glow of his body lit up my portion of the dorm. I had transformed him even while I had been sleeping.

"Twain," I whispered. Then I wiped my forehead free of sweat. "I'm sorry... I, uh, was having a nightmare."

He floated around as a weird sea snail. Tiny tentacles dropped down from his slug body. "Why did you change me into Ushi?"

"I..." After a deep inhale, I forced myself to relax. "I had to escape the nightmare. Sorry, buddy. I'll try not to do that again in the future." I reached out and grabbed Twain from midair. He didn't struggle as I pulled him into a soft embrace. The glow of his inner light warmed me.

Twain wiggled his tentacles. Once I released him, he landed on the nightstand. "Okay. But make sure to get lots of good sleep. No more spooky nightmares. That was our goal, remember? I don't know if my heart can handle any more jump scares in the middle of the night."

I felt the same way.

# CHAPTER 30

## A LESSON ON TRUE FORMS

The next day was Professor Helmith's class. She had yet to arrive, but everyone headed into the room regardless.

Most people arrived in the morning with a groggy expression, including Ashlyn, Nasbit, Raaza, and Phila. It was too early to study, in my humble opinion. I stumbled my way to my seat and exhaled as I sat. The nightmare had drained me. Although Twain had been there, and I had felt safer, I never managed to get back to sleep.

Sorin was clearly not in a great mood. He had been quiet all morning, even through breakfast.

Nini didn't sit at our table. She went all the way to the back of the classroom and sat with Raaza. I wasn't sure if she was doing that to be dramatic, or if it was because Raaza smiled and offered her a comforting word. Either way, it obviously bothered Sorin.

"This is all your own fault," I whispered to him. "If you had just told Exie *no*, like I said to, this wouldn't be happening."

Sorin shot me an icy glare. His gray-blue eyes, same as mine, really conveyed hate when he wanted them to. "Thanks, *brother*."

I glanced around. Exie had yet to arrive.

After I petted Twain, I stood from my seat. "I'll be right back." And then I walked out of the classroom. I wasn't going anywhere—I just stood outside the door and waited, my hands in my trouser pockets.

It was quiet. Most arcanists were already in class and hard at work.

Exie was easy to spot.

She sauntered down the Academy halls with her erlking fairy fluttering behind her. She had a radiant beauty that refused to be hidden by her robes, and she strode forward with a confidence that told everyone she knew it.

I stepped forward and intercepted her a few feet from our classroom door. "Exie."

"Gray." She went to step around me, but I intentionally moved to block her. "Is there something you want?" she demanded.

"You're not using my brother, right?" I asked, not even bothering to beat around the bush with pleasant conversation—or even a simple *good morning*.

Exie and her erlking both crossed their arms at the same time, as though they had rehearsed the very actions. "How dare you? I would never. Your brother is a kind and generous man who just so happens to be helping me. *That's all*. We're good friends. Ask him yourself."

"Uh-huh." I met her gaze and didn't look away as I said, "My brother is also a naïve hopeful who thinks everyone is secretly wonderful, and I would be very upset if someone intentionally shattered that delusion for their own shallow, petty gain. If anyone *did* do that, I'd take it upon myself to make sure they regretted it every single day for the rest of their time at Astra Academy. Am I making sense? Because you look like someone who might need things repeated in a slow voice before they truly sink in."

Her face grew red, and her eyes narrowed, but she didn't move. Rage radiated from her—but it didn't match mine.

"Is that a threat?" Exie asked in a controlled voice.

I shrugged. "You said you and Sorin are good friends." I stepped away from her. "So I guess that was more of my own personal daydream—since it's nowhere close to reality. Right? Right. Well, I'm so glad we had this conversation." I grabbed the door and held it open for her. "After you."

Exie flounced past me, not another word to offer. Her erlking stuck his tongue out as he went by, but I didn't bother to respond to that.

Once we took our seats, the door opened again to reveal Professor Helmith and her father. I had forgotten he was going to teach us a class, and when he stepped into the room, I sat a little straighter.

Nasbit softly gasped. Even his golem pointed and motioned as though this was an amazing event.

The Warlord of Magic, Volke Savan, stepped up to the front of the classroom and smiled. His black clothing, and dark scabbard, gave him an intimidating demeanor, but the look in his eyes reminded me what I already knew. He was a kind man. Strong and confident without being too imposing.

His arcanist mark glowed with a white inner light. Several people in the room pointed.

"Hello, class," Volke said. "I'm your professor's father. You can call me Volke. I'm here to speak to you about *true forms*. Every mystical creature has one, but not all arcanists will be skilled or virtuous enough to see their eldrin transform."

He leaned against the desk and took up a casual stance. When he glanced over to me, he offered a slight nod of his head. I returned it, but it felt odd to be acknowledged by him.

The shadows in the classroom, from the far corners to the ceiling, moved and fluttered with new life. Was it Volke's knightmare? It had to be.

Sorin sat up, his attention squarely on Volke. "Do you have a true form knightmare?" he asked.

"That's right."

Professor Helmith went to the chalkboard and wrote a few words.

*Geas*
*Virtue*

Volke motioned to the board. "Just as there are two ways mystical creatures can be born—through progeny or through fable—there are two ways mystical creatures can achieve their true form. The first way is through a *geas*."

"What in the abyssal hells is a *geas*?" Raaza asked.

Volke responded with a nervous chuckle. "That's a great question. A *geas* is a quest or obligation. Think of it as a task you need to complete in order to get your mystical creature all the power it needs to achieve its true form."

Nasbit shot his hand into the air.

"Yes?" Volke pointed to him.

"When a creature achieves their true form, do they transform right away? Or gradually? Or what happens with that?"

Again, Volke chuckled. He rubbed at the back of his neck and mulled over the question. "So, why don't we look at the difference between the normal creature and a true form creature, hm?" He motioned to Sorin. "Would you mind calling out your knightmare?"

Sorin stood from his seat, and the shadows around his feet expanded outward. Thurin stepped up out of the darkness, the empty suit of armor only partially complete. Parts of Thurin were missing, like one of his bracers and a portion of the shoulder guard. Otherwise, he was hollow, and his black cape twirled in a nonexistent wind.

Before anyone could comment, the shadows around Volke's feet stretched out across the classroom floor.

A knightmare stepped out of the darkness, one far more imposing than Thurin. It was a hollow suit of plate armor, but it was complete. It also had a cape, but *its* cape was lined with a night sky. The majesty of the twinkling stars caused most of the class to ooh and aah.

And then the cape *ripped itself in half*, each side becoming a bat-like wing. The knightmare flapped them, the inner star lining twinkling brighter than before. The creature had a wingspan of over fifteen feet. It was impressive.

Volke's knightmare was also covered in spikes—especially on the left shoulder, like some sort of defensive measure, though it seemed sinister. The gauntlets and boots were clawed, and every inch of the knightmare had a deadly appearance.

"This is Luthair," Volke said. "My eldrin."

When Thurin and Luthair stood next to each other, the differences were plain to see.

Luthair was slightly taller, more armored, he had wings, and every inch of his shadowy body moved with power. While Thurin was impressive—he was still a knightmare—he was plainer, a little shorter, and his cape was just a cape.

A true form knightmare...

It made me wonder what a true form mimic would look like.

A bigger cat? Or maybe something else...

"As you can see," Volke said as he stepped around his eldrin, "there are notable changes. First, true form knightmares gain these wings fashioned from their capes." He pointed to his knightmare.

Again, the knightmare flapped his mystical wings.

"They also become stronger." Volke glanced back at the class. "All mystical creatures can evoke something, manipulate something, augment something—but they also have a *true form ability*. You see, true form knightmares, and their arcanists, can tell when someone is lying to them. It's just an innate power that comes along with the true form."

"And true form phoenixes can revive people," Nasbit chimed in.

Volke nodded once. "That's true. Normal phoenixes can't, but true form phoenixes have a limited number of revives." He pointed to Raaza. "And you asked if the change is sudden or all at once? With *geas* true forms, the change is gradual. The more you complete the mystical creature's quest, the more they transform."

"Can you give us an example?" Ashlyn asked.

"Uh, sure. I can." Volke rubbed at his chin. He had no stubble or beard, which gave him a youthful appearance, even though he had to be over a hundred years old. "So, manticores have a geas requirement. They need to eat the eyes of children in order to achieve their true form."

Everyone in the classroom balked or gagged.

"Why are so many mystical creatures gross?" Exie asked with a frown.

"The other way a creature can achieve their true form is through a virtue." Volke held up a finger. "Unlike the geas, which requires a task to be completed, a virtue true form happens the moment you embody the virtue of the mystical creature. For example, sovereign dragons value autocratic power above all else. And if the arcanist also values power more than anything else, the dragon will transform. Right there on the spot. It could happen the moment they bond, or years afterward—the arcanist just needs to share the same virtue."

"What kind are knightmares?" Nasbit asked.

"Virtue," Volke replied without hesitation. "As soon as I embodied the ideals of a knight, Luthair transformed."

"The ideals of a knight?"

Once again, Volke nervously chuckled. "Well, to be honest, a lot about mystical creatures' true forms are still a mystery. I've gone out of my way to classify the two types, and to compile all the information I can on them. When I say *the ideals of a knight*, I mean the selflessness that knights are supposed to embody. Being willing to die for others, or to uphold a cause at your own detriment. If you hold their ideals in your heart, a bonded knightmare will transform."

Twain and I glanced at each other at the exact same time.

"So which are you?" I whispered. "Do I need to embody a virtue? Or do I have to do some sort of epic quest?"

"I don't know," he replied, his voice hushed. "I didn't even know what kind of Trial of Worth I was supposed to have, remember? I'm broken."

I patted his little orange head. "Heh. You're not broken. Don't say things like that."

"What about stone golems?" Nasbit asked. "Do they require a virtue or a geas?"

Volke held up both his hands. His knightmare strode around the room, its shadow metal armor clanking across the floor.

"I don't know every mystical creature," Volke said. "But I do know that stone golems have a geas. From what I've gathered, it has to do with a special kind of metal that can only be found underground. The golem must absorb it."

Nasbit furiously wrote in his notebook. He didn't even bother looking up when Raaza raised his hand.

"Yes?"

Raaza motioned to his kitsune. "What about my eldrin?"

"I'm not sure about kitsune," Volke admitted. "But there's no need to ask me for every creature, either. Your textbooks on mystical creatures should have a section dedicated to true forms, and everything we have documented on them."

Phila raised her hand. Volke motioned to her, and she asked, "Is that why your arcanist mark is glowing? That's the real sign you achieved a true form?"

Volke nodded. "That's correct."

"Why does your mark spark red sometimes?" Nasbit asked.

Everyone stopped what they were doing and stared. Volke rubbed at his forehead, his gaze distant. Sure enough, when I focused on the glowing mark, a flash of red sometimes streaked through it. Was that normal? Nasbit had asked the question as though it wasn't.

It was so subtle...

I hadn't seen it when I met Volke in the basement.

"You don't have to worry about that," Volke said, his tone darker than before. "Just trust me when I say that my mark is a little different than others." He forced a smile. "Astra Academy has an amazing record of helping their arcanists achieve a true form with their arcanists. I hope some of you will attempt it."

Nasbit nodded several times. "Oh, I will!"

"B-But don't get obsessed with it," Volke quickly added. "I knew someone who was so consumed by their quest to transform their eldrin, they forgot everything else."

"Oh, I'll be okay." Nasbit went back to making notes.

Professor Helmith stepped around her father and faced the class. "Now that you've heard the basics on true forms, I'd like you all to turn to the back of the book and study everything we have about true forms in other creatures. It'll be on the next test."

Everyone happily did as they were asked.

Before Nini started studying, however, she got up from her seat and wandered back over to my and Sorin's table. She took a seat next to my brother and silently went back to her reading.

Which made Sorin infinitely happier.

# CHAPTER 31

## ANCHOR ISLE

T sat in the dorm room, reading the book about the abyssal hells.

When I got to the section about the Death Lords, I almost skipped over it. I didn't want another nightmare with Deimos whispering about how he planned to torture me to death, but I knew it was the intelligent move to learn everything I could about him.

The page that detailed the Death Lords read:

And lo, there exists a realm beyond the reach of mortal man, a place of darkness and despair in the deepest depths of the ocean. In this cursed domain dwell the Death Lords, arcanists who gather souls for their own personal power.

They are masters of the abyssal dragons, creatures born of misery, who long to control the world. When outside the abyssal hells, the dragons are a blight upon the land, bringing famine, disease, and death in their wake. They delight in the suffering of *those who defy them, reveling in the torment of their souls.*

*So let it be known that the third abyss is a place only for the wicked, ruled over by the vengeful Death Lords. May the righteous avoid their grasp and find peace in a rebirth that brings them closer to their true and final life.*

I grazed my fingers across the page, staring at the information for much longer than necessary. I wished I knew more about *Deimos*, not just about the Death Lords and their dragons. Why didn't any of the books in the library have anything I could use?

Sorin had stayed with Nini out in the common areas. I figured they want to spend the time alone, so I had left as soon as I had an opening.

I was alone. Except for Twain. He sat at the end of my bed, his eyes fixed on the far window.

"There's no other mimic here at the Academy," he whispered.

"You don't know," I absentmindedly muttered as I turned the page of my book. "Professor Zahn turned out to be a mimic arcanist, remember?"

"Very well..." Twain glanced over at me and frowned. "I don't have any mimic friends. How am I supposed to learn about my true form or my Trial of Worth if I don't know any other mimics?"

I shrugged. "Does it matter? You're amazing. The best eldrin I've ever had."

"I'm the *only* one you've ever had."

We both chuckled. I continued reading, half my thoughts on Twain's problem. Where would I go to meet more mimic arcanists? I didn't know any personally...

The dorm door slammed open. I sat up on my bed, my back straight and stiff.

Knovak hurried into the room. He went straight for his trunk of clothes and rummaged through everything. He chortled to himself the entire time, more delighted than I had ever seen him.

"Let me guess," I said as I rested back onto my bed. "You finally got invited?"

Knovak grabbed a pile of shirts and trousers and threw them onto his bed. "Exactly, Gray. *Exactly*. I convinced Nasbit to invite me—even though he absolutely refuses to go. Which is fine, because I would love to meet an eligible bachelorette."

I fake clapped for him before returning to my reading.

"Now the most important decision is upon me." Knovak spread out the shirts. "What should I wear?"

"I think you have far greater decisions to make than your choice of clothes," I muttered as I read about the third abyss. "But maybe I'm crazy."

"The Kross Cotillion is almost upon us. There are no other decisions as important as this until then." Knovak stood straight and stared at me. "What're you wearing?"

"When is it?" I asked, ignoring his question.

Had anyone ever told me?

"It's in three weeks."

"Three weeks?" I slid off my bed and stood. "Seriously?" While I wasn't as obsessed with clothing as Knovak, I knew that wearing an appropriate outfit was important. I had thought we had months before this event. *Three weeks?* How could I make enough coin, purchase something, and then have it tailored in that short a timeframe?

"*Now* you're worried." Knovak rolled his eyes. He sifted through his clothing, his frown deepening as he continued. Then he shoved all his outfits onto the floor. "None of this is good enough."

The clop of hooves drew my attention to the window. Starling galloped into the dorm room, his white coat shining in the moonlight. With mystic beauty, the unicorn went straight for Knovak. A hat was perched on Starling's horn—one of Knovak's giant signature pieces.

"My arcanist?" Starling said. "I brought you the one I like the most! I told you I had it in the treehouse."

Knovak glanced over, his hands on his hips. "You took it?"

The unicorn stopped and drooped his head. "Well, I wanted something of yours to keep with me in the treehouse. You have so many hats, I figured you wouldn't miss it..."

Knovak took a deep breath. Instead of yelling at his eldrin, or even being disappointed, he nodded once. "Very good. I don't mind that you took it, so long as you kept it in good shape. That's my *shopping hat*. And I'm going to need it."

"You're going shopping?" Starling tossed the hat onto Knovak's bed. "May I accompany you?"

"Of course. I'll need to leave Astra Academy in order to find a shop with a decent tailor." Knovak snapped his fingers until I gave him my full attention. "You, too, Gray. On our free day, I'm taking you—and I *suppose* your brother—to Anchor Isle."

Anchor Isle?

I had heard of the place, but I had never gone. It was known for its unique marketplace, but that was about it. From what I remembered, the isle was actually quite small.

"Wait," I muttered. "You're *taking* us? Is that what you just said?"

Knovak used his fingers to comb back some of his plain hair. Was it brown? Sandy blond? It was just plain. "You have made quite a show about how you grew up as a candlemaker's son. I assume you're not swimming in coins and banknotes? As a *thank you* for offering advice when I was down, and to better exemplify a noble nature, I figured I would purchase you and your brother a cotillion-suitable outfit."

"We can't just wear our Academy robes?"

Knovak and Starling both laughed. Genuine laughs—like this was a hilarious joke—but I had been quite serious. Once they took deep breaths and calmed themselves, I chortled.

"All right. Shopping it is."

I stood outside the professors' lounge, Twain on my shoulder, my attention on the door handle. I now had an invite, and a plan to get an outfit, but I hadn't yet asked Professor Helmith if I could attend the cotillion. Technically, she had asked that I stay inside the Academy to avoid activating the gate fragments with my presence...

If she told me I couldn't attend the cotillion, I wouldn't. I had no intention of disobeying her, but I deeply hoped she would allow me to go. While this celebration didn't sound *that* amazing, I did want to see Ashlyn and make connections with arcanists who apparently thought I was too lowborn to even bother with.

I would show them that they were wrong.

Someday, I would be an arcanist worth learning about in a classroom.

I knocked on the door.

It opened, and Piper was there, leaning half on the wall. Her long hair spilled over her shoulder like an inky waterfall, and her robes were pulled open slightly in the front, exposing some of the flesh just beneath her collarbones.

The instant she laid eyes on me, Piper straightened her posture. Then she pulled her robes tightly closed.

"What're you doing here?" she asked, her tone bordering on anger.

"I'm a student," I quipped.

Piper narrowed her eyes. "Don't sass me. Why are you here at the professor's lounge?" She huffed and then asked, "Did you see Professor Ren on your way here?"

"No. But I'll tell him you're waiting for him, if you want."

"No. No." Piper stepped away from the door. "That's silly. I wasn't waiting." She motioned to someone else in the lounge. "It's Gray. I think he wants to speak with you."

I patiently waited as Piper moved away from the door and Professor Helmith came to greet me. Her lavender eyes were as bright as ever, and the moment I met her gaze, I couldn't help but smile. Helmith stepped out into the hall with me, her movements delicate. When she closed the door to the lounge, there was no sound.

"Gray?" she asked. "Can I help you?"

"Yeah..." I patted Twain. He purred.

"What's wrong?"

"Well, I was hoping to travel to Anchor Isle with some of my fellow arcanists." Before she could speak, I added, "I know you said I shouldn't travel around, but I figured if I was with everyone, it wouldn't be as much of a problem, and Anchor Isle is so small, there's no way a gate fragment is there, right? I mean, that's silly." I added a forced chuckle at the end, but it only made me sound desperate.

Twain narrowed his eyes at me. His disapproval radiated like heat from his body.

Professor Helmith giggled. "You may go to Anchor Isle."

"R-Really?"

"Yes. Headmaster Venrover has taken it upon himself to find all the nearby gate fragments—either around the Academy or around our Gates of Crossing. He's already gathered a total of thirteen."

Thirteen fragments? Just around here? It really put everything into perspective.

"How?" Twain asked. "Is *he* a twin or something?"

Again, Helmith giggled. She covered her mouth and shook her head as she did so. "No, no. Nothing like that. He's an all-seeing sphinx arcanist. His magic allows him to glimpse the location of people and things, given he has enough time to focus."

"Oh, wow," I muttered.

I would have to remember that, too. What would I need that ability for, though? And how was he using it? It wasn't an evocation or manipulation... Was the all-seeing sphinx's augmentation ability somehow related to finding things?

"So, you may go to Anchor Isle." Helmith tucked some of her hair behind her ear. "And you may go to the Kross Cotillion."

Again, I chuckled—this time more genuine. "You knew I would ask, huh?"

"It doesn't take genius levels of observation to see where the conversation is going."

With a snort and a laugh, I just stared at the floor. "Thanks. I'll try not to get into any trouble."

"I would appreciate that." Professor Helmith turned back toward the door. "If you don't have anything else, I'll be going over my notes for the next few classes. You have a test, remember? Make sure to study."

"I will." I would try. "Thank you, Professor."

On our free day, Knovak led me and Sorin down the grand stairway in front of Astra Academy. The docks in the Academy's lake already had several boats prepped and prepared to take students through one of the Gates of Crossing.

It seemed an expensive way to travel. Every time someone used a gate, they consumed a star shard to activate the magic. As Nasbit had mentioned several times, a single star shard was worth more than a whole family made in a year.

We took the steps at a leisurely pace. Knovak's unicorn clopped alongside him, the clack of the hooves echoing down the mountainside.

Twain, who seemed determined to live on my shoulder, kept his claws hooked into my shirt. Occasionally, he nodded off, but right now, he was wide awake. The morning breeze was crisp and the sun warm.

It was a beautiful morning.

"Wait for me!"

The cry reached us once we were halfway down. We all stopped and turned.

Exie hurried down the steps toward us.

"What're *you* doing here?" I asked.

Sorin shot me a glare.

I cleared my throat. "Uh, I mean, what a pleasant surprise! To what do we owe this pleasure?"

"You're going to drown her in your insincerity," Twain quipped.

We all patiently waited as Exie descended the steps. She slowed her pace as she reached us, her white sundress dirty along the bottom hem. She brushed her dress clean and then smiled. "You can't go to Anchor Isle without me, obviously." Then Exie turned her attention squarely to Sorin. "We have to have matching outfits."

"Uh, all right." Sorin half-smiled and then motioned toward the rest of the stairs.

We walked as a group of four arcanists. Exie's erlking fluttered along behind us, never making a sound. He had feathered wings like a peacock, but they were so small, and flapped so infrequently, it was difficult to hear them.

When we reached one of the two-masted ships, I caught my breath.

There were dozens of arcanists aboard. And not just the arcanists—

their eldrin, too. Several beasts took up the deck of the ship, including several pegasi, a yeti, one bear that half resembled an owl, and three other stone golems. One was a limestone golem, half-gray, half-yellow.

Sorin, Knovak, Exie, and I walked up the gangplank and practically had to push ourselves through the crowd of students. They wore robes of all years, but I didn't see anyone else from our class.

"This is popular," Sorin said. He was the tallest among us, and easily glanced over the heads of the other arcanists. "Is Anchor Isle exciting?"

"Very," Knovak said as he straightened his silk tunic. "You'll see once we arrive."

The ship's crew didn't wait much longer. After a few minutes, they pulled up their anchor and stowed the gangplank. The ship sailed for one of the gigantic silvery gates out on the lake, the winds always filling our sails.

"Nini is okay with everything?" I whispered to my brother, my voice practically lost in the sea of conversations happening all around us.

Sorin leaned down. "Nini forgave me. She's so amazing. She understood why I wanted to help. And she trusts me. And also, we're sweethearts now." His face shifted to a pale pink as he rubbed at the side of his neck.

"Ha!" I elbowed him. "Your *honeysuckle*, you mean."

Sorin wistfully sighed. "Then we shared love's first kiss—a moment cherished, pure and bliss."

I pinched the bridge of my nose. "Why?" I muttered. "Not everything needs to rhyme."

"I couldn't help it." Sorin wrapped an arm around me. "Once you've become a man, you'll understand. It's a special moment."

My irritation silenced me. *Sorin* had kissed a woman before me? My "little" brother? The one spouting off poems as often as he took breath? I sometimes didn't understand the world. Then again, he and Nini had been close for some time...

The gate was large enough for a boat, and it made me realize the gate to the abyssal hells had been just as massive. The fragments... There were probably hundreds of them out in the world.

Once the ship sailed through the ring, we were teleported in a flash of silver, glitter, and a rush of wind.

I blinked back the sensation, my heart pumping. Then I forced my eyes open and glanced around.

The wind was warmer here.

I rubbed my forehead and widened my eyes.

There it was. Anchor Isle. We weren't far at all—the location was only a few thousand feet away. And Knovak was correct—it *was* interesting.

Anchor Isle was a tiny island. It had white sand, a few dunes, and two palm trees. That was it. Several piers were built off the beaches, but the real fascinating design choice came from the ships.

Twenty sailing ships, ranging from one-masted vessels to three-masted vessels, were all permanently anchored to the piers. They were likely decommissioned vessels, or derelict ships—things no one wanted to take out on the waves. But they were now permanent buildings here. Each was tethered to the other.

Bridges were built from the deck of one ship all the way to the deck of the other. Ropes held everything in place. So did posts in the water, and chains hooking the larger ships to the rocks beneath the waves.

"Here we are," Knovak said as he lifted both his arms in dramatic fashion. "That's the *Flotilla Marketplace!* Isn't it amazing?"

"Why is it out here?" I asked.

Normal ships were parked in separate piers. Merchants and traders disembarked and then headed for the anchored ships.

They were...

Shops. Stores. Places to buy and sell goods.

It made me laugh. All these ships were tied together to form a massive marketplace?

"You see, Anchor Isle is so small that it was never claimed by any nation." Knovak smiled as he held a single finger up. "Because of this, no one claims taxes on the goods bought and sold here."

"Why doesn't someone claim it now?" Sorin asked.

"Now that it's worth something, two nations are arguing over who should hold power over it, but they haven't come to an agreement. Therefore, it's still free trading, so we'll enjoy it while we can."

Our ship went for the only open pier. The sailors threw down the anchor and tied off the ship before laying the gangplank. The arcanists of

Astra Academy hurried from the deck and headed for the "bridge roads" of Anchor Isle.

"This is pretty amazing," Sorin said with wide eyes. He walked down the pier with a goofy grin. "I bet we can find some interesting things here..."

"All sorts of illegal things are traded through here," Exie said, her nose wrinkled. She grabbed her fairy and held him close. "That's what my mother says, anyway."

That made me *more* excited for the Flotilla Marketplace. I stayed close to Sorin as we headed for the first decommissioned ship.

I didn't have any coin, but perhaps Knovak could be convinced to help me find a book or scroll on the abyssal hells...

# CHAPTER 32

## THE FLOTILLA MARKETPLACE

As a second-year student marched by—one with a small moon rabbit hopping by her side—I held out my hand to stop her.

"Hey," I said. "Do a lot of students shop here?"

The girl nodded. The arcanist mark on her forehead also had a rabbit, and I wondered what kind of magical abilities she had...

"A lot of merchants stop here to sell smaller quantities of their merchandise." She shrugged as she hurried toward the first ship. "But that means they're gone pretty quick, so you have to go fast."

I allowed her to rush off before I made my way closer to Knovak.

"There's a tailor here?" I asked.

He smiled as he placed a hand on my shoulder. "One of the best, actually." He leaned in closer to me. "Don't tell anyone I said this, but everyone is convinced that Jack is an escapee from a far-off prison, who works here to keep a low profile."

The amount of information I didn't want to hear was staggering.

Sorin grabbed me and pointed to a boat further down the line. "Look! That one is cooking food."

The students of Astra Academy had mostly funneled into the Flotilla Marketplace, leaving us with some space. Exie stood closer to my brother and waved away his comment. "Sorin, we should really head over there."

She pointed to a boat three down. The deck was filled with fine cotton fabrics and silk sashes. "Come, come. We shouldn't stay here any longer than necessary."

Exie practically clapped her hands as she strode forward. Her erlking *did* clap his hands.

Sorin and I exchanged a quick glance. He grimaced as he shrugged, but then he headed out after Exie.

"This way," Knovak said.

Starling stomped his hooves. "Hurry, Gray."

With a sigh, I followed after the man and his unicorn.

We crossed a bridge made of thick rope and wood planks. The creak of the ships, and the walkways, gave me pause, but the bridge held up, even when golems stomped across. We made our way across one deck, and then another.

Everything about the ships had been repurposed to become a better shop or living area. There were stands, shelves, and even walkways down into the holds to show off wares.

"Are there ever storms here?" I asked.

Knovak pointed to the waters just beyond the railing of the ship. Bones jutted out of the waves, some of them as large as the ships themselves.

"That's a leviathan skeleton that has been made into a magical artifact," Knovak said matter-of-factly. "It's set around all of Anchor Isle —the body is so large—and it calms the storms whenever they get near. It'll rain here, but never anything that would destroy the ships."

Whoever owned this island had obviously thought of everything.

Knovak and I crossed another bridge, this one ricketier than the last. It shook as we crossed, and Twain clung to me tighter than ever. Once we were at the "tailor" ship, Knovak headed down into the hold.

"This is Jack's," he said.

Starling had a difficult time going down the narrow steps, but the unicorn refused to give up. Once in the hold of the ship, he glanced around at the myriad of fabrics and sewing materials that hung on the bulkheads of the ship.

"Wow," Starling muttered as he swished his tail.

A man sat at a sewing desk in the back. He stitched a shirt shut as Knovak approached him.

Jack, I assumed.

He wore a red vest studded with sapphires, and a gold chain hung from the pocket down to the belt of his trousers. His tricorn hat had a blue feather. Was it from a blue phoenix? I wondered…

Jack also carried a pair of scissors, a set of needles, and a spool of white thread on his belt. He sat in his chair without any proper posture, his back in a hunch, but he didn't seem to care. His skin was burned dark tan from a lifetime in the sun.

His forehead…

The design was a fairy with a crown.

A queen fairy.

Sure enough, when I glanced up at the support beams built into the deck, I spotted the elusive fairy. Unlike Exie's erlking, this was a female fairy who wore a long golden dress. Most people didn't realize that the "clothes" of fairies were actually part of their body. While the tiny fairy appeared to be a majestic princess, the dress was more akin to scales.

"Oh, what do we have today?" Jack asked, barely glancing up. "Another arcanist from the Gentz family?"

"It's me. Knovak." He stood a little taller. "We've met a few times."

Jack stopped his stitching and gave Knovak his full attention. "Oh. Yeah. I remember you. But… you weren't an arcanist before. As a matter of fact, your mom thought you might never be an arcanist… If I remember correctly."

Knovak stepped close and completely ignored everything Jack said. "We're looking for outfits befitting a cotillion."

"Uh-huh."

"The Gentz family will pay. But I need two."

"What about Sorin?" I asked.

Knovak half-shrugged. "Exie told me she would get Sorin an outfit."

That didn't sit well with me.

Neither did this shop. It seemed shadier than I had first imagined. Was there such a thing as a mass-murdering tailor? Because that was the feeling I got when I glanced around. The scissors were larger than normal, and several pairs hung on the walls. The fabrics were all darker colors—and a lot of them were suspiciously dark red.

The queen fairy watched me with eyes that practically glowed scarlet.

Jack stood from his chair and gathered a measuring tape. Then he motioned Knovak close. Without words, the man took measurements. Then he motioned for the unicorn.

Starling's ears perked up. "Me?"

"You want to match, doncha?"

Starling smiled wide as he pranced over. "Oh, my. I'm so excited."

"You want to wear something?" Knovak asked.

"You wear such magnificent clothing all the time, my arcanist. I want to be more like you."

"O-Oh." Knovak gestured for Jack to continue. "Give Starling whatever he wants."

Once the pirate-tailor was done measuring Starling's neck like he needed to craft a noose, he motioned for me. I hesitantly walked over and complied as the man held up my arms, measured everything twice, and then wrote it all down.

Jack eyed Twain on my shoulder. "What's that?"

"My eldrin," I said. "A mimic."

"Eh. *Mimics*." Jack waved me away. "It gets nothin'. Damn beast will rip up anything I put on it if it transforms."

"That is a true statement," Twain said. "Also, I prefer being naked."

"Don't say that." I shot him a glare. "It sounds weird! Curse the abyssal hells, you're on my shoulder."

"I'm *naked* on your shoulder."

I grabbed Twain. He meowed as I yanked him off my tunic and placed him on the floor. With his orange fur puffed up, he hissed. Then I patted his head and brushed back his fur, calming him down.

"Knovak, you have this handled, right?" I glanced over.

He held a tangle of multi-colored fabrics. "Hm? Oh, yes. I'll pick something out for you."

I eyed the bizarre color choices and then muttered, "Hey, do you know anything about the Kross family? Like, do they have a crest? Or family... flag? Or something?"

I didn't know. Some noble houses had emblems or a crest of arms, but

I had never cared. Most of it was silly, anyway. Who needed an emblem for their family?

Knovak slowly turned his gaze to me. "*Oh*. I get it. No need to worry. I'll make sure you match."

My face heated as I walked over to the staircase. I wanted to look around the Flotilla Marketplace, but without any coin, I wasn't sure what I would do if I found something. I decided to search regardless. What was the harm of looking?

The Flotilla Marketplace buzzed with activity. Twain chased after me as I strode onto another rope bridge. He leapt onto my robes and then clawed his way to my shoulder. I patted him, but he snapped at my fingers, like this was all my fault.

With a chuckle, I glanced at the first shop.

Magical items were on display. Shoes that allowed someone to walk on water. Gloves that improved handwriting. A dagger that cut through stone without effort.

It was all... varied.

"This is all unique," the arcanist watching over the wares stated. "Careful now. Don't touch. We wouldn't want to get the enforcers involved."

"Enforcers?" I asked as I stared at the knife. The blade sparkled like a diamond cut in multiple directions.

"The arcanists who run this little isle. They don't take kindly to thieves."

I nodded once and turned away from her wares.

Made me wonder what kind of arcanists they were. Then an idea struck me. I closed my eyes and felt through the dozens of threads of magic. There were so many arcanists nearby that my choices were damn near endless. What did I want to transform Twain into? Nothing big, since he was on my shoulder, so I picked the moon rabbit.

When I tugged the thread, my mark changed, and so did Twain. He shifted and bubbled, until he morphed into a bright white bunny. His blue eyes sparkled, and his ears twitched.

"What is this?" he said, his voice squeaky.

I shrugged. Then I held my hand over the side of the ship and focused on my magic. "Let's find out." When I used my evocation...

A puff of light and glitter sailed out toward the water.

That was it?

Twain snorted. "I think moon rabbits aren't really *combative* creatures. Don't they bring good luck? You just shot luck magic all over the waves. Gross."

I snorted and laughed. Then I exhaled and strode toward the next ship. The bridges varied in quality, but none of them gave out. I thought I would just head back to Jack's when a ship further down caught my eye. There was a bookshelf positioned in the middle of the deck. Several leather-bound books lined the shelves.

I walked over, pep in my step. Once I was close, I quickly sifted through the titles. Nothing caught my eye.

"What're you looking for?" Twain asked.

"Something about the abyssal hells..."

"Oh! Interesting. I bet you can find unique books here. Nothing you can find at Astra Academy. Or maybe just junk." Twain twitched his ears. "Yeah. Probably junk."

"We should look regardless."

I headed down to the hold. Once down below, I found *several* bookshelves. Smiling the entire time, I ran over to one and began my search.

There were several other arcanists from the Academy here, each reading thin little books. I wondered what they were studying... But I didn't have time to ask. I focused all my attention on the titles of these tomes, trying to find something relevant.

Most were cookbooks.

A few were about preserving dead bodies.

One was about... ancient legends. It was titled: TALES AND LEGENDS FROM A TIME BEFORE TIME.

A "time before time" sounded intriguing. I grabbed the book and flipped through the yellowed pages. It smelled of perfume and grass. I almost sneezed several times as I got deeper and deeper into the text.

Then I found something called *The Tale of Death Lord Calisto*.

I stopped sifting through the book.

Twain glanced down. "I guess that's *close* to the abyssal hells. That's not the right Death Lord, though... It's one of the other ones."

I flipped the page and held my breath.

*The Tale of Death Lord Deimos.*

Fascinated by my find, I dove into the story, barely hearing anyone or anything around me.

But it was short. Painfully, miserably short. It read:

*Deimos was born of the seventh consort of Vyrain, first of twins, their emergence bloody. Forged in the fires of war, Deimos was among the mightiest champions of battle. Undefeated during his time, Vyrain was forced to acknowledge his son's prowess.*

*But the Third Hevron War decimated the empire. Deimos, recorded and witnessed, committed patricide, gutting Vyrain and making his skin into a banner Deimos carried into battle.*

*When Deimos was offered a chance to undertake the sixth abyssal dragon's Trial of Worth, he refused. He stated, recorded and witnessed, that he would only bond with the seventh dragon, as was his destiny and birthright.*

I finished the short tale and flipped the pages, hoping I had missed something.

Nothing. That was it. That was the tale. A bloodthirsty lunatic who fought in a few wars, killed his own father, fashioned said father into a flag, and then bonded with a disease-ridden dragon. Deimos sounded like a real winner.

I slammed the book shut and placed it back on the shelf. A chilly wind blew through the hold. Or maybe that was my imagination.

"That was pretty depressing," Twain whispered.

Everyone on this ship was so quiet. I understood why Twain would want to keep his volume low.

"I didn't learn anything helpful," I murmured.

"You learned that Deimos is trained in battle."

I glared at Twain. "I know. I watched him throw a trident from the back of a dragon with such astonishing accuracy it would make the stars blush."

Twain huffed. "I'm just saying..."

Although there were several bookshelves I hadn't checked yet, another chill sent a shiver down my spine, and I no longer felt motivated to search. Carrying Twain on my shoulder, I went for the stairs and leapt up them two at a time. Dread trickled into my thoughts.

I needed to see my brother.

After a deep breath to calm myself, I headed across a series of rope bridges. Twain held on and purred, his presence comforting. I patted him a few times, and enjoyed the rays of the morning sun.

Everything was fine.

Nothing was here.

I just had to relax.

Why did I feel so cold?

# CHAPTER 33

## THE TRUE TALE OF DEATH LORD DEIMOS

I stumbled across a wood-plank bridge and came to a stop on the deck of a three-masted warship. The cannons were on display, but the barrels were rusted and there were no cannonballs in sight. The stairway down to the lower decks was filled with conversations, and a welcoming glow emanated up, inviting patrons to enter.

I ambled my way over and carefully took the steps.

The cold never left me.

The steps were steep, and I glanced around, searching for my brother whenever I passed a deck. The third one down, I heard Exie's voice. She had a distinct and haughty tone that was hard to ignore.

"I love that one," she said with a giggle. "Really, it's amazing."

They were probably trying on outfits or some nonsense.

I walked down the narrow hall of the third deck and stopped once I heard Exie's voice on the other side of a door.

"Aren't you going to finish it?" Exie asked.

"I don't know," Sorin replied.

I pressed against the door and peered in through a crack. Sure enough, Exie and Sorin were together in a room with trunks upon trunks of clothing. Not only that, but shoes hung from racks on the wall, and accessories were on display in birdcages. Necklaces and bracelets hung from perches, some glinting in the glow of the lanternlight.

"I think you should," Exie said. She sat on top of a clothing trunk, her legs crossed. "You have a real talent for word-smithing. You shouldn't leave something incomplete."

"Well, I tried..." Sorin walked around the room, the shadows dancing around his feet. "I start with... *Her hair, a red, elegant smoke, like the threads of her reaper's cloak...* But smoke? That doesn't seem right. I could say... *Her hair, a red and tangled mess...* But it's never tangled, you know? So it's not even close to reality."

Exie's erlking sat on top of a birdcage, watching with bright eyes and a smile.

Same with Exie. She listened to my brother ramble without so much as a cough to interrupt. Once he was done, she said, "Maybe you should start the poem in a different location? Perhaps something like... *I watch her from afar with awe, her beauty without flaw.* Or something similar." Exie brushed her shimmering hair. "I mean, no girls want to hear about their messy hair."

Sorin nodded once. He rubbed his chin. "Yeah. You're right." He playfully tapped his own forehead. "Think, Sorin. You can't insult her."

"Don't be too hard on yourself. You're doing fantastically."

Fantastically?

I almost couldn't believe my ears.

Did Exie... *actually* like listening to my brother's poetry?

Exie waved her hand, and the messy room became a little more cluttered. Illusionary pictures floated through the air. They were false oil paintings of Nini and her reaper. Exie pointed to one where Nini stood by the walkway to the treehouse. "Here. Look, I have a picture to help you think."

Sorin stopped and examined the floating oil painting. "This is really good. You made this with just your illusions? From memory?"

Exie's cheeks brightened to a pink. She held her head a little higher. "I did, thank you so much for noticing."

"Why don't you make more illusions in class?"

"I have this dreadful fear that the others will mock and ridicule me if I make any sloppy illusions. I'd rather not deal with their judgment."

Sorin huffed a laugh. "Your illusions are amazing. No one would make fun of you. And even if they did, it would only be because they're jealous."

Exie rubbed at her face, a slight smile tugging at the corner of her lips.

"This looks exactly like Nini..." Sorin admired the picture.

And Exie admired Sorin.

I stepped backward, intent on leaving, but the floor creaked underfoot. Twain hissed at it, like the ship had betrayed us.

"Is someone there?" Sorin called out.

I slammed the door open and shook my head at Twain. "That's why we can't fashion two dinghies together to make a mega-dinghy," I said, pretending to have an ongoing conversation. "Oh, hey! I finally found you, Sorin." Then I half-nodded to Exie. "And you, too, I suppose."

Exie narrowed her eyes. "Oh. Gray. What a pleasant surprise." She snapped her fingers, and the oil paintings vanished. "Let me guess? You've come to collect us."

"That's right. Sorry, but... I think I need to return to the Academy."

"*You* need to return?" Exie frowned. "What does that even mean?"

Sorin hurried to my side. He grabbed my upper arm and then examined me. "Are you okay, Gray? Did something happen? Deadly dream monsters? Undead creatures from beyond the abyssal hells?"

"Just a normal day for us," Twain quipped.

"Nothing like that," I said as I yanked from his grip. "I just have a terrible feeling. I really think we should go."

"Okay," Sorin said, no hesitation.

Exie slid off the clothing trunk. With a huff, she headed for the door. "Very well. I already purchased everything we need anyway." She barely glanced in my direction as she exited the room. Her erlking fluttered after her, but only after giving me a side eye.

I wanted to be irritated, but now I just felt bad for Exie.

Sorin gathered her things and walked to the door, his mind likely still on Nini.

Visiting Anchor Isle had been draining. The sun, the sights—it left me tired.

Not Sorin, Exie, or Knovak, though. The moment we returned, the three of them went off to discuss everything they had seen, and the outfits they were planning. I couldn't muster the energy to join them. Cold and exhausted, I returned to the dorm to take a nap.

Twain joined me. He, too, was tired.

When I curled up in my bed, Twain balled himself into the blankets near my feet. After only a moment, I closed my eyes and allowed sleep to take me.

Dreaming...

Again, I found myself lost in a dream.

This time, I floated on the ocean waves just outside Anchor Isle. There were no clouds, no gulls, no storms—just endless blue skies and pleasant waters. With my back submerged in the ocean, and my face and stomach above the water, I stared straight up.

The warmth of the afternoon sun didn't help me, though. I was still cold. And as the dream progressed, the feeling worsened.

Then the voice returned.

"Mimic arcanist," Death Lord Deimos whispered, his gruff words echoing in my ears.

I closed my eyes and said nothing.

"Have you given my words thought?"

"Leave me alone," I whispered.

Deimos chuckled. Again, it felt like his teeth were practically on my ear. I splashed the water, rubbing at the side of my head.

"I know all about you, *Death Lord*." I gritted my teeth and shook my head. "I know who you were born to, and that you killed your father. You're insane. Why would anyone *want* to bond with an abyssal dragon?"

For a long moment, the Death Lord was silent.

When he spoke again, anger iced his words. "Is that all? What a pathetic summation of my life told by someone who lived centuries after my time. *You know nothing of me.*" He lowered his voice as he whispered, "I was born to Mayardi the Harlot, a woman the emperor fancied. He already had a wife and six consorts, but he took whatever, and whoever, he wanted."

I kept my eyes closed and envisioned the words he spoke.

"I shared the womb with my brother, and we were brought into the world together on a river of blood. Our mother barely lived, but our father thought a birth of twins was a weakness. Children who shared the womb are smaller, frailer... or so he claimed. When our mother gave birth a second time, to yet another pair of undersized babes, our father had their skulls bashed in. He said it was the price our mother had to pay for disobeying him."

I held my breath, the sounds of the ocean water fading.

"Disobeying him?" I asked.

"He commanded Mayardi to never again carry twins, yet she did regardless."

What a terrible reason to kill his own infant children.

"When she mourned for her children, our father had her head bashed in as well. Then he sent me and my brother away to die, to train with the warriors of his vanguard, far from his seat of power."

The beat of war drums pounded in my ears. Was I making this up? Or was my dream just taking on aspects of Death Lord Deimos's story?

"I kept us alive from the soldiers, but it was my brother who understood magic. He was an arcanist before me, yet never a warrior like we needed. I learned all manner of weaponry, while he learned to read and write. When war found us, my brother crafted the schemes, and I carried them out. In our first real battle, we encircled the enemy in a canyon, and slaughtered them from all sides. I led the charge—faced the strongest opponents myself, and won the respect of our legion."

The book I had read mentioned the Third Hevron War, but I had never heard of that before. How old was Death Lord Deimos? Too old for me to even picture the battlefields he had fought across.

"My brother insisted I bond with a sovereign dragon—to claim my rightful place as an heir to the empire—but my father wanted me dead." Deimos chuckled straight into my ear. "He knew the grudge I harbored, and he was afraid."

This was a much different story than the one I had read.

"Grudge?" I asked.

"He slaughtered my birthmother, and delighted in the death of my siblings. I made no secret of my hate."

If someone killed Sorin and the rest of my family, no matter the reason, I would never forgive them.

Deimos whispered, "So when I bonded with a sovereign dragon, the emperor reluctantly claimed me as his own. Not my brother—only me. And during the ceremony in the capital, I ordered my legion to burn the city to the ground."

The screams echoed in my ears, as though I could hear the destruction in the capital city from just outside the walls. The roar of flames, the clash of steel... I shuddered.

"During the destruction, I gutted my father and slayed his dragon. With the scales of his eldrin and the skin of that old man, I made a banner *no one would forget.*"

In my mind's eye, I pictured it all.

The red and black scales of a sovereign dragon mixed with the graying, dead flesh of a man. A fabric of death.

Deimos growled. "In my time, the gates to the abyssal hells could be opened and closed. To be chosen to bond with an abyssal dragon meant you would become one with the cycle of rebirth. It was an honor. A privilege. A duty of the highest order."

Bonding with a disgusting dragon was an honor? It didn't feel like it.

"Abyssal dragons were sacred, and so was their charge." Deimos's voice became softer. "Those who bonded with them became Death Lords, the keepers of souls. And once they had served their time in the depths of the abyssal hells, they emerged to the surface to rule with the wisdom they gained among the dead. It was their reward for maintaining the balance in the third abyss—the very middle of the hells. The one abyss that required someone pass judgment."

That made the Death Lords sound... noble.

"I was chosen, and my sovereign dragon took his own life in order to allow me to bond. But after I did, the Death Lords were betrayed." Deimos's anger returned. "The gates were sealed forever to prevent the abyssal dragon arcanists from returning to the surface."

"Why?" I asked.

"The arcanists in the mortal world wanted us to toil in the abyssal hells—suffering a lifetime of misery—and stay there forever. They didn't want to relinquish their rulership, and hand it over to abyssal dragon arcanists. They wanted to forget our place in the cycle. They wanted the abyssal hells to be a land of torment far beyond their thoughts."

None of that surprised me. History was filled with all sorts of betrayals.

This felt worse, somehow. Apparently, Death Lord Deimos was the kind of man who held onto a grudge *forever*.

"Cycle?" I asked.

The ocean waters lapped over me. In an instant, I was pulled under. Fully submerged, I floated downward, away from the light.

Despite the fact that we were underwater, Deimos spoke into my ear with perfect clarity. "Souls enter the abyssal hells. Some are reborn, others are not. The number reborn is dwindling, and the number of abyssal dragons born and thrown into the fourth abyss is staggering. There's no one is here to bond with them. Now they're monsters—elder-creatures who hate all life. This wouldn't have happened if the gates had remained capable of opening."

I struggled in the water, but I couldn't swim upward.

"My brother..." Deimos chortled. "He's the only one who understands. While I was locked away in the abyssal hells, he toiled to help me escape. He communicated with me, formed an organization to bring back the true order of the world. You think I'm evil? I'm insane? You've barely lived a life on this world. *You don't know the lengths I'll go to have my revenge.* I'm owed rulership, and I'm done waiting."

The tides pulled me lower and lower. When panic set in, I flailed.

"Don't you know death follows the rule of threes?" Deimos asked, amusement in his voice. "You'll perish if you go three weeks without food, three days without water, or three minutes without air."

How long had it been since I took a breath?

This was a dream. It was. *It was.*

If I needed, I could transform Twain into an ethereal whelk and save myself. That fact comforted me. As soon as my anxiety waned, I floated back toward the surface of the water. I emerged from the waves, and took in a deep breath.

"Dreams are when you're the closest to death in the waking world," Deimos whispered.

I blinked my eyes. Clouds blotted out the sun. The ocean waters were getting colder. I rubbed my arms and found I was fully clothed in the ocean.

"Mimic arcanist," the Death Lord whispered. "Tell me your name."

"Why?" I said as I coughed up water.

Deimos hesitated before saying, "You know more of me, and the more I know of you, the closer we can come to reaching an understanding."

I shook my head. "My name... is Gray Lexly."

"*Gray.*" Deimos scoffed. "How the standards of naming have fallen."

Although I wanted to make a sarcastic quip, I held back. Instead, I replied with something more earnest. "My mother named right before she died. It's the only gift she gave me, so I'll treasure it forever."

For long moment, Deimos was quiet, but his presence wasn't gone. The ocean waters grew icy.

"Ah. I see," Deimos eventually said. "Your mother is already in the abyssal hells. Died in childbirth. How unfortunate for you... Very fortunate for me."

I shot up, my heart pounding. My blankets strangled me, and I fought to free myself. Twain meowed, and it wasn't until I was free that I managed to gulp down air.

"Gray?" Twain hopped around the dorm floor, his back arched, his fur on end. He hissed and spat and spun around, but there was nothing to direct his ire at. "W-What's going on?"

I wiped my face of sweat.

It was a dream.

I glanced around the room. Everything was as it should be. Nothing out of place. Just me, Twain, and a bunch of empty beds. Sorin, Knovak, and Raaza would return soon. I didn't need to panic.

"Sorry," I said, my voice shaky. "I've been having a lot of nightmares lately." I scooped up my eldrin and hugged him close.

"Not with any soul catchers, though, right?" Twain twitched his ears.

"No. Just... normal nightmares." I exhaled. "I should probably stop reading so much stuff about Death Lord Deimos. My subconscious can't stop focusing on the man."

Twain un-puffed himself and then yawned. "Yeah. Probably."

I sat on the bed. "Let's... go back to sleep. I'm sure things will look better in the morning."

# Chapter 34

## Persistent

S now fell beyond the edge of Astra Academy.

It was an odd sight to see. The flurry of snowflakes landed on the trees and rocks just outside the Academy, but never on the buildings or the shrubbery itself. We were in a bubble of fair weather, protected from the elements. The winds still howled by the windows, and occasionally we had rain that pattered the roofs, but the extremes— storms, snow, hail—never touched us.

It reminded me of the leviathan bones around Anchor Isle.

Did Astra Academy have the same protections? Or did we have something else?

Between classes, I noticed more and more students discussing the Kross Cotillion. Apparently, second-, third-, fourth-, and fifth-year students weren't invited unless they hailed from specific families. Cotillions were for younger arcanists, and that seemed to disappoint a lot of the older ones.

History and Imbuing with Piper was just as dull as the other days. Today was extra special, because she wasn't here. Instead, her eldrin, Reevy, sat on the front desk, watching us. He kept his forearms crossed, and his eyes half-lidded in irritation.

"You *will* be tested about the information on page three hundred,"

Reevy muttered.

It was interesting having a rizzel as an instructor. He was so small, his voice didn't carry far into the classroom. And when he impatiently tapped his foot, it sounded like someone softly poking the desk.

His white fur and silvery stripes were beautiful, though. No dirt or smudges anywhere on his small ferret-like body.

The room was so quiet that when Brak shifted its weight from one boulder foot to the next, it sounded like a rockslide. Everyone glanced over their shoulders, and the stone golem bowed its head slightly, as if to apologize.

Nasbit patted Brak's arm. "It's okay, buddy. It wasn't your fault."

The stone golem lifted its arm made of stones and pressed a rock hand gently on Nasbit's back. Brak "massaged" Nasbit while the man read his book.

Most everyone else's eldrin were asleep. Ecrib was curled up in the back of the room, his fins twitching as he dreamt. Phila's coatl was coiled on top of him, as cute as a snake could be. Miko, the adorable kitsune, sat in the corner, her breathing even, the flames on her feet mere embers.

Even Starling the unicorn was barely keeping his eyes open. He sat next to Knovak at his table, yawning more than once.

Nasbit raised his hand.

Reevy sighed. "Yeah?"

"Where is Professor Jenkins?"

"Just call her *Piper*, and she's not here. Obviously." The rizzel huffed. "What? I'm not good enough for you? I'm not big enough?" He puffed his little chest. "I have this class under control, thank you very much."

"Uh, that's not it... I just wanted to ask Piper a question." Nasbit frowned. "Can I call her *Professor* Piper, at the very least? It seems disrespectful to just address her by her first name."

Brak continued to massage Nasbit, never stopping even as he had a conversation.

"Look..." Reevy glanced at the door and then back to the class. He lowered his voice as he said, "You didn't hear this from me, but Piper doesn't want to be referred to as *Jenkins* anymore because she married into that family, and now she wants to... disassociate with it."

Exie perked up, her eyes wide. "Oh, my. What a scandal." She leaned forward and smiled. "What happened?"

Reevy stomped a single foot. "That's really not the point."

"Did she have an affair? Is she being kicked out?"

With a glare that could kill, Reevy stared at Exie. His fur stood on end as he growled, "My arcanist would never do that! It was her mate who betrayed her, thank you very much. If I could, I'd throw him into the abyssal hells, but since Piper married into *his* family, she's the one who is shunned! Unfair. Disgusting. I'm angry all over again thinking about it."

Wow. This was a lot of information about Piper's personal life that I hadn't cared to learn. That sounded rough. And explained her drinking problem. And her general lack of enthusiasm lately.

I raised my hand.

Reevy practically hissed as he turned his attention to me. "Curse the abyssal hells... No more questions about my arcanist!"

"Oh, I wanted to know if you knew anything about the *Third Hevron War*?" I asked. "I mean, Piper is the history professor, and you're her eldrin... Maybe you know?"

"It's the last of the Hevron Wars," Reevy stated matter-of-factly. "Hevron fought against Tharage, and when Tharage finally lost, their cities were razed and their lands charred into a desert. But that was over two millennia ago."

Phila brushed some of her hair back. "Tharage was turned into a desert, huh?" She lifted an eyebrow. "How did that happen?"

Reevy held up a forepaw and then squeezed it into a tight fist. "Hevron took no prisoners, yielded no ground, and showed no mercy. Their anger was as cold and harsh as the iron of their weapons. *Hevron charred the lands of their enemies so thoroughly, they became wastelands of sand.*" Reevy lowered his paw and shrugged. "That's a direct quote from historians of the time."

That seemed to fit with the Deimos of my dreams. The man seemed... thorough. In everything. Especially his revenge.

"Anything about Deimos?" I asked. "The Death Lord."

The whole class went silent. Everyone knew about my run-in with the man, so why was this a shock? They all should've known this was coming.

"Deimos... I don't know anything about him." Reevy rubbed his tiny nose. "Those wars were a long time ago. The heroes and generals and warlords of those battles are probably long forgotten. Even Hevron no longer exists. It fell apart, and its lands are now a part of different nations."

I turned to my brother, ready to ask him something, when a pop of air and puff of glitter heralded Reevy's sudden appearance on my table. He *poofed* in front us, his ears up, his eyes narrowed. His teleportation had startled me. I leaned back, and he glared harder. His little angry expression was quite cute, but I doubted he wanted me to say that.

"This is reading time," Reevy growled. "If all you *cheese wheels* don't stop talking and asking questions, my whole afternoon will be ruined." He threw his little paws up in the air. "Think of my peace and quiet! You're killing it right now."

With a chuckle, I returned my attention to the book. "Yeah, yeah. It's fine. Sorry I disturbed the peace."

Then I stared at the pages of my book and dwelled on my dreams.

Perhaps Professor Helmith would know what to do.

I sat on my bed in the dorms, listening to the sounds of night just beyond the window. The hooting of owls amused me. What were they doing out there?

I tried to focus on the books I had checked out of the library, but nothing was helping. I was gathering information, but was any of it useful? War record after war record... What was I even looking for? Confirmation that Deimos was a warrior? I already knew that. What else was there to find?

What could I use against him? Or the abyssal hells? Perhaps it would be best to push it all from my mind and just focus on my studies. Once I became a better arcanist, I would have the tools to handle this. Currently, I was still weak. Twain maintained a new form for less than fifteen minutes, and I still hadn't mastered all the basic magic functions.

The door to the dorm slammed open, and Knovak stepped in with a small wooden chest held in his hands. It was the length of an arm, and nearly a foot deep. Knovak placed the chest on his bed and threw open the lid.

"Aha! Just as I suspected. Our outfits have arrived."

Starling clopped into the room a moment later, swishing his ivory mane from side to side. "Is my garment in there? I'm a majestic unicorn, and unicorns deserve majestic clothing."

"I suspect so." Knovak closed the door and smiled. "I've never seen a unicorn in anything other than armor, so this will be a treat."

I slid off my bed, careful not to disturb Twain. My little mimic was asleep on the tippy top of my pillow, his whole body curled like a loaf of orange bread.

He was adorable.

Then I walked down to meet Knovak. The man carefully removed every single piece of clothing from the chest and laid them across his bed in a careful fashion. He counted everything and then turned to me with a frown. "Are you ready to try everything on?"

I shrugged. "Sure."

"Good. Because these are yours. A vest, shirt, long cloak, and a pair of trousers. I thought Jack would've crafted you some gloves, but apparently not." Knovak held up a finger. "But if you need some, I have extra."

"You have extra *gloves?*" I huffed a laugh. The only time I had worn gloves was when handling large animals. Who wore gloves to a celebration?

"Here, Starling." Knovak tied a vest collar around the unicorn's neck, and then fastened a bow around the base of the horn. "This is your outfit."

The foal pranced around in front of us, his long, thin legs lifting high with each step. "Do I look dapper?" he asked.

"Very," Knovak replied.

I nodded once. "Dapper. Sure. It suits you."

While Knovak and his eldrin complimented each other, I headed for the door.

"Gray? Where are you going?"

I stopped once I grabbed the handle. "I want to shower. I'll change in the bathing rooms. Okay?"

"Very well. Just make sure you show me the results."

With my new outfit in hand, I headed for the bathing rooms. The Academy was mostly quiet, since it was just before curfew, but I wanted more time to myself. Sorin and Raaza would return to the dorms soon, after all. Showering and then changing gave me more time to be lost in my thoughts.

Perhaps I was overthinking things, though.

Headmaster Venrover was a powerful arcanist. He was already locating some of the gate fragments. And my discussions with Deimos were just dreams obviously brought about by my obsession with what was going on.

I barely saw anything as I stepped into a shower and blasted myself with semi-cold water.

My thoughts swirled in my head. I didn't want to rely on everyone else to solve this. The gate exploding was my doing, and the fragment that had gone into my hand...

I glanced at my palm as water ran over me.

Was it even there anymore?

I stepped out of the water and pulled on my new clothes. Silk felt amazing against my bare skin. The entire outfit was an icy cloud gracefully rippling over my body. For a long moment, I just rubbed myself, surprised by how much I enjoyed the sensations.

I probably looked ridiculous.

But I didn't care.

The vest was white, but the shirt and the pants were black. The pocket of the vest had an odd symbol stitched into it. A moon, a star, and an *X*. What was that? I rubbed at the symbol. It was interesting, to say the least.

When I observed myself in a mirror, I nodded once.

"Who's looking dapper now?"

My voice echoed in the large and empty bathing room. It made me flush with embarrassment when I realized I was just speaking to myself.

I did look good, though. The outfit made me appear more muscular than I was. Somehow. The magic of well-tailored clothes, I suspected.

All by myself, and with my old clothes in my arms, I stepped out of the bathing room.

A thought struck me as I turned to head for my dorms. Instead of returning to Knovak, I went straight for the girls' dorms. I already knew what Knovak would say, but it wasn't his opinion I cared about.

When I reached the room where Ashlyn stayed, I knocked on the door.

Phila answered, her eyes wide, her expression gentle. She wore a long nightgown made of feathery white material. She smiled, and then her gaze investigated me from shoulders to boots. "Oh. Gray. How lovely of you to visit. Are you looking for Nini? Because she's still out with Sorin."

It was late for that, but I trusted my brother. He was probably just singing to her or something.

"I'm here for Ashlyn," I said.

"Oh. I'll tell her."

Phila shut the door. I wished she would've let me inside. I hadn't seen the girl's dorm before. It honestly intrigued me, though I knew it was against the rules.

When the door opened a second time, it was Phila again. "Ashlyn said she'll meet you out on this floor's eastern balcony, just beyond the sitting area. Do you know it? Near the fireplace."

"I can find my way," I said.

"She'll be there in a few minutes."

That was strange, but she probably had to change or something else. I had disturbed her right before bed, obviously. I offered Phila a bow and then went straight for this mysterious balcony. The fireplace before the door outside was quite massive, which made it easy to locate.

I pulled open the door, stepped out into the night air, and closed the door with some effort afterward.

The twinkle of stars kept the balcony illuminated. The massive redwood treehouse, with dozens of eldrin, was just around the corner. One of the tree's branches wrapped around the Academy and went over the balcony, the bark walkway practically creating an overhang.

The Academy seemed alive sometimes. Organic. When I stared up at the branch, I wondered what had been done to get such a massive tree to grow this way—to intertwine with the stone walls and not destroy them.

I dropped my old clothes near the door and then walked over to the railing. It was too dark, and the mountain valley too far away, for me to see the ground. It was like standing at the edge of a dark ocean.

The door opened, and I turned around.

Ashlyn stepped out onto the balcony.

# CHAPTER 35

# FIRST SON, SECOND DAUGHTER

Ashlyn wore a surprisingly crisp outfit of tight, white trousers, and an even tighter black shirt. Her hair was neatly tied in a ponytail, exposing her neck, and I wondered if she had carefully done her hair before coming out to see me.

I had never seen her in such a curvy outfit.

With a smile, I stood straight and held out my arms. "Ta-da. How do you like my new outfit?"

Ashlyn looked me up and down, her blue eyes stopping on the odd symbol on the vest pocket. Then she sauntered over to the railing and rubbed her chin. With a sarcastic *hmmm*, she circled her finger through the air, silently asking me to twirl.

I complied.

Why not? I wasn't a very good show pony if I didn't put on a show.

"Don't keep me waiting for your verdict," I said as I finished my twirl and faced her.

Cold night air blew over the Academy, but it wasn't too chilly. I stopped myself from shivering, but I did step closer to Ashlyn.

We were alone out on the balcony. Just the two of us.

"I like it," she eventually said. "But why do you have my family's crest on your outfit? I mean, it's flattering, but odd. Everyone will ask you about it."

I pointed to my vest. "Is that what this is? I didn't know."

Ashlyn huffed a laugh. "Oh, I see. It was all a surprise."

"Knovak did it for me."

"Why would he do that?"

I stepped closer. Only a few inches kept us apart. Ashlyn never backed away or even avoided my gaze. She had this hard look about her, like she was daring me to get closer—daring me to try something.

It was hard to articulate the feelings she stirred in me.

But I liked them.

"I asked Knovak to give me an outfit that fit with the whole *Kross family aesthetic*." I shrugged. "I thought it would be cute if we matched."

Ashlyn chuckled, her smile refreshing. "That's mighty bold of you to think I would want to dance with a man who wore a matching outfit."

"What can I say? I'm a bold guy."

Her smile faded as she locked gazes with me. For an uncomfortable amount of time, she said nothing. The way her eyes searched mine, I knew she wanted to speak, but it seemed difficult for her. Finally, right before I moved, she whispered, "But are you bold enough, I wonder?"

Everything was a challenge with her. Even *this* felt like a dare.

She didn't think I would make a move.

She was wrong.

I leaned forward. We were almost the same height, and she wasn't that far down. But I still slowed as my lips neared hers. With my eyes half shut, I waited. Ashlyn didn't move. She didn't close the distance, but she didn't protest.

She was beautiful, especially as she fluttered her eyes closed.

I pressed my lips against hers, surprised by the warmth. Everything about her consumed my thoughts. Her sweet scent, the way she brought a hand up to the side of my neck, holding me in place for a moment longer.

When I slowly pulled away, I touched the hand she had on my neck.

"Gray," Ashlyn whispered. Then she dropped her gaze to her boots. "I..."

"What is it?" I asked, keeping my voice low.

Ashlyn exhaled, her shoulders slumping. "Gray... This..."

I forced myself to smile. When she didn't respond, I lifted an eyebrow. "What's wrong? Do I ruin all other men for you?"

She laughed once and then looked up at me. "I can't be with you."

I removed my hand from hers and then took a step back. The words twisted in my thoughts, and I wondered—for a split second—if this was because I wasn't good enough for her. Being lowborn was too much of a disgrace.

Ashlyn crossed her arms and half turned away. "I'm betrothed to someone. My father made that decision a few weeks ago. Right before we went camping." She didn't look at me. "I'm sorry. I couldn't think of a way to tell you."

"Seems pretty easy to say, actually," I said, trying to keep my anger in check.

"Okay, I didn't *want* to tell you," Ashlyn replied, her voice growing louder and hotter. "But there's no hiding it anymore. Everyone will find out at the cotillion."

The winds sailed by again. The night air smelled of damp earth. Owls hooted in the distance, but it wasn't enough to distract me from my mounting anger. I took a moment to pace beside the balcony railing.

That didn't help.

"I'm sorry," Ashlyn said again, this time her voice growing quieter.

I stopped pacing and faced her. "And that's it, then? You're going to marry someone? Who is he? Have you even met him?"

Ashlyn shrugged. "His name is Valo Fitzroy, and I met him when I was ten. I don't remember the meeting. He was just *there*."

"Why?" I demanded. "Why marry him?"

"My father thinks he'll make an important addition to the family." Ashlyn had spoken every word through one continual sigh. Then she rubbed her face. "My father... he really wants the Kross family to become powerful. He wants people to marry in... To make *us* stronger."

"And you're okay with that?"

Ashlyn glared at me. "I didn't say that."

"But you're going to marry him, aren't you? Seems like you're okay with it."

She stormed over to me, her anger manifesting in slight bits of lightning that flashed around the balcony, crackling like sparks. Her typhoon dragon magic was powerful—all dragons were—and it seemed whenever she got too angry, her evocation had a life of its own.

"*You don't know what you're talking about,*" Ashlyn said, on the verge of shouting. "You have *no idea* the standards I have to live up to, and all the pressures I have to make sure I'm not an embarrassment. My *brother* had an arranged marriage, and he never complained. My father and mother both believe Valo is an amazing arcanist with skills beyond my imagining. What should I say? Should I forsake my family just because they arranged a talented suitor for me? Is that what I should do, Gray?"

I didn't have a response for that. My stepmother and father didn't have any influence over my life now that I was attending Astra Academy.

Ashlyn turned on her heel, her body tense. In a harsh whisper, she said, "I've given thought to running away."

"Really?" I asked.

"But where would I go?" She shook her head. "I'm just being childish. My family is powerful, and wealthy, and... and what am I even complaining about?" Her gaze fell, and so did her shoulders.

All the lightning crackling through the air ceased.

After a powerful exhale, Ashlyn said, "I'm sorry. I... really like you." She half-smiled, but she didn't look at me. "I know this sounds stupid, but you're one of the few people who consistently make me laugh. I look forward to spending time with you. I don't have that with a lot of people. They're always... lying to me. Pretending. They just want something from me."

My chest filled with both agony and butterflies, the tiny insects battering their way out of my body. Why did she have to tell me all this if she was going to go through with marrying a man she didn't even know?

Perhaps she wanted me to try harder.

I gently grazed my fingers up her shoulder to the base of her neck. Only then did she glance over.

"You're amazing," I said. "No one will deny that. And..." I chuckled to myself. "You want to know what's really childish? I liked you since the first time I heard your name. Ashlyn. *Ash.* The gray flecks left over after a fire... I thought we matched in that aspect."

I had never met anyone who shared my name. But *Ash* was the closest

to *Gray* I had heard. And I liked it. It was like a beautiful sign. Good luck
—or perhaps an omen, since she was destined to marry another.

Ashlyn shook her head. She stepped away from me and walked to the
door of the balcony. "Gray. I'm sorry." She placed her hand on the handle
and waited. When no more words came, she just entered the Academy and
left me alone out in the cold night air.

I walked back into the dorm room, my body numb as I contemplated
solutions to my unusual problem.

Raaza, Knovak, and Sorin had all returned. Each of them sat on their
own bed, quietly reading—or in Knovak's case, sorting through his many
outfits.

"Gray!"

Knovak leapt from his bed and hurried over. His unicorn
accompanied him, and the two surrounded me the instant I was two feet
into the room.

"You look dashing," Knovak said as he examined me. "Jack did an
amazing job. And the colors match the Kross family. I bet you like
that, hm?"

I nodded once. "The outfit is great." But I couldn't offer any more
enthusiasm than that. "Thank you, Knovak. I appreciate the time."

My brother knew me too well. The moment I spoke in a melancholy
tone, Sorin stood from his bed. He walked to my side, his brow furrowed.
He grabbed my shoulder and examined me, obviously disregarding my
fancy new garment and only searching for some sort of injury.

"What's wrong?" he asked.

Knovak frowned. "What do you mean, *What's wrong?* Look at him.
He's great."

"Did something happen?" Sorin asked, ignoring Knovak completely.
He lowered his voice as he added, "I'm here for you. Just say the word."

I jerked out of his grip. "It's nothing, Sorin. Don't be dramatic."

"You're never like this unless it's serious."

"Like what?" Knovak interjected, clearly not understanding.

I pushed my way past my brother, Knovak, and Starling. Why were they so demanding? Couldn't they just leave me alone? I had to think. Nothing was over yet—I could think of a way to solve this if I just had enough time.

"Gray," Sorin said, his tone low.

I turned on my heel. "Fine. You want to know what's the matter? The girl I care for is going to marry someone else. There. You have it now. Everyone happy?"

Sorin stared at me for a long, silent moment. "But... Professor Helmith is already married."

Knovak frowned at my brother. "He's talking about Ashlyn."

"Oh," Sorin muttered. "She's already getting married? Interesting."

Raaza, who hadn't gotten off his bed, just watched me with an emotionless expression. The scars that marred his face almost looked like waxy blemishes in the dim illumination of the glowstones overhead.

"You know, you wouldn't have these problems if you just focused on your studies and training," he said, disinterest thick in his tone.

"I didn't ask you." I stormed past his bed and headed for my own.

"Pathetic melodrama like this is why you're struggling with tests and quizzes. First the problems in the basement, and now all this courtship nonsense."

Knovak held up a finger. "Wait a moment. One of the reasons to attend Astra Academy is to find someone of quality to wed. Everyone knows that."

"Nonsense."

"It's true. Think about it. Major houses want to add talented arcanists to their ranks. Lowborn arcanists want to join powerful houses. If you *aren't* involved in some sort of courtship, you're a fool."

Raaza clicked his tongue. "Tsk. I'd rather focus on what's important. Listening to the Lexly twins have relationship troubles every other night is exhausting."

"For the record, I'd like everyone to know I *don't* have any problems." Sorin glanced around between us. "Nini and I are sweethearts. Officially."

"You should have stuck with Exie." Raaza rolled over onto his side, showing his back to the rest of the room. "At least she's a noble with beauty and wealth. You gain nothing by courting the reaper girl."

No one responded to his statement, but I knew Sorin didn't care for it. Instead of engaging further, I took a seat on my bed. Sorin jogged over and lay on his bed directly next to mine. No matter what problem I was going through, my brother wanted to be there for me, which I was thankful for.

"Will you be okay?" he asked.

I nodded once. "Yeah. I already have a plan to solve this mess."

"Really? What is it?"

I glanced over my shoulder and half smiled. "I just have to convince Ashlyn's father I'm more talented than *Valo Fitzroy*."

# CHAPTER 36

## DREAM MEETING

I n the morning before Helmith's class, I arrived at the classroom early.

She sat at the front desk, seemingly all alone, but I knew better. Her ethereal whelk hid in the light of the room, effectively invisible, but present. I walked over and smiled, and Professor Helmith glanced up, her purple eyes catching the morning sun just right and sparkling.

Helmith wrote some notes in a small notebook, her handwriting elegant. I didn't know what she was doing, but she stopped as I entered the room. With Twain in my arms, I approached her desk.

"Gray," she said. "How are you?"

"Good, good." I nervously chuckled. "I'm glad you're here early, though. I wanted to speak with you."

Professor Helmith set her pencil down and pushed the notebook to the side, giving me her full attention. "About what?"

"Do you know much about abyssal dragons? As in... are they progeny creatures? That have eggs or something? Or fable creatures? Like they're born from some sort of circumstance."

Helmith shook her head, her eyebrows knitted. "No, I apologize. Most comprehensive studies of mystical creatures don't have any information on abyssal dragons. They aren't around for us to observe. Why do you ask?"

"W-Well..." I couldn't stop myself from sounding anxious, even though I didn't want to seem unsteady in front of Helmith. "In one of my dreams, I was talking with Death Lord Deimos. And he was angry, because he was saying the cycle of rebirth, and the balance of the abyssal hells, or something, was ruined because the gates were closed. He mentioned the abyssal dragons, and how more were being born, but they had nowhere to go."

The quiet of the early morning settled in around us. For a long moment, Helmith said nothing. She smoothed her silky black hair and then turned her gaze to the desk.

"Is everything okay?" I asked.

"You've been speaking with Death Lord Deimos?" Helmith whispered as she brought her gaze back up to mine.

"Well, not the *real* him. That would be impossible." I shrugged.

Twain snorted. "Remember when monsters in your dreams hurt you in real life? I feel like nothing is impossible."

Professor Helmith frowned. "If you believe it's a normal dream, why ask me?"

"I don't know," I muttered. "As soon as he said it, I thought it had some legitimacy. What *is* happening to all the new abyssal dragons? In my dream, Deimos said they were becoming elder-creatures, or monsters, basically, and I wanted to know if that was real or if my imagination is just... running wild."

Helmith stood from her chair. Then she strode around her desk and pointed me toward my desk. I said nothing as I took a seat. Professor Helmith walked over to my side and stood next to me, her movements fluid, but serious.

"I think I should see your dreams," she said.

I placed Twain on the table. "Right now? Or later tonight? When I'm sleeping."

"It'll only take a moment."

Professor Helmith reached out and touched the side of my face. The instant her fingers grazed my skin, a tingle ran through my body. Then my eyelids grew heavy, and my breathing even. I set my head down on the top of the table, and Twain just watched me with wide eyes as I drifted into a forced sleep.

I, paradoxically, awoke in a dream.

The mists of a waterfall floated along with the wind. I sat up in a green field of perfectly cut grass adjacent to a river that ran over a distant cliffside. The water in the air created rainbows that reminded me of the three waterfalls by Red Cape.

And of Ashlyn.

I shook the thought from my mind as I glanced around.

Professor Helmith sat next to me. I hadn't seen her at first, and I flinched when I realized how close she was.

"P-Professor," I muttered.

She turned her attention to our surroundings. Everything was perfect. The clouds were fluffy, the weather calm, and the distant forests were a vibrant green I had only ever seen in my dreams. She was a master painter when it came to creating a dreamscape for us to relax in.

A flock of butterflies with orange-and-black wings took to the sky.

"Deimos?" the professor called out. "If you're here, show yourself."

But no one answered.

I rubbed my ear, half-expecting him to speak, but there was nothing.

When the silence stretched on, Helmith turned to me. "Hm. I don't sense anything."

I shrugged. "I probably made it up. All I do know for sure is that he said a few things that made me wonder. I'm sorry. I didn't mean to waste your time."

"You're never a waste of my time, Gray."

My face heated, and I glanced away, pretending to be enthralled by the butterflies. "I just have an overactive brain, I suppose."

"Or perhaps the Death Lord is communicating with you some other way. I'm not sure how, but we know he must've been in contact with Zahn." Helmith exhaled. "I think it might be time that Headmaster Venrover improved the defenses of Astra Academy."

I snapped my attention to her. "For me? That seems... excessive."

"I'll speak with him about it once he returns. It's not just about you. It's about everything that's happening. I'm worried this problem will grow like the choking weeds of a mire." She grabbed a lock of her hair and played with it.

"What about your father? Do you think he can help?"

The butterflies fluttered all around us. They made no sounds—they were tiny and featherweight—but they tickled my nose and ears as they landed on me.

"Dad has already left," Helmith whispered. "He's a busy man, and he is more of a warrior than someone who would unravel the mysteries of the abyssal hells. I think I will need to call a different expert to help us."

I huffed a laugh. "Hasn't Astra Academy trained someone?"

"We do have a few alumni... But I wonder if they'll answer my summons." Before I could say anything more on the matter, Helmith glanced over with a smile. "But you really shouldn't worry, Gray. You need to focus on your studies. I will look into abyssal dragons, and you will free yourself of these troublesome thoughts, understood?"

"What if the Death Lord is actually speaking to me?" I whispered.

"For the time being, let's assume it's your fears getting the better of you. From now on, I will manipulate your dreams. You won't hear his voice while my magic protects you. All right?"

I nodded once, and a dozen butterflies floated off my head and shoulders. "All right. Thank you, Professor. For everything."

Professor Ren's class was always a surprise.

The man wasn't even pretending to be modest anymore. He wore his button-up shirt and robes fully open as he strode around the classroom, his hands tucked into his pockets. His many silver earrings always caught my eye as he walked by, more so than the glittery rune tattoos he had on his body.

Today, each student had their own pestle and mortar with them at their table. Professor Ren had passed out chunks of occult ore, and we all had to grind them up into a fine dust.

"This dust is what's used to create the magiborne runes you see on my body." Ren motioned to his chest and shoulders. The swirls of fire were bright. "*Enchant* is the verb, and *rune* is the noun. So, when you talk about these in academia, you would say, *I enchanted myself to have firebrand runes.*" He held up a finger. "They're *magiborne* runes because they only work on living things."

The rough grate of rocks in bowls made it difficult to hear him properly. The constant scraping filled the air of the classroom with a fine dust that also had people sneezing on the regular. It was an odd class.

To make things more interesting, Professor Ren's eldrin, the creepy spider, Trove, would sometimes go completely silent. It scuttled from one location to the other, click-clacking across the stone, but then it would be dead silent, like none of its needle-like legs were even touching the floor.

Bizarre.

"Think of it like this," Professor Ren said as he sauntered over to Ashlyn's table. "You use star shards to imbue inanimate objects with permanent magic, and we use occult ore to enchant living objects with permanent magic. Get it? Yes? Good. Everyone understands."

Nasbit breathed heavily as he crushed his ore. "Uh, Professor Ren? What, uh, do your magiborne runes do?"

Ren quirked a half-smile as he touched a red rune across his arm. "Well, this is from a true form phoenix arcanist. And this one here is from a salamander arcanist. You see, I now have minor fire abilities alongside my treasure cache spider magic. Unfortunately, while I can improve my natural magic—making it more potent through training—I can't improve the magic within these runes."

"Could someone..." Nasbit ground up more ore and grunted. "Have *all* magical abilities on them? If they got enough runes?"

"First off, the runes take up physical space on your body—the stronger the magical ability you want, the larger the rune." Professor Ren pulled his robes and shirt open even wider, showing everyone that none of his runes overlapped.

Exie and Phila both glanced up from their work, both of them with flushed cheeks and coy smiles. Ashlyn rolled her eyes. Not at the professor, but at the other two girls. When I glanced over at Nini, she was half-hiding in her overcoat, like Ren's gesture was somehow frightening. That was probably the most puzzling reaction anyone had to the professor's complete lack of shame.

"Additionally," Ren continued, "just like some objects can't handle a vast amount of magic being imbued into them, most human bodies will reject magic being grafted to it at a certain point. So, you should think long and hard about permanent magical enhancements you would want before you go through the process of enchanting yourself with magiborne runes." He smoothed his clothes back over his body.

"The occult ore only started appearing recently, correct?" Nasbit sat a little taller. "It only showed up after the last God-Arcanists War? Can you tell us about that?"

Professor Ren half-smiled. In an overly dramatic tone, he said, "So, during the war, there was a *blood plague* that spread from arcanists to mystical creatures. It drove people insane—turned them into monsters. But the god-arcanists changed the very nature of the plague to be beneficial."

The entire class paid a little more attention than before. Even Exie seemed intrigued by the professor's words, not just his body.

"The plague transformed into magiborne runes, which, as far as we can tell, infected the very planet." Ren waggled his fingers. "And that's how the ore manifests."

"Because the world is infected?" Phila asked as she raised a hand to her mouth.

"Basically." Professor Ren shrugged. "It's a theory. The ore didn't appear until after the war ended and the plague disappeared. All creatures infected with the plague just had blank runes on them. You can still find those, but they're rare. Now we need ore."

Raaza stopped grinding and lifted his head. "Does the Academy offer enchanting services?"

"Artificer students, as part of their education, will enchant or imbue things for a fee." Professor Ren motioned at him to continue. "Which is why you're making this fine powder. For them to use."

I sneezed and then rubbed my nose. Twain sniffled and also sneezed. My brother caught his breath, but he managed to hold back. That caused

Nini to giggle, and I was glad to see she was no longer hiding in her clothing like a nervous hermit crab.

"Professor?" I asked.

Ren strode over to my table and lifted an eyebrow.

"Do you think there's a rune that would be best against things like... the Death Lords?"

After a quick huffed laugh, Professor Ren shrugged. "Well, I suppose there are mystical creatures in the world that ward off death. If you found, maybe, something undead that had an augmentation against poisons and killing touches. Have you heard of a *grim reaper?* They're a variant of the standard reaper, and have weapons that kill on contact."

That sounded awful.

I just blinked at him and shook my head.

Ren smiled. "Grim reapers aren't really friendly chaps. Might be hard to convince one of their arcanists to help you."

"I didn't say I needed help." I returned to grinding up the ore. "I was just curious."

The professor walked up to the front of the room. His spider hid behind his desk, his clicking legs mostly quiet, especially when the room was drowned by the sound of ore being crushed.

"Most arcanists think long and hard about a rune that would complement their current skill set with their own magic." Professor Ren snapped his fingers, and a small burst of embers fluttered from his fingertips. "You see, treasure cache spiders don't have a powerful evocation. They evoke *webs.* They're sticky. They make great traps. But they don't hurt anyone. With my runes, I have a slight ability to evoke flames. I've given myself options to defend myself."

Raaza shot his hand up into the air.

Ren turned around and gestured to him.

"What's the most offensive evocation you can think of?" Raaza asked. "The strongest one."

"I suppose it depends on what you want. Instant death? King basilisks evoke a venom that will kill almost any living thing. But just like grim reaper arcanists, they're rare, and not very excited to enchant others. The Lamplighter Knights, who are mostly king basilisk arcanists, have rules about who they'll allow to have their runes."

"What about—"

Professor Ren held up a hand and silenced Raaza. "Just think about it, all right? You want magics that complement your own. And keep in mind you can never improve the runes once they're on you, so you definitely want something that meshes."

Everyone returned to grinding, and my thoughts drifted to combinations.

What would go well with my mimic powers?

It was more difficult a question than I cared to admit...

# CHAPTER 37

## TRUE BEAUTY

The few days leading up to the cotillion sent electricity through the Academy. It was all anyone could talk about. The older students, still irritated they couldn't attend, whispered unkind things about the Kross family as I strode through the halls.

"Everyone knows they're just collecting arcanists," someone muttered.

"I heard the archduke has been talking larger plans," another responded.

"Oh, I've heard that. Someone joked about him becoming a king."

"Shh!" A round of giggles followed as I headed to class. "You don't want to get caught saying things like that."

I didn't know much about the Kross family outside what I had heard within the Academy walls. It was obviously biased information—either people admired the family or they hated them, there was no in-between.

And while I had feelings for Ashlyn, I was starting to dislike the sound of her extended family. However, if I was going to impress her father—enough to ask for Ashlyn's hand in marriage over *Valo*—I would have to play along. If Archduke Kross fancied himself a king, it was best I didn't say anything to the contrary.

The morning of the cotillion, the dorms were filled with an energetic bustle the likes of which I hadn't seen before.

I rolled out of my bed just as the window slammed open. Starling galloped into the room from the long walkway outside. He leapt from the sill and clopped his way over to his arcanist's bed.

Miko came prancing into the room afterward. Her kitsune fire flashed brightly as she leapt onto Raaza's sleeping form.

I half expected a whole parade of mystical creatures to enter, given all the noise coming from the treehouse, but those were the only two who entered our dorms. After stretching, and grabbing my clothes, I got dressed.

Apparently, the Kross Cotillion was taking place at a dockside amphitheater in a port named Freestorm. I hadn't heard of it, but from what I was told, the waters around the city were crystal clear. Other students claimed they could see the seabed, even while standing on the deck of a ship.

We would need to take the Gates of Crossing again.

Twain yawned and then walked his way over to me. I scooped him up and placed him on my shoulder. "Don't mess up my vest," I said.

"Hm. *Good morning* to you, too." He yawned a second time. "But I'll forgive you this one time. We have a woman to woo."

"There's no *we* in this."

Twain twitched one of his large ears. "Excuse you. Everyone loves me." He purred as he said, "That's half the reason Ashlyn fancies you, I'm sure of it."

I chuckled as I headed for the door. But then I stopped once I realized Knovak and Sorin were fully dressed. They both had the word *dapper* down pat.

Knovak sported a short shoulder cape, black slacks, a red vest, and a black shirt. He wore a bowtie and a short top hat, and for some reason, carried a cane made of ebony. His arcanist mark, the star with the elegant unicorn, was prominent for everyone to see.

He tapped the brim of his top hat and turned to me. "How do you like it?"

"It's something," I said.

Sorin, on the other hand, definitely had more of a warrior's appearance. He didn't wear a vest, but he did have a decorative shoulder guard. His black shirt and white pants were rather striking—and at least the shirt wasn't being torn apart by his bulk.

My brother hadn't gotten a hat, but he did have a puffy collar frill that stuck out on his chest. He resembled a pompous rooster from the right angle.

"I'm not a fan," Sorin muttered.

The darkness around his feet shifted. "If you need me, I can always be your armor," Thurin said.

Sorin sighed. "I'll think about it." He fidgeted with the ruffles. "I wonder what Nini would think. Maybe I can see her before we leave."

"You need to hurry," Knovak said, waggling a finger. "We don't have much time."

My brother smiled and then dashed for the door, his knightmare keeping up with him. It amused me that, on the day of a fancy cotillion, Sorin only had thoughts for one woman, and it wasn't the one he was attending the event with.

Although we had several hours before the cotillion even started, I knew the ship would leave after breakfast. For some reason, excitement filled every inch of my being. This would be the first time I ever attended a celebration of this nature, and the thought of seeing Ashlyn in elegant attire brought about odd thoughts I never felt like sharing with anyone.

With Twain in my arms, and Knovak in tow, I headed for the dining hall.

The trek to Freestorm, and the marvelous amphitheater, made me nervous.

Of everyone in our class, only six of us were attending the cotillion. Sorin, Knovak, Exie, Ashlyn, Phila, and me. Of the six of us, only three of us were on this boat. All the girls had gone to the event with their own mode of transportation, though I wasn't sure what it was.

Sailing through the Gates of Crossing bothered me, if only because I knew we were further from Astra Academy than I liked. Professor Helmith had seemed certain that the headmaster had gathered up nearby gate fragments, but I still fretted.

But we didn't just go through one set of gates... we went through two.

When the ship arrived on the other side of the second gate, I had to stop myself from gasping.

This gate...

I had never gone through this one before.

We appeared just outside a tropical bay. The crystal-clear waters were exactly as the others had described it. Schools of silver fish darted away from the ship as it teleported onto the waves.

"Oh, wow," Sorin said. "Our island isn't near as beautiful as *that!*"

Soft white sand surrounded the crescent-shaped island. Palm trees and vibrant flowers of all colors dotted the landscape leading up to the small town, but the most impressive feature was the amphitheater built out into the bay.

The open-air design of the amphitheater allowed for the refreshing sea breeze to wash over everything. And the architecture was something else. Sure, it was built with sturdy wood, and marble pillars, and a large center stage for entertainment and dancing, but it was the smaller details that took my breath away.

Even as I stood on the deck of the ship as it sailed into port, I noticed the many vines and flowers that had been delicately wrapped around the pillars, support beams, and seats all the way around the structure. Everything smelled of tropical bliss. Each breath was its own mini vacation.

Twain perked up, his ears erect. "This place is amazing," he whispered.

A whole gaggle of greeters awaited us on the docks. None of them were arcanists, but they carried confetti made of small paper designs of mystical creatures. They threw the confetti as the gangplank was lowered and students funneled off the ship.

I stopped to pick up a flake of the confetti, astonished by the detailing in the paper.

Who had made this? It must've taken them hours. And those greeters just threw it all over the docks and into the pristine waters.

Seemed like a waste.

Knovak stepped off the ship with his unicorn close. "Oh, it's been too long since I visited Freestorm."

"This place is awesome," I said, still in awe of our beautiful surroundings. "This island seems too small for a town, though."

"It's more of a vacation location for several richer families." Knovak motioned for us to follow. "This amphitheater is used for grand celebrations and breathtaking performances. You should see the arcanists who really know how to craft illusions. They put on a spectacular show."

The water in the bay was teeming with colorful marine life. Fish, sea urchins, coral—it took all my willpower not to just stare into the waters.

But then I spotted something large beneath the crystal waves.

A typhoon dragon.

And not a hatchling dragon, like Ashlyn's. This was a fully grown dragon of epic proportions. It had to be the size of a three-masted ship, and its fins were gargantuan. The beast's glorious scales came in every color of blue and green. If the waters had been normal, it would've blended in, but this bay didn't allow for that.

The dragon opened its yellow eyes and glanced up at me from the waters, its slit pupils contracting into a thin line. I offered it a shaky wave. Then the beast snorted bubbles and returned to a restful state.

It was bored. I'd bet coin.

"This way," Knovak called.

Sorin hurried to keep up. The walkway from the docks into the amphitheater was a long one that stretched around the entire megastructure, but it wasn't one I could get lost on. There wasn't anything here on this island other than thatch-roof buildings and a few warehouses. The island existed for the theater and the beaches.

I didn't follow Knovak. Instead, I took my time walking along the dock, observing the waters.

"We're getting left behind," Twain whispered.

"That's fine."

"Are you going to have me transform into a giant dragon?" Twain eyed the beast in the bay. "Because I don't know if I can grow that large..."

"Nah, not that one. Your transformation would be way too noticeable."

"Hm."

I patted his head. "I have a couple other ideas to impress people, don't worry."

My eldrin purred.

When other ships arrived, I took a moment to count the guests and glance at their eldrin. One woman had a tanuki—a cute raccoon-looking dog—and some man had a sapphire drake—a wingless dragon with frost around its mouth and claws.

They were young, and small, and they walked past me without giving me a second glance.

Cotillions were for new arcanists, I supposed. Their small eldrin made sense. It required time for mystical creatures to get larger, and they only started to grow once they were bonded.

The last person to exit the ship surprised me. I held my breath as Exie walked down the gangplank, aided by several of the sailors. They brushed the wood of the dock, cleaning it before she stepped down.

Exie...

The woman wore an outfit that grabbed everyone by the eyes and refused to let go. If she wanted attention, she had it in cartloads.

Her dress had a daring cut down the sides, revealing skin from her legs up to her waist. As if not to be outdone, her neckline was equally low, revealing to the world that her flesh was just as soft, and smooth, everywhere.

I barely noticed the color of her gown. It was white. That was honestly the third or fourth bit of information that hit me, and it took a moment. It shimmered as she walked, her shoulders bare, her toned back exposed.

Her chestnut hair was styled in a tight ponytail where the back was curled into waves that cascaded to her shoulders. Her arcanist mark, the star with the erlking, was also clearly visible, and rather unique.

Her erlking wore a tiny black cape, little shoes, and a long tunic. He was the size of my fist, so the details were difficult to make out, but I knew from the way he moved, he thought he was glamourous.

Exie turned her attention to me, her eyes widening. She wore makeup with as much drama as she got herself into.

When she strode over, I made sure to keep my eyes on hers.

"Good afternoon, Gray," she said.

I nodded once. "You look beautiful, Exie."

She touched the side of her neck and smirked. "I know."

"Sorin's not going to care."

Exie hardened her expression into something neutral. She didn't respond right away to my statement, but her erlking did flutter around me with angry beats of his feathered wings.

"Sorin will say nice things about my choice of clothing," Exie eventually stated.

"He would say those things even if you were wearing a moldy bag."

"That's one of the reasons I fancy him." Exie shifted her attention to the clear waters of the bay. "When I asked Sorin to join me here, I told him I needed protection from the catty court drama that would ensue if I came alone. He agreed in an instant—a true knight."

"I'm sure you could've handled it without him."

Exie rolled her eyes. "You don't know what it's like. It's more than just jealousy. Some individuals can't keep to themselves. I want someone I can trust. Sorin is the epitome of trustworthy."

"You could've easily gotten someone else besides Sorin."

"But I don't want someone who isn't Sorin. Don't you understand, Gray? Sure, I *could* have gotten a drunkard from the bar, but... Sorin is different—he agrees to help me, even to his detriment. That's the kind of beauty you can't see with your eyes."

I tucked my hands into my pockets. "Yeah. I know."

"So, I like beautiful things, Gray. That's my thing." She eyed me and waited.

But she obviously didn't understand. "Sorin isn't the kind of man who will leave one girl just because a prettier one comes along."

"Perhaps after tonight, he'll change his mind."

"Good luck," I muttered. But I didn't mean it. Of Nini and Exie, I was rooting for Nini.

"Well, he's going to spend the whole night with me, isn't he?" Exie glowered at me as she stepped away. "I'll have time to prove to him that I'm just as amazing as the reaper girl. And do me a favor and stay away from us tonight, Gray. You're exhausting."

I watched her go, but then tore my attention away to stare at the water again.

It reminded me of...

Of the water that had poured out of the Gate of Crossing when Zahn opened it to the abyssal hells. I didn't know why, but I felt cold again. A deep, terrible chill.

Hopefully the cotillion wouldn't last long.

# CHAPTER 38

## THE KROSS COTILLION

I walked into the amphitheater and was met with another round of greeters.

"Invitation?" one asked before I could step inside.

I reached into the pocket of my vest and withdrew Professor Ren's invite. The parchment was softer than any I had handled before, and if someone claimed it were made from the fluff of clouds, I would've believed them. When I passed the invitation over, the greeter took it with special care. He examined the seal on the bottom—one with a moon and star emblazoned on red wax.

"Everything is in order," the greeter said with a rehearsed smile. He wore a tunic and pair of trousers that were pale green and matched the island. "We're so pleased a representative of the Ren family could join us. And so very pleased *you* could join us, Gray."

Professor Ren had signed his name on the invitation and listed me as the guest, so obviously I was with *his* family, but it hadn't occurred to me until right then. Would it matter? I doubted it, though it was odd he had said my name with such enthusiasm. It wasn't like he knew me.

The greeter offered me a glass of wine. Although I wasn't much of a drinker, I threw back the contents in one go and then returned it.

The greeter frowned as he took the empty glass.

The alcohol hadn't killed my dread. That was unfortunate.

"Please enjoy the opening show," the man shouted as I entered the theater. "The performers will continue until the beginning of the cotillion dance."

I waved in acknowledgement, though I didn't care.

My fears grew with each passing moment. Was there a gate fragment around here? If so, where?

Twain and I entered the massive structure and walked along the edges of the theater. There was no roof, which allowed for a clear view of the beautiful day.

More and more arcanists joined us for the cotillion, and a few mortals as well. Most were fresh arcanists, with faint marks on their foreheads, and smaller eldrin. I was surprised by the variety. Several will-o-wisp arcanists, a single grifter crow, two pegasi...

They were weaker creatures. Most tier one or two. The strongest eldrin I had seen was the typhoon dragon out in the bay, which was clearly a tier-four beast, capable of powerful magics. I hadn't yet seen Ashlyn or Ecrib, but I hoped I would soon.

Phila entered at one point, her coatl unique. She wore a dress made of lime-green silk, and it flowed with the beauty of a river as she walked around the amphitheater. Half of her gown was sheer, and it took on the appearance of mist whenever the gentle island breeze got a hold of it. She had a mystical presence about her, but I turned away, preoccupied with my own thoughts.

A dance started up on the stage, performed by a single pixie arcanist and ten mortal dancers and singers. Apparently, a cotillion was to last from midday to daybreak. First a show, then a dance, then some food, and finally, a speech. The food and dancing wouldn't occur until the evening. From now until then, we were meant to mingle and flirt, but I didn't care about any of that.

Knovak and his unicorn mingled with the others, though. He laughed so hard I heard from across the amphitheater. His unicorn nickered and showed off his clothing, happy to be paraded around. My brother found Exie, and the two of them stood together near one of the large wine tables. A crowd had gathered to speak to Exie.

It was odd that she thought she would have been ridiculed. Perhaps I didn't understand the behaviors of nobles. She seemed so popular—especially among the men, but some of the women, too—so why had there been any fuss?

I kept glancing around, wondering if I could spot a gate fragment in a bizarre location. They were small, after all. Easily missed. But if I didn't locate it, the cotillion could be interrupted by strange creatures from beyond the realm of the living.

Which would be funny, but only in hindsight. What if someone was hurt?

"Keep your eyes peeled for a gate fragment," I whispered to Twain.

My mimic nodded his head. "Aye, aye."

I placed him on my shoulder as I did another loop.

The center stage itself was a work of art, with beautiful wooden fixtures and bamboo detailing. The performers, dressed in dazzling costumes of red and blue, gracefully twirled and swayed to the beat of elegant music.

The longer the performance went on, the more my feet hurt. I walked around the theater three times, and I still hadn't found anything. My anxiety worsened, so I figured I was close, but I found nothing. Was I imagining things? Perhaps my nerves were getting to me.

As the day waned, the moon appeared in the sunset sky, adding to the magic of the evening.

"You should mingle with people," Twain whispered to me as I walked in the narrow space behind the main stage. "You're missing the celebration!"

"I know there's one here." I glanced into the darkest shadows and even felt around under a lip of the stage, though I was careful to make sure my sleeve covered my whole hand. "We can't just let it sit around."

"What's the worst thing that could happen? A couple of shambling ghouls crawl onto the stage? There are dozens of arcanists here. Those corpses will be dispatched quickly." Twain laid his ears back. "You and Nini handled a couple without any problem. You're worrying too much."

Twain was right. The monsters I had seen hadn't been too dangerous, and we were surrounded by arcanists. Even if most were young, and their eldrin considered weaker, there was still a fully grown typhoon dragon in the bay. *Someone* here was a powerful and accomplished arcanist.

We weren't in any danger.

"Maybe I should tell someone," I muttered as I stood and brushed off my slacks.

I stepped around the side of the stage and froze when I heard a small group of people rolling with laughter. It was just three arcanists, all men, all clothed in long capes that swept across the ground behind them. Their capes carried family crests, but I didn't recognize two of them. One wore the Kross family crest, though. I was quickly becoming very familiar with the moon, star, and *X*.

When I stepped closer, I noticed the three men had arcanist marks.

One had bonded with a *stoor worm*. A vile type of sea serpent that everyone agreed was a bad omen to see. They were powerful, but venomous.

Another had bonded with a *mermaid*. Beautiful creatures with powers to dazzle and persuade. I had never seen one, but my father claimed to have seen many when he had ridden on a ship many years ago.

The last arcanist had bonded with a *leviathan*. Powerful creatures of the ocean, generally regarded as some of the most legendary combatants.

"I've seen better cotillions, but this one has quite the venue," the stoor worm arcanist said. He held his wineglass close and swirled the dark contents.

The mermaid arcanist chortled and nodded. "I don't care about the quality of the cotillion. I'll always attend if I can."

"Oho! I've seen the way you speak with all the young ladies. It's obvious you can't get enough."

The mermaid arcanist chuckled. "Young debutantes are fantastic company. Wouldn't you agree, Valo? A shame you're getting married so soon."

Valo...

The leviathan arcanist turned in response to the name. "Here's the thing," Valo said. "Girls twenty-two or under, they smell massively different from a girl of twenty-eight or so. Girls sixteen to, say, twenty-three, have this creamy, buttery, and slightly sweet smell that is unbelievably magnetic."

"Yes!" The mermaid arcanist laughed and patted Valo's shoulder. "This man understands. And he articulated it so well!"

And here I had been worried I wouldn't get to size up Ashlyn's fiancé. Who was this man? I needed to know if I was going to prove to Ashlyn's father that I was the superior arcanist.

When I closed my eyes, I was bombarded with dozens of magical threads. It took me a solid ten seconds just to sort them in my mind's eye. Thankfully, every time I used this magic-sensing ability, it grew a little better. I felt the creatures, and their rough power, and their types, as though their information were written on the threads.

Like Sorin's knightmare... I felt that one.

And Knovak's unicorn.

The leviathan was still young. Its thread told me it was just a hatchling, which meant Valo probably wasn't particularly powerful right now, even if one day he would be.

I also felt Ashlyn's typhoon dragon.

After a short sigh, I set Twain down on the floor and motioned him to the back corner behind the stage. He nodded and scampered over there, not because I needed him hidden, but because I didn't want anyone to see him transforming. Once he was mostly out of sight, I tugged on Ashlyn's thread, and my forehead burned.

Twain transformed into a typhoon dragon. He grew in size in the darkest corner of the theater, and two of the singers gasped and interrupted their song when they spotted him, but afterward they went right back to singing.

I sauntered over to the group of three arcanists.

"Evening, gentlemen," I said as I approached.

They all glanced over at me.

The stoor worm and mermaid arcanist didn't interest me whatsoever. I only paid attention to Valo.

He wore an outfit similar to mine, though the cape made him stand out. His vest had the same crest as mine, but his slacks weren't dirty from kneeling and searching under a portion of the stage. Otherwise, we were very similar. His hair was that as blond as Ashlyn's, but his eyes were the color of extra-wet mud, and his expression was of a man who realized the wetness was urine.

To my irritation, Valo was slightly taller, but he was as thin as someone could get without being emaciated.

"Good evening," Valo said, lifting an eyebrow.

The other arcanists lifted their glasses. Once they saw my arcanist mark, their eyes went to the symbol on my vest.

"Are you a member of the Kross family?" the stoor worm arcanist asked. "I'm Lekker Jenkins."

Jenkins? Was this Piper's husband? Or perhaps one of his family? That explained the man's grimy attitude if it was her husband. I almost laughed, but I kept that to myself.

"That's right, I'm a member of the Kross family." I motioned to the surroundings. "This is hardly the celebration I thought it was going to be, though. I haven't been home in ages, and this is all we're doing for our cotillions? Hm."

I tried to replicate their condescending tones, but I wasn't as naturally adept at snobbery. My statement must've worked, though, because all three men relaxed.

The mermaid arcanist smiled. He had the slimiest expression, no matter what he did with his face. "Well, after all that work Septimus put into his son's cotillion, I seriously doubt he wanted to do that all over again. Some shortcuts had to be taken."

Who was *Septimus?*

I was about to ask, but I bit my own tongue. Obviously, it had to be Ashlyn's father, the archduke. I would blow my disguise if I asked inane questions. Best to let these weasels do all the talking.

"I appreciate what Septimus has done," Valo chimed in. "Being welcomed into the family with such open arms has been a refreshing experience."

"Of course he would want someone of your talent," Lekker stated. His eyes were set so close together, it was like they were trying to outdo his unibrow.

But he didn't say *what* talent.

Valo sighed. "I thought his daughter would seek me out this evening to speak with me, but she's yet to show herself."

"Probably playing coy. You need to chase down young ladies if you want their attention." Lekker rubbed his hands and gestured to the crowd flocking around Exie. "I can't wait to corner that one for a moment."

While Exie wasn't my favorite person in the world, I was tempted to walk over and tell her to avoid this man at all costs. Perhaps *this* was what she meant by needing someone at her side. Sorin wouldn't allow Exie to be "cornered" while he was around.

Then again, if Exie focused more on her magic, perhaps she could've crafted illusionary duplicates of herself to interact with everyone here. Then she could've escaped every situation.

I made a mental note to tell her that.

Valo smoothed his short, blond hair. "I thought Ashlyn would have more manners than this. Avoiding her own future husband? It reflects poorly on me if I have to search this whole island for her." Valo eyed me. "Have you seen her? And I apologize, I don't think we've met. I'm Valo Fitzroy."

I smiled. "I haven't seen her. And I'm Cymon Kross." I made that up on the spot, and it almost sounded like it, but no one called my bluff. I offered Valo a slight bow of my head. "But I think I need a drink of my own. If you all will excuse me."

Without waiting for any replies, I headed through the crowds of people filling the amphitheater. Ashlyn wasn't here. I had searched the whole area, after all. Valo was right—I would have to search the island if I wanted to speak with her. That was fine. She was worth it.

And beside the fact that Valo was bonded with a leviathan, he didn't seem that impressive at all. The real problem was *how to prove that*. Obviously, I needed to do something to show my worth. But what? I'd need more time to think about it.

"Welcome, welcome," a booming voice said, blanketing the area.

I glanced over my shoulder.

Ah. Septimus himself, it seemed.

The man's typhoon dragon arcanist mark was so prominent, I noticed it from halfway across the amphitheater. His short, blond hair, shaved short on the sides and kept longer at the top, marked him as Ashlyn's father. Either that or his piercing blue eyes, which rivaled the turquoise of vibrant ocean waters.

He wore a long, white cape and clothing that resembled armor underneath. Thick-studded leather, dyed black, covered his shoulders and protected his upper legs. His silk shirt and vest were the same as many others, but everything carried his family's crest. The moon and stars were a theme he clearly adored.

Septimus had a short beard, but since it was blond, it was difficult to see fully.

"This year's cotillion is to celebrate my one and only daughter, Ashlyn." The archduke motioned to the festivities. "As a typhoon dragon arcanist, she will help shape the world with her might and magic. Please, raise a glass for my daughter and make sure to wish her well... whenever someone spots her, of course."

His little comment at the end seemed to be said in both an amused tone and a genuinely irritated one. It was clear Ashlyn should've been here a while ago.

The crowd laughed at the comment, though.

But I didn't care for it.

I turned on my heel and headed for the door, even as Septimus continued speaking.

I released the thread of magic, and my arcanist mark returned to a blank star. Twain dashed through the celebration, weaving between people's legs as he hurried to me. Once close, he leapt, and I knelt enough to grab him in my arms.

Together, we left the theater and headed out onto the small crescent-shaped island. The door greeters waved, but I didn't call out to them.

When I closed my eyes and felt the threads of magic, I tried to focus even harder. Perhaps I could feel the general direction Ashlyn was in? If I could, that would help me find her. But it was difficult to focus with music and boisterous conversations filling the air.

"Did you fool people?" Twain asked with a chirpy giggle at the end of his words. "I bet they had no idea you were a mimic arcanist."

I patted his orange head. "I think I tricked them, but what matters right now is finding Ashlyn."

"First that gate fragment, now Ashlyn... This whole celebration, you've been doing nothing but searching for things. We haven't had any fish! And I smell it, too." Twain sniffed the air. "Oh, my... There's so much fish, Gray. *So much.*"

I hurried to the white sand beach and closed my eyes again. Ignoring Twain's rumbling belly, I focused on the threads. It was difficult to sense the direction of something, but a faint hint of Ashlyn's location flashed in my senses. Following my instinct, I turned and headed for the far pier.

A burst of music and cheering issued from the amphitheater. Archduke Kross must've said something spectacular. Or perhaps he had officially kicked off the celebrations. The cotillion was supposed to last the evening, after all.

I understood why Freestorm was the perfect location. Even as the sunlight died in the distance, it was still pleasantly warm as I strode toward the pier. The tropical weather was a delight that few places knew.

It didn't take long to reach the pier. Ashlyn stood halfway down, her eldrin in the clear waters of the bay. And while Exie was striking in her dress, Ashlyn stole the prize for the most beautiful.

Her dress resembled silver scales. When she moved, even slightly, everything shimmered, like a school of fish in the water. It hung from her shoulders all the way down to her ankles, but diamond-shaped holes had been carefully crafted into the sides of the dress, creating windows that highlighted her feminine curves and athletic build.

She wore a blue belt fashioned to resemble a typhoon dragon around her waist, but I didn't notice that until I was much closer. Ashlyn's blonde hair was loose and hung around her face, perfectly framing her in just the right way.

Ecrib poked his head out of the water as I approached. He didn't seem angry—none of his scales flared, and he didn't flash his fangs—which was probably a good sign.

"Ashlyn?" I asked as I drew near. "Do you mind if I join you?"

When she turned to face me, she forced a smile. "Gray. I'm surprised you came."

"And miss you in this dress? Never."

I walked down the pier, my footfalls causing the wood to creak. I wanted my approach to be quieter, but everything around us was so still. The amphitheater had enough noise for an entire parade, though.

"I told you, I'm betrothed." Ashlyn returned her attention to her eldrin in the bay. "You shouldn't say things like that."

"Oh? Maybe I should say things like your fiancé and talk about how —" I cleared my throat to better mimic his voice, "—*young ladies between the ages of sixteen and twenty-three smell of sugar and cream, nom*

*nom.*" I made the last two noises like I was eating something, my mouth full.

Twain and Ashlyn both laughed, but Ashlyn was the first to stop.

"He didn't say that," she muttered. "Jealousy doesn't suit you, Gray."

I said nothing in response. I *was* jealous, and Valo had *definitely* said that, but arguing about it wouldn't get me anywhere.

"I think your father is irritated you haven't shown yourself for the cotillion." I motioned to the front door. "Don't you want to speak with everyone?"

Ashlyn didn't reply. Ecrib stared up at her with large eyes, his pupils practically circles.

I set Twain down by my feet and rotated my shoulders.

Soft music replaced the upbeat singing that had dominated the celebration previously. It was a romantic melody, something so tender, it evoked thoughts of romance after just a few notes. The warm breeze, and the scent of island flowers, made everything perfect.

I held out my hand. "Well, if you don't want to go to the cotillion, maybe we can avoid all our responsibilities together and just dance here?"

Ashlyn once again chuckled. When she turned to me, it was clear she was fighting with herself, trying not to smile. "If anyone saw us, I would never live it down. There'd be whispers of my infidelity. I'd be a walking embarrassment."

"They'd have to catch us first."

For some reason, the taunt in my words seemed to resonate with her. Ashlyn glanced over at me. I didn't lower my hand. Her blue eyes were filled with a mix of indecision and action, but all hesitation left when she stepped forward and took my hand. I gently pulled her close.

Then I swallowed hard. In my head, this worked perfectly because *in my head, I knew how to dance.* As we stood together, her body practically pressed against mine, I realized that was all a delusion.

I did *not* know how to dance.

But did Ashlyn know that?

Nope.

With as much confidence as I could fake, I slowly swayed us. At first, it worked. She leaned into me, and we went with the music. But after the first minute or so, it was clear she expected more. So I twirled us. One little circle, and we were done with that. Ashlyn half-smiled at me, like she knew my terrible secret, but she said nothing. She was as classy as she was beautiful. Could there had been a better combination?

"Gray? *Gray.*" Twain scrabbled across the pier and stood by my feet. "Something is wrong."

"No, it's not," I muttered.

"I'm so sorry, but it really is."

Ashlyn released me, her attention on the bay. I turned as well, disturbed by the inky cloud that stained the water and made it impossible to see fish or the sand. The second I realized I wasn't dancing with Ashlyn anymore, the same sense of dread overcame me. Something was here.

Ecrib growled as he stepped out of the water and pulled himself onto the pier. His scales flared as he said, "There's a creature in the bay. Something as big as my father."

*His* father?

Was the gargantuan typhoon dragon in the bay *Ecrib's* father? That made his bonding with Ashlyn a little more interesting.

"What is it?" Ashlyn whispered.

The music in the amphitheater died the next moment.

A pair of enormous tentacles, the size and thickness of small, one-masted boats, lifted out of the bay and lumbered toward the center stage. Screams filled the air. Someone shouted at everyone to run. The tentacles were blackish-blue, and they sparkled in the moonlight, glistening with the inky waters.

Then they crashed onto the amphitheater, exploding their way through the walls, smashing the wood, crushing a few palm trees, and shattering everything they touched.

# CHAPTER 39

## THE MIDNIGHT DEPTHS KRAKEN

"Ecrib!" Ashlyn shouted.

Her dragon leapt to her side. Even wearing an elegant dress, she grabbed his back fin and hung on. Ecrib leapt into the water, his arcanist clinging tightly, and swam for the amphitheater.

Twain clawed his way up my pant leg and jumped to my shoulder. I took off toward the theater, running along the long walkway, my attention completely consumed by the ongoing destruction.

Four more tentacles rose out of the bay and smashed the side of the massive structure. The waters were as dark as a starless night, and I wondered if it was ink. Was that a kraken? It looked like it, but it was so much bigger. And the skin of the beast was bizarre.

Barnacles and sharp bits of coral clung to the sides of the massive tentacles. The small lights of anglerfish poked out of open pores on the kraken's body, like it *was* the night sky, and each star was actually a trap luring you to your death.

That wasn't what normal krakens looked like.

Mortals, arcanists, and mystical creatures poured out of the half-ruined amphitheater. The screaming filled the night with terror.

As I neared the structure, waves of people practically trampled me in their panic and haste to flee the scene. Everyone went straight for the boats, but it was clear they would have to exit the bay—and get by the kraken—if they were going to reach the Gates of Crossing.

What was going on?

The typhoon dragon—Ecrib's father—lifted his massive body from the bay. The black water ran from his body in waterfalls, crashing back to the bay and creating a roar of water. The beast had fins along his spine, arms, legs, and tail, and when he opened his fang-filled mouth, a storm's worth of lightning formed.

An explosion of light brightened the whole island as the typhoon dragon evoked a blast of lightning. When Ashlyn and Ecrib evoked their magic, it was nowhere near as powerful, or as potent, as that. Clearly, they were still young and inexperienced.

But *this dragon...*

I felt sorry for the kraken.

I shoved my way through the fleeing crowds, heading for the theater itself. Twain clung to me, his claws digging into my skin. He never let go, and I made it to the door right as the tentacles reached up and grabbed the large typhoon dragon around his long neck.

These gargantuan monsters were large enough that if they rolled over the building, I was dead. Fortunately, they grappled each other right at the edge of the ruined amphitheater, neither heading toward the beach.

Only a few arcanists had stood their ground around the theater's main stage.

Septimus was one of them.

He held up his hand, and just like his dragon, he evoked a hurricane's worth of lightning. It crackled outward in a burst that almost hurt my eyes; the light was so intense. The lightning struck the tentacles of the kraken, burning off a chunk of its bizarre flesh.

Another tentacle lifted from the bay and smashed another portion of the amphitheater's wall. A rain of broken wood and bamboo shot across the area, hitting me, Septimus, and a few other arcanists.

Sorin stood his ground in the building, his knightmare on his body, the two merged into one single being. Sorin dug through the rubble and pulled out some of the greeters who had been trapped by the falling debris. When he couldn't lift the wood with just his strength, Sorin manipulated the darkness to help him.

Exie stood close by. "We should go," she shouted.

"I can't leave these people," Sorin yelled back, his voice mixed with Thurin's. "*Get to safety!* I'll be there soon."

But Exie refused to leave. Although her outfit was not something that would accommodate digging through debris, she knelt and started helping regardless.

Several support beams holding the amphitheater snapped. The whole structure tilted forward and sank down, crashing into the bay. I held onto the wall and kept my footing, but the devastation was taking an ugly turn. Water rushed up onto the floor. If people were trapped under rubble or beams of wood, they would now soon drown.

The mighty typhoon dragon roared as he dug his claws into the kraken. Blood as black as the kraken's skin spilled out into the water, filling it with more oil-like liquid.

Then the main body of the kraken lifted out of the bay. Its mouth... It was a circle of teeth that reminded me of a lamprey. Its eyes were like jellyfish—otherworldly and shimmering—and practically the size of barrels. The vile kraken screeched with the intensity of a banshee, its cry so unsettling, I shivered. It was... some sort of magic.

I couldn't move.

Neither could Septimus, or Exie, or even the gigantic typhoon dragon. The *fear magic* gripped my chest and threatened to steal my breath.

But Sorin could still move. He pulled more mortals from the rubble, quickening his pace to fight the rising tide.

I closed my eyes and tugged on the thread of magic that was my brother's knightmare.

Twain transformed into the dark suit of knightmare armor. He was hollow and tall, and he fell off my shoulder and hit the ground from the sudden transformation. And as soon as *I* was a knightmare arcanist, the kraken's screaming didn't affect me like it had. Knightmare magic warded off the fear, just like Knovak's unicorn magic gave him more stamina.

Twain dove into the darkness and then rose up around me. The knightmare armor covered my normal clothing in an icy sensation of power. I ran forward and grabbed a few individuals under a beam by the half-crushed main stage.

Once I had pulled them out, I shoved them toward the door, but they trembled with fear.

The kraken bashed the typhoon dragon with its tentacles. The large beast was struggling to move.

I couldn't ignore the battle and just save people. I had to stop the kraken from screeching. But how? What did knightmares evoke? They also evoked fear. But they could manipulate darkness.

After a deep breath, I reached out my hand and controlled the shadows like they were an extension of my body. Unfortunately, Thurin was still young, and his magic undeveloped. I couldn't manipulate *much* shadow, but I managed to form a short spear of inky blackness and then took aim. The kraken was too large to impale or kill with a single blow. I had to be smarter than that.

I aimed for its eyes.

Then I manipulated the shadows and lanced the short spear straight into the monster's right eye. When my attack struck, the kraken stutter-screamed, and its fear magic over the area dropped.

The typhoon dragon, and Septimus, returned to pummeling it with lightning. They distracted the kraken so it couldn't turn its focus to me.

I glanced over at the destruction of the theater. There were more people trapped than I had originally thought. They were slipping into the bay, and the water was now so black that once they were submerged, I couldn't see them at all.

But typhoon dragons could manipulate water...

Septimus and his typhoon dragon were busy. And when more lightning fired up from the other side of the bay, I knew Ashlyn was joining the fray, trying to help her father fight this bizarre kraken.

I closed my eyes again.

Twain unmerged from me. He was once again a hollow suit of armor that moved around on his own.

Then I shivered. I felt the thread of magic for Septimus's dragon, but also felt the thread for the kraken... But I couldn't tug it. This thread was similar to those of the corpses I had fought in the graveyard. It was a thread of magic that led *nowhere*. Why couldn't I tug it? Was this kraken somehow undead?

No.

It had come from the abyssal hells...

Which meant the gate fragment I had failed to find... This was my fault.

I swallowed hard and shook my head, dispelling the terrible thoughts. Now wasn't the time. The amphitheater rumbled as it began fully breaking apart. My footing was shaky, and I didn't have much time.

"Twain, get to the water!" I shouted.

Still in knightmare form, Twain slipped into the shadows and only stepped out once he was in the bay. I knew he hated the water, but he did it regardless.

I tugged on the thread of magic that led to the giant typhoon dragon.

My forehead burned as Twain bubbled outward. He grew, and grew, *and grew*, until he was the size of the other dragon. Twain's knightmare armor became blue scales, and his body morphed into something with fins and fangs.

Twain was an exact replica of Septimus's eldrin.

Unfortunately, Twain was still young, and the massive dragon was not. The magic required for my mimic to take this form was taxing. Every time I had done this in the past, using the magic had hurt me. My body wasn't used to it. But I couldn't complain—I just had to save the people from drowning.

With my teeth gritted, I waved my hand.

The water answered my manipulation. Half the bay slid away from the theater, receding outward, like a swell of the ocean before a major wave. Once the water had rushed out, the people who had been trapped underneath coughed and gasped for air. Then they shouted for help.

Twain, in mighty dragon form, used one of his massive claws to lift the rubble and wood. With his other claw, he scooped up individuals and unceremoniously dropped them onto the amphitheater floor. Some of them could stand and walk, but others had been injured.

One of them was Valo. His hatchling leviathan was nowhere to be seen, and I wondered if it was fighting the kraken. A dark thought crossed my mind—what if we just put him back in the rubble? But that was petty.

There were others still trapped. Twain couldn't get them all.

I stumbled forward into the bay, my head hurting from the magic coursing through my body.

*Focus.*

I just had to reach them and help them to land.

But that was when I saw something strange. Someone had been lurking *in* the bay near the kraken, and now that I had moved the water, they were exposed. The strange man held a gate fragment, the silver glitter of the metal artifact plain to see. But it wasn't a small piece, like the things I had seen before. This piece was the size of my forearm. It was a twisted fragment, practically in the shape of a crescent moon.

And the man holding it...

He didn't look right. He wasn't even wearing much clothing. He wore a tattered pair of trousers and a bizarre smile. And that was it.

His skin was blue and pale, almost translucent, like he had been in the water for months and was now waterlogged. His bloated face and yellowed teeth told the same story. Was that why I couldn't find the fragment? It had been somewhere in the bay?

Had this strange man brought it here?

"*You're here,*" the man said, his voice almost lost to the sounds of combat. With a gleeful smile, he shouted, "I don't have to search for you! I will finally be the new *Seven*! I will earn my place by my lord's side."

What the?

He ran forward, his bare feet half-sinking in the white sands of the bay floor as he headed for me.

When he was closer, I noticed his arcanist mark was a seven-pointed star with a water sprite wrapped around it. A weak creature—tier one— and known for their ability to slip through rivers. Why was he using what little magic he had to help this kraken?

The man *threw* the gate fragment.

My first instinct was to catch it, but the intelligent part of me knew that was a mistake. I stepped to the side, avoiding the large chunk of silver. I watched it sail by me and hit the sand. But then when I glanced back, I realized the waterlogged man hadn't stopped running.

He crashed into me. We both hit the ground, but I was winded.

The gate fragment sat mere inches away...

"I will see real magic enter this world," the lunatic man shouted. "I will serve our great and powerful Death Lord!"

He clawed at my face, his soggy nails too soft to cut me, but his fingers slid close to my eyes.

In a moment of panic, I evoked lightning.

And not a tiny amount of lightning—I had no control over the storm's worth of power that ripped through my arm. It felt as though the magic had come straight from my heart, and it was burning its way out of my body.

*It was too much.*

I obliterated the man on top of me, but my chest, my arm, and some of my neck felt like they had been dragged through a bonfire. The typhoon dragon magic I had borrowed was so powerful, and I wasn't accustomed to wielding this kind of raw destruction...

The charred corpse of the lunatic spasmed and then collapsed on top of me. I took deep breaths.

The ground rumbled. The kraken and the others were still fighting, the screams of their combat ringing in my ears. I couldn't maintain my hold on the dragon's magic. Twain transformed back into a kitten. The bay... Without my typhoon dragon magic, I couldn't manipulate it anymore.

The water rushed over me.

I tried to stand, but the movement of the bay caused my feet to slide. Where was Twain? I needed him. We had to get back to land before we drowned...

"My arcanist! *My arcanist!*"

A water sprite fluttered overhead. It was an orb of water, similar to a will-o-wisp, but made of crystal-clear liquid. It pulsed when it spoke, its voice bubbly.

"You killed him! *You killed him!*" The sprite practically boiled with its anger.

I ignored it.

"Gray! *Gray, help!*"

Twain tried to run, but a wave of water cascaded over him. He twirled in the current and then tried to swim, but he was much too small. He flailed his little kitten legs, but bits of wood and debris were rushing over the water, battering him and nearly knocking him below the surface.

I sloshed through the rising waters. Once near Twain, I grabbed him and headed toward the wrecked portion of the theater. If I could just... climb back up...

"No!" the sprite bubbled. "My arcanist won't have died in vain!"

The creature manipulated the rushing water and threw a glob of it at me.

The gate fragment was in the glob, but I didn't see that until it was too late. And when it struck my arm, the glittering silver fragment melted into my skin, filling me with a sense of overwhelming dread.

And a new presence entered my mind.

# CHAPTER 40

## VIVIGÖL, SILENCER OF THE DAMNED

I couldn't think straight.

The bay crashed over me in a giant wave. Once I was under the water, my sight was stolen, too. What was I doing? I held Twain close, but a headache bloomed in my skull, starting with my forehead and working its way backward.

For some reason, my limbs wouldn't function. I couldn't swim, and when I opened my mouth, I inhaled water.

I was going to drown.

Someone grabbed my shoulder. I was lifted out of the bay, and then a blast of ice solidified the liquid beneath me, stopping it from rising any further. Before I could ask what was going on, I was dragged up onto the ruined amphitheater.

Through a fit of coughing, I hacked up all the water in my lungs. I glanced up to see the headmaster's assassin—Fain—my once-invisible bodyguard. He had saved me.

"Where have you been?" Twain shouted. "We need you! Don't let my arcanist die!"

Fain pulled me farther away from the frozen waters. He didn't answer Twain. The man was muscled and powerful, and with a single arm, he could've carried me all the way to the boats. But his fingers were blackened, practically dead, and so were the tips of his ears. He had a hard look about him—an expression free of fear.

"That's a *midnight depths kraken*," he said, his voice gruff. Icy mists covered his exhaled breath. "Don't allow it to touch you. C'mon."

The headmaster's assassin yanked me to my feet. I shuddered. Something was wrong. I couldn't walk. My head wouldn't stop swimming.

Fain didn't notice or didn't care. When I didn't move, he grabbed my upper arm and practically carried me across the rest of the amphitheater. It was difficult for me to focus, but I noticed the water sprite giving chase. It tried to manipulate more of the bay to break apart the rest of the theater. Was it trying to knock me back in?

When the sprite got close, Fain whirled around. He evoked a blast of ice that created a five-foot wall. The icy crystals struck the orb of water and froze it solid. When the sprite fell to the theater floor, it shattered, dying instantly.

Before we could celebrate, the midnight depths kraken slammed one of its tentacles onto the floor next us. The limb shattered the floor, but before it could collapse into the bay below, Fain evoked his ice in a sheet across the splintered wood. His magic stopped the floor from breaking further, and he dragged me across, his footing surprisingly solid for running across such a slick surface.

When we dashed by the kraken's tentacle, I spotted dozens of creatures living in the creature's flesh. Small crabs, angler fish, and even some eels. They poked their heads out, each one as dark and unsettling as the last. For a split second, I thought they were happily living in the kraken—like the giant creature was protecting them—but then I realized the creatures couldn't escape.

The kraken's body was like a living tar pit. The small creatures were stuck. They were reaching out, trying to grab freedom, but couldn't.

I could only imagine what would happen if I touched the beast.

Then Fain jerked me forward, and I returned my full attention to escaping.

Sorin and Exie had saved as many people as they could, but neither of them seemed to see Fain as he hurried for the pathway to the ships.

I closed my eyes again, trying to think of something that would help me. When I felt around for threads of magic, I sensed several different creatures, but what did I need?

In a moment of clarity, I picked the unicorn. My mark shifted, and Twain transformed. He didn't need me to carry him anymore. Twain fell off my shoulder and then galloped alongside Fain, but that wasn't why I had picked Knovak's eldrin.

It was because unicorn arcanists could manipulate their own emotions and regain their stamina. I picked confidence as the emotion, and I tried to shake away any and all fear. It worked—for a split second, I felt no terror or dread at all, and my body answered my commands, my stamina returning in full force. My headache lessened.

"Why didn't you help us before?" Twain shouted. With his new unicorn stamina, he was ready to yell at Fain the entire trek.

"*You two* ran off into the crowds," Fain growled.

"We needed to help people!"

"Until you transformed, I had no idea where you flew off to. Next time, *head to the damn boats.*"

Fain brought me to one of the piers. Several ships had already set sail, each of them heading straight for the Gates of Crossing. Two remained behind, not yet full of guests.

Where was Ashlyn? Surely, we wouldn't leave without the others in my class?

The typhoon dragon tore off one of the kraken's tentacles. The scream almost deafened me. It was clear who would win this fight, but the mighty beast of the ocean depths grew desperate. It flailed its remaining tentacles, thrashing about with such force that the monster slammed the beach and practically created a crater.

"My brother," I said. "I can't leave without him."

But...

It wasn't *me* who had said it. Sure, the words had come out of my mouth, and it had sounded like my voice, but it hadn't been my choice to say those things. What was going on? I couldn't even force myself to say something—to warn everyone.

Fain glanced down at me, his dark eyes calculating. "Wait here," he commanded. "As soon as I find your brother, we'll leave together."

The man wrapped himself in invisibility, disappearing from my sight.

I heard him run off, no doubt wanting to grab Sorin as quickly as possible. But instead of waiting, like instructed, I turned and hobbled toward the nearest ship.

Again, it wasn't me.

What was going on?

"Gray?" Twain clopped over. He followed me to the gangplank of a ship and stayed close as I practically stumbled onto the deck of the ship. "What're you doing, Gray? Fain said we should wait. Don't you want him to get Sorin first?"

"I need to return to the Academy," I said.

The ship's crew seemed to be nothing but cotillion greeters. They all eyed me with strange expressions, and several of them whispered to one another. I wanted to shout something to them—to warn them I wasn't myself—but I couldn't seem to do it.

Someone ran up the gangplank.

I glanced over my shoulder and spotted Knovak. He and his unicorn leapt onto the ship.

"Gray?" Knovak asked. "What's going on? Are you leaving?"

The cotillion greeters exchanged knowing looks before untying the ship and lifting the anchor.

My heart hammered in my chest as panic set in. Someone was controlling my body while I watched like a passenger behind my own eyes. What was going on? Was it the gate fragment? It had to have been. The presence in my mind had only taken root after my skin had absorbed the fragment.

Was this...

Death Lord Deimos?

Twain untransformed. He returned to his kitten form, but that didn't make him happy. He ran to the railing and glanced back at Freestorm. Then he turned his attention to me, his eyes big and his ears laid back.

Without the emotion manipulation of the unicorn, fear settled back into all my thoughts. For some reason, that gave me a slight bit of control over my hands. They shook, and I managed to rub my forehead—that was *my* doing, not Deimos's—but it wasn't enough.

"Gray! We can't go."

I glanced over. "I *need* to return to the Academy."

Knovak stepped close. "Gray? What's wrong?"

"Stay quiet," I said, my tone low and icy, "and I may allow you to live."

Knovak, Starling, and Twain all stared at me with large eyes. Although I barely had control over my body, I rubbed my face again, trying to wrest control over my thoughts. I moved away from them.

Knovak grabbed my shoulder and turned me around to face him. "Gray, this isn't humorous. What's happening?" I had never seen him look so serious.

Moving against my wishes, I reached up and grabbed Knovak's wrist. Although Twain wasn't transformed, magic flowed through my body. It wasn't mimic magic, or unicorn magic, or anything mundane. It was terrible—a type of magic that burned me.

I recognize it, because I had wielded it once before.

Abyssal dragon magic.

A sinister white-and-blue energy crackled from my touch. Abyssal dragons evoked raw magic, but what did they manipulate?

Knovak clenched his teeth and then tried to yank away. I kept my grip on his wrist, and then I felt Deimos manipulating Knovak's very soul. Abyssal dragon arcanists could graft people to their dragons, after all...

"Leave my arcanist alone!"

Starling lunged forward, horn first. His crystal horn stabbed me in the side, slicing through my clothing and puncturing my side. Crimson blood splashed onto my slacks and boots. I laughed as I grabbed Knovak by the shoulder and slammed him over the railing.

He fell into the water, barely moving.

When Starling wheeled around and tried to stab me again, I held up my hand. Deimos was going to evoke his powerful blast of magic. Starling wouldn't stand a chance.

But...

The injury, coupled with my own dread, seemed to be enough for me to pull control away from Deimos. I managed to lower my hand and shake my head. I couldn't allow the Death Lord to kill Knovak's eldrin. I couldn't allow him to do *anything*. I had to resist him!

Starling dashed past me and then also leapt off the edge of the boat.

My eldrin watched the whole thing but didn't move. Even now, as I struggled, Twain just watched, his eyes wide.

"Gray..." he whispered.

"He's the one," a greeter on the ship shouted. "They were right. Our new lord will soon return."

The other "sailors" all muttered agreements. The one at the helm turned toward the far Gate of Crossing. Had the greeters been in on this attack? Was that why they had been so happy to see me? Had... these people... been planning on giving me the gate fragment? What was going on?

I dug my fingers into my scalp as I tried to free myself from Deimos's control.

"Twain," I managed to choke out. "Go get... help... *Please*. This isn't me!"

Twain's large ears stood straight. He shivered, his brow furrowing. He glanced back at the island, and then at me. I didn't know why, but he ran to my leg and pressed himself against me. "I won't leave you."

"But..." I groaned as a lancing headache ran through my skull. "Twain..."

He didn't move from my side, even as the ship sailed straight for Astra Academy.

It took all my willpower just to keep Deimos from having full control.

Blood wept from my injury, but only for a few minutes. Arcanists had a natural ability to heal over time, but that didn't mean the pain faded. My body was weaker as well. Blood didn't replenish itself so quickly.

Our ship went through two Gates of Crossing, using up star shards to make the travel. The farther we went, the fewer ships we spotted. Apparently, most of the fleeing cotillion guests *hadn't* headed for the Academy. Why would they have? They had probably wanted to stay nearby, so they could gather up the injured, or perhaps help Septimus after he defeated the kraken.

The treacherous sailors of our vessel never really spoke to me. They refused to make eye contact, actually. They muttered things about their new lord, their voices barely above a whisper. A few of them bowed. Who were these people? I wished I had more control over my body—I would've demanded answers.

When the ship reached the edge of the lake just outside Astra Academy, my heart fell.

Why did Death Lord Deimos want to return here? This whole place was filled with his enemies.

"I need to see... Professor Helmith," I said to Twain, hoping he would find someone to help. I grunted as I grabbed at my chest. Everything hurt, especially my heart and my head. When I glanced down at Twain, he nodded once, but he didn't say anything.

Although Professor Helmith wasn't the most powerful combatant, there was no one else I trusted as much as her. Surely, she would help?

The ship docked at the pier, and I stumbled off. The mortals didn't say anything to me. They watched me go, their expressions equal parts fear and hope. What did they want from me? Why do all this?

The pathway was illuminated with lanterns and glowstones. It was still night, and most of the creatures in the Academy and in the treehouse slept. The eerie quiet only added to my desperation.

No one was around to stop me.

I took the first step up the long stairway to Astra Academy, but through sheer determination, I stopped myself from going up any further. Although I didn't know what Death Lord Deimos wanted in the Academy, I wouldn't allow him to have it.

"Stop fighting me," I said through gritted teeth.

Well, *that* wasn't me.

I was talking to myself—Deimos using my mouth to communicate. When he spoke, he had my voice, but he said everything with a harsher edge, one that was somehow authoritative.

"Never," I managed to reply.

To Twain, I must've appeared insane.

My eldrin watched with his ears drooped low, his frown prominent. He said nothing, but his two-colored eyes observed everything.

"I thought you might resist," Deimos said through me. For some reason, he half-smiled as he said, "I underestimated you. I wanted you to cease to be..." He forced my body to take another step up the stairs. "But I've never lost a battle of wills with anyone."

I shook my head and forced us to stop. "*No*. I won't let you..."

"If you persist in this futile attempt to hinder me, your mother's soul will be shredded to empower my eldrin."

Twain gasped. Again, he said nothing, but he mewed a soft noise of concern.

Deimos's words twisted in my chest. What was I supposed to do? What *could* I do? Death Lord Deimos existed in a realm of souls, far beyond my reach. I couldn't save my mother—but Deimos could destroy whatever was left of her.

Sweat dappled my face. It dripped off and hit the stone steps around my feet.

I didn't want my mother to suffer because of me.

"Fine," I ground out. "Fine..."

I walked up the steps, no longer fully fighting for control. Deimos took the steps two at a time, hurrying up toward the front gates of the Academy. It was quiet. When Deimos opened the door, and it groaned halfway through, it sounded like the blast of a rifle that was how silent it had been before.

"What's happening?" I managed to whisper.

"It will be over soon," Deimos replied in my voice, keeping it low.

"I don't understand..."

Deimos walked us forward. Our steps were shaky, and I feared we would fall over at any moment. Twain kept close, but he never came close enough that we would step on him.

"The Gate of Crossing is tied to *me*," Deimos said, "and fixed to my soul. Zahn used other souls to tie the other end of the gate, and it seems I'm now able to astrally project some of my consciousness through these fragments."

Curse the abyssal hells...

It was like *my body* was a gate he was using. Deimos's soul—even his magic—could spill forth from my being.

I huffed a laugh. I would never be free of this nightmare. Ever since Zahn had set out to open this gate—and he had picked twins to kill for his ritual—my fate had been sealed. Either I stopped Death Lord Deimos from entering this world, or I would be destroyed.

We stumbled toward the inner staircase, my stuttered footfalls echoing in the hallway. The dim lighting was enough for me to see by, but not far. When someone walked our way, we froze.

Nasbit emerged from the shadows. He had a book in both hands, his lips pursed in tight concentration. Brak was nowhere to be seen, but that made sense. The stone golem was likely staying in the treehouse.

"Hm?" Nasbit glanced up from his reading material and spotted me. His eyes widening told me I didn't look well. "G-Gray? I thought you were at the Kross Cotillion?"

"It was pretty bad," I managed to quip. With a half-smile, I added, "But I..." I gulped down air and couldn't finish the sentence. Deimos didn't want me to speak.

Magic coursed through me. Deimos half lifted my hand, but I managed to stop him.

"*No,*" I growled, trying to keep my voice low. "*Don't hurt him.*"

Twain leapt forward. "Don't worry, Nasbit! My arcanist was feeling really under the weather, that's why we left early. We need to see Doc Tomas. There were some really bad fish at the cotillion!"

I didn't move. Sweat dripped off my chin and hit the floor.

Nasbit stared for a long time. Probably too long. I felt Deimos's agitation long before Nasbit closed his book. "Right. Well, it seems irresponsible to use star shards for trips back and forth to the Academy. I hope you'll keep in mind that those are valuable resources."

He chuckled.

No one else did.

"We'll try not to be wasteful," Twain said with such fake cheeriness, I wondered if he was trying to blow our cover.

Nasbit took wide and hesitant steps around me. "O-Okay. I hope you feel better, Gray." He quickened his pace once farther away.

I didn't reply. Instead, I continued on my way to the stairwell, thankful I hadn't hurt Nasbit like I had Knovak.

We were heading for the Academy's basement. My heart hammered in my chest as we took the stairs down. Now I knew what Deimos wanted—

he had come here for all the gate fragments Headmaster Venrover had collected.

With gulped breaths, we made it to the bottom of the stairs. Then we went straight for the imbuing room. How did Deimos know where to go? Had someone told him? I scrunched my eyes closed, but Deimos opened them again.

Someone in the Academy had put the gate fragment in the cave during my class. Someone had known I would be attending the Kross Cotillion. Someone had definitely informed Deimos about the fragments being collected.

Or perhaps multiple people.

"Besides Zahn," I managed to choke out, "who—why—are these lunatics helping you?"

"They know the true order of things," Death Lord Deimos said as he grabbed the door handle and pushed the door open. "There are still followers of the old ways. Priests of the abyssal dragons. Worshippers of the Death Lords."

So... crazy people. Fantastic.

We walked into a large and mostly empty room, my steps still unsteady. The table with the gate fragments sat at the far end, near the back wall, but Deimos didn't angle us in that direction. Instead, Deimos walked toward something else.

The trident.

With a chuckle, he strode for his weapon.

"I've missed you," Deimos said—not to me, but to the golden trident perched delicately on a display stand. "But we were always destined to be reunited... Vivigöl, Silencer of the Damned."

We grabbed the shaft of the trident, and my thoughts filled with panic. Only Death Lord Deimos could wield this weapon, and since this body wasn't his, would the weapon reject me?

But nothing happened. We pulled Vivigöl from its perch, and Deimos spun it once with the expertise of someone who had done it a million times before. The trident practically whistled through the air as he held it close.

The power...

The trident pulsed with recognition and purpose. My body felt better with the weapon in my hand. Vivigöl itself had added its might to me.

Twain meowed, but it was soft and sad.

The door opened a second time, and I knew this wouldn't end well. Someone was going to try to do something. And now that Death Lord Deimos was wielding Vivigöl, Silencer of the Damned, who could possibly stand against us?

# CHAPTER 41

## TRAPS AND GAMES

Nasbit stepped into the room and pointed.

Professor Ren and Professor Helmith followed him in. My mouth went dry the moment I saw her. I had wanted to see Helmith before Deimos had retrieved his weapon, but now that he was armed, I wanted Professor Helmith to run as far away from here as possible.

Ren's spider eldrin click-clacked across the floor behind him, staying mostly out of sight. It was such a thin and spindly spider, it probably didn't need to stay in the treehouse.

"See?" Nasbit whispered. "*There he is.* Gray's not himself."

Professor Ren stepped forward. Neither he nor Helmith had their robes on. Instead, he only wore his trousers and an opened button-up shirt, not even boots. His runes glittered as he strode toward me.

"Roark," Professor Helmith said, her voice filled with concern. "Wait."

Ren stopped halfway across the room. He never took his eyes off me. When he tensed, I realized he understood—I was dangerous.

I glanced over to the table. Thirteen gate fragments sat on top of it, each the size of one of my fingers. What would happen if my body absorbed all of them? Would Deimos just take over? Would I have no control at all?

"Gray?" Professor Ren asked.

"You should... get away from here," I managed to say. Then I inched toward the table.

Ren tightened his hands into fists. "Don't touch any of those gate fragments. If you attempt to get close to them, I'll stop you."

"I can't wait to see you try," Deimos said with my voice. Then I took another step closer.

Professor Ren opened both of his hands and swung them forward. He evoked *webs*, a sticky substance that flared outward. With expert skill, he created them like a net and threw them across the room. They blanketed nearly everything, including my body, sticking me in place. Ren didn't let go of his evocation, though. He held on to the edge of the webs from his position halfway across the room.

Deimos struggled to move. He managed to twist his wrist, and his trident, Vivigöl, broke apart a small portion of the webs, as though the abyssal coral couldn't be tethered by this magic. Once my arm was free, Deimos held it up and pointed my palm at Ren. A beam of raw magic—blue and sickly—blasted across the room, crackling with immense power. Ren managed to lean to the side, just barely dodging the insidious attack, but the magic pierced the far wall and sliced through the stone, creating a hole as wide as someone's head.

Deimos's evocation would effortlessly puncture through a person in an instant.

"All right," Ren said through gritted teeth. *"Let's get serious."*

He evoked fire from his hands, and it spread across the webs in a flash. The threads of his treasure cache spider evocation lit up like a bonfire, and the flames flashed down to the ends of the strands. The fire burned me, but it also weakened the webbing.

My heart raced. I would've panicked.

But Deimos apparently felt no need to worry. Once both arms were free, he spun Vivigöl and cut through the remainder of the web. Then he threw his weapon at the table. Vivigöl smashed through the wood and stabbed into the stone, the gold shaft and tines sparkling in the light of the flames now scattered across the room.

All the gate fragments fell to the floor and scattered outward.

Two twirled across the stone in my direction. I knelt and touched them, the fragments melting into my skin as though I were a sponge and they were water. The moment they filtered into my body, Deimos had more control. My body didn't jerk or stutter.

Deimos smiled.

Professor Ren dashed through the flames. He evoked more webs and threw them over me. The sticky substance glued my arms close to my sides and bound my feet to the stone floor. When Deimos attempted to move, it was like walking through tar. He couldn't go far.

When Professor Ren was closer, more of his runes glittered. Then the webs shifted from silky, sticky to metallic. The strands of the webs hardened and solidified. He had ensnared me with some sort of trap.

I was so thankful.

But then Ren evoked his flames again. The web heated, the metal strands glowing bright. They burned through my clothes, then seared my skin. The agony was intense—and if I'd had full control, I would've screamed. But not Deimos.

Professor Ren ran over and reached out as though he wanted to touch me. And although Deimos couldn't lift my arms, he didn't seem to care. Like a dragon himself, Deimos opened his mouth and evoked his deadly beam of raw magic.

I hadn't known that was possible.

The beam was smaller than the one he had evoked before, but it was just as potent. It blasted through a portion of Professor Ren's chest, disturbing his runes, carving a hole in his body the size of a gold coin, and knocking him backward.

"Roark!"

Since Ren was no longer concentrating on his magic, the webs faded and the fires in the room dulled. Deimos pulled himself free of the weakened trap and ran for his weapon. Once Vivigöl was in his grasp, he knelt and grabbed two more gate fragments. They absorbed straight into my skin, empowering Deimos and robbing me of more control.

My skin was mangled, and I had lost blood... Normally, I'd be too injured to move, but somehow, through this bizarre connection, I *felt*

Deimos pushing those fears to the side. His willpower dominated everything, even his ability to feel the pain.

Professor Helmith hurried to Ren's side. She knelt and tried to help him up, but Ren shook his head.

"*Damn*," he muttered. "Caught me... by surprise..."

"Don't move," Helmith whispered. She pulled off his shirt and tried to bind it over his chest—somehow stopping blood from gushing out the gaping hole in his chest. "E-Everything will be okay."

Nasbit hovered by the door, one foot in the room, one foot in the hallway. His eyes were large, like he couldn't decide on the best course of action. Stay here? Or go get help?

He remained frozen with indecision.

Twain, on the other hand, dashed from the room, running as fast as his little kitten legs would take him. I wasn't sure where he was going, but I hoped it was someplace safe.

Deimos walked around the room, searching for the silvery fragments hidden under the embers and strands of fading webs. Every step reminded me my leg was weak, but Deimos soldiered through that as well.

When Deimos turned to grab another fragment, something happened. I couldn't see it, but the pain that lanced through my leg and chest was almost blinding. I staggered forward and then glanced down. Long needle-like metal poles were jammed through my body. When I glanced over my shoulder, I realized it was Trove—Professor Ren's eldrin —who had crept around the room and stabbed me when I hadn't been looking.

With gritted teeth, Deimos whirled around. He stabbed at Trove, but only caught the nimble spider with one tine of the trident. It was enough to tear through the spider's metal skin, and even pop out one of the rough emeralds.

Trove skittered away, his body wrecked.

The injuries across my body were mounting. Deimos took a deep breath, but he wasn't deterred from his goal.

Nasbit finally ran into the room. He went straight for Helmith and Ren, and offered to help with his injury. Professor Helmith allowed him to help, though I wasn't sure what he could do. He was a stone golem arcanist. They weren't known for their healing.

"Wait here," Helmith whispered as she stood. When she turned to face me, it wasn't with smiles or acceptance. She had an expressionless face I had never seen before. "You're Death Lord Deimos, aren't you?"

I stopped searching for fragments and faced her, Vivigöl tight in my grip. "Submit, and you will be spared the suffering I've promised my enemies." And although it was *my* voice, it was darker than it had been before. Menacing.

"You have one of my students—let him go."

Deimos ran a shaky hand down my chest. My blood-soaked shirt stained his hand with crimson. He laughed once. "Your student is weak, his body frail. I'll be done with him shortly."

"If you won't release him, I'll take him by force."

Again, Deimos smiled. "*I can't wait to see you try*," he repeated, this time more amused than he had been when he had said it to Ren.

Professor Helmith brushed back some of her black hair and strode forward.

When Deimos held out his hand and evoked another beam, Helmith waved her arm. The pink runes on her shoulder glittered as a shimmering barrier appeared around her. It was a personal shield, and when Deimos's attack struck, the raw magic dissipated across the barrier. Helmith had protected herself.

Then she hurried closer. She had no weapon, and ethereal whelks only evoked light. What was she planning? To touch me and put me to sleep? Why? It was so risky—she should've run. Deimos had a weapon. Would her barriers save her from that?

The instant Helmith was close, Deimos stabbed with Vivigöl, aiming straight for her heart. Helmith tried to use her barrier, but just like I had feared, the tines of the trident shattered her protection. Fortunately, she staggered back, away from the stab.

But if she got closer again...

There was no doubt in my mind that Deimos would kill her instantly.

"You've sealed your fate by defying me," Deimos said with my voice. He held his trident close, and he pushed magic through it. Was he trying to empower the weapon? But something odd happened. The trident shifted slightly, as though trying to rearrange itself.

The movement reminded me of Twain whenever he transformed.

Had Deimos inadvertently pushed some of my mimic magic into the weapon?

This obviously surprised Deimos as well, because he stopped and stared.

"Gray, I need your help," Helmith whispered as she stepped closer.

She was speaking to *me?* She wanted *my* help? Her calm and singsong voice reminded me why I had always admired her. Professor Helmith... She was mystical in a way others weren't.

Helmith hurried forward again.

Deimos readied Vivigöl. "What a fool."

But when he went to thrust his weapon, I fought against his control with all my might. I tried—as much as I could, with all the concentration I could muster—to shatter Deimos's hold. It wasn't enough to take full control, but I stopped him from perfectly attacking. Vivigöl struck lower, rather than perfectly forward, missing Helmith's heart and instead striking her body. The tines of the trident sliced through her dress, her stomach, her organs, and then up to the bottom of her ribs, but Helmith didn't retreat.

She reached forward, bloodied and injured, until the tips of her fingers grazed my cheek.

And that was all it took.

Her ethereal whelk magic took hold. Sleep gripped my thoughts, and even though Deimos fought it, my body slumped to the floor.

And so did Professor Helmith.

# CHAPTER 42

## HOPES AND DREAMS

I awoke in my dream, shaken.

Then I stood and took in my surroundings.

It was a bizarre landscape. The sky was red, the sun closer than I had ever seen it before. Flares of fire circled the edge of the sun, lighting up the area with a blaze of scarlet. The ground was black rock that shimmered as though wet, even though everything was dry. Mists hovered in the distance, dancing on a breeze I couldn't feel.

What an unsettling area.

Professor Helmith stood next to me, only ten feet away. She wore a dress of white feathers, her long, black hair fluttering back. With poise and grace, she stood on her tiptoes, her bare feet not an uncommon sight when she walked through my dreams. She wore a silver anklet that jingled when she took a step forward.

Across from her, standing more than thirty feet across the flat, rock surface, was Death Lord Deimos.

He was the type of man who always stood in a combat stance, his dark eyes sharp, his black hair slicked back. He was muscular—and taller than anyone here. Probably the most disturbing detail was his armor, which was crafted out of twisted bone and steel. The man wore full plate that covered his whole frame.

He had no helmet, but I doubted he cared. His arcanist mark, prominent on his forehead, showcased his bond with an abyssal dragon.

Deimos didn't have Vivigöl.

"What have you done?" Death Lord Deimos demanded, his attention on Helmith.

"I'm here to make sure you leave my student," she said, calm and unhurried.

"Heh. You're on the edge of death, hag. Your heart beats weaker and weaker in the waking world."

Helmith shook her head. "Doesn't change why I brought you here."

"But it will determine how this ends."

"You're just a fragment of a soul—not strong enough to free yourself from my sleep."

Deimos half-smiled. "For millennia, I have gathered power, grafting souls to my eldrin, empowering him beyond everything thought possible. My *fragment* is more than capable of defeating you both."

Light from the raging sun formed into something solid next to Professor Helmith. It was Ushi, her ethereal whelk. The sea snail floated in the air around her, Ushi's tentacles dangling.

I closed my eyes and felt for threads of magic...

I caught my breath. There were only four.

The ethereal whelk.

The treasure cache spider.

The stone golem.

And *the abyssal dragon.*

Since a small part of Deimos's soul was in this dream—part of my being—the thread of his magic was *right there*. But would it work in this dreamscape?

Deimos held up his hand and unleashed a blast of bluish, raw magic, the hue sickly, especially in the light of the dying star overhead. Helmith's runes flashed, and a barrier formed around her. The magic slammed into the shield and then faded, splashing away like water.

That answered my question. His abyssal dragon magic worked here.

But I had to be careful. Last time I had transformed Twain into an abyssal dragon, the monster's magic had started to kill me from the inside out. If I was going to use it, I had to be certain of my shot.

Helmith waved her hand, and the rocks beneath our feet shifted. A wall jutted up in front of Deimos, blocking his view. Then Ushi evoked an orb of bright, shining light. The little whelk threw it into the air. It hovered overhead, growing in size, practically becoming a second sun.

Deimos blasted a powerful beam of magic through the wall of stone. Helmith stepped to the side, dodging.

I ran around our arena until I had sights on Deimos himself.

The rock wall transformed into trees, and vines shot from the branches, moving with dream-like fluidity. The vines grabbed Deimos's arm, and flowers blossomed across the vegetation before hundreds of butterflies poured out of them.

Deimos growled his irritation, but I couldn't make out his words.

A sickly haze of bluish mist rolled from his body. The butterflies caught in the fog began to die. So did the trees, and the vines.

The orb of light that Ushi had created finally reached its peak. The little whelk dropped the ball, and it crashed down into the wet rocks, the light blasting outward with the force of an explosion. Deimos held up his arm, shielding his eyes.

But that was when I tugged the thread of magic for the abyssal dragon.

My forehead burned as my arcanist mark shifted. In the next instant, while Deimos was still blinded, I held up my hand and imagined the evocation leaving my palm like I had seen Deimos do time and time again.

The blast hurt—more so than the typhoon dragon's lightning—but I gritted my teeth and used Deimos's attack against him. The beam of raw magic ripped through his body, creating a hole straight through his chest.

I stumbled backward, shocked it had worked.

The blue mist faded.

More butterflies took to the sky, so numerous, they created a black cloud that almost blocked out the intensity of the red sun. Then the butterflies scattered, and the weather shifted to something pleasant. Blue skies, a gentle breeze... I breathed easier.

Perhaps this would be over now.

Deimos stood, even with a hole through his chest, and evoked his raw magic at me.

I hadn't been expecting it. There wasn't enough time to dodge. The blast sliced through my shoulder, and my body instantly went numb.

"Gray!" Helmith shouted.

"H-How?" was all I could ask as I collapsed backward, stunned the Death Lord was still standing.

"You're all fools," Deimos said, his gory hole stitching itself up. Not with flesh, but with the bluish magic that coursed through his body. The injury healed, but it looked like slime—or ooze. It reminded me of the souls grafted to the abyssal dragon I had seen.

"I'm a master of death," Deimos shouted, half-angry, half-amused. "*I can't be killed by the likes of you.* We can fight in this dream world for five hundred years, and I would never yield—and you would never win. Sooner or later, your will shall break, and I will emerge the victor."

Professor Helmith headed to my location.

My chest hurt. I couldn't breathe. I wasn't going to die, was I? Here? In this dreamscape? The abyssal dragon magic... I had just watched Deimos stitch himself up. When I glanced at my own injury, I realized bluish liquid was filling my chest, "healing" me like it was with Deimos. It hadn't been a conscious decision. The magic worked on its own, similar to my own arcanist healing, through which injuries closed themselves without me willing it to happen.

And the abyssal dragon magic wasn't killing me like it had before. Why? Was it because a fragment of Deimos was technically in my body?

Before Helmith reached me, Deimos turned his deadly magic on Ushi.

He blasted her ethereal whelk and shattered a portion of the little creature's shell. Ushi fell to the ground with the weight of a leaf, fragments of her iridescent shell floating all around her.

Helmith hardened her expression. Then she waved her hand. Stones shot up from the ground, surrounding Deimos. They formed into bars and crossed above him, forming an *X*, and trapping him in a naturally made prison.

Then she made it to my side. "Gray, are you okay?"

I placed a hand on the oozing part of my chest. "I don't know," I croaked, my lungs hurting.

Deimos blasted himself free of the cage. He laughed as he did so, clearly amused by our efforts to stop him. "Did you think this would work? Was *this* your plan? Pathetic."

"I don't care if we're locked in combat for five *thousand* years, I'll never let you have Gray," Professor Helmith said as she stood to face him.

Ushi, half broken, her shell barely there, floated close to her arcanist. The ethereal whelk couldn't maintain her levitation. Helmith took her into her arms.

When the numbness in my chest waned, I pushed myself to my feet. Being locked in dream combat for longer than five *minutes* sounded like a torture I didn't want to experience, but I would never leave Helmith—not now, not ever.

Death Lord Deimos held up his hand.

Before he could evoke his magic, I blasted another beam—no aiming, just as fast as I could summon it. The pain that flared through my body caused my beam to veer off. I missed, but Deimos had stepped to the side, hesitating.

The world shook. The ground, the sky, the mists in the distance. As I stumbled back to the ground, I watched as everything trembled and then started to break apart.

Deimos chortled. "You're dying, ethereal whelk arcanist. I can feel it in the waking world. And even your grasp of this dream is slipping through your frail fingers."

"This is the realm of dreams," Helmith whispered. She cradled Ushi close. "Anything is possible here. Even the hope that I'll live to see this through."

"Your determination is admirable but misplaced. Fear not—for your bravery, I'll honor your soul and allow it to go through the rebirth."

But Helmith's eldrin...

Ushi glowed a bright white. Her whole body. This dream world pulsed and solidified again, the ground bursting into emerald grass, the sky shifting to night, with a moon so huge, it was effortless to see the craters that marked the surface.

It was brilliant and exhilarating.

And then Ushi grew larger. She started at the size of a human head, but light sparkled around her, adding to her width and height. She became the size of a fully grown human, but her silhouette was so strange, I couldn't describe it without using the word *bizarre* at least twice.

When the glow faded, her body was revealed.

Ushi was a combination of many creatures. She had the spiral shell of a whelk, the long body of a serpentine dragon, the talons of eagles, the face of a cat, and the tail of a lion. Her skin, shell, and "fur" were all the iridescent hue I had known before. She shimmered like a beautiful diamond cut into the creature I saw before us.

Ushi... was like a living dream. A mishmash of thoughts and images, but playful and happy. A true dream.

*A true form ethereal whelk.*

Professor Helmith's arcanist mark glowed with the same inner power. Her mark, the seven-pointed star, was now adorned by an image of this strange dream creature.

Helmith lifted her hand, and silvery rocks blasted out of the ground, startling me. They formed a prison again, surrounding Deimos and then solidifying into place. Only this time, when Deimos attempted to use his magic on his new prison, it didn't work.

His beams shattered on the rocks, and his deadly mists did nothing...

"It's no use," Professor Helmith whispered with a smile. "You may be a master of death, but I am a master of dreams. Nothing will work here unless I allow it to work."

"This won't stop me," Death Lord Deimos growled, his voice echoing in his stone cage. "*Nothing has ever stopped me.* I will be free—from this prison, and from the hells."

Helmith twisted her hand into a tight grip, and the rocks closed in tighter.

Then the dream weakened. It shook and shattered. The ground broke, the sky cracked like glass, and the moon paled, its glow draining away. All distant images wobbled and swayed like mirages. The rocks beneath my feet finally gave way.

But Professor Helmith's prison remained intact. It had been created from her new true form magic, and remained unharmed, even as the rest of the world evaporated around me.

Everything else disappeared.

And then I woke up.

# CHAPTER 43

## ABYSSAL TIES

I sat up, my heart beating slow, but hard. With a shaky hand, I rubbed at my chest, half-expecting to find a hole where Death Lord Deimos had struck me. Thankfully, my body was whole.

Had it really been a dream?

I glanced around, surprised that Deimos wasn't trying to take hold of my body. Perhaps *everything* had been a dream. That thought actually got me to chuckle. If someone told me the cotillion was tomorrow, I would've laughed like a loon.

But then I realized I was in the Academy's infirmary, and that everything had been real.

This giant room was familiar to me. Three dozen individual beds were positioned along the length of the two longest walls, with windows at the far end of the room—windows that stretched from the floor to the ceiling. The curtains were tied back, allowing the morning sun to trickle inside.

The view was something else. The infirmary overlooked a nearby mountain range. In the morning light, I realized how some individuals could be struck with inspiration to paint their surroundings. I wasn't artistic, but I wished I could capture the imagery for all time.

Then I rubbed my face and spotted two interesting things.

Firstly, Twain was sleeping on top of the covers between my legs. His orange fur was smoothed down, and his long ears to the side. He took even breaths. I patted him, and he stretched himself awake.

Secondly, I spotted silvery gate fragments on the nightstand next to my bed. They were the fragments I had absorbed—I only knew that because the crescent-shaped fragment from Freestorm was among them. It was so uniquely shaped that the rest had to be the other smaller pieces that had gotten into my body.

Twain blinked his eyes open. "Gray? Are you awake?"

I nodded. "Yeah. What happened?"

"I went and got Doc Tomas to help you." Twain stood and shook himself off. "But it seemed you were healed by the time the doctor and the headmaster arrived in the basement. And no one could remove—"

"I don't care about me. What about Professor Helmith? Is she okay? Where is she?"

Twain tilted his head to the side. "I don't know. Helmith and Ren were taken away. They were both badly injured." My eldrin frowned. "Does it hurt, though?"

"Does *what* hurt?"

"The thing on you. No one could remove it."

Thing?

I glanced down. I wore a white tunic and a matching pair of trousers. But there was something around my neck. I had been so disoriented after the battle in the dream, I hadn't realized. With a shaky hand, I pulled down the collar of my tunic.

A band of gold metal was wrapped around a good portion of my upper body. It started on my left arm, wrapped around my bicep and then over my shoulder, and then it wrapped around the base of my neck and continued to my right shoulder and bicep. It was the most intricate and strange piece of jewelry I had ever seen.

When I touched it, power pulsed through my fingertips.

I knew that feeling.

This was... Vivigöl, Silencer of the Damned.

"No one could get it off you," Twain whispered. "They tried, but everyone who touched it got hurt. They didn't know what to do..."

I grabbed the gold abyssal coral around my neck and yanked. Shockingly, the jewelry shifted. It had been as hard as metal a second ago, but the instant I wanted it off my body, the whole piece of jewelry became malleable. It molded to my grip.

After a second yank, the coral came off. Then it *click-click-clicked* into a new shape. Similar to Twain's transformation, the jewelry changed back into its trident form, longer than the bed, and tipped with three frightening tines.

It was light, though. It was still a strain to hold my arm out completely straight, but the trident wasn't as heavy as I had thought it would be.

Twain gasped, his fur puffing up. "What're you doing?" he shouted.

In a moment of panic, I dropped the weapon. It clattered to the ground with several *bangs*. I took a deep breath and calmed myself. The trident wasn't dangerous. It hadn't burned my palm or even injured me.

"You have the Death Lord's trident?" Twain shook his head. "Why? What is everyone going to say when they see you with it?"

I threw off the covers. Most of them flew on top of Twain. He meowed and swiped them with his claws. Then I slid off the bed and picked the trident back up.

Vivigöl...

The weapon pulsed again once I touched it, as if reaffirming who I was. The trident didn't consider me an enemy. Was it because Deimos had wielded it with my body? I wasn't sure. And how would I reason with an abyssal weapon, anyway? It wasn't like I could explain the situation.

"You shouldn't hold it," Twain said.

"What else am I going to do with it?" I asked. "Hide it?"

The sarcastic part of me wanted to disguise the weapon as a broom and prop it in the corner. Ingenious! It would get a few laughs, at least—before some unsuspecting mortal touched it and died.

That one playful thought seemed to resonate with Vivigöl. It shifted and *click-click-clicked* into a new shape, remolding itself even while in my hands. My mimic magic... The weapon seemed to take on the properties of my powers.

And then...

Vivigöl was a broom.

A terrible broom, mind you, since the bristles were as sharp as needles, and the handle was curved slightly to accommodate a two-handed grip, but it was still a broom.

Twain stared at it.

I stared at it.

Silence was our only other companion.

"How are we even going to explain this to the others?" Twain whispered. "I feel like I'm losing my sanity just trying to wrap my head around the situation."

With a nervous laugh, I swished the deadly broom around. "No, I get it... Vivigöl takes the shape I want."

As soon as I thought about it as a trident, the weapon *click-click-clicked* back into its original weapon form. The clicking was the coral shifting itself into place. The weapon wanted to be metallic, and changing shape was clearly not its original design. The hard and sharp pieces snapping into place caused the sound.

Now that it was a trident, I stared at the tines. "But this will be hard to explain," I whispered.

Twain nodded. "No one is going to let you keep it."

With a frown, I imagined it as jewelry again. I was pleased, and surprised, when Vivigöl shifted onto my body. It clawed its way up my right arm and then across my shoulders, like it had been before. It was almost chain-like, and capable of moving whenever I lifted or dropped my arms.

It was neat. But frightening. I didn't like that the sinister weapon was wrapped around the base of my neck, but there was so much coral, it had to be over a good portion of my body so as to stay on me and not be cumbersome.

The far door opened.

I leapt back onto my bed and pulled the collar of my tunic over Vivigöl.

Headmaster Venrover walked into the infirmary, followed by a thin man with a tiny pair of spectacles. Behind that man was something I had never seen in person before. It was a mystical creature, but one so amazing, I widened my eyes just to make sure I was seeing it correctly.

It was a pile of rubble in the shape of a dragon. Well, perhaps not entirely rubble.

The "dragon" had broken stained glass wings, flakes of copper for scales, gold coins for a mane, broken pottery for its legs, wrought iron for its claws and spikes, and shattered stone for the rest of its bulk. The debris was all held together with magical strings, almost too gossamer to see.

It was large, at least as tall as a house, but since it was nothing but broken and discarded objects, it could shape itself as it moved. The dragon poured through the door and then regained its dragon shape once inside the infirmary. It clicked and clacked and banged around as it moved, but once it stood still, it was majestic.

A living piece of art.

I loved it.

Headmaster Venrover walked over to the side of my bed, but I barely saw him.

"Gray," he said. "Do you know what a *relickeeper* is?"

I blinked and then turned to him. "It's a mystical creature. We learned about them in class."

"That's correct." Venrover motioned to the thin man with spectacles. "This is Samuel Muldoon, a researcher who used to work with me in Ellios. He is the relickeeper arcanist who extracted the gate fragments from your body."

Samuel Muldoon stepped forward. "You may call me Dr. Doon. Everyone does." He offered a slight bow of his head.

I returned the gesture and then hesitantly turned my attention to the gate fragments on the nightstand. "Should those be out like that?"

The headmaster half-smiled. "Relickeepers are mystical creatures of magical items and objects. They can keep things in stasis, to prevent the use of magic for a short period of time. I went to retrieve Dr. Doon once I realized we would need powerful destructive magics to rid ourselves of these strange fragments. I figured, if we couldn't destroy them immediately, we would need to render them inoperable."

I nodded once. "Does that mean... Dr. Doon is staying here at Astra Academy?"

The doctor stepped forward. He wore a suit of all black and gold. His shirt and trousers had gold trim, and his short cape had a shimmery golden lining. The man also wore gloves that covered his hands from the tips of his fingers to his wrists.

"I'll be here teaching magical theory to the imbuing students," Dr. Doon said matter-of-factly. "That way, if any more of these fragments show themselves, I can disable them." He walked over to the nightstand and fingered a few of the smaller pieces. "These are fascinating. *Very* fascinating. As soon as Adelgis told me about this magical phenomenon, I had to see it for myself."

The headmaster chuckled. "I was pleased to see the relickeeper's ability to pull magical items toward them worked with the fragments in your body. It was fortunate."

I rubbed my chest, relief washing through me. The headmaster had gone out of his way to find arcanists to solve this problem? I was lucky—perhaps even blessed. Death Lord Deimos wouldn't take me.

Then I glanced up. "What about Professor Helmith?" I whispered. That was the one piece of information I had been waiting for. Almost nothing else mattered.

"Rylee? She's taking time to recover in her quarters. Her husband will return to the Academy to care for her, and take over her duties as professor in the meantime."

"But she's okay?" I asked, my volume rising with each word. "She's not going to die?"

Headmaster Venrover shook his head. "Both Rylee and Roark will live. Or should I say, Professors Helmith and Ren. You see, Ren's injury was less significant than Helmith's. Professor Ren should be resuming his teaching by tomorrow."

Why were Professor Helmith's injuries so significant? I had been sliced open by Vivigöl in the past, and I had made a full recovery. Well, I still had scars, but I hadn't been bedridden long. Why was it different for Helmith? Perhaps the fight in the dream had taken a lot out of her.

Or perhaps... since I had been an abyssal dragon arcanist when I was struck with the trident, my injury had healed differently.

I didn't know for sure.

"Professor Helmith's eldrin changed," I whispered. "It became true form. Why?"

Venrover genuinely smiled this time. It was rare—the man didn't seem to show a wide range of emotion. Ever. "Do you know how ethereal whelks are born?"

"I think we read about that in class as well... I can't remember, though."

"When a child drowns, there's a small chance an ethereal whelk will form near their body." The headmaster rubbed at his own arcanist mark as he spoke. "You see, ethereal whelks are the last dreams of children. The final piece of hope they will be saved from death. It's that hope given form that creates the whelks. Therefore, an ethereal whelk's true form is achieved when the arcanist fully embraces hope that life will get better—that you can make life better if you strive for it."

"So... ethereal whelks have a virtue as a true form," I muttered, remembering our class on the subject.

Professor Helmith had fought against the Death Lord with me, never wavering from her goal to stop him. Even as she was dying. Had it been that hope that she would succeed that had changed Ushi from a small snail to a living embodiment of dreams?

I wondered.

"Do you know what's required for a mimic to achieve its true form?" I asked.

The headmaster glanced over at Twain.

My eldrin tilted his head to the other side this time.

"No," Venrover said. "I've never seen a true form mimic. I apologize. Perhaps you will discover it for yourself one day."

"Right..."

The headmaster motioned to the bed. "You should rest for now. Tomorrow, you can rejoin your fellow students and resume your studies. Please try to rest. I know you've been through a lot, but I will do everything in my power to make sure this Academy is safe from outside influences, even if I have to hire the most powerful arcanists to build protections around the entire campus."

I nodded along with his words. "Thank you, Headmaster. I'll try."

Before Venrover and Dr. Doon left, the headmaster stopped at the end of my bed. "Oh, I should mention... The abyssal coral around your body seems to be attuned to your soul. Please take care not to allow it to touch anyone. I'll find another arcanist who can remove it, but in the meantime, you should be aware that it's dangerous."

"I can remove it," I said, no hesitation. "If you want it, you can have it."

I wasn't sure how I felt about Vivigöl. Half of me wanted to get rid of it, while the other half wanted to keep it, as a form of protection. But it wasn't *my* weapon, it was Death Lord Deimos's.

"It answers to your magics?" Headmaster Venrover asked.

I nodded.

For a long moment, he said nothing. Then he replied, "Best you keep it for now, then. Someday soon, I'll have a method for growing the abyssal coral, but I'll need the weapon if I'm going to do it."

Vivigöl weighed heavy around my neck and shoulders. I rubbed at the gold coral. "All right." Then I held up a hand. "Wait. What about... the rest of my class? What about Knovak?" Memories of the events around the cotillion swirled in my head. What had Deimos done to him?

"They have recovered. Knovak as well. He was shaken, but not permanently injured."

"That's good," I said with a sigh. "Even my brother? He's safe? And Ashlyn?"

"All safe."

"What about your assassin?"

The headmaster stared at me, his dark eyes searching mine. "My *what*?"

I nervously shook my head. "Uh, Fain? The wendigo arcanist. He's your assassin, isn't he?"

Venrover laughed, his face growing pink. "Oh, well, you may refer to him as *my assassin* if you wish, that's fine. I'm certain he would prefer it. He's gone by many names, and many titles, but he's never objected to that one. Yet."

"Is he okay?" Twain asked. "He pulled Gray right out of the bay! He saved us. Even if he was late about it." My eldrin stamped his paw on the bed.

The headmaster glanced over to the empty space next to him. Then he half-smiled as he returned his attention to me. "Yes, Fain is fine. He wasn't injured during the battle at the cotillion, and he did manage to collect all our students."

The headmaster spoke the words as if reassuring a child. I didn't care. I just needed to know they were all alive and fine.

"Now rest," Venrover said. "Please. Professor Helmith insisted you have all the time you need to recover."

I stayed in the infirmary for the rest of the day, Twain by my side.

When night finally settled over the mountains, and classes had ended, the door to the infirmary opened to reveal Sorin and Nini. They were practically exact opposites as they entered the room. Nini, small and covered in layers of clothing, hesitantly made her way in. Sorin, lumbering and confident, nearly twice her height, headed straight for me.

"Gray!" he shouted.

It was a good thing no one else was in the infirmary with me, because they would've been woken by his raucous yelling.

He jogged to my bed and half-lifted me into his arms for a tight hug. I tensed, worried he would touch Vivigöl on accident. Fortunately, my tunic covered the deadly piece of jewelry. Sorin released me and then held me at arm's length, his hands gripping my upper arms.

"You made it," he said, breathless.

"I'm okay," I said. "Everything is fine. Helmith defeated the soul fragment of Deimos, and the headmaster found an arcanist who could remove the gate fragments from my body, so... I think it's all over."

Twain stood on his four feet and nodded. "Yeah! Now we can just go to class like normal arcanists and eldrin. *Finally.*"

Sorin released me and stood tall. With a smile he said, "*But you refused to go without a fight, and with all your might, you summoned the light. A blazing fire from within your soul, a force that a Death Lord can't control.*" Then he rubbed his nose. "They're going to write epics about you. And if they don't, I will."

I chuckled. "Thank you, Sorin. But I don't think anyone should write about me." For half a second, I almost told Sorin about Deimos's threat to harm our mother. But I kept that to myself. I didn't want to upset him.

Deimos could still do it. But I didn't want to think about that.

Nini stood at the foot of my bed. She smoothed her red hair and then straightened her glasses. Her reaper hovered by the door of the infirmary. I didn't remember seeing Waste enter the room, so I wondered when he had.

"Are you feeling okay?" Nini asked. "I heard the Kross Cotillion was so thoroughly destroyed that they'll have to rebuild most of Freestorm."

"I'm fine." I glanced between them. "Ashlyn isn't here?"

"She went back to her family's compound," Sorin whispered. He crossed his arms and shrugged. "I'm sorry, Gray. She said to tell you she would be back soon, but apparently her family was concerned about the attack."

"That... makes sense." But I didn't like it.

Sorin grabbed Twain and lifted him up into the air like a human infant. Twain mewed in surprise, his eyes wide. "Are you okay?" Sorin asked. Then he cradled Twain and rubbed his soft belly. "Nothing happened to my favorite kitten, right?"

"S-Since when am I your favorite kitten?" Twain swiped at him with all his claws. "Put me down! I'm a mighty mimic! You can't treat me like an adorable pet!"

Sorin didn't care if Twain slashed him up. The cuts were shallow, and my brother's pain tolerance was rather high. He chuckled as he rubbed Twain even more. The hissing and spitting practically filled the whole infirmary.

"Who's the cutest kitten in the world? *You are.*" My brother spoke to Twain like he was a grumpy infant.

"Gray! Transform me into something big so I can teach your brother a lesson!"

With a smile, I closed my eyes. The threads of magic were more distinct now. Every time I sensed out my surroundings, I gradually became better at it.

But then my heart jumped into my throat as I realized what all creatures were nearby.

Sorin's knightmare...

Nini's reaper...

The infirmary doctor's golden stag...

And Deimos's abyssal dragon.

I grabbed my chest, my panic sudden and al- consuming. Was he nearby? Was he here in the Academy? I glanced around, my eyes wide. Sorin was too busy messing with Twain to notice my dread, but Nini furrowed her brow.

"Gray? Are you okay?"

I took deep breaths and closed my eyes again. I could sense the direction of creatures. Was the dragon in the basement?

No.

Sorin's knightmare was by my bed, and Nini's reaper was by the door, and the golden stag was in the room over... But the dragon...

It was me. The thread led back to me.

I opened my eyes, realization settling over me like dust across the room. The soul fragment of Deimos was locked away in my body, and with it, a small window to the abyssal hells.

The thread of magic that led to the dragon was just *there*, dangling close to me.

Forever.

"Everything is fine," I said, more to myself than to Nini. "I was just surprised, that's all."

She stared at me and then slowly nodded. "O-Oh. Okay."

"Gray!" Twain playfully shouted. Sorin had begun tickling him, and he couldn't break free. "Help me, Gray! Don't leave your favorite eldrin to suffer!"

I tugged on the thread that led to Sorin's knightmare. Twain transformed and freed himself, but I barely paid attention to any of that.

My thoughts dwelled on the implications of always having the abyssal dragon as an option. I wondered what it meant, and I knew I'd have to discuss this with Professor Helmith as soon as she was better.

Until then, I tried to return my focus to my brother and my eldrin.

I just wanted some normal Academy life. Perhaps for a few weeks. That would be excellent.

THANK YOU SO MUCH FOR READING!

**Please consider leaving a review**—any and all feedback is much
appreciated!

**Gray's story continues in *Abyssal Arcanist*!**

**To find out more about Shami Stovall and Astra Academy, take a look at her website:**
https://sastovallauthor.com/newsletter/

**To help Shami Stovall (and see advanced chapters ahead of time) take a look at her Patreon:**
https://www.patreon.com/shamistovall

**Want more arcanist novels? Good news! <u>The Frith Chronicles</u> is where is all started! Join Volke and the Frith Guild as they travel the world.**

# About the Author

Shami Stovall is a multi-award-winning author of fantasy and science fiction. Before that, she taught history and criminal law at the college level and loved every second. When she's not reading fascinating articles and books about ancient China or the Byzantine Empire, Stovall can be found playing way too many video games, especially RPGs and tactics simulators.

Shami loves John, reading, video games, and writing about herself in the third person.

If you want to contact her, you can do so at the following locations:

**Website:** https://sastovallauthor.com
**Email:** s.adelle.s@gmail.com

 facebook.com/SAStovall
twitter.com/GameOverStation